The Angels Are Flying So Low

Will Appiah

Before the Crown

The Angels Are Flying So Low

Reprint: Crown Edition, 2023

The child who is not embraced by the village will burn it down to feel its warmth…
-African Proverb

This book is a dedication to my wonderful grandmother, as I write this in her eightieth year. You are the matriarch of the family and I will build a world around your love.

I also write this for my beautiful and caring mother, who used to gather her children in bed with her to read us Junie B. Jones books before bedtime. These were the best nights that will forever remain a positive imprint in our minds.

Lastly, I dedicate this book to my father. The man who sacrificed so much for his children. You once told me that 'we need more heroes in the world.' I will never forget those words and will dedicate myself to actualizing our vision…

…to create more Angels.

Also by Author:

The Purposeful Oliver Burke

Scars Serve As Reminders

Table of Contents

Me·da·se – "Thank You"
(Origins: Twi)
God Bless Our Homeland Ghana

The Angels Are Flying So Low

PART I
MAHLAH

CHAPTER 1:

US OR THEM

Inmate 0713 aka "Mahlah"   *Manhattan, 1986*

"You can't have an extra scoop of anything, nigger," barked the officer in disgust. "I don't care if your stomach starts eating itself and you fuckin' starve to death. Keep your mouth shut, keep your eyes low, and eat what we feed you. You should imagine anything you want and cry yourself to sleep because as long as you're in here, you'll never get it... ever! I don't care who you fuckin' know. One thing I will promise you is that as long as you're an inmate in my detention center, I will make your life a living hell."

The corrections officer laughed as he walked away from the sitting inmate, who proudly wore the ridicule like a bullet that just missed one's heart. Despite the embarrassing scene, the young man continued to force his calm attitude while aiming his chin high with pride. His lips and eyes twitched as he fought back this sudden rush of anger. With a smirk on his face, he peered over at the others who sat at his lunch table for their implicit backing. In them, he needed to know he had made it out of that ordeal the victor, but he only saw their frightened faces looking away. The prison was already tough as it is, and they knew they didn't need any other issues with the guards to make it any tougher.

*****

"**Inmate 0713**," was a quiet, but frightening, member of the juvenile detention wing at Port Authority Correction Center, also known as PACC, in New York City. Although he was serving a two-year sentence for gun possession, on the surface, he seemed like any other gentle soul who was in the wrong place at the wrong time.

He did not walk around with his chest out like a big shot, like most others at PACC, but was regarded as such because of his known affiliations, temperament issues, and the stories about his life before incarceration. The young inmate did not enjoy being a member of the correction center and often found himself trying to stay under the radar to avoid issues. He knew he had a short temper and did not want that to lead to an extended sentence. Fortunately for him, he had grown used to the Corrections Officer's treatment.

Before he arrived, fourteen months before that day, many of the prison's senior gangsters were forewarned about his arrival. Most of the inmates in the corrections center were directly or indirectly aligned with a street gang or organized crime family, so he was welcomed by the blacks, the Italians, the Hispanics, the Irish, and the Japanese. Because of their existing arrangements on the streets of Brooklyn, it was in their best interest to ensure he was taken care of. Each of these race crews had various groups within them, some that got along and some that didn't, but they all fell in line when needed. The crew leaders were not against open discussion if it meant business would not be interrupted.

When he arrived, inmate 0713 was welcomed with reverence and guaranteed protection from other inmates. After his arrest, the judge and prosecutor attempted to get him to snitch on others involved in the crime he was convicted of and those still within the underworld, but he refused and accepted his punishment. He knew there was a greater benefit to not snitching and gladly took what they threw at him. This helped provide him the protection he grew to know at PACC.

Before arriving, he also believed he had a friend in PACC, but after months of being locked up, he could not seem to find him anywhere and no one seemed to know anything. It was as if his friend had just disappeared into thin air.

Despite that, he still had no plans to make any new friends in prison and simply wanted to do his time and go home. He didn't care for the gangster life anymore and as time went on, he realized that prison was just like the streets he'd left behind. There were rules in place to keep order and limit any disruption to their way of life. A set of three bylaws governed the juvenile inmate community of PACC. Each of the crews had its own set of prison laws, but the three bylaws applied to them all.

1. ***Noi O Loro ("Us or them")*** - *Inmates were inmates and guards were guards. There was no intermingling of the two.*

2. ***Deuteronomy 19:21- ("Life for a Life")*** - *Murder will not be tolerated unless previously agreed*

upon as punishment. Anyone found responsible for the murder will pay with their life.

3. ***Women and Kids are off limits*** - *No respect will be given to anyone who has sexually assaulted a woman or child.*

It was a "by us, for us" arrangement that ensured everyone's time at PACC was cohesive. If any of the bylaws were broken, the punishment was determined by the leaders of each of the prison crews.

The neo-Nazi loyalist group was the only crew who was against the relationship the other groups had with each other. They did not like anyone who was not them but needed to compromise to keep a seat at the table. Their leader had a vote when punishment was required, so they too adhered to the code – when necessary.

When inmate 0713 first arrived, he was approached by a captain within the neo-Nazi group, Hagan, who was also regarded as one of the group's main enforcers because of his history of violence on the outside. During this encounter, Hagan approached inmate 0713, with three others trailing behind him, and told the teen he "owned the entire prison" and the kid should "stay away."

"I'd advise you to keep to yaself, boy. You in my house now and I don't care who the fuck you know. I'm ya master in here," he remarked with a smile that displayed his missing teeth.

Inmate 0713 could feel the man's hatred and knew he wanted no problems. He did not want to associate with the gang culture of prison so he turned around and walked away. He figured he wouldn't have had any issues adhering to Hagan's command because he committed to giving up the life that got him incarcerated. Unfortunately for inmate 0713, Hagan had a short temper and saw the inmate's gesture as his blatant disrespect for the neo-Nazi's command. He attempted to follow the inmate but saw a guard approaching and turned around. From that day, inmate 0713 had avoided Hagan at all costs.

Unfortunately, outside of Hagan, there was another at the correction center who wasn't very happy to see any inmate with so much power. Officer Kellerman had no respect for the street life and had zero tolerance for any of its gangsters. He was a tall, white man with tattoo sleeves that stretched from his fingers up to his neck, a big beard, and an even larger belly that hung over his belt. He was the lead guard, which meant all other guards in the male juvenile wing fell under his supervision. He also had a cordial relationship with the neo-Nazi leader because of their profitable business arrangements.

In PACC there was a total of 200 individuals which included juveniles and those on the psychiatric wing. The juvenile wing made up a little less than a quarter of the total number of inmates. Being Manhattan's largest and toughest corrections facility, they took on some of the most violent inmates and shipped others to some of the sister centers around the state. Although the adult wing was tough, Port Authority housed juvenile inmates with lesser crimes.

PACC was also known to have a zero-tolerance policy that forbade inmates from fraternizing with guards, or inmates from fraternizing with other inmates at different security levels or genders.

The inmates wore a single name on their uniforms, but to the guards, they were nothing more than the numbers assigned to them. The policy to keep the different security level inmates separated was strictly enforced. Maximum security inmates, who wore numbers that began with "99" were housed in a separate and more restricted building from the general population. This was the case for both the male and female prisons. Level one inmates had a few more rights and their numbers began with any two-digit number combination between "00" and "88". The juvenile detention camp was no different and housed both men and women separately. For juveniles, there was a bit more leniency. Their large recreation yard was separated in half with men on the north side of the fence and women on the south. The only thing separating the two yards was a heavyweight chain link fence that stretched from one end of the facility to the other.

Both the male and female wings also had an isolation chamber, which was an 8 by 8 ft. shed with high concrete walls, no roof, and no windows. There was nothing in this space besides a thin mattress pad, a thin blanket, a bucket stained with remnants of feces, and a condensed version of a Bible that laid under the pillow. The space did not hold heat well and the corners of the rooms were filled with dead cockroaches. All inmates feared being put into the isolation chamber because of the lack of human interaction. The extreme isolation drove many inmates crazy and created dreadful stories to pass along to others.

*****

That day, after the verbal abuse from the guard and the meal period ended, the inmates were herded outside for one of their two optional sixty-minute recreational periods. Most guards loved to watch the inmates amble in from the recreation period because it meant they were going back to lockup and the fun was over. This especially brought joy to Officer Kellerman, who ensured he never missed it.

Inmate 0713, who also wore the name "Mahlah" on his uniform, turned his gaze from the guard. Still embarrassed from being berated in front of the other inmates, he whispered to himself, "I'll see you later, Kellerman." But he had no plans for retaliation. He was more than halfway through his two-year sentence and knew he did not need any bad behavior to extend his already horrible stint. His goal was to stay out of trouble and mind his business in hopes of being released on time or early. Although he planned to remain cool, he knew his anger issues would be the thing to land him in trouble. He thought it best to avoid issues at all costs.

He walked toward the basketball court for his regular five-on-five pickup game. Basketball was his favorite way to pass time during the recreation period because it allowed him to be physically active while keeping him from sitting idle. When he was free, he was used to going to battle on the court and enjoyed every opportunity he could find to relive those memories.

After losing their first game, Mahlah and the other four members of his team made their way off the court to sit with the other waiting inmates.

"Y'all are trash," he said in a demeaning tone. He was furious with his teammates and how their game had only lasted fifteen minutes. They lost twenty-one to sixteen, and he had scored all their points. *These fuckin' dudes are trash. I can't believe they couldn't even make a single basket.*

Basketball had always been his favorite sport and he thought he was great at it. Unfortunately, he did not feel his teammates, who were also selected by their team captain, were as skilled as he was, nor were they as committed to their victory. Most guards placed bets on the games and despite not seeing any of the winnings, it made it more exciting to Mahlah to know he was playing for something.

As he made his way off the court, he looked over to the court's far end and noticed a group of four guards staring and pointing in his direction, and laughing. His anger was instantly triggered and quickly rose as his head began to become warm. His breathing sped up and he dropped his head, focusing his eyes on the ground in front of his feet. As he motioned forward, he turned his attention up toward a group of inmates sitting on a bench in front of him. At the center of them was Hagan who wore a crooked smile as he stared down Mahlah. Hagan whispered to others in the group, and they all erupted in laughter, which Mahlah noticed and assumed was also due to their embarrassing basketball game. *They never picked up a basketball. Fuck them.*

He shook it off and shamefully continued forward belligerently. He was going to just park himself on the bench until he heard his teammates joking and giggling. He looked over at Hagan, again, and saw him still laughing and now pointing. He could no longer take it.

His embarrassment quickly turned into anger, and inmate 0713 snapped.

He turned and shoved the closest person to him, which was one of the other players. The teammate, who was a larger Hispanic male, fell to the ground but quickly shot back up to his feet and rushed Mahlah. He reciprocated the force and pushed Mahlah back, which caused him to also stumble backward. The Hispanic teammate followed his shove with a swing of his fist, but Mahlah was able to dodge his jab and quickly stung him back in the right-side rib.

The guards' attention had already been turned back to the basketball court, so they didn't see the altercation when it first began. It wasn't until others waiting on the bench began rushing to the scene that the guards also began to run over with their batons in hand. By the time the four patrolling officers had arrived at the scene, it had grown from a two-man altercation to an all-out melee. Teens from all corners of the yard began to clash as the guards rushed in attempting to separate them.

Blacks fought whites. Hispanics fought Asians. Blacks even fought other blacks as they clashed in the yard. It didn't matter who was associated with which crew or what bylaws existed, they all had to stand their ground because this was a chance for everyone to make a power play. Reputations were made or destroyed in these moments and everyone wanted to give themselves a story to tell.

Mahlah continued swinging at anyone within arm's distance and as each punch landed, his anger softened, and his satisfaction grew with it.

"I told you to stay out of my way, boy," an inmate snarled at Mahlah as he delivered a strong uppercut into Mahlah's stomach, forcing the breath out of him. When he looked up, he saw Hagan standing over him and watched as the neo-Nazi captain quickly followed it up with an overhead punch that connected on the left side of his face, bringing him down to the ground.

As he fell, Mahlah felt his face begin to burn and his vision blur. He touched his upper lip and wiped the blood running down from his nose and out of his mouth. When he looked back up, he saw another inmate lunging at his assailant, which provided him a moment's rest. Hagan neutralized this man and then turned his attention back towards Mahlah. He rushed in and kicked the inmate in the ribs, further exhausting what little breath he had left in him.

As he clutched his midsection, Mahlah looked up and could no longer see the details of his attacker's face but saw the multiple swastika tattoos both on his neck and bald head. In Hagan's hand was a shank pulled from his boot. He motioned towards Mahlah and just as he was about to reach in and stab him, another black inmate rushed in and stabbed Hagan with his shank over and over until his body hit the concrete.

The teen threw his weapon under his uniform and extended Mahlah his hand to help him to his feet.

"Don't worry. We ain't lettin' nothin' happen to you in here. You protected in PACC."

Just as Mahlah began to thank this young man for saving him, multiple gunshots erupted accompanied by the panic alarm. The two men fell to the ground— chest down. Officers quickly stormed the yard in riot gear. A guard was yelling through the loudspeaker.

"Get on the ground! Lie face down on the ground! Shut up, no talking! Interlace your fingers behind your head!"

The two men obliged and from their grounded position, they saw others around them also executing the guards' command. After minutes of waiting on the ground, they were all brought to their feet and ambled back inside. Mahlah was separated from the others and delivered to the isolation chamber, where he would spend the next seven days with nothing but his thoughts. This would be his punishment for inciting this incident.

CHAPTER 2:

ALONE

Mahlah

The seven days that followed the brawl were by far Mahlah's toughest and most trying at PACC. For twenty-two hours every day, he sat alone in a small isolation chamber with no human contact or form of entertainment to keep his mind busy. He received one small meal in the morning and one larger meal in the early evening, which typically was left-over from what was served in the chow hall. The remaining two hours of the day were offered as "free" time, which only meant if the guards were in a merciful mood, they would allow sequestered inmates to step outside of their isolation chambers for an hour or two.

At first, Mahlah struggled with the loneliness because he was alone with just his sprawling thoughts. He finally received "free" time after day two, which gave him some reassurance that the guards had noticed the fruits of their punishments were paying off. On day four, they removed the permission and returned him to a twenty-four-hour lockdown. He knew this was a mental tactic of theirs.

Because of the horrible things he saw when he slept, he forced himself to stay awake during most of his time in isolation. When he did sleep, he could see the blood. It was his hand holding the gun and all he could see were bodies sprawled on the ground around him. In his dreams, he was reminded of the person he was when he was free—a person who lacked confidence and struggled to find purpose. A person who aligned himself with some very dangerous people in order to fit in. This was a person he was trying to leave behind.

*****

When Mahlah was finally released from the isolation chamber, he could barely open his eyes. His taste glands had dried out and when he was finally provided a glass of clean ice water, he drank every drop until he was using his straw to suck the bottom of an empty cup. Because the darkness from the room had become home for so long, he cringed at the foreignness of the lights and the brightness of the sun's rays.

On this day, he was being escorted by Officer Kellerman, who paraded him through the halls as a trophy while also using the inmate's battered body as a warning to the others. Although he didn't say it, the message was clear: the guards run the facility and anyone who doesn't align with that would find themselves receiving similar, or worse, treatment to persuade them.

When they arrived at his cell, Mahlah was dumped on the cold ground and laid there until he heard the cell door behind him slam shut and lock. He crawled to his bunk where he stayed for days, skipping meal periods and rec time.

Just as the sun began to set that early evening, one of the crew leaders stopped by Mahlah's cell to check on him and gave him an update on Hagan.

"I heard that racist mothafucka died while they were takin' him to the hospital. The kid who stabbed him is still in iso, probably for his protection. I heard the neo-Nazis had a hit on both of you. Kellerman was going to set you up but that's been handled. We paid the debt to keep you alive. Well, not 'we.' More like your guardian angel on the outside paid your debt. He paid off the neo-Nazis and told me to tell you to keep your head down and stay off the radar. You don't need any more enemies in here."

*****

About a week after his release from isolation, Mahlah found himself getting back into the swing of things. He had begun eating and drinking as normal and even began taking advantage of his recreation period again. He was determined to avoid going back to isolation and told himself that he would steer clear of playing basketball to avoid getting angry.

I don't need to give Kellerman any excuse to throw me back in there.

He sat there in the bleachers and watched as others ran 5 on 5 pick-up games to entertain the guards. After watching the first game, which also ended with one team dominating their opponents, he decided he couldn't watch anymore.

This is wack.

He grew to favor his time alone and decided to take a walk just to give himself peace of mind. Walking was used as a calming mechanism, and he didn't want any reason to get angry.

While walking around the yard, the young inmate decided to walk a different route from his regular path.

He had walked the same route so many times over the last fourteen months, and wanted change. He intended to make today different.

While proceeding back from the walk, Mahlah noticed a lawn equipment supply shack, which was off the beaten path. It was still in the recreation yard but was near the fence connecting the male and female yards. It was in a blind spot from the guard towers and seemed almost unnoticeable. He knew PACC ran a tight ship and did not leave any room for error. The correction center prided itself on having one guard for every five inmates in the juvenile detention center. In the adult prison, there was one guard for every three inmates.

I don't know about this.

The closer he got to it, the more he realized that he could not see the front of the guard tower, which was his confirmation that the shack was indeed out of their view. He continued walking forward, and the closer he got, the higher his anxiety became. He found himself at a crossroads between curiosity and fear. When his curiosity to learn more about the shack outweighed his fear of punishment, he forced himself to proceed forward.

While moving closer toward the shack, he began to feel perturbed about where he was going and what he was doing. Because of his dealings with Officer Kellerman, he knew it would be difficult to talk his way out of being caught roaming. He thought about it for a moment longer and decided he didn't feel comfortable moving forward.

Shit, if Kellerman or any of the guards catch me here, I'm done. I don't need that.

He turned around and proceeded back toward the basketball court.

As he walked back, he continued to deliberate his thoughts.

It's highly unlikely that there would be any real estate that's unaccounted for on this prison ground. I should stay away and get through this stint without any issues. Yeah, that's probably best.

When he arrived back at the basketball court, he watched two other games before heading back into holdings.

*****

The next day, the young inmate woke up with the mysterious shack still at the forefront of his mind. He had never ventured this far into the yard and could not stop thinking about it since his "almost" visit the day before.

I need to know what's over there. Maybe I can go one of these days.

*****

After wrapping up three sets on the bench, Mahlah looked over at the others with him.

"Yo, I'm going for a walk. I'll be back."

Just then, one of the prisoners working out with the group rose to his feet to join him but before he could fully stand, Mahlah interjected. "Nah, I'm good. I'm walking alone."

Others in the group looked around at each other then turned their attentions back to their workout as Mahlah moseyed away. Walking was normal for him since he stopped playing basketball and the others just nodded their understanding.

While he moseyed the grounds, Mahlah peered around until he was able to confirm all other guards were in their normal positions. This was his confirmation that the unattended equipment shack was still his targeted destination. When the inmate finally arrived at the shack, he first looked around and saw the main door was bolted shut. The windows all had bars on them and were slightly frosted to prevent any outsiders from peering inside.

I really shouldn't be here. There's a reason there are bars on the windows. How will I explain this?

Just as he was about to turn around and proceed back, the inmate heard rustling coming from behind the small shack. He had assumed he was alone so the sound frightened him and caused him to look around nervously.

Maybe it's a rodent? Maybe something more.

Before long, Mahlah's apprehension turned to curiosity, and he wanted to see what was back there. He crouched down slowly and made his way to investigate. When he arrived at the corner, he saw a young female inmate planted on the other side of the fence. She was sitting with her legs crossed between two bushes and a notepad and pencil in her lap.

He found it unusual but realized this potential "quiet spot" he had stumbled upon had already been discovered by another.

Maybe it's not so private after all, he thought. *It's probably best to avoid it altogether.*

Before walking away, he peered around the corner one more time to look at the mysterious woman.

I haven't seen any other women besides the tough-looking corrections officers. She's kinda pretty. Maybe I can say hi?

He could not completely see her full profile from around the corner, but from what he could tell she was a caramel-skinned African American girl with short, braided hair.

As he approached, the startled young woman faltered backward in fear. She fretfully looked around for others and then quickly grabbed her items.

"Don't be scared," Mahlah remarked in a low and gentle tone. "I'm not here to hurt you and I didn't mean to frighten you. I was looking for a quiet place to get away and came across this equipment shack. I saw you and came to say hi. Please don't be scared."

The young woman, still startled, continued to look at Mahlah with eyes full of panic and puzzlement. She didn't break her gaze, stood, and grabbed her notebook. Without saying a word, she turned around and started away.

"Wait, you don't have to go," he begged. "Please don't go. I didn't mean to scare you. What's your name?"

The woman stopped and peered back with hopeful eyes. She noticed his still demeanor, passive eyes, and gentle smile. It calmed her to see this. Like him, she had seen how frightening some of the other inmates were and as she looked at him, he could see she felt he was somehow different. His eyes held her gaze and she also noticed his low voice, which was somehow harmonic. Mahlah slowly planted himself on the ground and crossed his legs to show he was harmless.

The girl continued to stare until her face finally softened, and she decided to turn around and stay put. They still had some recreation time left and sensed, like himself, she had nowhere else to go. She slowly sat back down between her two-bush nesting spot, smiled over at him, and spoke."

"Here the guards call me inmate 0207, but my real name's Salena… Salena Brown."

"Nice to meet you, Salena. Over here, they call me inmate 0713, but my real name is Oliver Mahlah. Nice to meet you."

"Nice to meet you also Oliver *Mahlah*," she joked as she emphasized his last name with an accompanying giggle. "Mahlah… is that French or something? It sounds like I should be eating some escargot when I say it."

Oliver smiled and gave her a playful look back.

She's starting to feel comfortable. Good.

"I don't know where it's from. That's the name I was given so I'm kinda just stuck with it. Glad to hear you think it's funny," Oliver replied sarcastically. "What are you doing here Salena? You seem too nice for this hell."

"I should be asking you the same thing, Oliver Mahlah," she emphasized with a smile. "How did you find this place? I've never seen you here before."

"I kinda just stumbled on it. What about you?"

"Well, this is where I come to write and think."

"That makes sense. I am a walker and kind of just found it during my walk yesterday. This correction center is fuckin' intense. I saw this shack and finally decided to check it out."

Although he explained his hope for the shack to be a place he could get away, it was much deeper than that. In prison, Oliver was in the company of convicts and gangsters, which he knew was not who he was. Every day, he found himself performing for the company he was surrounded by. He was protected by gangsters and knew the only way to continue to remain protected was to maintain an image. He didn't mind this but found a greater solace in the time he could spend by himself. He knew when he was alone, this was the time when he could be who he really was. Scared and lonely, angry, and emotional. His isolation showed him that.

"Aww man…did anyone follow you?" she questioned. "I've been coming here for weeks now and I hope you didn't ruin it for me."

"Don't worry Salena, no one followed me. I made sure of that. What are you writing about?"

"I write poetry. I usually come here to write my thoughts down and transform them into poetry. I write about everything: this place, the food, the people, the grounds. Anything I observe or feel like writing."

"That's cool. What are you going to write about me?" he joked. "Handsome? Dashing? All of the above?"

"Oh please. You're alright but far from dashing."

"Yeah…yeah… Anyways," Oliver offered lightheartedly as he looked around. "I should write also but I kinda just want to do my time then get out of here. Wouldn't even know what to write."

"You could write about anything," she remarked as she pulled the pedals off of a flower she picked up. "You can even write about this flower."

"Flowers? I'll pass."

"So, what do you do to pass time?"

"I used to play basketball but had some problems with that. Now I just lift weights, keep to myself, or sometimes sing with my boy…"

"You know, I thought I heard some harmony in your voice," she stated excitedly as if she had discovered an unknown truth about her mysterious new friend.

At that moment, Oliver chuckled as he bashfully looked down at his wristwatch. He saw recreation time was wrapping up. He knew he needed to get back before the guards began asking questions.

"Looks like our rec time is over. It was nice meeting you, Salena. Maybe I'll see you around."

"You too, Oliver. See you around."

He then slowly proceeded back towards the recreation yard unnoticed and made it back just as they were calling for inmates to return to the building. As he got in line, Oliver realized that his conversation with Salena was the first one he'd had in a while that did not include any talk about prison, his sentence, the guards, or why he was locked up.

That was nice and light. Hope I see her again.

Thanks to his prison sentence and failed relationships, Salena was the first woman he'd opened up to in over a year. He didn't think he had feelings for her—he didn't want to. The last woman he had loved had hurt him, badly. But maybe Salena could be a friend. She was the first person he had met since he arrived who didn't know about his troubled past. She was the first person to see him just as Oliver... just a person...

CHAPTER 3:

SLÁINTE

Oliver Mahlah

The following day, Oliver could not wait for his recreation time. He woke up with no interest in basketball or lifting weights and instead looked forward to taking a walk.

I can't wait to talk to her again.

The prison offered two recreation periods – one AM and one PM – and when he entered the yard that morning, it was exactly as he thought – mostly empty. Most inmates stayed inside which meant the guards who were on duty outside were more attentive. Although he was curious if Salena was at the shack that morning, he did not want to risk anything by making his way back there.

I'll just have to come back after lunch when there's more people around.

*****

As he sat at his lunch table listening to the other inmates talk about new ways to make money and how they planned to "change their lives on the outside," Oliver's mind drifted.

Salena seemed nice but can I trust her?

Despite the many prisoners who knew him in juvie, the young inmate did not feel he had anyone he could fully depend on. He learned a lot about trust before coming to PACC and realized over time that as long as he was a prisoner, he was not going to find anyone he could fully open up to. *Maybe it's for the best.*

Although he was hopeful that Salena could be a friend, he knew that he needed to be cautious around opening up to strangers – no matter how nice they were. In PACC, he knew his fate could be determined by his fame, his anger, or his reputation, and believed he needed to tread carefully if he wanted to survive the remainder of his sentence. He was determined to keep his head low, anger maintained and just finish his time unscathed.

Just as he was about to look at his wristwatch to check how much time he had left for lunch, he felt a heavy hand slap the back of his head causing his face to land on his lunch tray. It was Wednesday which meant they were serving mashed potatoes, mystery meat drowned in beef-based gravy, and an excessive amount of snow peas, which covered most of his tray. This made the scene exceptionally more embarrassing.

As he separated his face from the food on his tray, his embarrassment and anger began to rise. There was a collective "gasp" from the others at the table as they eagerly peered at the humiliated teen for a reaction. All inmates knew Officer Kellerman as a strict, no-nonsense bully who got his excitement from reminding juvenile inmates who was in charge.

"Whoops, you accidentally ran into my palm," badgered Officer Kellerman. "Finish your lunch and get the hell out of my chow hall."

Oliver quickly shot up from his seat and wiped the gravy from his eyes. His jaw was clenched, his eyes were furrowed, and his hands shook as he attempted to hold back his trembling balled-up fists. His breaths were now very heavy, and his piercing stare shot right through the corrections officer.

"What the fuck do you think you're gonna do, nigger?" barked Officer Kellerman with a sound of pure aversion and detestation in his voice. He clicked his tongue and continued. "Your head ran into my hand as I walked by on my usual patrol. You should be more careful next time. Wouldn't want to accidentally knock you unconscious for being in my way."

As Oliver stared intently at the officer, he noticed other guards slowly making their way to the scene. He instantly remembered the handicapped position he was in and exhaled one last sigh filled with disappointment as he deflated himself back to his seat. He knew he was in no position to dispute the officer's harassment and did not want to go back to isolation. Instead, he proceeded to sit back down as if nothing had happened. He had no intention of extending his sentence any further and knew he would not allow Officer Kellerman to bait him into reacting.

"That's what I thought," berated the officer as he proceeded to walk away while smirking in satisfaction.

After Officer Kellerman was gone, Oliver looked at the other inmates, shaking his head in disbelief. To his right was one of his favorite people in prison, Letieus, who went by the nickname "Preacher" because he always sang choir songs. To his left was Connor Kelly who handed Oliver a napkin and reassured him to keep his head up.

"I hate this place," stated Connor. "One day, someone's going to mess that guy up. He can't treat people like that."

"Well, that one day ain't today, and that someone ain't me," replied Oliver in a fearful yet reassuring tone. "The last thing I need is to go to war with a CO when I got less than a year left in this place. It wouldn't make sense. I'm sure someone's gonna give Kellerman what he deserves, it just can't be me."

"I understand you, man. You can't go around treating people like that. If we were in the streets, my crew would have sliced into him by now. Hopefully one day someone beats him bloody and knocks him unconscious. We'll see who's laughing then."

"Thanks, Connor," replied Oliver in a joking manner. "I can always count on the Irishman to make me feel better by inserting some violence into the conversation."

"Well, you know you can always count on me for something, man," joked Connor. "Sláinte!"

When the inmates finally completed lunch, they were taken outside for their recreation period. Oliver had no intention of doing anything but going back to the shack. He was around nothing but hardened young men and cynical guards all day, and was looking forward to being around this new stranger who seemed docile and calm. His curiosity was piqued and he wanted nothing more than to be in her presence.

As he looked around the yard, he saw everything was moving as normal. The basketball court and weightlifting spaces were both filled, and as usual, the guards were focused on ensuring their gladiators, who were behind their bets, were performing as expected. Once Oliver confirmed he was in the clear, he casually began his walk and made his way in the direction of the shack.

When he finally arrived, Oliver gave one final look around, then proceeded toward the back. As he approached, he began to whisper Salena's name but there was no response. He did not see her in her previous spot.

Something doesn't seem right. Maybe she got scared?

Just as he was about to turn tail and leave, he heard a rustling sound coming from the other side of the fence through the bushes. When he looked over, he saw Salena motioning towards the same spot he met her only 24 hours before.

"Hey, Salena," said Oliver as he approached with obvious excitement in his look. "Thought you wasn't coming."

"Hey…I had some issues with the COs over here. Nothin' I can't handle though. You been here long?"

"Nah, not long. I just wasn't sure what time you typically get here. I know exactly what you mean about the COs," he admitted. "There's one over here who gets on my nerves. I swear he's waiting for me to punch him in the face so he can lock me away forever."

"Wow!"

"Yeah. I just try to stay away from him, and when I see him, I try my hardest to keep from reacting. The last thing I need is to get more time in this fuckin' place. There is nothing for me here."

"Yeah. There's nothing for me over here either. Every morning when I wake up, I can't wait to take advantage of the *full* hour away from the guards and those angry bitches."

Oliver nodded in understanding. "Yep, I feel the same about the thugs over here."

"It's just been so frustratin' cause the guards treat us like we're less than human. There's no respect and they don't even allow us to speak unless spoken to. I shouldn't be here, but when I tried askin' if I could speak with someone about my case, I got brushed off."

"The guards on this side probably ain't no better than the guards over there. It's just like the guard I mentioned before. I'm sure it's because he was a weak fuckin' loser on the outside so he became a Corrections Officer in juvie to feel superior. Couldn't deal with real inmates in a normal prison. Anyway, I've got about ten months left in this place and I remind myself every day that I need to stay on track to get the fuck out. What are you here for?"

"It's so stupid, I don't even want to tell you."

"You can tell me. It probably ain't stupid. Tell me. You can trust me."

"Well…a few months ago, one of my friends told me that her daddy taught her how to drive as practice. He was in and out of prison, so my assumption was he taught her while he was out. Because she was a few months away from turning sixteen, she told me he wanted her to practice."

Oliver thought he heard someone and turned his attention and looked around. When he was sure they were alone, he turned his attention back to Salena's storytelling and listened as she continued.

"So, one day, she pulled up to my house and was driving a car that I never seen before. She told me that her daddy's friend let her borrow it to continue to practice with. When I asked her where she was driving to, she said, 'anywhere we want.' I should have seen this as a red flag. At first, I was like, 'this ain't right,' but she looked so cool and I was so excited to drive with her. I should've said no but I got into the fuckin' car anyway."

Salena was wringing her hands as she spoke. Oliver could sense her remembrance was making her uneasy.

"You don't need to continue if you don't want to."

"No, it's okay. I feel like I can talk to you."

"Why?"

"I don't know. Guess you're better company than these bitches over here. Anyways, as we drove for a few minutes, I could tell she wasn't ready to drive on her own. She wasn't driving anything like how I had seen others driving. Her driving was faster and jerky. I was gonna tell her to let me out when a police car pulled up behind us with the lights on. She told me not to say nothin' and that she was gonna handle it.

"When the officer walked up to the window, he seemed shocked to see two lil girls driving. He asked my friend for her driver's license and registration. She looked at me with this dumb look of shock and turned back around and told him she didn't have either on her.

"I could see her hands trembling and saw there was no key in the ignition. Instead, there were a few wires twisted together under the steering wheel. That's when I knew the car was stolen. That bitch lied to me. The officer called for backup and when the other cop arrived, they told us to get out, put our hands on the hood, all that, and put us in cuffs. They then asked us how old we were and who the car belonged to. I was so scared and kept quiet. That bitch lied and said she was twenty years old, and the car belonged to her friend.

"The first officer walked my friend away and continued asking her some questions. The other officer began to check the car. When he opened the trunk, he called the first officer to the back to look at something. There was a pile of radios. Fuckin' radios."

"Wow," Oliver interjected as he shook his head.

"Then, they separated us by taking us to different police cars and the officer asked me whose car it was. I told him that I was told that the vehicle belonged to a friend of my friend's daddy. He then asked me if I knew what was in the trunk and I told him no. He seemed genuinely good. Some are, you know? Acting like he was my friend or something. He asked me for my name and age. I truthfully told him both and he told me that he was arresting me. He said I could call my mom when we got to the station, but I think I was more afraid of her than I was of the cops."

"Why?"

"Because she always told me if I got pregnant or dropped out of school, she'd disown me. Guess I took that to heart. Anyway, I thought my friend would confess to the whole thing and they would let me go but was wrong.

"As the other officer was speaking with my friend, who was now crying, the one talking to me told me that my friend said it was my idea to drive the car. He said she told him that I knew whose car it was and that I knew about the radios in the trunk. I can't believe she lied on me like that. Ughhh… I get so mad thinking about it!"

"Yeah, I would too."

"The same cop from before told me real quietly while he was booking me that he knew my friend was lying, but there was not much he could do."

Shock was painted on Oliver's face as Salena continued. *Guess we both got taken advantage of.*

"The officers first took us to booking and let me call my parents. My mom didn't have any money so she couldn't bail me out. I told her what happened and she just started crying. I was originally told I would be receiving fourteen days. I was ready to do my two weeks and come home. Unfortunately, things didn't play out that way.

"As we both stood in the courtroom, the judge saw my friend's attitude and wanted to punish us. She sentenced us both for possession of the stolen property and grand theft auto. I couldn't believe it when the judge announced my charges. They transferred us here.

"Shortly after arriving here, I found out that she did know what was in the trunk. She was trying to create some cred for herself and was telling people she stole the car. I saw her in the chow hall and went up to confront her. We got into this huge fight."

Oliver sat there in disbelief. He could not fathom how angry he would have been if he was betrayed this way. He thought back to his old life and his old crew and if others would have made the same decisions to not snitch as he did. He wondered if they would have traded his freedom for their own.

"After that fight, PACC threw me in isolation. While there, I couldn't stop thinkin' about how betrayed I felt. What made it worse was I heard she was tellin' others I snitched on her. Ughhh…I was so angry. I wanted to kill her."

Salena paused and lowered her voice back to a whisper.

"I'm not a thug, I'm not a bully, and I'm not a thief. You're actually the first person I shared that story with. Everyone else looks at me like a tattletale and some have even threatened me, so I mostly keep to myself. I can't wait to get out."

"Wow, that's crazy. Did your friend ever apologize?"

"No, she did NOT! That bitch claimed she told me to keep quiet. We grew up in the same neighborhood and were around the same group of kids for most of our lives. We weren't really friends, but because we was around the same people, I saw her as an acquaintance. Guess I wanted to believe we were friends but that was a mistake. Now, look at me. Fifteen years old and locked in this juvenile detention center. Even when I get out of here, I won't have a life. That will haunt me."

"What do you think happened to her after isolation?" inquired Oliver.

"I really don't really care where she is, to be honest. I'm just happy I don't have to see her lyin' ass anymore."

"Well, if you were to see her today, what would be your first reaction?"

"I don't know," replied Salena as her face softened in confusion. "There have been so many emotions that have run through my mind since that day. The days after I got out of isolation were hard. I woke up feelin' angry every day. I felt sad and frustrated. Lonely and defeated. I was constantly thinking about the 'what if's' and even considered doing something rash."

She paused, lowered her eyes, and shook her head.

"Rash like what?"

"I don't know. Just something that could stop everything. Fortunately, I didn't 'cause one day when I was at one of my lowest points, my cellmate invited me to some church service she was going to. I grew up attending church with my family, so it wasn't that hard to convince me to go. The focus of the service was forgiveness. The pastor spoke about the importance of letting go of grudges. He said a grudge is like a black cloud that hovers over your head. It doesn't bother the other person very much, but you always walk around in a shadow.

"He spoke about the past, and regret and forgiveness and stuff. A bunch of stuff that made me think."

As Salena wiped the few tears that began rolling down her eyes, she looked at her clock and noticed recreation time was wrapping up.

"I'm so sorry. We spent this entire time talking about me and now we have to go back inside. You going to be back tomorrow?"

"Uh... yes…I'll be here tomorrow."

"Great! I wanna hear your story. I wanna hear what brought you to this horrible place."

Oliver wasn't used to anyone taking such a genuine interest in his life nor anyone opening up so much about their own life. The actions of the people in his life were driven by greed, anger, and violence. This had forced him to close himself off from certain parts of this world. He had been closed off for so long because of it and was not used to making connections. Salena shared her story with him and in doing so, he realized how invested he was in hearing about it. He realized he hadn't lost his temper once nor did he feel the need to put on the tough-guy exterior he had become accustomed to. He felt comfortable with her and wanted more.

CHAPTER 4:

THE OTHER SIDE OF THE FENCE

Oliver Mahlah

As he made his way back to the main yard, Oliver thought about what Salena told him. Despite the anger and frustration she felt toward her friend, she still found some way to forgive her for the wrongdoings. He thought about how powerful her story was because he knew how difficult it would be for him to forgive that type of wrongdoing. *How could Salena forgive those things? How could anyone forget that type of betrayal?*

Just as he was about to think back to the beginning of his long and troubled path that led to PACC, he heard one of the guards yelling.

"Inmate!... Inmate!... Step to the side!"

When Oliver looked over, he saw Officer Kellerman standing with another guard, both staring and pointing in his direction. They both had roguish smirks on their faces and Kellerman was signaling for Oliver to walk toward him.

Oh shit. This can't be good.

"Where you been inmate?"

"Ummm… I been in the yard like everyone else," replied Oliver avoiding his eyes. "I didn't see any open spots on any basketball teams, so I decided to just go for a walk. I usually walk to clear my mind."

The officer clicked his tongue and smirked. "Are you telling me that you couldn't play basketball like a little monkey, so you went walkin' alone? Like a sad, lost puppy."

"Just because I walk alone doesn't mean I'm lost, sir," Oliver replied now turning his gaze toward the officers.

I need to keep calm. I can't let him get to me.

Officer Kellerman laughed and nudged the other CO as if Oliver made a joke.

"You must take us for some fools," remarked Kellerman sarcastically. "I was looking for a stress ball to make me feel better about monitorin' you shitheads. Since I couldn't find one, I came looking for you instead. To my surprise, you weren't at the basketball court with the other monkeys. After wasting my time looking around, I thought to myself, *'where could this scrawny nigger be?'* Just as I was beginning to think you stayed inside during this rec period, you show up casually walking toward the building. Now here you are."

Officer Kellerman then walked toward Oliver until he was right in front of him. He was staring into the inmate's eyes with a piercing gaze begging for a reaction. Oliver could smell the stench of stale cigarettes and coffee on his breath as he displayed his stained, yellow teeth.

"This is your only fuckin' reminder. You don't breathe without my approval first. I should be the first person you think about when you wake up and the last person to cross your mind before you shut your fuckin' eyes. Any decision you're thinking of making, you should think, *'should I run this by Officer Kellerman first?'* If at any point the answer to that question is yes, then I'd highly advise you to stop what you are doing. Now get the fuck inside before I smack the black off your face until the white meat shows."

Let me just go inside. Fuck this guy. It's not worth it.

Oliver continued to stare intently at CO Kellerman who still had a huge grin on his face.

"Did I fuckin' stutter, shithead? Didn't your Momma teach you how to respect your elders? Maybe I need to bring her in and show her a thing or two about respect," he said with a wicked smirk and a wink.

Oliver had taken Officer Kellerman's harassment before, but he felt this time, the CO had gone too far speaking about a mother he did not know. Although Oliver grew up an orphan, something in Kellerman's threat triggered him. He was so angry; his fists were balled up as if he was squeezing the life out of them. The pace of his breathing had picked up substantially and his head was now warm. Without thinking, Oliver blurted the first thing that came to mind in his angry state.

"You're just a soft, fuckin' loser who preys on inmates who can't do anything because of the constraints the judicial system placed on us. If we were out of these walls, you'd be my bitch. Actually, you wouldn't even get that honor. You probably would have been handled by now. That disrespect would have got you killed outside of these walls, and I swear you're lucky."

Officer Kellerman had a look of disbelief on his face and gave an uncomfortable laugh. He then looked at his younger white colleague, Corrections Officer Rubinak who also wore a look of shock on his baby face. Officer Rubinak saw how much the harassment had affected Oliver and was equally as surprised at his reaction as his older, racist colleague. Just as he was about to make a statement, Officer Kellerman interrupted.

"Did you just threaten me, inmate?" questioned Kellerman. "I think you just threatened me. I think that warrants some time in isolation. Officer Rubinak, don't you agree?"

Officer Rubinak once again turned his attention to Oliver and saw the anger and frustration on his face. He watched as Oliver's eyes did not break their gaze from Kellerman and the teen was fuming. His nostrils were flaring, and his body language was combative. The toll of Kellerman's harassment had finally hit its apex with the young inmate and Rubinak felt stuck.

"We should just leave this kid alone. He's nothing," he remarked as he turned his attention to Oliver. To live up to Kellerman's expectations of him, he forcibly demanded Oliver make his way inside with the others. "Get the fuck inside, inmate."

Officer Kellerman looked over at Rubinak with hesitation at first but reluctantly agreed, turning his attention back to Oliver.

"You're lucky Rubinak saved your life because I was ready to put you into isolation for the next ten months. Get the fuck inside you black fuckin' bastard. Go!"

Oliver slowly unballed his fist and wiped the few anger tears that had formed in the corners of his eyes. He proceeded toward the building and as he walked, he realized he was almost ready to jeopardize the remainder of his sentence for Kellerman's harassment.

Since he arrived at PACC, it was difficult for him to sleep through many nights. His anger and nightmares had always been his issue. He now realized his fatigue had also caught up to him. *What did I almost do? I almost fucked up my entire sentence over Kellerman. Thank God for Officer Rubinak. I can't do this anymore. I need to get out of here.*

He decided to take Kellerman's threat seriously. He knew the CO was keeping an eye on his movements, which worried him. He did not want to risk Kellerman finding his hiding space or even worse, finding out about Salena. Even though he promised her he would return the following day, he knew he needed to tread carefully. He decided that as long as Kellerman was closely watching him, he had to avoid the shack.

After Oliver walked through the building doors, Kellerman pulled Rubinak to the side and stared intently into his eyes.

"Rubinak…. you're a smart guy. I can tell." His voice grew cold and threatening as he peered into the eyes of the young CO as if he was speaking directly to his fear. "Don't ever take sides against me. If you ever embarrass me like that again, especially in front of these fuckin' spics and niggers, I will have you working security at K-Mart. You fuckin' got that?"

Rubinak froze in his place and nodded his head in agreement. He watched Kellerman proceed into the building.

*****

Over the next few weeks, Oliver watched as Kellerman monitored his every movement. The CO closely supervised as the inmate ate lunch, walked the halls, and even as he entered the restroom. Kellerman had Oliver feeling uncomfortable, which meant he had him right where he wanted him. He was fulfilling his promise to make Oliver's time at the correction center a living hell.

Since the day he first learned about Salena's story, Oliver had been trying to make his way back to the shack. As time went on, his appetite for the risk grew smaller and smaller and he found fewer opportunities. He knew he could not do anything with his new shadow following him everywhere. Although the treatment was unjust, he was unbothered by Kellerman's antics. Instead, he felt horrible that he could not follow up with his new friend on the other side of the fence. Something about their conversation had calmed him. He was determined to make his way back to the shack and finally found an opportunity after five and a half weeks.

*****

On this Monday morning, Oliver woke up to the news that his oppressor, Officer Kellerman, was on furlough. Everyone at PACC knew Kellerman as the terror of the juvenile wing so anytime he was not around, news spread like wildfire. For almost two months, the teenage inmate had lived under Kellerman's tormenting eye which meant he had to be on his best behavior. Although his behavior changed, he still was the same troubled, fearful young man. He planned on taking advantage of Kellerman's absence and knew he may not receive a better opportunity to see Salena.

After lunch, Oliver was the first one outside in the recreation yard. It was as if he felt a fresh breath of air due to his seemingly newfound freedom. Just like the previous five weeks, he first stopped by the basketball courts to ensure he kept to his routine. He confirmed the normal guards were at the court and invested in the games before slowly making his departure. As he walked away, he began to think to himself, *something doesn't feel right.* He'd gotten so used to avoiding walking in the direction of the shack, that he felt the anxiety building by him walking there on this day. Despite his hesitation, he knew he may not receive another opportunity, so he continued.

When he arrived at the shack, there she was. Sitting with her legs crossed just like he left her five weeks prior. As he approached, Salena raised her head. His gentle eyes caught her gaze as they exchanged smiles.

"Wow…. Would you look who it is. Where you been, stranger? You told me you was coming back and I ain't seen you for weeks now."

"Well, you remember how I told you about the one guard who has it out for me? After we spoke that day, he stopped me before I could get into the building and pretty much told me he was going to make my last few months a living hell. Since then, he's been following me like a hawk. I didn't want him to know about this place or you, so I've avoided it."

"Damn, what an asshole," she said, and was suddenly anxious. "Wait… how'd you make it here today? Did he see you?"

"Well, I heard he's on a vacation or something like that. Actually they said it's a furlough so I used this as an opportunity to come by."

"A furlough?" replied Salena with a confused look on her face and skepticism in her voice. "What's that?"

"I heard it's when the guards take off. Something like that."

"That's weird but okay. Well anyway, let's catch up. You still need to tell me—"

Just as Salena was about to finish her sentence, the lockdown alarm sounded in the male juvenile detention wing. Oliver and Salena quickly looked at each other and both got up and made their way back to their respective yards. As he ran back, Oliver worried because the only time this alarm sounded was if there was a riot, a fight, or an escape. Being that his wing was minimum security, a riot or escape was very unlikely. *There must be a fight.*

As he got closer to the main yard, what he saw shocked him. All the other inmates were laying face-down with their fingers interlocked behind their heads. Standing above them all were the guards and standing out atop all the guards was Officer Kellerman with his nightstick in hand and a cigarette in his mouth.

When Oliver got to the basketball court, he dropped to his knees and placed his chest on the ground. He locked his fingers behind the back of his head. Kellerman then flagged a colleague in the guard tower who turned the alarm off. As Oliver lay face down on the hot concrete, he heard heavy footsteps approaching. He did not care to look at who was walking toward him, but he had an idea. As the footsteps grew closer, so did his dread and terror. He laid there, his mouth so dry, he could feel the lump of fear that rested in his throat.

He quickly looked up and saw Kellerman staring right at him and assumed his punishment would be more time in the isolation chamber. Surprisingly, this didn't scare him. He realized he wasn't afraid of spending time in isolation because he was afraid. No, his fear came from the fact that he would be away from Salena, who at that point he believed to be the only person in prison he may have been able to talk to as himself.

When the footsteps arrived directly in front of Oliver's head, the guard crouched down and whispered something in Oliver's ear.

"I warned you, nigger. I told you that you shouldn't breathe without my approval first. I told you that any decision you're thinking of making needs to run through me first."

"I was just on a walk around the—"

Just as he was about to finish his statement, Officer Kellerman struck the teen in the rib cage with his nightstick which forced the breath out of him. The officer then looked back in the direction from which Oliver came running and vaguely saw the figure of a female standing in the distance. The fence was not close to the basketball court, but the corrections officer could see that it was an African American woman on the other side. She was staring intently at what was occurring, and Kellerman realized what was going on.

"Ohhh… I see now… You got yourself a little nigger girlfriend. Does she know you're already my bitch? Maybe I should walk over and let her know. Or maybe instead, I should show her what a real man looks like. How 'bout that, nigger? Would you like that?"

Oliver wanted to get up and react, but he was still holding his ribs from the nightstick attack.

Kellerman then blew his whistle and announced recreation time was over and the inmates were to make their way back inside. Oliver began to rise to his feet and Kellerman used the bottom of his boot to push the inmate back down. The guard then crouched down again and placed his hand on the teen's shoulder.

"Hope you like the dark 'cause you'll be spending the rest of the week in isolation for insubordination."

He then carted Oliver to the isolation chamber where he would spend the next 96 hours.

*****

When Friday afternoon arrived, the doors to the isolation chamber finally opened and instantly shot a beam of light into the small room, blinding Oliver. He covered his eyes with his weak hands as the silhouette of a large man approached and forcibly grabbed him from the ground. Although he couldn't see the look on Kellerman's face, he could feel him grinning with satisfaction. He could sense the CO was beaming to see his plan had broken the inmate.

He was so weak he could barely keep up as Kellerman once again dragged him back into the main building to his cell. When they arrived, Officer Kellerman dropped Oliver on his bottom bunk bed and walked toward the exit of the cell. Before exiting the room, he turned around and looked at Oliver.

"Hope you learned your lesson, boy. I don't like doing things like this but some inmates, like yourself, respond better to violence and this type of treatment. This will be your final. Fuckin'. Warning. Don't even think about doing anythin' other than what I allow… Oh yeah, by the way… I visited your girlfriend." The evil guard rubbed his hands and licked his lips. "She was nice and tight just like I love them. She won't be needin' you anymore, so don't even think about trynna see her."

He then turned around and laughed as he made his way out of the cell. It was lunchtime so everyone else in the wing was in the chow hall but Oliver could not bring himself to eat. Instead, for the next twenty minutes, he silently cried in his bed.

I need to get out of here. I can't do this anymore.

He wasn't sure if his tears were derived from anger, fear, or resentment, but he thought about how he got to his current point and felt broken.

I can't win against this guy. I just want to leave.

As he lay there, he heard someone whispering his name from the entrance of the cell. When he turned around and looked over, he saw Officer Rubinak, standing by the front door. At first, he thought it may have been another one of Kellerman's tricks and turned back around.

"Oliver…I'm sorry about what happened to you. Kellerman is the devil, and this is his special version of hell. The rest of us live in it just like you all do. I know you probably don't trust me, but I want you to know not everyone here is like him. Some of us want to see this place emptied till there are no more inmates to house here. You don't have that much longer left in your sentence and I would hate to see another young black man lose himself in this place. I can tell you're destined for a lot more and I want you to ride out the rest of your time here."

This is another one of Kellerman's tricks. Why won't he just leave me alone? He thought as he continued to disregard the Corrections Officer's plea.

"Listen…. Oliver…that's not the reason I'm here. I'm here because of Salena."

When Oliver heard Salena's name, he slowly craned his head and then his entire body toward the guard.

Wait, what?

He picked his weak body up from the bottom bunk and carried himself towards the cell's door.

"What do you know about Salena?"

"After taking you to isolation, Kellerman went to the female side and spoke with some of his CO friends over there. They found out it was Salena who you were friends with. So, Kellerman took a few of us over to speak with her. He asked her what the two of you spoke about. She told him you did not speak about anything and the two of you had just met in passing. He didn't believe her and told her if she didn't tell him the truth, he would have to do unpleasant things. She stood by her story and reconfirmed that the two of you did not speak about anything and that you barely knew each other. He felt she was lying and had us leave. Before we all left, he laughed and placed his dirty heavy hand on her shoulder. This was his way of showing his dominance over her. The others didn't know it but I knew this was a threat. He told her that he believed her and wished her well for the remainder of her time at PACC."

Oliver looked around nervously to see if anyone else was with Rubinak and when he was sure the guard was alone, he finally looked him in the face as the CO continued.

"As we all walked out of the room and made our way back to this side, we passed a few of the COs on the female side who Kellerman knew. They looked at each other and nodded in what seemed like some sort of nonverbal agreement. Kellerman told me and the other guard to keep going and that he would catch up. As I walked away slowly, I overheard Kellerman telling his friends to find out what she knew and send him any updates. I assumed this meant just a follow-up conversation but was unfortunately wrong."

Rubinak looked back when he heard a noise.

"I don't have much time but yesterday, Kellerman brought the two of us to the guards' break room and locked the door. He told us that his people in the female wing interrogated Salena to find out what she knew. In doing so, she was beaten so badly that she went into cardiac arrest and, well…. she died."

Oliver's face changed. He couldn't believe what he was hearing. Rubinak continued.

"Kellerman claimed he only asked them to rough her up a bit, but they took it one step further. He claimed he just wanted information, but you never know with this guy."

Officer Rubinak then pulled out a polaroid from his pocket and showed it to Oliver. In the picture, it showed Salena with her face badly beaten with her eyes seemingly open.

"I learned that Kellerman told the guards over there to take a picture with her eyes open to make it seem like she was beaten up by another inmate and was still alive. I shouldn't even have this, but I see how he treats you and knew you wouldn't have believed me without this photo. I wish I could've done something, but I was too late. I'm just trying to do my time and I suggest you do the same.

"Avoid Kellerman when you can and in the moments he confronts you, bow out. He's a power freak that needs to feel like he controls everything. The reason he made you a target is because you get along with everyone and he thinks that makes you scary. Every time you or any other inmate rebels or talks back to him, it fuels him up and makes him want to embarrass you even more. I suggest you quietly do your time and get out. I'm stuck here for now because it's the only job I could get, but I see you have so much more ahead of you. Again, I'm sorry about your friend. I have to run but remember what I told you."

Oliver took one last look at the picture and then placed it back in his pocket as he walked back to his bed. As he lay there, he began to think back to his last full conversation with Salena. They did not know each other that well but he felt somewhat responsible for her death. He never laid a finger on her, but still felt she was gone because of her association with him. His regret became anger as he thought about Kellerman and the role he played. *He cannot get away with this. Something needs to be done. How could this happen?*

Tears—the silent kind—slowly painted his cheeks as each drop ran from his eyes off his face. *We can't do anything about the past and should move on. Don't be a prisoner to it.* Salena's words echoed in his mind.

There was nothing he could do about the past and he did not want to worry about what the future had in store for him. He knew his best option was to remain in the present and focus on getting out. They had barely known each other, but her death hit him harder than he expected because to that point, she had been his only beacon of peace after a life of strife.

Maybe she would want me to put this past me the way she did with her "friend." Maybe she would want me to just focus on getting out.

*****

Over the course of the next few months, Oliver did just that. He kept his head down, his mouth closed and his eyes straight. He did not want any more unnecessary attention and was committed to finishing up his stint without any other issues. Officer Kellerman noticed this change in inmate 0713 and continued harassing him for a few weeks after Salena's death. After the CO noticed his treatment did not beget a response from the inmate, he got bored and found other, more rebellious, inmates to focus his attention on. Based on rumors and what Rubinak told him, Oliver knew that Kellerman only bullied because of the reactions his treatment triggered. He knew that deep down inside, the Corrections Officer's greatest joy came from knowing he had broken others down. Oliver quietly watched as others were berated just as he was. It angered him but also relieved him that he was no longer the target.

In his final days at PACC, Oliver struggled with how to deal with the Kellerman situation.

I'm almost out. I should just leave. I need to just leave.

He was torn on what to do because he wanted to avenge Salena's unjust death, but he also could not bring himself to address it directly.

I want to just leave but he had Salena killed and he needs to pay for that. I can make him pay. I don't want to get back into that life, but I need to act. He can't continue like this.

Oliver didn't want to hold a grudge but finally decided that he couldn't let this one go. On his last day, he met with the leaders of each of the associated prison race crews to thank them for everything during his time in juvie. He reassured them that he would ensure their hospitality was known on the outside and ensure it was repaid. He had no intentions of going back to that life but knew it would sound good to say on his last day.

Before walking out, he left each of them with a letter and told them to open it when he was gone. The day after he departed from PACC, the leaders met and opened their letters together. In each of the envelopes were two photos and a letter. The first photo was a picture of Officer Kellerman with one hand on Salena's shoulder. The second picture was the same picture Rubinak had shown Oliver months before in his cell. It was a photo of Salena's beaten face. Both were time-stamped on the bottom which clearly showed how they occurred roughly around the same time. There was also a letter in each envelope. The letters were all the same and read:

1. ***Noi O Loro***
2. ***Deuteronomy 19:21***
3. ***No respect will be given to anyone who has harmed a woman or child.***

On this day, two of the three bylaws that govern our juvenile population at PACC were broken. Officer Christopher Kellerman selfishly decided to have an innocent woman raped, beaten, and murdered because she refused to perform sexual acts on him. The life of an innocent prisoner, serving a sentence like each of us, was unjustly taken at the hand of a corrupt prison guard who lives his life on a constant power trip. A life was taken and now a life is owed. I leave it to all of you to decide the punishment of this perpetrator but encourage you to issue a just and swift reprimand to continue to hold the integrity of the bylaws. The future depends on it.

See you on the other side.

Signed,
Oliver Mahlah (Inmate 0713.)

PART II
ORIGINS

CHAPTER 5:

FORGIVE ME

Sixteen Years Prior   *Manhattan, 1970*

On August 26, 1970, the city roared with activity on both sidewalks and streets. Taxis filled the busy New York City streets while Jamaicans occupied the sidewalks with carts filled with beef patties and roti. As per usual, the corners of each block slowly became overwhelmed by the smell of incense candles as local drug dealers clocked out from their overnight shifts and cart pushers clocked in.

With the nation still in transition after the Civil Rights movement, which was at its pinnacle only a decade before, New York City was at the forefront of the nation's progressive change. Suburban neighborhoods became packed with individuals of many different races while the city centers busted at the seams with white businessmen. The country's newly elected president began his term by placing a heavy emphasis on education and the youth, in hopes of selling a more bountiful future that could hopefully erase a stained past filled with segregation.

According to the country's leader, the plan was simple. To correct a broken institution, they needed to commit all available resources to it. "How could we fail?" he would often say.

Unfortunately, his high optimism and low acumen for strategy became more and more obvious. As certain resources were identified and dedicated towards education, holes were created in other areas that opportunists quickly noticed and took advantage of. To them, it didn't matter if you were black, white, yellow, brown, rich, poor, smart, or dumb; if there was a product to exchange, the only color that mattered was green.

As time went on, the rise of the drug trade began to replace a once broken education system, creating new challenges for a country formerly crippled by division. The fine line between success and failure began to dissolve, and one problem replaced another.

Many of the young children were a result of their parents' acceptance of the change. Many played together in the playgrounds while parents gazed from afar. As their children played, parents discussed the positive changing landscape of the New York Tri-State area, which was defined through recent political announcements.

Two months prior, just over the Hudson River, Kenneth Gibson was announced as the first black mayor of Newark, New Jersey. This positive change showed Brick City's commitment to its recovery after the 1967 Newark Riots, which resulted in roughly ten million dollars' worth of damage. It also resulted in the relocation of the white middle class, leaving the broken city to poor minorities, failing business owners, and drug fiends who had no interest in kicking their habits. This was a trend that all the five boroughs in New York found themselves in.

*****

On this morning, a young African American woman wandered the shadows of Brooklyn looking for a place to rest, panting rapidly. As she exhaled her exhaustion and fatigue, she leaned against an available wall in an empty alley in an effort to gain control of herself. She began to feel dizzy and slowly lowered her body onto the ground beside a dirty dumpster.

As she closed her eyes and attempted to gain control of her breathing, she reached into her pink backpack to grab a bottle of water which sat beside her lightly used 10th grade mathematics textbook. She took a long drink until the bottle was empty then took an even longer exhale. Her hope was that the water would help with the dizziness she was feeling that warm morning. She was wrong.

As she placed both hands on her forehead, the young girl sat silently in the alley as if she was in deep thought. After a few minutes of pondering, she slowly moved her hands from her forehead to her eyes as she began quietly sobbing. Her crying became hysterical, and she sat alone until a passerby saw her in the alley and walked toward her.

The girl did not notice this person at first but jumped back when she saw the shadow of a figure draw close. When she looked up, she noticed a white man, dressed in an ill-fitting suit with dilapidated black dress shoes approaching. With tears still running down her face, she was hopeful that the man would turn around when he saw she was crying. Instead, when the man reached her feet, he dropped a few dollars on the ground and leaned in to place one hand on her shoulder. The young woman jumped back and slowly wiped her eyes as she peered at the multiple $1 bills sitting within arm's length. When she looked up at the man, she listened as he requested that she stop crying.

There was a concern in his tone and somehow, it comforted her. That comfort was swiftly removed as his tone changed and he then suggested that she quickly perform a sexual favor so he could be on his way.

As she wiped the remaining tears from her face, the young woman continued to look at the man with the guise of impatience before turning her attention back to the dollar bills in front of her. She pondered, quickly totaled the sum of the money in her head, then with the same look of disgust, she looked back up at the man standing impatiently.

"Go away. I have nothing for you," the girl demanded. "I'm not working and even if I was, I wouldn't touch you, old man. I'm not no two dolla' hoe."

"You better learn some respect when you speak to me, girl," barked the man while reaching to grab her thick hair. As he tightly gripped it with a full fist, he forcibly jerked her head forward and made her watch him unbuckle his pants with his available hand.

"Don't you ever think you're better than me. You're nothing in this world and if it wasn't for the public service you're about to perform, I'd have you killed for speaking to me like that."

"Please, sir! I don't want to," cried the young woman using both hands in an attempt to free herself from his grip. "Please just leave me alone. I just want to be alone!"

"You have no rights here, girl. If my money is green and you need it, I'm in charge. Besides if it wasn't for me, you'd still—"

Just as the man was about to finish his statement, he heard rustling coming from the dumpster. He stopped unbuckling his pants and turned his attention to the sound. After a few seconds of silence, the man assumed it was possibly a rodent looking for breakfast and turned his attention back to the young woman. Before he could make his next statement, he again heard a noise coming from the dumpster. This time, it sounded as if it were the sound of a crying baby. It was hard to hear but it slowly became more palpable as she jerked back away from him.

The man turned his attention back to the young girl just as she began crying frantically again. He assumed she may have been hysterical from the act he was about to make her perform but he then focused his attention back on the dumpster and his face dropped.

"Stop!" cried the young woman as she attempted to grab the man's arm, but he forcibly knocked her off. As he approached the dumpster, it became more obvious and he was now certain the sound he heard was, indeed, a baby crying. With arched eyebrows, the man gave one shocked look back at the young woman and then turned back towards the dumpster.

Right there in front of him was an object tight wrapped in a baby blanket sitting on top of bags of garbage and newspapers. As he reached in to unwrap the baby blanket, the man inhaled and then exhaled a deep sigh of disbelief. There in front of him was a baby no more than one-month-old crying and sweating profusely from the cocooned body wrap it was in. That summer morning was hot enough, but it was obvious the baby was overheating from the covering. The now worried man slowly began to back away from the dumpster while staring at the young girl in shock. Her shaking hands were still over her eyes as she cried.

"Oh my god. You're crazy. Is that your baby in the trash? You need help," the man stated as he slowly backed away towards the alley exit. As he began to walk away from the sitting woman, he gave one final glance at his dollar bills on the ground, then turned around and ran away.

After the man was gone, the young woman proceeded to wipe her eyes and then picked up the cash. As she pocketed the money, she got up and walked towards the trash, and stared at the crying baby. She watched, with disappointment on her face, as the baby cried uproariously. With her head down, the young woman reached in to pick the baby up.

She held the child in her arms and looked uncomfortable—as if she was holding it for the first time. Her vision was still blurred, and her thin, weak arms shook as she held it. She brought the baby close to her body for a hug then in a very low and sad voice the young woman whispered, "Forgive me."

She placed the baby back down in the dumpster then dropped to her knees and began sobbing harder. The pain for the act she was about to commit fell from her 10th grade educated brain to her broken heart, and she questioned her value. She thought about how for the longest time, she had been told she wasn't worth anything now nor would she be later. *How could anything I care for be worth anything? How could anything in my life turn out okay if I barely have control over it?*

She cried beside the trash for a few more minutes before standing to her feet. She picked up her backpack and began to slowly move toward the alley exit, in the direction that she entered less than twenty minutes before. When she reached the exit, she turned around and gave one final look back toward the dumpster containing the wailing infant. She dropped her head then turned around and disappeared into the sidewalk traffic. The sounds of a baby crying disappeared as the overbearing sound of cars honking and people talking became prevalent.

*****

Roughly fifteen minutes later, another individual entered the empty alley. Instead of searching for a place to rest, this middle-aged, bone-thin black woman arrived and proceeded straight towards the dumpster. She knew what she was looking for and went straight for it. She climbed inside the dumpster and started desperately rummaging through the trash in search of something to eat. She began tearing bags of garbage open and checking empty food cartons for crumbs of anything edible. She could smell the leftover food under the stench of the trash and hoped she would be able to separate the two once found.

As her search continued, she began furiously scratching her neck and body. She then began twitching and speaking out loud as if she was conversing with another. She had multiple marks on both of her bone-thin arms, signaling entry points for her highs.

She continued digging through the trash until she reached the far-left side of the dumpster. She froze at what she saw. There in front of her was a sleeping baby, wrapped in a damp blanket. The woman was confused and began nervously looking around the alley for anyone else. She turned her attention back to the sleeping child and stared. For a moment, she considered continuing to search around the baby in hopes of achieving her original objective of finding food or something of value she could sell or trade for heroin.

Why is this damn baby sleeping in this dumpster? Is there someone here? There has to be someone here watching me. They trynna set me up. They won't eva set me up.

Her paranoia grew.

Despite the hiccup, the woman was still hungry and knew she still had a lot of garbage left to search so she resumed her digging. She quickly decided that the baby was not worth anything of value and if someone was, in fact, watching her, they would instead worry about the baby and not her. She continued with her search and just before she tore into another garbage bag, the woman stopped and talked to herself.

"This baby probably been here for a while and ain't no one come for it. Maybe it's lost. Maybe I can get some money for it."

She convinced herself that there had to be a worried mother desperately searching for her missing child. She decided she wanted to benefit from the ordeal.

She was desperate for the cash and was committed to doing what she could for it.

I should sell the baby. I'm sure Lefty can find the parents and maybe even give me sum money for it. Wait… he may ask me questions. Fuck!

She considered putting word out on the street and waiting on someone to come looking for *her* but knew she did not have the luxury of time on her side.

I need cash now! I can't take it to the police because they gonna try to lock me up for being high. I just gotta give it to Lefty and beg him for money or H.

The woman hopped out of the trash and lifted the sleeping baby out behind her. She wrapped the baby's head with the wet blanket and just as she was turning around to leave, two white police officers walked into the alley and proceeded towards her.

The woman had previously shot up heroin that morning and was in no condition to have a straight conversation with officers.

I should run. Wait. Where the hell can I go? They too close for me to get away. Let me just lie. These dumb ass cops can't prove nothin'.

"What the hell are you doing?" demanded the older of the two officers, who wore the name "M. Moran" on his badge.

"I'm just here with this baby I found and was… plannin' on bringing him to the… precincts, ya hear," lied the twitching woman as she slurred her words. "I hear there's a reward for its return here and I wants it. Can I collect that from you sirs?"

"Do you want us to believe that you came into this empty alley and found a missing baby?" replied the same officer in a sarcastic tone. "How do you know there is a reward?"

"The streets talk, sir. You just need to know when to listen."

"Well, I don't believe you, lady, and we're going to have to bring you and the baby into the precinct until we get this sorted."

"Wait, wait, wait, wait, wait," the lady said shaking her head. She was getting nervous and began to sweat. "I bet not… be under arrest for… findin' this baby here and commitin' myself to bringin' him… in fo' my reward. I am doing… my public services… to better my community.”

“Lady, if you didn’t do anything wrong, you have nothing to worry about. We just need you to come with us so you can collect your reward from the precinct.”

The lady looked at Officer Moran with a skeptical and distrustful look, then turned to glance at the other cop who was a younger officer with the name “C. Smith” on his badge. She then looked back at Officer Moran and her look of skepticism morphed into an expression of hope. Her expectation was that she was not being misled and that the older officer would “look out” for her best interest.

“Ok, sirs…as long as I am not under arrest here. Just make sure… I gets my reward at the precincts, ya hear?”

“Don’t worry, as long as you cooperate, we’ll keep our fancy bracelets away and send you on your way with a reward,” confirmed Officer Smith.

The woman then looked back at Officer Moran and made one final plea.

“I’m trustin’ you, my brother. Make sure I gets my reward.”

Just like that, the three of them proceeded towards the alley exit with the baby in the hands of one of the officers. The woman cooperatively entered the backseat of their police cruiser, and they were off.

When they arrived at the precinct, the patrol officers introduced the twitching lady to one of their investigators.

“Ma’am, we will be asking you a series of questions before we can give you any money for your information. The information MUST pan out though or we won’t give you anything.”

They assumed she knew more than she was telling them back at the alley and were hopeful that time and breakfast would help her high wear off and her information to spew out.

They took her into a quiet corner of the main floor, and the two officers and investigator brought her a bagel, black coffee with a few bottles of water. The baby was left with another one of the officers on the other end of the floor.

"Where's my money?" demanded the lady.

"Be patient, ma'am," replied the investigator. "We need your help and are just going to get some information from you then send you on your way with your reward. Shouldn't take more than thirty minutes and you can enjoy breakfast while we speak with you."

"No one mentioned no questioning. Where's my money!" the lady again reiterated this time in a bolder tone. Her stuttering had also disappeared which was their indication that her high was wearing off.

"You'll be paid, but not a second before we get some information that will help us locate the baby's guardians. You've helped us come this far, help us close this."

The lady looked at all three officers then softened her glance as she nodded her head in agreement.

During their questioning, the officers asked the lady about how she found the baby and why the baby was in a wet blanket. Assuming they were placing blame, the lady once again became very paranoid and aggressive. She threw her hands up defensively, assuming they were questioning her as if she did something wrong. She very assertively shot up and once again began asking for her money.

"Settle down, ma'am. Again, you will be paid after we get some questions answered. Before then, we cannot give you anything besides breakfast."

With distrustful eyes, she looked at Officer Moran and again rudely demanded her money.

"You told me I'd be paid for coming down here. You didn't say anything about all these damn questions, my brother."

"Ma'am, we need you to sit down and answer a few questions before we pay you anything," reiterated the investigator in the same calm manner. He then turned his attention to the two officers and threatened loudly, "She's uncooperative. We shouldn't pay her a thing. Let's let her leave without anything."

"Wait!" she demanded. "Let's make this quick. I gots some places to be."

With her eyes bulging, she first looked at the two officers then turned and looked at the investigator before slowly sitting back down.

"Great, now we are getting somewhere," joked the investigator. "Did you see who left the baby in the alley?"

"No."

"Why was the baby so tightly wrapped in a damp blanket when it's so hot out this morning?"

"I found him like that and didn't touch him."

"But we saw you with the baby in your arms lady," replied Officer Smith in a tone that sounded less accusatory and more inquisitive.

"Yeah, because I picked him up like that. I was gonna bring him to y'all for my money."

"Okay, and you did not see who left the child."

"Like I said before, no!"

They spent the next hour questioning the woman before giving her an envelope with $30 in it. They told her there would be a lot more if she could help them find the baby's parents or guardians. She looked in the envelope with a disappointing glare and then rushed out of the precinct.

*****

The officers spent the first 72 hours searching for any evidence they could find. They went through all the open cases involving missing children and kidnappings but found nothing. Normal protocol dictated the first three days the most crucial because of the integrity of the evidence. They also feared for the baby's guardians and were committed to doing what they could for them, even if that meant arresting them. They hit the streets hard and by the end of the third day, they came back with more questions than answers.

Before throwing him into the social service system, the officers reached out to a good friend of theirs in the community.

Ms. Mabel-Ara was a community organizer and activist who had regularly petitioned to take a tougher stance on prostitution, drugs, and gun violence in Brooklyn. She had seen the boom of all three as the country focused its attention on education. She was also very involved in the civil rights movement and prided herself on being able to march on Washington D.C. with Dr. Martin Luther King. Her connection with Brooklyn was simply that this was her birthplace.

Her stepfather had been a police officer—one of the good ones. He and Officer Moran had been good friends on the force. Ms. Mabel-Ara's stepfather left the force to become a diplomat and moved with his family overseas, but they kept in touch. Now, when Officer Moran and his young partner Officer Smith had a particularly sensitive problem—like this abandoned baby—they turned to Mabel-Ara for help.

The two officers reached out to her to seek some guidance on what to do with the baby. When the officers introduced her to the baby, she instantly fell in love but knew she did not have the time and could not make a commitment to foster a child. She had a goal to one day open a small foster home but wanted to build that in a better Brooklyn. She wanted to take things step-by-step.

She had seen so many cases like this mysterious baby's and felt the best way for her to make a difference was to try to end the issues at the root. In this instance, the root was the street life that had claimed so many people. She recommended a few foster programs within the city and worked with them to create a list of homes the child could be filtered through.

Despite their helpful list from Mabel-Ara, they still wanted to find the child's parents or guardians because they believed that was best for the baby. They found challenges with this and after a few days, allowed child services to take the child and issue him a home and name. The once mysterious baby was given the name Oliver Mahlah, which was inspired by a popular story about an orphan named Oliver Twist. The last name "Mahlah" was randomly selected for the child by the social services director. After working with social services on a name, they then found his first placement. The baby would live with a nice foster family who had a few other children around the same age. The police officers then went back to the streets, determined to find answers.

Because they were still committed to locating the baby's guardians, they made regular rounds through the neighborhood where Oliver was found in hopes of finding someone who knew something. The lady who turned the baby in was normally found in the streets of that drug-ridden Brooklyn neighborhood, so the two officers regularly checked in with her during their rounds with hopes of getting more information.

"This lady's not giving us much," remarked Officer Smith one day after an unsuccessful visit.

"Yeah, I think we need to drop her stipend this week. Her information isn't panning out like she promised it would."

"I'll tell accounting to cut it by fifteen dollars. That'll show her."

Over that same period, there were multiple drug-related busts and deaths in Brooklyn. Heroin, cocaine, and marijuana were now the booming drugs, and overdosing on heroin was, sadly, a regular occurrence in New York. Another growing vice that plagued the streets was prostitution. There was a market for drugs and sex in New York and Brooklyn saw its fair share.

Violence also became very prevalent during this period. Most drug dealers saw drug addicts and prostitutes as second-class citizens and there were many instances of violence toward prostitutes and addicts. Because prostitution was frowned upon as a career choice, prostitutes were regularly beaten and robbed. Over time, and because of the frequency, calls regarding prostitution became less significant.

Prostitutes defended their pimps and the police got nowhere. There were just too many of these calls and many precincts decided to turn a blind eye to low-level drugs and prostitution.

*****

During their rounds one October morning, the two officers noticed a crowd in the middle of Paxton Avenue, which was located a couple of blocks away from where the baby was found two months earlier. As the officers approached, they forced themselves through the crowd and saw two young black women dead in the middle of the street, both with gunshot wounds to the head. When they surveyed the entire scene, they saw a pink backpack sitting a few feet from one of their still bodies, its contents scattered throughout the street. Among these contents were one unopened bottle of water, a melted candy bar, one mathematics textbook, one English textbook, a baby's bib, and over two dozen small packs of what looked like cocaine. Each of these small packs had a cursive "C" on them which was written in red font. It was obvious now that the young teens were murdered after a failed robbery attempt. The officers saw the baby bib and began to piece clues together.

CHAPTER 6:

NEW YORK TIMES

Oliver Mahlah

Over the next eight years, the officers continued to passively monitor Oliver's development. They were assigned to the rough neighborhood in Brooklyn where the brown baby was found and took a special interest in him. The situation which brought them together was an unfortunate one they had never seen before, so they focused on the baby's continued well-being while still working to prevent any other similar cases. After a while, it became difficult for them to fulfill that commitment because of their growing workload and diminishing support.

Midway through the eighth year, Officer Smith became the senior cop on his detail after Officer Moran suffered a career-ending injury. He'd been shot in the spine during a routine call and was now wheelchair-bound. Officer Moran had hand-selected Officer Smith's new partner straight from the force, and when the youthful replacement, Officer Jalacie Jefferson arrived, Officer Smith noticed he had the same youthful expression that he, himself, wore close to a decade prior. He was on the younger side, no more than thirty years old, with a sprightly face, dark goatee, and athletic build.

Officers Smith and Jefferson made it a point to stay close to Officer Moran and visited him in his Westchester home regularly.

"Looking good, old man," Officer Smith joked while wiping his eyes at the sight of his old partner.

"I can still take you out any day." Officer Moran traded as he turned to Officer Jefferson. "Hey young man. You doing okay? I know this guy can be an asshole."

"He's alright. Worst thing he's done so far is he got me into eating glazed doughnuts. My wife hates it!"

"Don't let him slow you down with his poor diet." He smiled as he continued. "Hey listen, how's the kid? Mahlah."

"We haven't really been able to keep tabs. Things have been crazy and we've been swamped. We're trying to keep it all together and do our best."

Officer Moran traded looks between the two officers before continuing.

"That kid had nothing. I know how this story goes for people like him. He'll go into the system and disappear. Probably get killed or go to jail as he makes his way through the system. You've got to promise me you won't let that happen."

"Why? What's so special about this kid?"

Officer Moran's hand shook as he struggled to take a sip of his water. Officer Jefferson saw this and assisted before the injured officer continued. "Thank you. I've done a lot in my life. Some I'm proud of, some I'm not. As I think about how we found that kid. I just want to reach the end and know I did something good. Can you help me ensure that?"

Officer Jefferson looked at Officer Smith and they both nodded. "Yeah, we can do that. We'll watch over him."

"Thanks."

"What will you do now?"

"I don't know yet," Officer Moran said scratching his chin slowly. "Truth be told, there are some things that baffle me. The force isn't what it used to be and I don't know how high up it goes. I don't want to scare you but I'm done with that life. Think I'll just do what I can locally… Mabel-Ara still thinking about doing that youth center?"

"I think so."

Officer Moran looked around his home slowly then locked eyes on the officers. "Think it's about time I gave up all this and moved back to Brooklyn. This place is too big for Betty and I anyway."

*****

For the next six years, the two officers kept their promise. They followed Oliver all the way through the foster care system until he landed at Dunbar House when he was fourteen years old. This was his sixth house and over time, he grew a resentment towards families he saw as whole and happy. He became bitter and acted out his frustration in the form of temper tantrums, verbal assaults, and sometimes, physical altercations that kept him on a short transfer list within the database. Around this same time, Oliver realized it was difficult to control his anger but did not care.

The Dunbar Home was in the rough Canarsie neighborhood of Brooklyn, known for its heavy gang and drug activity. Inside of Dunbar House felt no safer than outside. Like Oliver, most of the residents who lived there grew up with scorn and resentment towards the outside world. They didn't trust many and isolated themselves away from others who did not share the challenges that only Dunbar residents knew. For those who did live there, they found it difficult to build trust because of the perilous environment that was encouraged by the house's supervisor, Ms. Janet.

Ms. Janet was a tough, butch lady who had zero tolerance for bad attitudes, disrespect, and stealing. Although her rules were strictly enforced, she was an antagonistic aide. When outside of the house, she recommended the residents find other forms of resolution as long as it didn't bring any unnecessary attention to the house or her program.

She would regularly threaten bad behavior with homelessness and would punish the residents by starving them. "Hunger builds strength," she would say. "How can you learn to appreciate the food if you've never been hungry?" When residents disagreed, she would advise they settle it themselves with "their hands" which often resulted in all other residents feeling unsafe.

There were also a few of the larger residents whom she favored because she was able to control them. They were older than sixteen, which meant Ms. Janet had arranged for personal accommodations to keep them in her program. When she needed to reinforce her position as leader of the home, she would usually have those in her command execute her directives.

Although she hated their weakness, she did care, in a twisted way, about her foster children. If they weren't tough, the world would tear them to pieces. She wanted them to be just tough enough. This came in the form of tough love. Her favorites got other forms of her love. She found herself inviting many of these favored residents to her bedroom for "sleepovers."

Despite any apparent care, she preferred to use her position as leader to keep her residents scared. She used this fear to cover up the fact that she was using only a quarter of the stipend the government was providing to the children. The rest was kept for herself.

*****

On Monday, September 10, 1984, Oliver Mahlah began his first day at Roman Reade Public School in East New York. The school was in just as rough a neighborhood as Dunbar House but was the only public school within a seven-mile radius. Oliver was excited to go to high school because, like other foster children, he looked for any opportunity to be out of the house.

On his first day of school, Oliver walked into Roman Reade wearing a black t-shirt, cargo pants, and Timberland boots. Loud outfits and nappy afro hair were the popular fashion choices, so Oliver's unique style caused him to quickly stand out amongst others in the school. He did not care to fall into the mold, and this was obvious.

Over the following days, it also became evident that he did not have any plans, nor did he care to be recognized on any high performers list. His agenda was to have no agenda. He moved at his own speed, ignored school bells, and followed his own rules. His nonchalant attitude towards his education also showed in the quality of his schoolwork—when he actually bothered to turn it in. His classmates admired his bad-boy attitude while his teachers detested it. They noticed his carelessness but assumed it was something he would grow out of after getting comfortable with his new surroundings.

By week four, both his teachers and classmates became frustrated with Oliver's cavalier attitude and blatant disrespect for them. Most teachers began locking their classroom doors to prevent any latecomers from coming in. This caused Oliver to miss class repeatedly.

Like the teachers, most other students at Roman Reade also took note of their Dunbar House classmates to avoid them. They thought Dunbar House residents were rude and dangerous. They were right.

*****

One afternoon that October, Oliver's history teacher Mr. Morgan forgot to lock his door and Oliver walked into his class twenty minutes late and sat in the back of the room. He had missed class or was late every day for five weeks straight but today Mr. Morgan decided enough was enough and took a stand.

"Where is your late pass, Oliver?" questioned Mr. Morgan in front of others.

"What?"

"I am asking where your late pass is for entering my class twenty minutes late, Mr. Mahlah," his tone grew as he used his full name to make a point that he was the adult. He was in charge.

"I don't have a late pass," replied Oliver in a dismissive manner. "Just go on with the lesson. I'll catch up."

"Oliver, I refuse to accept that as an answer. Why are you always late? You need to provide me a late pass detailing why you were late to my class and why you interrupted the middle of my lesson?"

"I'm sorry, but I can't give you that, Mr. Morgan. I will try better next time," Oliver claimed in an intimidating yet reassuring tone. "I will make it my goal to be early to every class moving forward."

"Thank you, Oliver. Don't let it happen again."

*****

The next day, Mr. Morgan purposely left his door unlocked. He was tired of being disrespected by Oliver. He decided that if the carefree teen, or any of his classmates, entered late, they would be sent to the principal's office for an in-school suspension. After completing attendance, he realized, Oliver was the only one missing. He was ready to take a stand.

When Oliver arrived to class fifteen minutes after the bell, Mr. Morgan stopped writing on the board and then motioned toward the door. He blocked the teen's path with his arms and looked at him with disappointment.

"Mr. Mahlah, yesterday you told me you would NOT be late to my class anymore," stated Mr. Morgan as he looked at his watch. "You are fifteen minutes late and I will pose the same question that I asked yesterday. Where is your late pass, Mr. Mahlah?"

"I don't got one. Stop playin', Mr. Morgan, I just want to get to my seat."

"I'm sorry, Mr. Mahlah, I cannot allow you to participate in today's lesson unless you can produce a hall pass which explains your tardiness."

"Well, I can't produce that, Mr. Morgan," he replied, staring Mr. Morgan square in his eyes.

"Okay, then I'm going to have to ask you to go to the principal's office and explain to them why you were late. They'll be expecting you and will give you details on your punishment."

"You serious, Mr. Morgan?"

"Yes, Mr. Mahlah. I am very serious. I will not allow you to walk into my class on your own schedule. Other students make it a priority to be in their seats on time and I cannot tolerate anyone who will disrupt that."

"This is bullshit. I don't want to be in school anyway. The only reason I'm here is that Dunbar fuckin' requires it. You can take that late pass and keep that shit." Oliver roared as he turned around and stormed out of class.

The entire class erupted in laughter and in his embarrassment, Mr. Morgan quickly ran to the classroom phone to inform the principal's office of the occurrence. He told them that they should be expecting Oliver momentarily since he just left the classroom. He remained on the line to confirm such and after three minutes of waiting, he asked the secretary to confirm Oliver's arrival. She informed him that Oliver had not yet arrived.

*****

After leaving Mr. Morgan's class, Oliver proceeded toward the principal's office to explain his case and demand to be transferred to another teacher. *He gotta have something against me.* Attending school was one of the requirements of residency at Dunbar House and despite his hesitation, he knew he needed to explain himself to the principal as part of his occupancy. He didn't care so much about Dunbar but was tired of bouncing around. He had grown used to Ms. Janet's rules and didn't care to go somewhere else where life may be harder.

As he walked, he saw another African American male student also wandering the halls aimlessly. Oliver had no interest in meeting or getting to know this individual but noticed, like himself, that the student was also not dressed like the rest of the kids in the school. The student was wearing a gray t-shirt with denim overalls with one strap off and a baseball cap on his head which was backward. The young man saw Oliver approaching and walked up to him. The two caught eyes before Oliver diverted his attention.

"Where you heading?" inquired the student as he looked at Oliver.

"I got kicked out of class so I'm heading to the principal's office to try to explain myself."

"Damn man…I got kicked out for falling asleep. I'm supposed to go to the principal's office also, but I really don't feel like gettin' a lecture today. I swear this school finds any and every reason to remind me that I'm a failure. I really don't need to hear that today. I'm probably about to ditch school for the rest of the day."

"And go where?"

"I got this place outside of school I like to hang at. When I want to leave school, I usually make some shit up so if they call my house, my Grandmama doesn't get mad. I'll just say I was in the nurse's office. If you sign in the mornin', they don't call home," replied the student. "I'm Lenny but my friends call me Lenox."

"Why do they call you that?"

"Well, you ain't my friend so ain't no reason for you to know," replied Lenny as he laughed in amusement. "What's your name?"

"My name is Oliver… But my friends call me… Ummm… Oliver Mahlah."

"Ahhh the infamous Oliver. From Dunbar House? I've heard of you. Your name's causing a bit of noise in this school. I hear you move on your own time and don't do the rules thing."

"Ain't no better time than my own," replied Oliver boastfully.

"Listen here, I'm about to connect with some friends outside of school," remarked Lenny. "You want to join?"

Oliver looked around and realized he also had nothing but lectures and punishment ahead, so he agreed. He had already signed in when he arrived that morning, so it was counted as a day in school. Now he could do what he wanted. He didn't trust this strange individual but knew he was better off leaving than sitting in the principal's office. The two of them walked right past the principal's office as they headed for a side exit through the gymnasium, which Lenny had become accustomed to using for his early departures from school.

*****

As the two teens walked the streets of East New York, they learned more about each other. Lenny explained how his nickname came from growing up in Harlem.

"Yeah, I came up around Frank Lucas and 'em," boasted Lenny. "My Grandmama moved me out to Brooklyn to live with her cause it was getting too dangerous back in Harlem. Nothing I couldn't handle but you know how that goes."

"But why do they call you Lenox?"

"Wait…you've never heard of Lenox Ave? You must have been living under a rock."

"Nope… never heard of it. Anyways, where are we going? I never been to this side of town."

"There's this clubhouse just around the corner from here. We can hang out there if you want."

"Whose clubhouse is it? They cool with me coming with you?"

"They cool if you cool, man. Don't be weird and you got nothing to worry about. Don't think many people are there anyway."

When the two teens arrived at a seemingly abandoned building on Flatlands Ave, Lenny signaled his arrival by giving the door a special knock and waving to the camera pointing directly at them. Seconds later, a large dark-skinned individual dressed in all black opened the door and stared at the two teens. He held his gaze and exchanged glances with both teens. Oliver's face shifted and his attention turned to Lenny, who continued to stare the large man down as if they were battling to see who looked away first.

Suddenly the large man and Lenny erupted in laughter, followed by a special handshake.

"Who's ya friend?" questioned the large man in his deep voice.

"He's cool, Croc. He's a friend from school. We both got kicked out, so I brought him with me. This is Oliver."

"You got kicked out *again,* Lil man?" he emphasized. "You know Rahzmel doesn't like you skipping days at school."

"Well, more like I left… Is Rah here? I'll explain."

"Nah, he's out with the others but still."

"Well, this will be our secret, Croc. If he comes in before I leave, I'll explain what happened. If he doesn't come in while I'm here, then this will stay between the three of us. Cool?"

"Alright, lil man," replied Croc as he chuckled in amusement. "You're lucky I like you. We got drinks in the back. Nice to meet you, Oliver. Go have fun."

When the pair entered, they walked down a long, dark hallway to the back room. The back room was brightly lit and was filled with couches, tables, a pool table, a large refrigerator, and large television. On the table was a white powdery substance that Oliver had never seen before and a few small bags of marijuana. On both ends of the main room were a few rooms with their doors closed. Two half-dressed black women were sitting on the couch watching TV and a third who entered one of the back rooms just as Oliver and Lenny had arrived. The latter was much older than the others and was fully dressed. On one of the tables, Lenny noticed a half-full bottle of Irish Whiskey and walked straight towards it, uncapped the bottle, and took a large gulp. He looked at Oliver and handed the bottle to him who stared at it with confusion. Oliver peered at Lenny then surveyed the room for further confirmation.

"It's just whiskey. Take a sip," joked Lenny.

Oliver switched his attention from Lenny back to the bottle and then proceeded to take a big gulp of the crimson beverage.

Suddenly, Oliver was hit with a hacking cough which lasted for seconds before he regained control of himself. "What was that? It burns," questioned Oliver as he cleared his throat.

"Just a little whiskey man. I'm assuming you don't drink?" replied Lenny as he held back his laughter.

"Nah, not really. I usually just chill."

"Well do you smoke?"

"Not really. I usually try to just stay low."

"No better way of staying low than to get high," joked Lenny as he pulled out a pre-rolled joint from his pocket. "I'm about to toke right now. You can join if you'd like."

"Nah, man, I'm actually good. I should be getting home. The school probably called Dunbar House so you know, I should go deal with that."

"Aiight, man. Maybe next time. Hopefully, your people don't go too hard on you, and I see you back at school soon."

"Yeah, hopefully."

Oliver made his way back to the exit and when he arrived, Croc extended him a handshake.

"Nice to meet you, man. See you again soon."

On his trip home, Oliver thought about how cool it was for Lenny to have the clubhouse as a hangout.

He gets to hang out with those older guys. They treat him like a friend.

Being that he had only been around others at Dunbar House, he was really impressed by the relationship Lenny had with Croc and assumed he had the same relationship with the others.

I wonder who Rahzmel is to Lenny. That guy seemed cool. Hopefully, I see him around.

*****

The school had contacted Ms. Janet about Oliver's behavior. When he arrived home later in the afternoon, she yelled so loud that the ringing in his ear kept him awake until well into the night. She also starved him from dinner and made him sleep in the basement which was poorly insulated and cold. He knew he did not want to deal with that type of reprimand again. Since all residents were required to attend school as a requisite to being housed at Dunbar, he knew he was going to need to adjust his approach to get what he wanted.

He also had an interest in continuing to hang out with Lenny and friends and knew he did not need any unnecessary attention monitoring his movements. For the first time in his life, he felt he had met someone to whom he could possibly relate to.

*****

As he proceeded to Mr. Morgan's fifth-period class the next day, Oliver quickly devised a story that he would tell the educator to explain his failure to reach the principal's office the day prior. He planned to apologize and muster up as much sincerity as possible.

If I gotta be in this school, might as well avoid problems with these teachers.

He arrived at the classroom five minutes before the bell and walked straight to Mr. Morgan's desk with his hand extended. As he firmly shook the instructor's hand, he looked into his eyes.

"Hello, Mr. Morgan. I'm very sorry for my actions yesterday," he recited as if he was coached on his apology. "I was having a really bad day and took out my frustrations on you. It wasn't right of me to interrupt your lesson and talk back the way I did. I didn't mean any disrespect in my actions."

Mr. Morgan nodded as the teen continued.

"After leaving your class yesterday, I began to have a small panic attack because of how bad I felt," he lied. "I ran outside for some air to clear my thoughts and must have lost track of time. I know I was wrong, and I truly do apologize. I plan to do better moving forward."

Mr. Morgan was surprised by Oliver's approach and thanked him for the apology. He then looked at his watch.

"Continue with this positive effort, Oliver. I see so much potential in you and I'm confident it can reflect in your performance. Now go find your seat."

The two of them shook hands again and Oliver proceeded toward his seat. As he made his way to the back of the room, he once again thought about how much he enjoyed hanging with Lenny.

Hopefully I see him later.

When the final bell rang that day, Oliver made his way straight toward the school exit to see if he could catch Lenny in passing. He waited for a few minutes and still no Lenny. He wondered if his new friend had even come to school that day and just as he was about to make his way towards the subway, which was also known as the MTA, he saw the main doors open and Lenny walked out, dressed in khakis with a button-down and a backpack on his shoulder.

"Yo, man!" blurted Oliver. "I've been looking for you."

"Sorry, man, I been in class and stayed after to ask my teacher some questions."

"Wow, look at us! Little scholars in the making! You even dressed the part I see," Oliver joked with an accompanying playful shove.

"Yeah. Shortly after you left the clubhouse yesterday, Rahzmel came by and found out I left school. Let's just say, it was not pretty. Last week, he warned me about leaving school and when he found out I left school *again*, he yelled at me. Bad."

"Damn, man. Ms. Janet from Dunbar chewed me out last night when I got home too. The damn school called her and told her what happened in class so I'm trying to be on my best behavior. I'm not trynna get kicked out. Who is Rahzmel to you anyway? Why did he yell at you?"

"He's no one, man. Forget I even mentioned his name. Listen… I gotta get out of here. I'll see you in school tomorrow."

The boys shook hands and went their separate ways.

When Oliver arrived back at Dunbar House, he saw a police cruiser parked outside. Because of his antics the day prior, he worried that he may have been in trouble for skipping school. *Did Ms. Janet call the police for yesterday? This is some bullshit.*

As he walked up the steps, the door opened, and out walked two officers with Ms. Janet. It was one older white cop who was followed by Ms. Janet and one younger African American officer.

"Excuse me," noted Oliver as he squeezed past the two men so he could enter the building.

The two officers and Ms. Janet craned their necks back into the house as the teen ran up the stairs towards his shared bedroom. When he got to the top, Oliver saw the three of them still staring in his direction but was relieved because it was obvious they were not there for him. Despite his confusion as to why they stared so intently, he continued towards his room to do his homework.

*****

Over the course of the next few weeks, Oliver and Lenny both continued with their "good behavior" during school and continued to hang out after school. Neither teen had any other companions, so they became fast best friends. Lenny told Oliver about what life was like in Harlem and the main contrasts between Harlem and Brooklyn. Oliver shared stories about Dunbar House and his tough childhood moving around in the foster care system. The boys became very comfortable with each other during this period.

On one Friday afternoon, the boys left school and decided to head to the corner store for some gum before heading to the park to play basketball. As they walked, Oliver inquired more about the mysterious clubhouse, which had been on his mind since they first visited.

"You still never told me about that clubhouse we went to a few weeks back. Who is Rahzmel and why was everyone so afraid of him? Even that big guy, Croc, seemed scared of him."

"Well, that's Croc. His real name is Cornell, but he got the nickname Croc when he was younger because he was always bigger than the other kids and had a bad attitude. From what I hear, he's calmed down A LOT. Now he's just a punk," Lenny joked, reassuring himself that they had the type of relationship where he could call Croc nicknames. "Truth is Rahzmel is my older cousin. The clubhouse is where he chills with his friends. Croc is his best friend, and he has a few others they run with who all chill ova there."

"So those girls were a part of the crew also?"

"I've never seen the two who were sitting down but the older one who left the room when we arrived was Angela. That's Rahzmel's girl. They've been together for a while also. Most of the girls who go there are friends with Angela, I think. It's nice to see some beautiful women in the clubhouse every now and then. Feel me?"

"Got it."

"Listen man. Those cats aren't people to be hanging around. Croc seemed cool at the door but he's like Rahzmel. Nice at first but not someone you should really be around. They're best friends which is why I kinda know him. Rahzmel used to live with my grandmama also until she kicked him out. Now she just lets him come by and visit every now and then. You think your upbringing was tough, they had it tougher.

They've been running in the streets forever and came up when crack cocaine was in its infant stages. They were around a very scary Brooklyn. It made them who they are today and as much as I love Rah, I also try to avoid him when I can."

"Why? That's your cousin."

"Truth be told, he's smart. He's like a businessman out here. Just like those cats on Wall Street, he reads the newspaper every day. That's what makes him so scary. New York Times, I think. Picture that, an educated black man running the streets of Brooklyn just like the mayor. He doesn't dress in these fancy suits like them but trust me, he knows his stuff.

"The only reason I took you to the clubhouse that day was that I knew he wasn't going to be there. I didn't account for Croc and the others. They're also a few others who you didn't see but I won't even speak about them. Just take my advice, don't ever go around there unless you're with me. I'm dead serious."

Oliver nodded in agreement as the boys arrived at the basketball court. The people he met at the clubhouse were cool and mature, but Oliver had no interest in visiting without his friend's approval. Up until that point, he hadn't had anyone he was close with, so he enjoyed the time spent with Lenny. He was happy to have finally found a friend who didn't fear him for being an orphan or avoid him for not looking like everyone else. He finally found someone he could call a friend.

CHAPTER 7:

WRONG PLACE, WRONG TIME

Oliver Mahlah   **November, 1984**

The following Monday afternoon, Oliver waited for Lenny at their usual meet up location. Although his relationship with Lenny was far from a trusting one, he knew Lenny was the closest person he had to a best friend. The two teens were in different classes during the day, so they generally did not see each other much at school. They typically would meet after school at the same gymnasium doors they used on the first day they met.

As he waited, Oliver felt something was wrong. He began to look at the clock in the hallway and after waiting fifteen minutes past their normal meet-up time, he assumed Lenny was either staying late for counseling, got afterschool detention, or did not come into school that day. *Maybe I'll see him tomorrow.*

The next few days were the same and Oliver began to worry about his friend. Despite their growing friendship, Oliver never spoke with Lenny about where he lived. All he knew was that Lenny was from Harlem and now lived with his grandmother in Brooklyn. He also had no way to get in contact with him. It was as if his friend had just disappeared.

By that Friday morning, Oliver convinced himself that something had happened to Lenny, and he was determined to ensure his only friend was okay. He continued thinking of possible scenarios which may have resulted in his friend's disappearance.

Maybe he got sick? Yeah, I think he's sick. Has to be if he's MIA like this.

Like himself, Oliver knew Lenny was also trying to be on his best behavior at school, so he didn't think he was suspended or expelled.

Guess I'll try again next week. He couldn't have just up and disappeared.

*****

On Monday, November 5th, Oliver proceeded with his school day as normal. By the end of the day, he once again found himself waiting at their usual spot, hoping to see Lenny. Unfortunately, this was to no avail. Lenny once again was a no-show so Oliver decided instead of sitting around dreaming up possible scenarios, he would go searching for his friend.

The only three places he knew Lenny to visit were the basketball court, the park, and the clubhouse. He visited both the park and the basketball court and confirmed that Lenny hadn't been seen at either spot in over a week. He then thought about the clubhouse but replayed Lenny's warning about never visiting without him. *What if he's in trouble? Maybe Croc or someone knows where he is or can help me find him.* He disregarded his friend's advice and made his decision. The clubhouse was his next stop.

When Oliver turned the corner and saw the clubhouse in his view, Lenny's warning returned. He stopped in his place and for a moment, the guilt of disobedience flooded his mind, until he once again thought about his missing friend. *He may need me.*

He continued forward and as he made his way closer to the entrance, he forced himself to relax. When he arrived at the front door, he thought twice and then gave a gentle knock as he peered up at the camera pointing in his direction. There was no response and after minutes of waiting, he figured his knock wasn't heard. He heard music playing on the other side of the door and then began to bang more assertively. The door flew open almost immediately and there towering over him was Croc with a still look on his face. That frightening blank stare turned into a look of confusion as his face softened. Oliver could tell Croc was trying to remember him but couldn't at the moment.

"Hey Croc…umm… not sure if you remember me but I'm friends with Lenox… Ummm… I mean Lenny."

Croc continued to stare at the teen with confusion before his look softened. It was obvious he was now remembering their meeting weeks prior.

"Oh yeah! You're Lenny's friend. How you been man?"

"I'm good. Just keeping up with this schoolwork and trying to stay out of trouble."

"Good for you, man."

"Hey, listen…have you seen Lenny? I haven't seen or heard from him in a while and I'm a little worried."

"You haven't heard? You should probably talk with Rahzmel. It really isn't my business to tell." Croc then looked back down the narrow hallway and yelled. "Yo Rah, Lenny's friend from the other day is here." He then turned back to Oliver. "Go on man, Rahzmel's back there."

Oliver slowly motioned through the door and past Croc until he heard the heavy metal door slam shut and lock. His legs grew weak and shook as he walked through the long, dark hallway towards the main room. He could barely conceal his terror and tried to compose himself, but when he saw Croc trailing him towards the main room, he froze.

"Go on," the enforcer stated.

Oliver took a deep breath, forced his composure, and proceeded forward. He knew he was now committed.

When he arrived in the main room he noticed the same two women from before were sitting on the couch. There were also two other men sitting at the table playing cards in the back.

"Who's the kid and why is he here?" barked one of the two men barely looking up from his cards.

"This Lenny's friend," replied Croc. "He was here with him the other day."

"I asked why he's here? I don't care if he's Lenny's friend," the same man protested in a bitter, disgruntled tone. Although his tone was assertive, Oliver could also hear a bit of apprehension as he watched the man spew his reply to the large enforcer.

Oliver walked up to the table with his hand extended.

"Hi, Rahzmel. I'm Oliver. I'm Lenny's friend from school."

Without shaking the teen's hand, the two men sitting at the table exchanged looks as they fought back their laughter. Oliver looked down at his idle hand and watched as the two men then erupted in uncontrollable laughter, slapping hands as if they had succeeded in pulling off a joke only they were aware of. Oliver stood there confused and embarrassed as he retracted his hand back.

"Is there something that's funny?" A loud, deep voice came from the next room. The two men stopped laughing as everyone looked over to the doorway. Suddenly a man much older than the two men at the table came out in a wheelchair and was being pushed by Angela. The man had thick braids in his hair, a full beard, and a mustache, which complemented his thick pink lips and gloves on both hands. In his lap was the outline of something hidden under a black towel.

"I asked what the joke was, Chino?" demanded the man as he approached the table. "Did you find something funny about what happened to my cousin?"

"Nah, man. I was just laughin' at the kid. That's all."

"But I didn't hear the young man make a joke, did you?" replied the seemingly handicapped man in a calm but frightening tone. Oliver stood there and continued to watch the scene unfold.

The man then removed the towel and unveiled a twelve-gauge shotgun that was resting on his lap. There was a collective gasp from the room as everyone went silent. The man stared at Chino intently for a few moments then turned his gaze back to Oliver. He requested that Angela remove the shotgun from the room and when she did, he removed his gloves and extended his hand to Oliver. The frightened teen could feel the rough callus as he used his shaking hands to grip the man's cold hand.

"Hi, man...Nice to meet you. Sorry about Chino and Rio. They don't know how to treat guests. You're Lenny's friend, right? I'm his cousin...Rahzmel."

Rahzmel looked down at Oliver's shaking hand then continued.

"Don't worry about the two of them. They're just jokers. Couldn't hurt a fly if they tried," he lied.

"Hi… uhmm… Rahzmel… I'm sorry to bother you but… uhmm… I didn't have anywhere else to look. I'm looking for Lenny. He hasn't been to school, and I was hoping he may be here. One time he brought me here and I was wondering if he may have come back."

Rahzmel sighed and then asked the others to leave the room so he could speak with Oliver privately. The entire room quickly emptied.

"You're a good friend. I can see why Lenny likes you. Listen, man… my cousin got picked up a few days ago and he's currently sitting in a cell in a juvenile detention center in Manhattan. He should be out soon, though, so don't worry about him."

The news came as a surprise to Oliver. This showed through his arched eyebrows and mouth left ajar at the news. "Picked up? What did he get picked up for?"

"I guess just being at the wrong place at the wrong time. It's okay though. He should be out soon. It was just a misunderstanding. Listen, man. Lenny told me a lot about you. He told me you're a good guy. Trustworthy and loyal. Trust is a very important trait in people. It makes them dependable and means their word is bond. The reason Croc, Chino, and the others are here is because I trust them. I don't want to bore you with a lecture, but you seem cool, Oliver. I look forward to seeing you again. It's always a great time here."

"Thanks for the update on Lenny, Rahzmel. I should go. If you speak with him, please let him know I said what up."

"Oh for sure. I got you."

"Thanks, man."

Rahzmel then stood up and to Oliver's surprise, he was able to walk. He wore his shock on his face as he learned Rahzmel wasn't handicapped. A look that softened as the others began to return into the room. Rahzmel showed Oliver to the exit and the two of them shook hands before he walked back to his peers in the main room.

Before leaving, Oliver gazed back and when he did so, he saw Rahzmel had pulled out what looked like a machete and had it to Chino's neck. He watched as Rahzmel held the sharpened blade against Chino's neck so that he could feel the cold, ridged edge of it, begging to pierce the skin. He could see a thin line of blood had appeared as if it was formed to compliment the perspiration that had formed on Chino's forehead out of fear. Rahzmel whispered something in his ear before forcibly releasing his grip and disappeared back into his room.

Oliver departed through the main door and headed home. As he rode the subway, he thought about how friendly, but frightening, Rahzmel seemed.

Stupid! I couldn't even stop stuttering. He probably thinks I'm a punk.

The scene with the shotgun seemed a little odd but Oliver assumed it was some sort of joke that he did not get. The scene with the knife was more frightening and he knew he was not supposed to see it so he convinced himself that it was okay. He saw Rahzmel as a proud man who simply demanded respect. He could tell this from the way he spoke and carried himself. Based on how Lenny had described him, he knew Rahzmel's demeanor was lighter than an ego but darker than insecurities, which made him unpredictable. Croc seemed no different. Although he knew the red flags were there, he convinced himself that his now incarcerated friend had it all wrong about these guys.

Over the next few weeks, Oliver went on with his day-to-day routine. He was determined to continue improving his standing at the school and made it a point to also be a better example at the Dunbar House. After being chastised by Mr. Morgan on the day he left school, Oliver committed himself to proving he was worth something. He decided that he wanted to stay at the Dunbar home past his sixteenth birthday and knew the only way to do so was for Ms. Janet to request it. He knew she had actually cared about him—even if it was by being tough on him. His goal was to also make Ms. Janet see his value.

*****

One following Wednesday afternoon, Oliver was leaving school and heading towards the subway. When he exited the building, he saw Rahzmel, Croc, and Chino sitting parked in front of the school. Oliver was not expecting them and thought they may have been there because of Lenny. He got excited and quickly ran over to the group to see them.

"Hey, Oliver. How's it going, man. How was school?

"Good! Is Lenny back?" he said excitedly.

"No, I think he's still in the detention center. Turns out there were a few complications but it's all good. It'll get figured out soon. We're actually here to see you."

"Me?"

"Yeah! We were passing by going to grab something to eat and figured we'd see if you were free to join us."

"I just got out of school and should probably head home."

"Aww, c'mon man. We're just heading down the street. Come by for a soda then we can drop you off at your house. Sound good?"

"Ummm…. I think I can grab something real quick then I really should head home."

Oliver then got into the car with the three men, and they drove off. While driving, Oliver learned Chino, Croc, and Rahzmel all grew up in the same neighborhood. They were childhood friends who continued hanging with each other through their teen years. He thought to himself, *now they want to hang out with me? How cool.*

He had never been worth anything and now the older guys wanted his company. He felt good. During the car ride, he questioned them as to what the clubhouse was for.

"Just a place for close friends to get together and hang out. Sometimes we talk business but for the most part, it's just a place where we can hang out without having to be on the streets."

"When we met, you were sitting in a wheelchair. Was that your wheelchair?"

Croc laughed from the driver's seat.

"No, it wasn't. Sometimes I like to play around in it," Rahzmel admitted. "It belonged to the former leader of the crew I used to run with. His name was Lefty. He was making so much money, he had two custom-made wheelchairs with his initials inscribed on the wheels. When he went to prison, one was left to me, and the other was left to another member of the crew who died about five years ago. I kept it around when he was in prison and even kept it after he died. I've been meaning to get rid of it but haven't had the chance."

The group continued to the local diner for a soda, as promised, then dropped Oliver off at Dunbar House. Before driving away, Rahzmel extended Oliver an open invitation to the clubhouse whenever he was bored and wanted to hang out. This confirmed Oliver's thoughts about Rahzmel being a nice guy. He did not have any siblings himself and assumed Lenny was overreacting when describing his older cousin. *I wish I had family like Rahzmel. He seems so cool.*

"Thanks for the soda and the invitation. Maybe I'll see you guys around."

"Hope so."

That night, Oliver thought back to his day. When he looked at Rahzmel, he saw a leader. He saw a man who could stand by any decision made because he had confidence spilling out of his ears. Someone he felt comfortable calling a friend. Oliver didn't know it at the time, but when Rahzmel looked at him, he did not see the same thing. In Oliver, Rahzmel saw an opportunity. He saw Oliver's lack of confidence and knew this would make him obsequious. It would make him a good soldier.

CHAPTER 8:

WE OWN THE NIGHT

Oliver Mahlah

The following day, as school was coming to a close, Oliver realized he did not have any plans for after he got out and he did not want to go back to Dunbar. He'd grown so used to visiting the basketball courts with Lenny that he felt unsettled with this small gap in his daily routine. He remembered his open invitation to the clubhouse and although he didn't want to come on too strong to Rahzmel and Croc, he did want to befriend them.

I'm way younger than they are. Why would they want to hang out with me? Probably only because I'm Lenny's friend…Well, maybe they think I'm cool. If I want them to like me, I'm going to have to show up. I'm going to go.

At the sight of the teen's familiar face, Oliver was let in by Croc. He made his way to the main room and saw Rahzmel in the back with Angela sitting in his lap. Chino and Rio were on the couch with two other girls sitting beside each of them and a joint being shared among the group of four. Three other young women were sitting on the adjacent couch sharing their own joint while watching television.

"Oliver, welcome!" remarked Rahzmel in an excited tone as if his guest of honor had finally arrived. "I'm so happy you're here. You get to enjoy our little get-together. You know, we were just talking this morning about what a cool young man you are. We don't really see too many cats your age who can keep up with us. As far as I see it, that takes a lot of maturity and is very commendable."

Oliver melted at Rahzmel's praise. He then watched as Rahzmel whispered something in Angela's ear and she got up from his lap and walked over to the group of girls sitting on the couch. Angela bent over and whispered something in one of the girls' ears, then went back to Rahzmel's lap.

The girl, who was wearing a red floral dress with her hair made up, then walked over to the kitchen to grab two beers then walked back over to Oliver and grabbed his hand. She escorted him to the table in the back of the space and then sat with him.

"My friends call me Minnie because I LOVE Minnie Mouse and polka dots. You're Oliver, right?"

"Yeah," he responded nervously.

"Don't worry, babe. I won't bite…unless you ask me to."

The pair spoke, drank, and laughed for a few hours until Oliver looked at the time.

"Sorry, I should be getting back."

"Aww, we were just hitting it off," remarked Minnie, grabbing his arm in a provocative manner that allowed him to flex his biceps. "When will I see you again, Ollie?"

"Umm … will you be here tomorrow?"

"I think so. I got work tomorrow afternoon but should be able to get out by 5 p.m. I can always ask Angela to get out a little early if you gon' be here earlier," she smiled.

"Oh, that would be good. I normally get out of school at 3 p.m. and can come by right after. Is Angela the boss?"

"Yes, she is, baby. She the boss," she replied with a smile exposing her beautiful, well-maintained teeth.

He wasn't sure, but assumed Angela worked in hair or beauty salons because of the way Minnie and the rest of the women took care of themselves. They all had their hair, nails, and makeup done which impressed Oliver and convinced him they were in the business of beauty.

The teen said his goodbyes to the group and even got a handshake from Chino, who had a much better attitude toward the teen. Minnie locked arms with Oliver and then escorted him to the door. She kissed him on the cheek and blew him a kiss as she watched him walk away. He thought about her the entire trip back home.

*****

As promised, Oliver returned the next day, then again, the following day. He continued visiting the clubhouse after school for the next few weeks and during that time, his friendship with Minnie began to grow. He began hanging around the clubhouse more and more and at that time, he noticed she was also coming around every day. He assumed she was coming for him and his attraction for her continued to increase. She told him how impressed she was with his role within Rahzmel's crew.

"Rahzmel really likes you. He reminds me every day to make sure I take care of you."

"Take care of me?" joked Oliver. "I can take care of myself. Anyway, I should be taking care of you. I'm going to make enough money with the crew so that I can take care of both of us. You watch!"

"Okay, baby," she smiled.

He was also enjoying hanging out with Rahzmel and his crew and loved how the others began to warm up to him. Rahzmel began offering Oliver some clothing to wear, a Motorola DynaTAC cellphone, which hadn't even been released to the public yet, and even offered pocket money to keep him from having to steal anything. Oliver knew he did not need any of those things and he was not used to receiving anything from anyone so he regularly declined the offerings, but Rahzmel insisted.

"It's a gift, Oliver," he said one day. "Everyone likes having you around. This is just our way of showing it. We look out for each other here. It's a family."

Oliver was not used to being a part of anything like this. He saw this as his opportunity to be a part of something larger than just Dunbar House. He began accepting Rahzmel's gifts.

"I want everyone in the crew to have a cellphone. You never know when I may come calling."

Oliver would soon learn that the day would come shortly after.

*****

One day after hanging out at the clubhouse, Oliver was heading home so Rahzmel offered to walk him to the subway. It had been weeks since originally learning of Lenny's incarceration so, during their walk, Oliver once again inquired about his friend's status.

"Oh, my cousin's good. He told me to tell you he's doing well, and he was happy to hear you're running with the crew now."

"That's good! Is there a way I can call or see him too?"

"Nah, man. The prison doesn't allow visitors or calls. Some security issues or somethin' like that," he lied.

"Oh, okay," replied Oliver. He then replayed Lenny's warning to stay away from the crew and although Rahzmel's information was conflicting, he disregarded it in an effort not to seem like he missed something he should have already been told. "Did he say when he's coming home?"

"No, he didn't. I'm sure he's running that place by now. With all the friends our crew has in Brooklyn, he's probably calling the shots in there."

The two of them stopped on the corner before Oliver entered the subway. Rahzmel grabbed his shoulder and pulled the teenager closer.

"Listen, man, I need your help with something. Tomorrow, I need somethin' picked up and brought back to the clubhouse. It'll just be a backpack, so it won't be too heavy. I or one of the other guys would do it but we have an important meeting tomorrow at the same time that we can't miss."

Without thinking twice, Oliver agreed to help. He was finally receiving the opportunity he had waited weeks for—a chance to prove himself.

"I can do it. I'll pick it up and bring it back."

Rahzmel then gave Oliver the details and told the young man that he only had two rules: "do not look inside the bag and if the police question you, don't ever mention anything about the crew."

Oliver agreed and the two parted ways.

*****

After school the next day, Oliver took the subway to Park Slope and walked to the address where Rahzmel told him the backpack would be. When he exited the train, he realized he was in the Irish section of Brooklyn which made him slightly uncomfortable. In his neighborhood, he was used to seeing mostly black people, so it made him a little uneasy to be around so many white people. He had never seen this many white people in one neighborhood in his life.

As he walked and looked around, his worry began to increase because of his obvious displacement. Shop owners and people passing by all stopped to watch the young, black teen pass through *their* streets. He had no confidence in his look, and it was obvious he didn't belong.

When he finally arrived at the edifice, he turned around and noticed he was followed by a couple of street-level thugs who had tailed him from a few blocks back. His fear quickly turned to anger as he prepared to defend himself. He had no weapons and knew his fists were going to have to be enough. *These guys want to mess with me? I got to fight back.*

What made it worse was the only instruction Rahzmel gave was to be at this address at 4:30 p.m. and it was now 4:25 p.m. He figured he may not last five minutes fighting the three street thugs who were now quickly approaching him on foot. He knew he was outnumbered and considered running but did not want to let Rahzmel down, and knew this was his burden to see through.

Almost immediately after he backed himself to a wall and balled his fist, three Irish men, driving a grey Buick Regal, pulled into the empty parking lot and drove toward the young man. The driver made eye contact with the three thugs and signaled for them to leave. They quickly obliged the nonverbal command and rushed out.

"Who are you?" questioned the man in the passenger seat. "Lenny's not back yet?"

"Rahzmel sent me. Lenny couldn't make it, so Rahzmel sent me instead."

"Rahzmel is one slick one," the Irishman remarked turning to the two others. "There he goes running with these puppies again."

The driver then went around to the trunk to grab a backpack. He threw it at Oliver's feet and got back into the car.

"Tell Rahzmel that I will reach out to him soon with the next order."

Oliver wasn't entirely sure what the man was referring to and had no plans to look into the bag. He promised Rahzmel that he would bring the bag back without opening it and he planned to stick to that promise. At first, he felt uneasy about what he may have been carrying but then remembered what Rahzmel said about trust. He trusted Rahzmel and assumed the gang leader would not put him in a dangerous situation.

He continued back to the clubhouse and when he arrived, Rahzmel, Croc and the others were there drinking beers.

"My prodigy returns!" remarked Rahzmel. "Did you have any issues?"

"No, I didn't," he lied. "The man sitting in the passenger seat of the car wanted me to tell you that he will reach out to you again with the next order."

"Great. Thanks for doing that. Our meeting got out early so we came back to celebrate. Someone get this man a beer."

Rahzmel then motioned for Oliver to follow him to the back room. He closed the door behind them.

"Did you open the bag?"

"No, I didn't. You told me not to, so I didn't."

"Great. Aren't you curious about what's in the backpack that I had you carry from Park Slope back here?"

"I don't think I want to know."

"Go ahead and look in the bag, Oliver. I want you to look."

When Oliver slowly unzipped the backpack, all he saw was a bunch of newspaper clippings. He peered over at Rahzmel and saw him holding back his laughter.

"Newspaper clippings?" questioned Oliver in confusion. "What's so important about newspaper clippings?"

"To be honest, it's not the newspapers that I wanted you to get for me. This was a test for you. I speak so much about trust because I believe it's important to surround yourself with people you love and trust. Every man in the next room is like a brother to me and I trust them with my life. Lenny's my younger cousin and like yourself, had to earn my trust to run with us. We grew up separately, so I wasn't sure about him at first. But he did all the same small tasks for me that you're doing. This allowed the crew to become comfortable with him. Trust can't just be given. It must be earned and if you were to earn it, I had to be sure you would do exactly as you were told. And you did."

"So, I'm a part of the crew?"

"Slow your roll. That was just the beginning. Not every bag will be filled with newspapers. To be honest, it will be easier for you to do these runs because you will simply look like a student walking home from school. The runs will always be for money and all you will need is your backpack. When you meet with the other crews on your assigned day, they will fill your bag and send you on the way. That's usually how people your age start in the game. By making these types of runs. In time, you will earn your spot. But the journey to joining the crew will be a fruitful one. If you do what you're told, you will continue to reap the rewards with the rest of us. I mean, we gave you Minnie, right?" Rahzmel joked.

"Is she here?"

"No, not yet. I think she's still working. You going to wait for her?"

"I really should head home. Ms. Janet's probably waiting for me."

"Ok man. That's cool. I'll tell Minnie you were here and that you asked about her. She'll be happy to hear you took care of this for me. She really likes people I like, and I like you. You remind me of myself when I was your age. I used to run with some older cats just like you are. They used to be all around Brooklyn and now I have my own crew. I think one day, all of this can be yours if you want it," he told Oliver. Although this sounded attractive, Oliver felt like he was in a sales pitch and Rahzmel was selling him a dream. He stood impressed.

"Thanks, Rahzmel. Tell Minnie I came by, and I will see her tomorrow."

CHAPTER 9:

THIS THING WE'VE BUILT

Oliver Mahlah

Over the course of the next few weeks, Rahzmel had Oliver continue running quick and easy errands for him around Brooklyn. During this time, Oliver learned more about Rahzmel's crew and the business they were in. Although he was now aware of Rahzmel's illegal activity, he continued to make excuses for why it was okay. Like he did when he mentally replayed Lenny's warning, he justified Rahzmel's behavior.

The process was put into place and became systematic as time went on. He was to attend school as normal then immediately after, go do a pick-up run before heading back to the clubhouse. The plan was for him to use his backpack so it would look like he was just another student leaving school. To avoid suspicion at Dunbar House, he told Ms. Janet that he was involved in an afterschool study program which usually kept him late. Because his grades had improved drastically, she saw no reason to assume he wasn't telling the truth.

After running for a bit, Oliver began feeling more and more comfortable with his responsibility within the crew. Everyone had a role to play, and he wanted to play his right. He wanted to do his part until he was on top.

Rahzmel was the obvious leader who was responsible for maintaining the high-level relationships with other crews, ensuring profits continued coming in, and took overall responsibility for their products. Croc was his driver and right-hand man. Because of his size and frightening demeanor, Croc was also Rahzmel's enforcer.

Rahzmel and Croc grew up together and had been running in the streets since they were both young. Both men became members of the former crew, led by Lamont "Lefty" Franklin, over a decade ago and left the gang together. After Lefty was murdered in prison, Rahzmel and Croc built their own operation. Rahzmel trusted Croc more than anyone else and Croc was the only one who had known Rahzmel before he became the leader of this street gang.

Chino and Rio also grew up with Rahzmel and Croc but joined after the men had already formed the new crew. They were both known as hotheads who lived by a "shoot first, ask questions later" motto. This made them very strong members of the crew but also made them huge liabilities to other crews whom Rahzmel had forged relationships with. They were appointed roles as lieutenants who ran the street-level operations. Their focus was profits and if it was coming in, they didn't care who they were calling boss.

Both men had soldiers under them who were responsible for the street-level drug deals. Rahzmel's goal was no violence between crews in Brooklyn, so he felt more comfortable leading the group and having them take ownership of the street-level activity as long as they followed his cardinal rule: no murders unless approved first.

Everyone had the same goal of getting paid so Rahzmel made it his focus to exploit peoples' strengths. Competition and territory were also something Rahzmel took very seriously. His crew had acquired most of the terrain Lefty's crew had so as time went on, and connections were formed, he leveraged land to forge new affiliations.

Rahzmel had created relationships built on trust with the Jamaicans, Italians, Japanese, Hispanics, and Irish, so his main focus was to ensure everyone continued to get paid. He titled this partnership between the other crews the "Collective," because of their collective agreement.

As time went on, Oliver learned the importance of his role. Rahzmel was heavily involved in the drug game and these regular money pickups were made by a member of each crew, on their assigned day, each month. Rahzmel trusted him to be that member.

Oliver began to admire Rahzmel's business acumen, his "everyone eats" motto, and the overall friendly demeanor that made his transition comfortable. He became more and more interested in what Rahzmel told him weeks before about the empire falling to him one day. He became more interested in one day leading the Collective.

*****

The Irish crew took responsibility for Park Slope. They were a lawless group of outlaws who ran a weapons distribution operation that stretched from Boston to New York. The Japanese crew was involved with prostitution and was based in Brooklyn Heights. Their business was massage parlors and beauty shops which doubled as brothels for the right clients. Many politicians found themselves on that "right clients" list.

The Jamaicans were based out of Bedford Stuyvesant and Brownsville and in addition to marijuana, they also controlled weapons and heroin. The Italians were based in Long Island but also had stash houses throughout Manhattan. In Brooklyn, the Italians were based in Bushwick and Brighton Beach. The Hispanic crew, who were based in Crown Heights, controlled the street distribution of cocaine, which was growing in popularity in New York. Rahzmel's crew ran Canarsie and East Flatbush and were also responsible for crack cocaine. Because they had assumed responsibility for the business relationships, Rahzmel's crew also took overall responsibility for the Collective's political connections. This ensured Rahzmel sat at the head of the table within the Collective. Oliver would later learn that Rahzmel's crew was also involved in prostitution.

Despite his knowledge of the Collective, Oliver was still very curious about Angela's role within Rahzmel's operation. He knew she was Rahzmel's girlfriend for many years but also knew she played a larger role in the full operation. She was much older than Rahzmel, but Oliver figured that was the kingpin's prerogative. Most times she was at the clubhouse, she was joined by a group of younger women who were usually dressed up and looked like they had just come from the dance club. He didn't care to pry but as his interest in Minnie grew, so did his curiosity about Angela and their purpose.

*****

One day after getting out of school, Oliver saw Rahzmel and the others sitting out front waiting for him. He assumed they were going to do a run and needed additional hands. As he approached the truck, he realized it was Croc in the driver seat with Rahzmel and Angela sitting in the back.

"You ready?" remarked Angela with a big smile exposing her gold tooth.

"Ready for what?" replied Oliver in a very muddled and suspicious tone. "Where are we going?"

"We going back to the clubhouse. We've got a surprise for you, baby. Rah talks about how well you've been doing so he set something special for you." Rahzmel smiled and then began kissing her neck. Oliver turned his attention back to Croc as they pulled away.

When they arrived at the clubhouse, Croc pulled up in front and gave Oliver a handshake and wished him good luck. Oliver was even more confused now and realized they were leaving him to go into the clubhouse alone. *What do they want me to do? Why did they drop me off?*

After the car pulled away, Oliver entered the clubhouse and noticed that all the lights in the main room were off, and music was playing very low on the speaker. "Get up, get up, get up, get up…let's make love tonight." He recognized the song that was playing was "Sexual Healing" by Marvin Gaye and, at that moment, had an idea of what was happening.

Oh shit…

There were candles lit but Oliver immediately turned the light on in the main room. He heard a soft voice from the back room tell him to "leave them off." When he looked towards the back, he saw Minnie approaching wearing nothing but a sexy red lace bra and panties with white polka dots.

She motioned toward Oliver in a seductive manner and grabbed both hands to walk him to the couch. She then climbed on top of him and began slowly kissing him from his forehead down to his lips. *Her lips feel so soft, and her skin smells so good,* he thought to himself while also trying to listen to the music for any guidance on what to do next. He had never been with a woman before and wanted to ensure his lack of experience was not obvious. He was so nervous, and he knew she could smell his sweat.

I can't disappoint Rahzmel. I can't look like a punk.

He excitedly grabbed her medium-sized breast and began kissing her neck, just like he had seen Rahzmel do with Angela. She grabbed his hands and whispered in his ear for him to "go slow." She began slowly riding his body to the tempo of the music and moaned her enjoyment for each of his soft kisses.

As he continued kissing her neck, Minnie pulled out a small baggie with what looked like the same powdery white substance he saw when he first visited the Clubhouse. The baggie had the letter "c" in cursive, which was written in the same red font. She used the tip of her pinky, which had a French tip, to scoop out a small amount and then snorted twice, once in each nostril. She then scooped out a third nail full and placed her finger under Oliver's nostril.

"Just sniff very, very hard, baby. Just like you were smelling something really good and wanted to smell it forever. Trust me…This that FIRE, baby."

Oliver had never tried drugs before and had no intention of starting now. He really liked Minnie and considered declining, but he knew word of his cowardice would get back to Rahzmel. Before doing as instructed, Oliver looked at her nostrils and saw the residue of her last two sniffs had left remnants. He finally sniffed the drug and instantly felt a rush shoot to his head. Although he could feel the pleasure senses the drugs had triggered, he was not a fan.

He watched as Minnie tossed the baggie onto the table and the pair resumed kissing. She slowly unbuttoned his shirt and slid back down from his lips to his neck. She continued to make her way down until she reached his hairless chest. He cringed in fear at each kiss she placed on his chest. She stopped then smiled at how intimidated he was. She then stood up and extended both hands to the nervous teen. When he placed his hands in hers, she walked them both to the back room and shut the door.

CHAPTER 10:

PROFESSIONAL

Oliver Mahlah

The very next day Rahzmel and Croc once again sat outside of the school waiting for Oliver. They were parked in the same spot but this time it was just the two of them. When Oliver entered the truck, the two men were laughing and praising the teen.

"Heard you had a good day yesterday," boasted Croc. "Anything you want to tell us?"

"Nah, I'm good," Oliver held in a bashful yet boastful manner. He wasn't sure what Minnie had told them and decided he wanted to let them drive the conversation.

"Listen…we spoke with Minnie, and she said she wants to see you again. She really enjoyed last night."

"She told you that?" Oliver replied shockingly.

"Yeah, man. She did," replied Rahzmel. "She really likes you and loves how you run with the crew. You're one of us. She likes that. Did you like her?"

"Yeah, she's pretty and cool to chill with. She's much older than me but that didn't seem to be a problem with her."

"Good to hear. She's a very good friend of the crew and you can have her when you want her."

"Nah, man. I'm enjoying just hanging out with her and you guys. I'm probably too young for her anyway. What's she like, twenty-one?"

"Don't worry about age, man. It's nothing but a number and if you like her, I'm telling you, she can be yours when you want her. The only thing I will say is don't fall in love. Girls like that are cool to have around and have fun with, but they aren't like Angela."

Oliver was determined to prove he was as tough as one of the others, so he laughed off the comment about falling in love.

"Listen, man… Croc and I need to make a run to this thing and want to know if you want to tag along."

"Yeah, Rah, anything you need."

Rahzmel smirked with satisfaction to hear this and they were off.

On their way, Rahzmel told Oliver that this was a meeting with the other crews, and he should not say a word without checking with him or Croc first.

"Don't worry. I won't say anything."

Croc then reached for the holster on his right hip and handed Oliver a 9-millimeter handgun and asked him if he knew how to use it.

"No," he replied shortly.

As he gripped the handle, his fear was beginning to settle somewhere in his stomach, making him feel nauseous.

"You okay?" Croc questioned.

"Umm… yeah. I'm okay."

Oliver had never held a gun before and worried about what he would need to do with the weapon he was given. He also didn't want to come off as weak to Rahzmel and Croc, so he forced confidence as he told Croc he was ready.

"Extend your arm until your elbow is straight then point in the direction of your target and pull the trigger. Always keep the gun on safety until you're ready to use it. Tuck it under your shirt and don't bring it out unless you need to. The person you're pointing it at may not think twice."

Oliver nodded so Croc continued.

"We aren't expecting violence, but it never hurts to be prepared."

Oliver fearfully looked at the weapon, which rested coldly in his hands, and tucked it away. He tried to settle his shaking hands and shoved them into his pockets to hide his terror from the others.

The three men arrived at the abandoned warehouse in Crown Heights and when they pulled up, they saw a few other vehicles there. When they entered and walked into the room, Oliver was relieved to see a few familiar faces he had seen during his pick-ups. It was then that he realized he was at his first Collective meeting.

The leaders of each organization all sat around a circular table with members of their groups behind them and spoke about a new gang that had begun encroaching on the Jamaican territory in Brooklyn. The crew was a Jamaican bunch from Queens whom they learned was looking to expand their distribution, so they began selling their product in various parts of Brooklyn and the Bronx.

"Unfortunately, dey did not check with any of us first before coming into our areas of Brooklyn," barked the leader of the Jamaican crew, Nigel. "I know where dey are right now and we need to send dem a message to leave Brooklyn or we will leave bodies in da blood clot streets!"

"Have you tried speaking with them?" questioned Rahzmel whose first instinct was always a nonviolent approach. "You know the goal of our arrangement is to avoid violence at all costs. That's what keeps us under the radar."

"Yes, mon. I sent one of my guys to speak with dem last week and dey sent him back with his clothin' ripped off and his pride in da pieces. Stupid bumboclaats think dey can fuck with us! Dere was twelve of em' on da corner and my one man couldn't do nothin' by himself. Dis why we have dis arrangement, no? To keep things cohesive? Well, den let's make it cohesive and send a louder message."

Each of the leaders from the other crews agreed and voted their agreement. Each crew assigned a member of their crew to join Nigel and the Jamaicans in sending a message. Rahzmel was the last vote and he confirmed that he, Croc, and Oliver would be joining them but once again beseeched them for no dead bodies. He reminded the others that the reason they can operate the way they did was because of their agreement of no violence. He knew breaking this agreement would mean a greater war within Queens and Brooklyn with its biggest gang—the police.

All men then went back to their vehicles and followed Nigel's crew to their territory in East Flatbush. When they arrived, the cars all parked around the corner from where the Jamaicans were staged. Nigel's crew would be leading the pack and would be followed by the Irish, Hispanics, Italian, Japanese, and Rahzmel's crew. Oliver stood between Rahzmel and Croc. Like before, Nigel first sent one man to attempt to speak with the Jamaicans one last time to request they leave Brooklyn. From their position, they watched as the man fearlessly walked toward the group of twelve gangsters and begged them to depart. The group of twelve then quickly taunted the man by pushing him back to where he came from. Oliver watched as they all laughed as the man retreated around the corner.

He saw Nigel look back at Rahzmel for confirmation. Rahzmel turned around and put one hand on Oliver's shoulder.

"Remember what Croc told you about shooting a gun. Stay behind us the whole time."

Oliver nodded his head and confirmed the message was received so Rahzmel looked back at Nigel and nodded his head in agreement.

All men then began moving toward the perpetrators with guns pointed. The Queens Jamaicans saw the men running towards them and began discharging their weapons in defense. As members of the Collective took cover, they also began returning fire toward the Queens Jamaicans causing them to duck for cover. The street erupted in gunfire.

Nigel and the others continued pushing and shooting back in their direction. Once the Queens Jamaicans realized they were severely outnumbered and outgunned, they began to retreat toward their vehicles, which were parked on the adjacent street. They knew their best chance at survival was to retreat and preferred to live to fight another day.

Oliver had never been in a gunfight before, so he nervously hid behind a vehicle as his hands shook vigorously from his fear. He was frightened by the gunshots and cringed as each sound rocked his core, again and again. He wasn't sure exactly why he felt that way, but it had scared him so badly that he could feel warm steam traveling down his pant leg. Croc and Rahzmel both saw him ducking and yelled for him to stay down until it was over. Nigel threatened in the direction of the retreating Jamaicans and yelled for them not to step foot in Brooklyn again unless they wanted a war. After that, he turned around and thanked Rahzmel and the others who supported them. Rahzmel and Nigel shook hands and all crews went their separate way.

During their trip back, Oliver apologized to Rahzmel and Croc for his nervousness during the shootout. He knew he was not prepared for what was being asked of him and did not want to lose their trust and respect.

"It's okay….," Rahzmel replied with a pause. "We never like to use violence to resolve problems unless the situation calls for it."

Oliver heard the reassurance in what Rahzmel was saying but could also hear a hint of sarcasm in the gang leader's voice.

"To be honest, that's why I wanted to bring you instead of Rio or Chino. I knew they would be quick to kill someone, and we don't need anyone being picked up for murder. Not now. This collective agreement between other crews only works if we all do our part and unfortunately, sometimes, the path to a resolution involves some violence…but not now."

The gang leader joked, "I saw you standing like Rambo. I may need to replace Croc with you. I really feel like you're fitting in very nicely. Good job. We will celebrate at the club in a few days. For now, we will drop you off at home. The gun is yours. We'll lock it away for you at the Clubhouse. The last thing we need is you to get caught with a gun at home."

Oliver assumed that by "celebrate at the club," Rahzmel was speaking about the clubhouse, so he didn't ask any questions and got out of the truck when they arrived at Dunbar.

*****

As promised, a few days later Croc and Rahzmel picked up Oliver from school and told him they were going to celebrate. Oliver assumed there were girls and beer waiting for them back at the clubhouse but when Croc parked the truck, he saw they were far from their clubhouse in East New York. In front of him was a standalone building in what seemed like a dark and quiet neighborhood with a brightly lit sign that read, "Delilah's" on the door.

Where are we?

When the three men approached, Rahzmel and Croc both shook hands with the two large bouncers who also extended a hand to Oliver. The three men proceeded towards the back of the club and as they walked, Oliver looked around in amazement. He had never been inside a strip club before and was astonished by the number of bare-naked women and the excess of old men parting ways with their money.

When they arrived at the bar, Oliver watched as Rahzmel kissed Angela on the lips, and she grabbed his hand to walk the three of them to the VIP section which was located on the next level. He continued to observe the room and when the group finally arrived in VIP on the second floor, Oliver gave a double look because he thought he saw Minnie.

On his second look, he confirmed what he saw. It was Minnie across the room in nothing but her pink polka dot panties, giving an elderly Hispanic man a provocative lap dance. He was in disbelief. *How could she betray me like this? I thought we had something between us. What the fuck is she doing?*

The waitress brought them a few cold bottles of beer, a couple of rolled-up marijuana joints, and a few small packs of cocaine which were in small baggies labeled with a cursive letter "c" in red font. Oliver looked over and saw Rahzmel and Croc celebrate the arrival of these vices with a smile. He quickly turned his attention back to Minnie. As he continued to watch from the distance, his anger continued to rise.

He watched as Minnie slid between the gentleman's legs while motioning her head around his crotch in the same sexual manner that she did with him only days before. She then slid back up and began kissing the man's neck, also as she did with him. Oliver knew they weren't exclusive, but he also knew the two of them had shared some very intimate moments. He realized that, against Rahzmel's suggestion about falling in love, he had feelings for her. In a very angry tone, Oliver tapped Croc on the shoulder and inquired why Minnie was there and dancing on another guy.

"Didn't she tell you before? She works here. She's a dancer, man. This is her job."

"No, she didn't tell me. She told me she worked for Angela, but I thought they worked in a beauty parlor or something."

"Nah, man. Beauty parlor?" he chuckled assuming Oliver was joking. "Did anyone tell you that? Angela owns this club. Minnie is a dancer here. This is an exotic dance club where these girls get money to make men feel good. Most of the girls who come to the clubhouse belong to Delilah's. I thought you knew that."

"No, I didn't nor did I ask. I thought they were just girls who followed you guys. Rahzmel once told me Minnie was a friend of the crew, so I thought she and the other girls were just people who came around like Angela."

"Nah. I'm sorry you're just finding out. Yes, those girls are friends of the crew, but they are just girls Angela brings with her from the club when she comes to the clubhouse. Girls like Minnie aren't girls who guys like us should fall for. She's a dancer. She's a professional who's all about getting her money and uses her body the best way she knows. She and the other girls come to the clubhouse to get high and get drunk. That's it."

Without responding to Croc's comment, Oliver again thought about how betrayed he felt. He felt a heaviness in his heart that he hadn't felt before and began to shake. Minnie hadn't told him about the work she did and neither did Rahzmel, Angela, or Croc. His face grew warm.

In his angry state, Oliver looked back at Rahzmel and saw him kissing Angela. Seeing them infuriated him further and he reacted by running down to the main area where Minnie was. He was undaunted by the fear of repercussions.

Oliver grabbed the Hispanic man by the neck and pushed him away from Minnie. He knocked him to the ground then climbed on top of the man and began punching him in the face. Minnie yelled for him to stop but he ignored her yells. Moments later, two other Hispanic men pulled Oliver off the floor and restrained him. Both men drew their weapons, and one of them aimed his gun at Oliver's face. Almost immediately as they did that, Rahzmel pointed his gun at one man's head and Croc pointed his weapon at the head of the other.

"Let the boy go unless you want us to mop the floor with your brains and blood," demanded Rahzmel. "I'm sorry for him attacking your friend but there will be no violence in my club."

"Rahzmel, your puppy attacked a member of our crew," replied one of the men as he lowered his weapon. "We have an agreement, and your intern broke that agreement. That will not be tolerated."

"I understand that, and I agree. That will not be tolerated, and I will handle it. I will speak with Cesar in the morning and get this settled. For now, just get out of here before this puppy bites again," he demanded.

The two men forcibly released Oliver and picked up their bloody friend from the ground. Right before leaving, Rahzmel tapped Croc on the shoulder and motioned for him to grab something from the office. Moments later, Croc came back and handed the three Hispanic men a small bag of money for their troubles. He told them it was to take care of their tab for the night and extra to compensate for the trouble. They irritably thanked Rahzmel and made their way toward the exit.

As this was occurring, Oliver pulled Minnie to the back room and asked her why she didn't tell him she was an exotic dancer.

"What does it matter? You're not my man nor are you paying my bills. You're just a kid."

"But what about the other day? We had sex in the clubhouse. Was I a kid then? Was I just another client?"

"Look, Oliver. I really like you but this my job and it's all I got. I can't be a gangster or drug dealer like the rest of you, so I use my body to make money. I'm sorry you thought this was something more, but we were just having fun. Angela told me to take care of you, so I did."

Oliver, who was holding back his tears, stared at Minnie and then shook his head. He angrily started to storm out of the room. When he opened the door, Rahzmel and Croc were both standing there, grabbed him by the back collar, and aggressively demanded he follows them to the truck.

"What the hell was that?" barked Rahzmel in an angry tone. "You attacked a member of the fucking Hispanic crew. They are members of our Collective. Those boys do not play, and we need them on our side. Why the fuck would you do that?"

"I saw him dancing with Minnie and got angry. I didn't know they were with the Collective," he said in his defense.

"Minnie? You're telling me that you attacked him because of Minnie? Let me remind you of something, young man. Minnie's not your girl and I told you not to fall in love with that bitch," remarked the kingpin in a tone intended to humble the teen. "She belongs to all of us and if I wanted to take her in the back room and fuck her, I would. This is her job. The only value she brings to this world is to make guys feel special enough that they are willing to part ways with their hard-earned money. That's her job and you nor anyone else will change that. Just forget about her."

"Why didn't you tell me this before?" he barked back. "When we had sex, it felt like something was there."

"Who the fuck are you talking to like we're peers?" Rahzmel roared. "You better remember who you're talking to."

Oliver deflated back and diverted his eyes from the kingpin's gaze.

"Trust me, it wasn't. I told Angela to have her suck your dick and if I knew you would fall this hard, I wouldn't have rewarded your loyalty by giving you a bitch. I thought you were mature enough to enjoy some of the nicer luxuries of your loyalty to the crew, but I guess I was wrong. For the sake of all of us, she won't be coming around anymore. You've proven you can't control your emotions. Now I have to go and deal with this mess. Tomorrow, I will speak with the Hispanic crew to figure this out. My hope is that they don't call for your head. Shit!"

"I'm sorry, Rahzmel."

"You just better hope I can talk my way out of this. I also want you to remember that nothing is more important than this thing we've built…Don't ever put anything or anyone above this crew. Your actions were selfish and if you ever act out like that again, I will place the barrel of my gun between your eyes and pull the fuckin' trigger myself."

This was the first time that Oliver was truly frightened by Rahzmel. The once caring gang leader who took him under his wing had disappeared and Oliver felt he had finally seen the version of Rahzmel that Lenny had warned him about. He felt the same chills that shot up his spine when he watched Rahzmel hold a blade to Chino's neck like it was nothing. He was frightened but knew there was nothing else he could do tonight.

As he made his way out, Oliver remembered Mr. Morgan teaching them about a saying from Sun Tzu. "Keep your friends close and your enemies closer." Oliver wasn't exactly sure which side he fell on at that moment but knew exactly where he needed to be. He was scared and believed the best place for him to be was next to Rahzmel. He had already seen Rahzmel's verbal wrath and didn't want to be on the tail end of the violence he knew he was capable of. He knew there was no turning back.

CHAPTER 11:

25TH HOUR

Rahzmel

The day after the strip club fiasco, Rahzmel met with Cesar, the leader of the Hispanic crew as a means to prevent a potential conflict. He knew Cesar's crew as a dangerous unit with some frightening connections in South America, and had no interest in going to war with them. They ran a tight cocaine circuit through New York that stretched through the various boroughs. Because of their reputation for violence, he knew he needed to negotiate a punishment for the youngest member of his crew that was fair and just. He did not want to seem weak or vulnerable and knew Cesar respected him because of his strength. His goal was not to seem overly dominant but still strong enough to warrant respect. He arranged for the meeting to be held at a location of Cesar's choosing and decided to come with an initial suggestion which Cesar quickly declined.

Cesar's counter suggestion was for Rahzmel to greenlight Oliver's murder at the hands of the crew member the teen attacked but Rahzmel believed that to be an extremely excessive punishment for such a harmless mistake.

"He's young and immature. It was just a bad decision from a kid."

"That's your problem, Rahzmel. Not mine. You choose to run with those kids and now this is the cost of that."

"I know and up until this point, there haven't been any issues. Let's be reasonable, Caesar. We've made a lot of money with this arrangement and this kid has been a part of that. His punishment shouldn't bring physical harm because it would send the wrong message to the rest of the Collective. To our money."

"What are you suggesting?"

"Let's find something that will prevent any long-term damage between us."

"Okay. I want $50,000 and I want the corner of Central and University."

"But that's one of my most profitable corners."

Caesar stared unamused and reiterated his demands. "It's either the money and corner or we kill the kid."

"Okay, okay. But no harm can come to the kid, and we act like this never happened?"

"Okay, deal."

Even though he also felt this to be a bit excessive, Rahzmel reluctantly agreed. He did not want any harm to come to Oliver and knew Cesar may not have had the patience or appetite to listen to other offers. They shook hands before departing.

Oliver will repay every fucking cent plus interest for this shit, the kingpin thought to himself.

After the meeting was over, Rahzmel left with Croc and during the trip back, he called Rio and Chino with updates. He told them that they would be giving up one of their distribution corners and suggested that they relocate their street soldiers to another vacant section of East New York. "Minor setback for a major comeback" is what he told them with frustration in his tone. Without questioning their leader, the two of them agreed and made the adjustment. They knew Rahzmel was always making deals, so they had learned early not to question him.

Croc was the only person who was aware of the truth behind the decision to relocate. He was at the negotiation with Cesar and during their car ride home, Rahzmel told him to never tell Oliver or anyone else the price he had to pay for the teenager's life. Because he knew he already had Oliver's loyalty, he figured it may be more beneficial to put Oliver in a position to make more money. He understood the mistake the boy made and did not want an excessive punishment. His hope was that in time, Oliver would regain his trust. But not without putting in overtime.

*****

Oliver

After what happened that night at the strip club, Oliver felt his relationship with Rahzmel took a turn for the worse. He was still welcomed in the clubhouse and continued to complete pickups, but he noticed the gang leader no longer took a particular interest in him and thought his role within Rahzmel's succession plan had disappeared.

Rahzmel would regularly hold meetings without notifying Oliver, which went against what he told the teen the night they attacked the Queens Jamaicans. He was determined to regain Rahzmel's trust because it made him feel valuable.

Oliver approached Croc and asked him how to regain Rahzmel's trust.

"Don't worry about it, man. The issue with the Hispanics was already handled. You just need to give Rah some time. Do as you're told and follow his plan to make this money. He's got some plans to grow and trust me when I say, you want to be on this side of the arrangements."

"Okay. Thanks. Just don't let Rah forget about me. I can do better."

Oliver knew Rahzmel as a businessman who was all about money, power, and unity. Rahzmel's rule for the Collective was that "everyone eats together as long as everyone is on the same wave." This spoke to his vision of an inclusive and profitable Brooklyn underworld.

"Okay. I'll do that. Thanks, Croc."

*****

About a month later, Oliver was heading back to the clubhouse after making a money pickup. It was the second Tuesday of September which meant he was picking up money from the Italians in the Bushwick neighborhood of Brooklyn.

During the visit, he had informed the Italians that he was working with Rahzmel on the expansion of their collective.

"Yeah, Rahzmel is expanding, and we got some big plans for everyone," he lied. "We gon' eat together!"

He did not have a plan or specific details but told them that the expansion would include more profits and more territory. They seemed excited to hear this and told the teen they were going to relay the message to their leader, Luca. His plan was to have this same conversation with the other crews during his upcoming pickups to show Rahzmel he was worth something. He was excited to get back and tell Rahzmel his plan and even more excited to tell him that the other crews were already on board.

After leaving the Italians, he began to head toward the train to get back. Before entering the station, he realized it was only 4:15 p.m. and he still had time before he had to be back, so he decided to take an alternative route in order to scout for corners that he knew were not already claimed by others within the Collective. He was going to bring this information to Rahzmel.

At that same time, he also realized he forgot his mobile phone at home which worried him at first but figured if he needed to contact anyone, he could run back to the Italian crew's stash house to get a message out. He knew the Collective controlled most of Brooklyn so he assumed he would be okay in most places he visited.

He proceeded forward and took the detour which led him up Bushwick Avenue. As he made his way, he took note of how much nicer this part of Brooklyn was from Canarsie.

Rahzmel would love this.

When he arrived at the end of the block, he saw a large group sitting on the stoop of an abandoned apartment building. He was not sure at first but as he continued closer, he couldn't believe what he saw. It was the same Jamaican crew from Queens whom they had run out of town weeks before. They were on the opposite side of the street playing music and joking around as if they weren't encroaching on territory seeking to disrupt profits.

Because he had not been in any meetings since the night of the strip club, he was unsure if Rahzmel and Nigel had come to some sort of agreement with the Queens Jamaicans.

Why else would they be back in Brooklyn?

He presumed the Italians and Rahzmel had already known about them being there and continued forward up Bushwick Ave.

As he walked, he avoided staring at the group. He had already confirmed it was them and didn't see any reason to make contact or acknowledge their presence. He also hoped they would not recognize him from the previous shootout.

As he continued, a few of the Jamaicans noticed the mysterious teen walking down the quiet street carrying a large backpack and ran across the street towards him. They were bored and he looked like he could be a customer or prey.

As they grew closer, Oliver was confident they did not remember him because of how they joked around. He felt worried—this kind of thing didn't usually happen. But he tried to reassure himself. *It's just bored gangsters messing around on the corner. Not a problem. The crew's got my back, anyways.*

They walked up to Oliver and first offered him drugs. "Hey, need anything, batty boy? We got what you need."

"Nah," Oliver replied dismissively as he kept walking. They kept following and asking if he wanted some drugs or women.

"You seem stressed, man," one said. "I got somethin' to help ya unwind. Where ya headin' so fast anyway, boy?"

"I'm on business for Rahzmel," replied Oliver, a bit haughtily.

They laughed at him. "Who's Rahzmel? We know no Rahzmel. Look at this batty boy, playin' like he's somethin' important."

Shit, this isn't right. I was wrong. Oliver was now afraid, and the Jamaican teens saw it on his face.

One of them yelled, "Hey mon, what's in ya bag, anyways?"

He ripped the backpack off his back and held it over his head. When Oliver turned around to grab the bag back, another one of them forcefully pushed him back to the ground. They tore the bag open and noticed it was filled with cash. Oliver was now terrified and embarrassed. He was desperate to run, but wanted to get the money and some dignity back if he could.

"Do you know who I am?" threatened Oliver. "That money belongs to some very dangerous people who would not be happy to hear that I was held up in delivering it to them."

"Unuh, come if yah come," replied one of the Jamaicans. "It's ours now."

Oliver knew Rahzmel's approach was to avoid violence so he wasn't entirely sure if his threats would actualize.

"Hey, give it back! Or else my friends will fuck you up!" His voice was shaky but held its volume.

The Jamaicans laughed as they shoved Oliver back to the ground.

He couldn't go back to Rahzmel, or the Italians empty-handed. He felt his head getting warm and was now furious.

I'd rather die fighting than just give up $20,000 of Rahzmel's cash.

He stood up and once again demanded his bag back.

"If I don't get that bag back, I will come back and light up your fucking block in bullets like it's raining," he lied.

They did not take kindly to this threat especially since they were shot at only weeks before.

The Queen's Jamaican's seemed much larger than he remembered, and their presence shook him to the core. Before he could get another word in, the men suddenly jumped on the teen and Oliver felt the space around him quickly shrink. He saw he was cornered and threw his hands up prepared to defend himself. The assailants charged straight for him, knocking him to the ground until he was curled in a ball of defense. One of the assailants used his dirty boot to deliver a forceful stomp across the teens head, which caused his vision to blur. He continued to cover his head with his arms as the perpetrators punched and kicked him lifeless. They landed each blow to his head and body, and Oliver could hear a ringing in his ear. He felt disoriented and helpless.

After a few moments of kicking and punching, the attackers lifted Oliver's barely lifeless body and dragged it into the empty alley near the overflowing dumpster. The teen could barely see anything but could smell the rancid trash inches from his beaten face. He spit up blood as the attackers rushed away and just as he attempted to rise to his feet to get back, he collapsed. From the ground, he gave one final hazy look at the street until everything went dark.

*****

Around 10:30 p.m., Oliver woke up to a male voice asking him if he was okay while shaking him. He was dazed and confused and when he realized where he was, he noticed it was two police officers who were standing over him, attempting to help him up.

"Are you okay, son?" remarked one of the officers as he reached in, but Oliver quickly retracted back. "I'm Officer Smith. Calvin Smith. Do you know where you are?"

Oliver stared at both officers and remained quiet. He looked into their eyes and as scared as he was, he somehow felt comfortable there with them. He wasn't entirely sure if it was because they were on Rahzmel's payroll or because they had seen each other before. They looked familiar but Oliver could not confirm where he remembered them from.

Because he couldn't remember, he knew it was best not to speak with the officers about anything involving Rahzmel or his operation. He then turned his attention away and attempted to stand on his own feet but when he rose, he collapsed back down on the ground. He was visibly bruised and beaten. What the officers didn't see were the wounds that were deeply buried in his soul. No one else could see them but Oliver was as sure about them as he was about his own existence. He was angry with what was done to him, but he was more afraid. Afraid of what he had gotten involved with. Afraid of what Rahzmel would do next. Even worse, he was afraid of what would be expected of him to do next.

"How did you get here and what happened to you?" questioned Officer Smith.

"You can trust us, Oliver. I'm Officer Jalacie Jefferson. We're here to help you," remarked the African American officer in a calm, and reassuring tone.

Oliver again looked up at the two officers.

"How do you know my name?"

"Ms. Janet has been looking for you all night. She called us earlier this evening when you didn't show up at the Dunbar House. We spent the past few hours driving around Canarsie and adjacent neighborhoods in search of you. What are you doing all the way out here in Bushwick?"

"I got jumped and the cats who beat me up brought me here. Can you take me back to Dunbar?"

"Yes, we can. Are you in any trouble?"

"No, I'm fine. I just need to get home."

"Okay, we can take you home. Before that though, we need to take you to the hospital to ensure you don't have a concussion."

The officers took Oliver to the hospital for a concussion checkup and when it was confirmed he had nothing more than a few bruises and scrapes, they drove him back to Dunbar. When they pulled up in front of the house, Ms. Janet came running outside and began yelling at Oliver from the distance. As she got closer, she saw the bruises and black eye and stopped yelling. She examined the teen's wounds and in a stern tone, advised him to go get some rest. At her request,

Oliver went into the house and left the officers to speak with Ms. Janet.

They explained what happened based on what Oliver shared. They knew there were a lot of details he was not telling them, but they left it for Ms. Janet to handle.

"Go easy on him. He's been through a lot tonight." She agreed and when she went to speak with Oliver, he told her the same thing he told the officers. He had changed so much since when he first came to Dunbar House, and she knew he may have been involved in something more than what he was telling her.

"Why the fuck was you on the other side of town? You told me you was at school," questioned Ms. Janet.

When he didn't respond, she threatened that whatever he was involved in better not make its way into Dunbar House.

"I'm not your motha' so I will tell you this once. I don't care if you go to jail or die in those streets."

He remained silent.

"If these actions ever make their way into this house, I will send you back to the foster care system and put a target on your back. I will drive you there myself and leave you to be someone else's problem. Also, don't forget that you're only here 'till you're sixteen. After that, you should be able to fend for yourself."

Right before leaving the room, Ms. Janet told Oliver he would be staying home to rest the next day and slammed the door. He didn't assume she was letting him stay home for his own well-being. He knew that deep down inside; she didn't want him to go to school where his teachers could begin to question his bruises.

*****

Rahzmel

Meanwhile, while Oliver had been working to rebuild his relationship with the kingpin, Rahzmel and Croc were on their way to lunch with Luca, the leader of the Italian crew. Rahzmel enjoyed meeting with the other leaders weekly. Today was Tuesday, which meant Oliver would be picking up from the Italians later in the day. Luca confirmed that there were no issues and told Rahzmel his crew would be ready for Oliver's arrival later in the day. They dined before the two leaders shook hands and went their separate ways.

When Rahzmel and Croc arrived back at the clubhouse, they hung out while they waited for Oliver to return with the Italian's contribution. Croc had seen how determined Oliver was to get back into Rahzmel's good graces and had hoped the gang leader had seen the determinations as well. He casually mentioned Oliver's efforts, but Rahzmel ignored him. Rahzmel had also seen the work Oliver was putting in but figured the teen wasn't going anywhere, so he was in no rush to acknowledge or commend the teen's work until he repaid every cent of the $50,000, lost to the Hispanics, in sweat.

By 6 p.m., Rahzmel came out of the back room and asked Croc if he had seen or heard anything from Oliver. It was unusual for the teen not to return to the clubhouse by 5 p.m. They assumed he may have gotten sidetracked and was still on the way so he disregarded it. Because of their existing arrangements with the police, they knew he would not have been questioned unless it was by the few officers who did not fall under their agreement. Even if he was arrested, the news would have made it to him by now. They gave him another hour to return.

By 8 p.m., Oliver still had not returned so Rahzmel began to worry for his money. He called Oliver's phone, but it was turned off. He then got on the phone with Luca to inquire about the status of the pickup.

"The boy left at 4 p.m. with the money. Said he was heading back to you," Luca remarked. "Is he not back?"

"No," Rahzmel replied shortly and irritably.

"Let me call the guys and see what's going on. I'm going to put some eyes in the streets to find out where your boy is."

"Thank you, Luca."

Chino and Rio were both back at the clubhouse by then, so Rahzmel dispatched them to the streets for answers while he and Croc headed to Park Slope. He informed them that they should all plan to return by 11 p.m. with either Oliver, his money, or their updates. His final instruction was that if anyone located Oliver before 11 p.m., they should call his phone. All the men agreed and headed out.

They started their search at Dunbar House but learned from another one of the residents, who was sitting outside on the stoop, that Oliver had not been back since morning. Next, they checked the school but by the time they had arrived, it was closed, and all lights were off. They figured it was unlikely he was there.

They continued to search the borough, driving from neighborhood to neighborhood. By 10:30 p.m., Rahzmel and Croc still had not found the teen and were ready to head back to the clubhouse to regroup. They had just left Luca's stash house 15 minutes earlier and hoped he was simply missing and did not run away with their $20,000 in cash.

Rahzmel was now angry when he realized Oliver was nowhere to be found and no one had any answers for him. *He's an orphan with no family or ties to Brooklyn. If he stole from us, I will murder him.*

Croc did not think Oliver was stupid enough to steal from them and told Rahzmel so. He knew Oliver was much smarter than that and believed the teen fully comprehended Rahzmel's lecture on trust.

As they continued their drive home from the Italians, they saw a parked police cruiser, with its lights flashing, parked beside a dark alley.

As they slowly drove by, they peered closer into the scene and saw the two officers speaking with a figure on the ground. *Can't be,* Rahzmel thought. From the passenger seat, he watched as Oliver sat on the ground speaking with the officers.

"Whoa, whoa…slow down, Croc. I think Oliver's there with them. Do you recognize them? Are they one of ours?"

"Nah, I don't. They might be new. Never seen them before."

They were unsure what was being discussed and were even more curious as to what had happened to cause Oliver to be speaking with two officers whom they did not know. They did not know if the officers were a part of their payroll, so they avoided driving to them. Instead of approaching, they parked a few yards up the street and waited to see how the scene unfolded.

Croc then used his cell phone to contact Rio and inform him that they located Oliver.

After about twenty minutes of waiting, they watched as Oliver entered the police cruiser with the two officers and drove off. They followed the car to the hospital where Croc decided it was best to call it a night. He assumed the officers were going to the hospital for Oliver and knew they probably would not have had a chance to speak with him. Croc suggested they go back to the clubhouse, but Rahzmel demanded they stay and watch.

"No, we aren't going anywhere."

"But, Rah-"

"But, nothing. That little bitch owes me $50,000 and is on the hook for today's pick-up. Where he is, my money's close so we aren't going nowhere."

They decided to park within eyesight of the police cruiser and were planning on taking turns sleeping because they assumed they were going to be there all night. Rahzmel had a ton of questions for Oliver and didn't want to let him out of his sight. The first question was—where was his missing money?

CHAPTER 12:

I WILL BREAK US DOWN

Oliver Mahlah

The following morning, Oliver woke up in his bed at Dunbar House and vaguely recalled the night before. He wasn't entirely sure how he made it home but remembered making the pickups from the Italians and how heavy the bag of money felt on his shoulders.

Wait…Did I see the Jamaicans last night? He felt the bruise on his ribs and cringed from the pain. His face was a horrid mixture of bruises, scrapes, and bumps. His already thick lips were swollen like a mushroom which matched his puffy right eye, which was slightly shut. Both cheeks had scrapes that were now beginning to scab over. When he hobbled over to the mirror, he could barely recognize himself. Still in disbelief, he brought his hands to his battered face, then slowly lowered them to his side at first touch. He was in so much pain.

Oh shit! Rahzmel's probably wondering where I've been with his money. He probably thinks I ran with it. Fuck! I better call him to tell him what happened.

When he reached under his bed for his box of items, he grabbed the dead cellphone Rahzmel gave him which sat beside the cash he had saved up. *Damn, I wish I had my gun last night. Those Jamaicans wouldn't have gotten a penny if I did.*

When he noticed the room was empty, he put a battery in the phone and then used it to call Rahzmel to tell him what happened. He told the gang leader about the Queens Jamaicans and how they were back in their territory. He stated they were the ones responsible for the robbery and the beating. Rahzmel replied by telling the teen that he was on the way to pick him up, avoiding speaking about any details over the phone.

Roughly five minutes later, Rahzmel called Oliver out to take a ride with him. Oliver found it unusual that he arrived so quickly but didn't want to question it. When he approached the car, he noticed Rahzmel was driving, and Croc was sitting in the backseat. He again found it unusual since Croc was normally the one driving. Despite his hesitation, he got into the passenger seat and the three men drove off.

"You a'ight man?" questioned Rahzmel in an accusatory tone void of sympathy. "You gave us a little scare yesterday."

"Yeah, just a few scrapes. Nothing's broken," he replied with his gaze and voice both stuck at Rahzmel's tone.

"That's good, Oliver. What exactly happened?"

Oliver sat quiet as he deliberated. *I don't want to say the wrong thing. I don't recall much.*

"You deaf?" Rahzmel barked. "I said what happened?"

"I'm sorry Rah. I'm still in a little pain." Oliver placed one hand on his left rib and the other on the door handle, then attempted to turn to talk to the kingpin.

"Don't turn around. Stare straight and talk."

"Ok…umm…I met with the Italians and picked up the money as normal. When I left, I was on the way back and noticed the group of Jamaicans in what I thought was the Italian territory. I hadn't been at any of the recent meetings, so I wasn't sure if you all had agreed on somethin' that I wasn't aware of. I continued to head back towards the train, and they approached me."

"Did they recognize you from when we ran them out of Brooklyn?"

"I don't think so. When they approached me, it seemed like they were just there to fuck with me."

He paused as he used his shaking hand to wipe his forehead.

"They saw me with the backpack, and I figured they would have assumed I was coming back from school. They must have noticed something else because the next thing I knew, they were rippin' the bag off my back and knocked me to the ground. I asked for the bag back and when I walked towards them, they attacked me again. I thought about how strong you both are and realized I could be that strong too, so I demanded the bag back again.

"You trusted me to be a part of this thing you've built, and I didn't want to let you down… *again*. When I demanded the bag back from the Jamaicans again, they all jumped on me and began attacking me until they knocked me out. When I woke up, I was in an alley with two police officers who seemed to have recognized me from somewhere."

"How did you know they recognized you?"

"One of them said my name."

"Did he say anything else?"

"No, just that they needed to get me to the hospital. I don't remember what happened after that. The next thing I knew, I was back home, and Ms. Janet was yelling at me."

"Did they say my name?"

"What?"

"Did they say my name?!?!" Rahzmel barked.

"I don't think so. They seemed really interested in me."

"Sorry you had to deal with that, Oliver. I appreciate you for trying to get my money back. I've called a meeting with the Collective this afternoon to discuss how we will handle this situation. The money was taken but that can easily be replaced. They will need to answer for putting hands on one of my soldiers," remarked Rahzmel in the same cold, murderous tone Oliver heard when he first met him.

"Rio and Chino are in the streets right now seeing if they can get eyes on the Jamaicans. They will call us when they find something. After stealing $20,000 of my money and putting their hands on one of my soldiers, I bet they're hiding out until this thing blows over. For now, let's go grab an early lunch and catch up. You're right, it has been a while since the last time we spoke and I'm sorry for that."

From his passenger seat, Oliver could see Croc through the side mirror. He saw the large enforcer shift in his seat to reach his right hip—where he wore his gun. It was at that moment that Oliver realized the danger he had been in. The answers he gave to Rahzmel's questions had determined whether he left the car alive.

*****

Around 12:30 p.m., Rahzmel got a call from Rio. He mentioned they'd received word that the Queens Jamaicans used a warehouse in South Jamaica, Queens. Rahzmel then called an emergency 2 p.m. meeting at the clubhouse with leaders from each crew. He told Croc to ensure Chino, Rio, and himself were all in attendance. He also told Croc to ensure Angela and her girls were not there. He reminded the enforcer that they were at war which meant they needed soldiers. Croc understood and made a few more calls.

*****

By 2 p.m., all the leaders and a few others with their crews filled every seat at Rahzmel's clubhouse. Rahzmel started by thanking all crews for joining on such short notice and immediately followed with a recap of what Oliver told him regarding the previous night's attack. He informed them that they knew where the Queens Jamaicans were hiding and because it was in Queens, it would be very dangerous for them to address. Luca immediately interjected by offering his apologies for his crew not locating the Jamaicans in their territory earlier. He was fully in support of responding with force and even offered assistance from their "family" members in Queens if needed.

"My assumption is dat dey popped up on an empty corner to steal business," barked Nigel. "Dey didn't get da message da first time and dis disrespect cannot go unanswered, brudda," he said, turning his attention to Rahzmel.

"Mi wan blood," demanded Nigel.

"We cannot and will not stand for this. Blood begets blood and they've spilled blood first," replied Rahzmel.

His tone was cold. Even colder than the night he yelled at Oliver and the teen felt chills at what was to come next.

Rahzmel walked down the aisles between the filled seats, making sure to look each gangster in the eye as he spoke. Once he finished walking, he stood in the back of the room where his audience would have to crane their necks in order to see him. Although subtle, this act spoke volumes only Oliver understood. Rahzmel needed to feel in control at all times, even if it meant with just the attention of his audience.

There was a unanimous decision that they strike hard, and they strike fast. Despite his original hesitation toward violence, Rahzmel was the first one to cast his vote in favor of it. He worked so hard to keep violence off the Brooklyn streets but knew this needed to be done. The fact that they would be going to Queens also made it more attractive to him because it technically wouldn't violate his agreement with the Brooklyn officials. They also were unsure how many men the Jamaicans had in their warehouse so each crew within the Collective offered at least five of their best men to address the hiding bandits.

From Rahzmel's crew, Croc, Rio, Chino, Rahzmel, and Oliver were planning to be their representatives. Croc ensured their street soldiers were all on high alert. The plan was set; they would all regroup at the clubhouse at 9 p.m. and set off with a total of thirty-five men. All ready for war.

Before leaving to head home, Oliver grabbed his gun from Rahzmel's closet. He never wanted to find himself in a situation like that again and knew he would not have been robbed if he had his gun. When he got back to Dunbar, he hid the gun in the box underneath his bed before taking a nap.

He wanted to ensure Ms. Janet saw him in order to create an alibi for himself. He knew this was him thinking like the leader Rahzmel wanted him to be. Early that evening, he went to speak with her and thanked her for what she said the night prior.

"I don't want to fall down the wrong path and appreciate you caring," he lied. "I'm tired so I'm going to skip dinner and go to bed early. Night"

At 8 p.m., he stuffed some clothing under his covers and quickly got dressed. He snuck out of the window from his second-floor shared bedroom. Fortunately, others were downstairs eating dinner so no one else saw him leave. He also made sure he left the window slightly cracked so he would be able to get back after the night.

When he arrived at the clubhouse, what he saw gave him chills. There on the main table were multiple hand pistols, automatic weapons, and bulletproof vests. He had never seen so many guns in one place and had a feeling that the night was going to end very badly for someone. Rahzmel handed Oliver a handgun when he approached and asked if he remembered how to use it.

"Yes, I do," he remarked as he gripped the cold steel. In reality, all he could remember was Croc's warning to "not think twice before pulling the trigger because the person on the other end wouldn't."

It was at this moment that Oliver realized he forgot his own pistol in the box underneath his bed.

Shit, I left my gun at home.

"I know you're scared," Rahzmel started, "but this isn't just to scare them. You gotta be all in. We need to send a message that they don't fuck with us."

As Oliver held the handgun from Rahzmel, his hands became weak and clammy. He did not want to seem like a coward but also knew he was not like Rahzmel or Croc. He realized he may have started something he could not walk away from.

I don't think I can do this.

Without saying anything, he nodded at Rahzmel to show his understanding.

I can't do this anymore. I'm not sure how but I need to get away from this. This isn't me.

Lenny's warning once again rang in his mind. Although their time together was brief, Lenny was the one person who was like him. He was the one person also searching for his place in this world. Oliver had wanted to ask about Lenny again, but the time was never right. And now, he knew Rahzmel was in war mode.

*****

By 9:45 p.m., the members of the Collective had arrived at the warehouse. One of the cars drove around the building twice to scope out the scene and when they arrived back at the larger group, they reported their findings. Their plan was to surprise the Jamaicans by entering from different doors and covering all exits. Because they were in unfamiliar territory in Queens, they did not want to be surprised by anyone, so they ensured men were also positioned by the vehicles.

As they quietly entered the warehouse, the group of men looked around and noticed a potent, stale scent of marijuana mixed with incense coming from one area. There was a light cloud of smoke throughout the building, and they knew they would need to be extremely quiet because of the Jamaicans' heightened sense of paranoia. They noticed a sound coming from one room in the middle of a long hallway on the second floor and crept forward towards it. They had men approaching from both ends of the hallway and when they arrived at the room, they quietly cracked the door, which was already ajar, and counted about twelve Jamaicans sitting around the television watching TV and smoking.

In addition to marijuana, there were half-empty bottles of rum everywhere. Stacks of money sat on the table with a few handguns around them. Rahzmel whispered to Oliver and asked if he recognized any of the men in the room. Oliver peered around the corner and nodded.

He wasn't sure if he recognized them from the robbery or a few weeks before, but his assumption was that because he recognized a few of them, this was enough confirmation that this was the group who robbed and assaulted him. Rahzmel then looked back and gave a thumbs up to Nigel who then signaled the rest of the group.

At Nigel's signal, they all charged into the room with their weapons drawn.

When they saw people coming, the Queens Jamaicans reached for the weapons on the table. Without giving them a chance, most were shot down until only four members of the group remained alive.

Oliver did not discharge his weapon but watched as the others made the cold gangster life seem easy. When the shooting began, he stood behind Croc with his entire body trembling. *What am I doing here? I shouldn't be here.* He looked around the room and saw all the dead bodies on the floor and was shaken. His breaths were rapid and he could not stop shaking.

The four men who remained were forced to the floor with their hands locked behind their heads. They shouted that they were unarmed as they begged for their lives. After 10 seconds of begging, Nigel laughed superciliously, pointed his gun, and shot one of the men three times in the back of the head. The sound of his gun emptying shook the room.

He then looked at Rahzmel and asked what he wanted to do with the remaining three. Without answering the question, Rahzmel looked at the money on the table, then looked at Oliver. He looked back at the three men, who were on the ground unarmed, and shot another one of them in the center of his head once. He followed up by shooting the man's face and body eight more times until he was unrecognizable. Oliver quivered as the sound of each of his gunshots echoed in the small room.

As Rahzmel's gun clicked, signaling it was emptied, Rahzmel put in a new magazine and unloaded another two shots in the man's body.

He did not even answer the question. Oliver thought to himself. *This was a complete blood bath. I thought Rahzmel was a businessman but now I realize he's a stone-cold killer. I need to get out of here. What have I done?*

Now two men remained and after peering around the room, they realized they were severely outnumbered and accepted their fates. Without being told to do so, they stood to their feet and lowered their hands. They held their chests out while they both stared directly at Nigel. They barked threats in their native language and spit on the floor directly in front of Nigel's Timberland boots.

One of the Italians brought the empty backpack to Luca who showed it to Rahzmel. This was their confirmation that these were the men who robbed and assaulted Oliver. Rahzmel showed the bag to the teen, who was still standing behind Croc, and reminded the teen that these men were the ones who beat him up the day before. Oliver knew what they did to him but figured this was the cost of the life he was a part of. The anger that embodied him twenty-four hours before had subsided and all he wanted to do now was leave. Rahzmel looked the teen in the eye.

"Do you have the gun I gave you?" he asked.

When he went to reach for it, Oliver realized he did not have it on him. *Oh shoot. I must have dropped it.*

"No, I think I dropped it."

Rahzmel shook his head. "Only you can get the revenge you deserve because you were the one these men wronged." He then pulled another handgun from his back and handed it to the young teen. As everyone watched, Rahzmel motioned for Oliver to take care of the last two men so they could leave. Oliver looked at the gun and then slowly raised his arm to point at the two men. He stood there for a few seconds as his hand continued to shake. The weapon was only a few pounds but felt like a boulder in his hand. At that moment, the men heard police sirens in the distance and grew anxious.

Nigel offered to kill the remaining two men, but Rahzmel stopped him.

"This needs to be done by Oliver," the kingpin began. "Everyone else should leave. Oliver and I will finish. Want to make sure this job is done."

Without any questions, Rahzmel, Nigel, and Oliver remained as the other men left the room and headed back to the car. Rahzmel watched as Oliver lowered his hand and head.

"I can't do it," Oliver stated in a low and frightened tone. "I cannot take their lives."

As angry as he was from the night before, he knew there was no coming back from taking someone's life. He felt like he was living in a dream which slowly became a nightmare as the characters became darker. He saw Rahzmel go from warm and welcoming to a killer who didn't ask questions. *I don't want to be like that anymore.*

He dropped the gun to the ground and watched as the disappointment in Rahzmel's face grew. It was glaring and Oliver knew there may have been no redemption from this type of letdown. Rahzmel was a very proud individual and Oliver could see the disappointment and rage growing in his eyes. His actions had embarrassed Rahzmel in front of Nigel and the others which he knew infuriated the drug kingpin.

The two men noticed this opportunity and turned around to attempt to reach for the hidden weapons they had stashed underneath the couch. Nigel saw this and used his own gun to let off several gunshots in their backs. Rahzmel also let off a few shots and then picked up Oliver's gun.

"Run!"

As they made their way out of the building, they noticed most of the other cars had already departed from the lot and the only two that remained were Croc's truck and Nigel's 1970 Chevy Impala. When they got into the truck, Rahzmel used a napkin to wipe the blood from his boots.

"We were never here," he demanded. "What comes next may be beyond our control and we need to lay low till the heat dies down."

Oliver listened to Rahzmel's warning but inside all he heard was his opportunity to separate himself. He agreed to the command and although he was happy with the directive, he knew the request came more from the gang leader's disappointment than his worry. When they dropped him off back at Dunbar house, Oliver snuck back upstairs through the window he left cracked and into his bunk. Fortunately, he did not wake any others as he laid his head down and went to sleep.

*****

The next morning, Oliver was ready to take Rahzmel's advice and lay low. He figured this was the perfect opening he needed to break away from Rahzmel's crew. His hope was to get back to the life he led prior to meeting Lenny and his plan was to go to school and then home every day. The street life was more than he could handle, and he was over it. His hope was that in time, Rahzmel would forget about him because of the teen's inability to adapt to their violent lifestyle.

I'm done.

As he prepared to get ready for school that Thursday morning, he remembered he did not have his backpack because of the robbery. In the melee of the night, he forgot to take the school bag home with him from the warehouse. At the moment, he did not see this as a big deal and figured he would use some of the cash he earned to purchase a new bag. When he reached for the cash, he saw his gun and reminded himself that he also needed to get rid of it when he got home from school later that day.

He went to school as normal and as his day commenced, he actively engaged in each class, was more friendly with his peers, and even offered to stay and clean the board after Mr. Morgan's class. Despite his new approach to life, he couldn't stop thinking about the faces of the men who were killed the night before. The entire night continued to play out in his mind.

After completing his day at school, he was determined to pick up a new bag and act like nothing happened. He knew it would be hard but all he wanted at that moment was normalcy. He wanted to be a teenager again.

When the final bell rang, his first stop was the local convenience store where he found an almost exact replica of his bag. After paying, he made his way home to next take care of the gun.

When he arrived at Dunbar House, he saw three police cars sitting in front of the building. The same thoughts ran through his mind as the night when he returned after skipping school. *Why are they here and why are there so many cars?*

He looked around.

One police car may have just been a coincidence but three…they are looking for someone.

After what happened the night before, he had an idea of what the reason may have been but was hopeful that there was no connection between the police cars and the incident at the warehouse in Queens.

He slowly approached the house and before he got to the steps of the entrance, the main door shot open, and out walked Ms. Janet with four officers. She was pointing at Oliver and told them that "this is the young man you're looking for."

It was that moment when Oliver realized he may have been found out. He briefly considered running away but knew he had nowhere else to go and all of his stuff was upstairs.

The group approached the teenager and one of the officers asked if he was Oliver Mahlah. He hesitated at first but once he saw Ms. Janet shaking her head, he knew there was no opportunity to lie.

"Yes. What's this about?"

"Turn around and put your hands behind your back," the officer commanded, his hand resting on his gun. They forcibly grabbed the teen and wrestled him into handcuffs.

"What's going on?" questioned Oliver.

Without answering, the officers then pulled out the backpack from the warehouse.

"Are you the owner of this bag?" questioned one of the officers.

His eyes shot open in surprise. He knew he saw the bag at the warehouse last and believed the only way they would have it was if they were in Queens and saw the dead bodies. He replied.

"Yes, that was my bag but I lost it a few days ago." He looked at Ms. Janet for confirmation

"Yes…apparently, he was beaten up and robbed," remarked Ms. Janet with skepticism in her voice.

One of the officers then pulled out his shoebox which he knew contained rolls of cash, a cell phone, and a loaded handgun. Oliver knew what was inside but looked at the box with shock. *How could I be so dumb and leave the gun in the house? I should have taken it with me this morning.*

"Do you know whose gun this is?"

"No," he replied shortly. "I've never seen that gun or that money before."

"We found both under your bed, Oliver," claimed one of the officers. "Last night, your backpack was found at the scene of a homicide in Queens which led us here. In our search for you, we unexpectedly found this. I don't think it's a coincidence. Where were you last night?"

"I was here yesterday. Ms. Janet saw me."

"I did see him around 6 or 7 p.m.," claimed Ms. Janet as she interjected. "He told me he was going to bed early and I didn't see him for the rest of the night. He claimed he was going to bed early but I don't believe him."

"Where were you after that, young man? Where were you after you left to go to bed?" questioned one of the officers in an accusatory tone. "Why did we find a gun in your bedroom?"

"I don't know! It's not mine. I've never seen that gun or that money before. It might be someone else's."

"We'll get this sorted out at the station. Oliver Mahlah, you're under arrest. You have the right to remain silent. Anything you say will be used against you in a court of law."

As the officers continued, Oliver's mind went blank. He couldn't even hear them reading him his Miranda warning and looked around fearfully. From the corner of his eyes, he could see something moving through the second-floor windows. He looked up and saw about six other residents peering at the scene. There were multiple pyramids of his housemates, the tallest lining the back row as their younger, smaller housemates stood in front.

"It probably belongs to one of them," he lied as he used his shoulder to point to the window.

Before they put him into the police car, Ms. Janet walked up to the handcuffed teenager and smacked him across his face. An officer put a hand on her shoulder and told her to step back. While he walked her backward, Ms. Janet was tearing up.

She yelled. "What did I tell you about bringing the street into Dunbar? If you ever get out of that hell, you are no longer welcome at Dunbar House. You're a lost cause."

Oliver looked over and saw one of Ms. Janet's "favorites" standing beside her. The teen had a look of satisfaction on his face and remarked. "Yeah, dummy. Now no one's ever going to love you!"

Oliver was fed up with Ms. Janet's doubt and treatment of him. Although she seemed like she cared at times, he realized she did not *truly* care about him or what was happening to him. In a very cold, emotionless tone, Oliver stared back at Ms. Janet and whispered back, "I will break us both down." He was then carted off.

The other residents of the home continued to watch from the windows as the officers placed Oliver into the car and drove off.

*****

Rahzmel

At 9:47 p.m., hazy-eyed Rahzmel was watching tv slouched in his robe while he drank his watered down bourbon. He sucked on his cigarette while dozing off as the local car dealership commercial came to an end. With a belligerent expression, he looked over at Angela, "Come give me some sugar, girl."

Before she could even get to her feet, an image of a warehouse with police caution tape appeared on the screen and instantly grabbed Angela's attention.

"Police are investigating a possible homicide at 45 Sycamore Avenue in Queens, New York."

Rahzmel turned to look.

"Authorities have two suspects in custody including a juvenile in connection to a homicide at a warehouse in Queens. In what appears to also be a robbery, several unidentified bodies were also found in what appears to be one of the deadliest murders the borough has seen in years. Tune in at 11 p.m. for more."

Rahzmel looked over to Angela with bloodshot eyes. His breaths were hurried and he was now sitting up straight. His voice grew loud.

"Shit!"

PART III
MEDASE MA

CHAPTER 13:

YOUNG MAN

Oliver Mahlah   **Brooklyn,** *1986*

In 1986, sixteen-year-old Oliver Mahlah was once again a free man, left to return to the Brooklyn streets he once roamed. After serving two years in what he called "hell," he knew he never wanted to go back. The streets made him doughty and intense, but he believed PACC was responsible for making him resilient and steadfast. From dealing with Kellerman's daily harassment to feeling partially responsible for the death of the one person he considered a real friend since Lenny, he knew his time at PACC reinforced the opinion he had of himself—he was destined for failure.

*****

When he was arrested two years prior, his public defender argued that he, Oliver, was a victim of a robbery which was why his backpack was not in his possession. Oliver explained the story about what happened with the Queens Jamaicans when he was robbed and made sure he left out any details incriminating Rahzmel and the Collective. He argued that when they robbed him, the last thing on his mind was what they were planning on doing with the backpack full of his "schoolbooks." The judge also was confused at this and understood where the teen, and his defense, were coming from. He showed compassion toward Oliver at first until the prosecutor introduced pictures from the scene of the homicide at the warehouse in Queens.

After reviewing the pictures of the brutal murder of the twelve men, the judge began to feel Oliver may have been more involved than he was leading them to believe. Once the loaded gun and money from Oliver's bedroom were introduced as evidence of his "street dealings," the judge decided it was in everyone's best interest to keep Oliver off the streets. He decided to sentence Oliver to 24 months in the juvenile detention wing of Port Authority Correction Center for unlawful gun possession. They also charged him as an accessory to murder, which he would later be acquitted for. The judge had good intentions for everyone's safety, but unfortunately, the teenager's absence from the street did not stop or slow down the violence that followed in the ensuing months.

Other members of the Queens Jamaicans learned of their Brooklyn rival's involvement in what happened in the warehouse and flooded Bedford Stuyvesant with violence. When they found out about Nigel's affiliation with the Collective, they went into their war chest for manpower and weapons. Like the Collective, they too were connected both in and outside of their borough, so it wasn't difficult to find people to aid their efforts for revenge. Over the period of Oliver's incarceration, the two sides went to war, which resulted in a substantial number of lives lost, stolen and damaged products, and a disruption to the guarantees Rahzmel had once promised the police and politicians.

When the war with the Jamaicans came to the Brooklyn streets, the chief saw what was happening and annulled his arrangements with Rahzmel. He seized control of the streets and placed officers on many of the corners that were previously occupied by drug dealers and street runners. He also made his officers do regular rounds throughout their neighborhoods. He saw that this war had become larger than either side was prepared for and Rahzmel could no longer control the outcome. This increase in police presence resulted in a substantial decrease in profit for the Collective.

About fifteen months into the war, Rahzmel calculated how much the war had cost him and it almost made him sick. He attempted to set up a meeting between Nigel and the leader of the Queens Jamaican crew in hopes that they would be able to come to a peaceful agreement. The costs for both sides were too substantial to continue to ignore and he was ready to put an end to it. Sadly, at first, both leaders were too proud to meet. Nigel was a gaudy, flamboyant, and arrogant man who refused to succumb to his rival's wishes. This infuriated Rahzmel as he strived for peace.

After a while, Rahzmel convinced both men to put their pride aside and sit down with each other. When he finally brought them together, he made sure they saw how much the senseless killing was affecting everyone. Because he was a businessman, he used charts to show the decline in profits as well as the increase in police activity since the war began. They listened as Rahzmel spoke and both agreed that it was best to put an end to it. They came to an agreement that ensured both crews would remain in their individual boroughs and if there was any encroachment, it should be brought to the leaders before anyone reacted with violence.

Once that was settled, Rahzmel spent the following nine months rebuilding the operation he once ran as king. He rebuilt relationships and set up more distribution routes than before. He squeezed every corner in Brooklyn to make up for the lost profit and respect. He was also forced to make a larger donation to corrupted officials up and down the chain. The way he saw it, he needed to be aggressive to gain the streets back and knew it was not going to be cheap.

*****

That Friday afternoon, Oliver walked out of PACC. For the first time in nearly two years, he stopped and listened as the birds chirped. He viewed this as them singing his freedom, so he stood and basked in their praise.

Although he was happy to be a free man, he knew he had nowhere to go. Even though Rahzmel ensured he was taken care of at PACC, he did not care to return to the street life or the kingpin's care. He stopped and began to think about all available options he had and realized he had none. He loathed the fact that the street life may have been his only choice.

When he walked out and listened to the heavy door slam behind him, he closed his eyes and took a deep breath filled with uncertainty and doubt. He then exhaled his hope, which forced a smile on his face.

When he looked up, he was surprised at what he saw. There, in front of him, were the same two officers who found him the night he was robbed and brought him back to Dunbar. They walked up.

"Hi, Oliver. Glad to have you back on this side of the wall. Do you remember us?"

"Yes, I do," replied Oliver in a rough, defensive tone. He was unsure why they had once again resurfaced in his life. After his experience in PACC, he was also a bit skeptical of authority.

"You're Officer…Jefferson and Officer Smith. Ummm… you're the two cops who found me after I was beaten up and took me back to Dunbar."

"That's right. How are you doing?" questioned Officer Jefferson. "I'm sure you're happy to be a free man, huh?"

"Good. It was fucked up in there. It's hard to describe but it was bad. I thought about this day every second I was in there. I can't believe it's finally here. It's like walking out of hell. Anyway, why are you here?"

"We are here to take you home."

"Ms. Janet said I can't go back to Dunbar. I have no home."

"Yeah, we spoke with Ms. Janet, and she was very adamant about you never returning to Dunbar," remarked Officer Smith. "We weren't planning on taking you to Ms. Janet."

"We actually have somewhere else we want to take you," chimed in Officer Jefferson. "Honestly, this should be a better place for you."

"No, I'm okay."

"Oliver…you have nowhere to go. We're not here to give you problems."

"What do you want?" questioned the teen.

"We have somewhere we want to take you. It's a safe place," remarked Officer Smith.

"Oliver…I'm sure you may not trust us after your experience in there but we're not here to give you any problems. Whatever happened with you in the past is over and we just want to help. We have someplace we think would be good for you."

"Where is it?"

"Don't worry, it isn't far."

"Look, what's the catch?" Oliver said defensively. "What do you guys want from me?"

"No catch, Oliver," replied Officer Jefferson. "We just want to help you."

They handed him a backpack and told him it was to carry the miscellaneous items he was holding in his hands and pockets. He cautiously accepted and thanked them. When they arrived at the police cruiser, Officer Jefferson leaned into Oliver.

"If you feel uncomfortable, you can leave now. We aren't here to hurt you. Trust me when I say, we are here to help."

Oliver's face softened as the officer leaned out. Something about Officer Jefferson's words and demeanor helped make him comfortable so he entered the police cruiser.

*****

When they pulled up to the house that evening, Oliver noticed how closely it resembled Dunbar House. In front of them was a beautiful two-story house with a red-tiled roof, a driveway large enough for two cars, and beautiful landscaped grass, shrubs, and flowers. The grass was perfectly cut and from the backseat of the car, Oliver could see the fabric curtains that hung inside the windows which hid the beauty Oliver knew was inside the house.

Judging by how well kept this house is, someone rich must live here.

After they parked, all three men walked up the path toward the main entrance which was a large roasted almond-colored door inside a black door frame. As they approached, the front door swung open before they could knock, and there in front of them was a middle-aged white woman with a head full of grayish hair, a slightly hunched back and a face somewhat shriveled like a prune. She wore a black apron, stained with red sauce, which read, "Feed thy Soul" and had a smile on her face that exposed her perfectly aligned white teeth.

She reached in and hugged the two officers as if they had long known each other and peered over at Oliver with a welcoming smile, again exposing her beautiful teeth. The officers introduced her as a "very close friend." She then wiped her small hand on her apron and extended it to the rough-looking teen. She introduced herself as Ms. Mabel-Ara.

"Hello, young man. I am very happy to finally meet you," she said in a soft, docile tone.

"Hello," he replied shortly while avoiding eye contact.

"Are you hungry? You look hungry. I just finished cooking dinner, so come eat."

She then turned and walked back into the house. Oliver looked at the two officers who smiled and began to follow. Oliver remained in the doorway, confused at what had just happened. He met this lady for the first time and now she was asking him to come into her home and eat. He wore his skepticism on his face as he stood by himself in the doorway.

After watching the officers disappear into the house, he entered and slowly trailed right behind them. His first observation was the sound the officer's shoes made as they walked on the newly shined hardwood floors. His second was the smell of a home cooked meal.

When they arrived in the dining room, Oliver saw a dining room table that had ten chairs around it. Five of the chairs had other teens in them, who all got up when they saw the visitors approaching. The officers seemed to know the five teens and they exchanged pleasantries upon arriving. The officers then introduced the mysterious visitor as Oliver, "a friend." The excitement of the five teens was shining on their faces and as they approached Oliver, he stepped backward in apprehension. He did not know them and did not trust their intentions on why they were approaching him this way.

Why are they smiling so much? Why did I come here? I need to find a way out. These fuckin' officers set me up.

Just as he was slowly backtracking toward the dining room entrance, Ms. Mabel-Ara came into the room holding a large, piping hot plate of meatloaf. She placed it in the center of the table then turned and directed the officers to the kitchen for the rest of the food while the teens all motioned back towards their seats. They ran back to help and returned with mashed potatoes, yams, salad, and gravy.

Everyone at the table was seated except Oliver, who was still standing at the doorway. Ms. Mabel-Ara turned to peer over at the rough-looking teen and requested he come sit down. She sat at the head of the table and offered him the seat right next to her which was empty. She patted the seat with her hand.

"Come sit before the food gets cold," she offered with a smile.

He was nervous and slowly walked over to the table, watching the others as they watched him. He sat at the dinner table and folded his arms.

When he looked back at the food, he reached in to grab some mashed potatoes but was rejected by a loud smack that Ms. Mabel-Ara gave his encroaching hand. He retracted it back to his chest and stared back at her, expecting anger. On her face, he didn't see any rage. In her eyes, he saw a gaze that was unfamiliar to him, one he had never seen before. She then reached out and forcibly grabbed hold of his clammy hands.

"We don't eat until we've said grace, young man," she remarked with a smile.

"What's grace?" Oliver thought to himself. He had never "said grace" before he ate and was confused by her command. He apologized silently with his hands still locked and watched as everyone around the table reached for their neighbor's hands, closed their eyes, and bowed their heads. Despite everyone's uniformity, he did not know if he was supposed to do the same, so he didn't and watched as they spoke.

"Dear Lord, we thank You for this meal You've allowed us to prepare and share with our friends. We thank You for our health and for allowing us to see another day on Your green earth. We thank You for bringing everyone together so we may feast in Your glory. On this day, we welcome a new friend, Oliver, who comes to us after fighting through one of Your toughest battles. We trust that You guided Oliver through that arduous period to ensure he received Your lesson and came out stronger. I am confident You've shared many lessons he has benefited from. On this day, we praise You. Amen."

When everyone lifted their heads and opened their eyes, Oliver looked at Ms. Mabel-Ara for her approval for him to eat. She looked back at Oliver with another smile and then reached in to grab the spoon for the mashed potatoes. She handed it to him. As he scooped food onto his plate, he thought to himself.

This is what a family must feel like.

At dinner, as they ate, Oliver sat mostly quiet as the rest of the group conversed and joked in a regular fashion. Oliver was shy and apprehensive, but Ms. Mabel-Ara continued with her normal resolve. As she joked about her seemingly overcooked meatloaf, she sat pleased as she caught Oliver stealing glances and occasionally chuckling at her humor. During dinner, a representative from Child Protective Services came to the house to check on Oliver. She knocked on the door and Mabel-Ara and Officer Smith went to address it. The officers had previously coordinated for Oliver to be taken into their custody, then passed over to Mabel-Ara. The CPS agent came to ensure they fulfilled that request.

After dinner, the officers thanked Mabel-Ara, then took Oliver to the next room. They told him that he had a home there with Ms. Mabel-Ara if he wanted it but needed to give up this "tough-guy" persona.

"Ms. Mabel-Ara is a kind, gentle and caring elderly lady who runs a very strong home because of the investment she makes in each of her children. She runs a youth development program designed to teach teens from the inner-city basic fundamentals like etiquette, money management, and simple economics."

As they spoke, Oliver looked around the room aimlessly as if he was not concerned with what they were saying. He noticed a few things he knew he could get money for and decided he would come back to this room when it was empty. They told Oliver that if he wanted to remain there with Ms. Mabel-Ara, he had to commit himself to give up the street life he once led.

"We aren't dumb, Oliver," claimed Officer Smith. "We know you were involved in things you didn't tell us about. Dunbar House is tough, and you needed to be tough to survive. Listen. We get it."

He stood there with his arms crossed.

"We know that the way Ms. Janet ran the house made it very easy for children to feel unwanted, which resulted in most of you seeking love and approval from the streets," explained Officer Jefferson. "Ms. Mabel-Ara is different. She doesn't run a foster home. She adopts all these children. It's amazing. She's successful because of the love and trust she shares with the teens who reside here. She doesn't work full-time anymore so she can give you the attention you deserve. I know you don't know us well and probably don't trust us, but I want to tell you that we know more about you than you may believe. Trust us when we say, this is the place you need to be. Ms. Mabel-Ara has been doing this for a long time and she knows what she's talking about. She will guide you to the place you need to be."

Oliver knew he had nowhere else to go and told them that he would stay one night to determine if he liked it. Unlike Ms. Janet, he got a positive feeling from Ms. Mabel-Ara and was hoping for a better living arrangement. He could not bring himself to admit this to them.

The three of them went back to the kitchen and Ms. Mabel-Ara walked the officers out. She then showed Oliver upstairs to a large room he would be sharing with two others. She reiterated what the officers said about him staying there. She wanted him to stay but did not want to force him to nor did she want the peace in the house disrupted. Oliver replied.

"I'll stay one night and decide by morning."

She nodded and then showed him to the bathroom. She told him to wash up before bed and ended by telling him that there was a clean set of clothes on his bed waiting for him.

When they arrived at the room, Oliver was reintroduced to his roommates, Jeremiah, and Isaac, who were in the room doing their homework. Oliver went straight to the bed where his clothes were and sat there quietly for a second. He thought about how surreal it was for him to get out of prison and be given a meal and bed. He didn't trust it one bit and again felt he was being set up.

The last time I was treated like this, I was lured into joining a gang.

The two other teens in the room were listening to the radio so Oliver did not bother to try and make conversation. Instead, he went straight for the shower and when he returned, he went directly to his bed and pulled the covers over his head. Like Dunbar House, he had no interest in making friends with his roommates and laid there until he was sure they were asleep. He didn't know them, therefore didn't trust them, and did not feel comfortable sleeping until they were asleep first.

*****

That night after everyone had gone to bed, Oliver lay there staring at the ceiling through the darkness. He was tired, but couldn't sleep because of the unusually soft mattress, warm blanket wrapped around his body, and unusual kindness he had encountered from everyone that evening. What they offered in PACC was very different and he had a difficult time adjusting. He also thought about the nourishing meal and warm shower he had that night but worried about the cost he was going to have to pay for them. He didn't trust anyone and was skeptical of Ms. Mabel-Ara's kindness.

When he looked over at the clock on the wall, he saw it read 1 a.m. He then looked at the other two teens in the room and confirmed they were deep asleep. He assumed everyone else in the house was also sleeping, so he decided to grab his stuff and depart. Despite how comforting it felt, he feared there may be an unknown cost to Ms. Mabel-Ara's hospitality and decided he wanted to leave before he found out what it was. He did not know where he was going but knew this was his best chance to leave.

He grabbed his items and crept out of the room and slowly down the stairs. Before leaving through the front door, he went back to the room from earlier and picked up a few of the items he thought he could pawn. After filling his backpack, he moved toward the main door. Just as he was about to reach for the door handle, he heard a woman's voice ask, "Why do you need to leave from a place you can call home?"

Oliver instantly froze where he was and looked around the dark room for the location of the voice. He saw a shadow sitting and when he squinted to look more closely, the light came on, revealing Ms. Mabel-Ara sitting in front of him with a Bible on her lap.

"Where are you going in the middle of the night, young man?"

"I'm leaving, so don't try to stop me."

"But leaving to go where?" she replied. "You only just got here."

"I'm going home."

"Which is where?"

"Not that it's your business, but my home is with my crew on the other side of Brooklyn."

"*Your crew?*" she emphasized. "Oh, you must be talking about Dunbar House?"

"No, not Dunbar. I stay somewhere else."

"You stay? Are you a dog?"

"No."

"Okay, so you don't stay. You *live* somewhere else," she corrected with a smile. "Dogs stay and you aren't a dog, are you?"

"Whatever," he stated, gripping his bag tighter as he glanced at it.

She looked down at his bag. "Do you have everything you need, Oliver? Can I get you anything else before you go?"

Oliver froze at the thought he had been caught stealing his first night out of PACC. "Nah, I'm good. You didn't really give me anything anyway," he lied.

"Okay. You're free to leave if you don't want to be here, but it was nice having you over for dinner. I hope you enjoyed my burnt meatloaf. As you could probably tell, it was my first time making it," she giggled.

"It was good. Thank you."

"You're more than welcome, young man. Well, don't let me hold you up from going to the place where you *live*."

Oliver slowly turned around and started walking back toward the main door. He grabbed the handle again and before he turned the knob, he stopped and thought for a second. Where *was* he going and what was so exciting on the other side of town that was making him want to leave at 1 a.m.? He knew he did not have anywhere to go and questioned why he was running.

Where am I going?

He thought about Ms. Mabel-Ara's joke about making the meatloaf for the first time and smiled. To him, it was perfect. It was the first real meal he'd had in a while and despite the dark, dry and crispy corners, he found it delicious. He realized he had no business out on the streets at 1 a.m. His bag with Ms. Mabel-Ara's property felt very heavy. Heavier than just the weight. He turned back around to walk toward Ms. Mabel-Ara. He placed the backpack at her feet and looked at her.

"What happened?" she questioned with a warm smile on her face. "I thought you were leaving."

"Why do you want me here?"

"I want you to be happy and safe. This is my home and I know it will be a great place for you. In my home, we all take care of each other. You've been through so much Oliver, and I know I can never understand how tough it's been for you, but I do want you to know that this is a place you can call home because it's mine."

"But why me? I lied and actually did steal your stuff. Didn't you see me?"

"Yes, I did…"

"Then why didn't you stop me."

"Is it my place to stop you, young man? If you want to steal, you will steal. If you want to lie, you will lie no matter what I say or do. Of course, I'd rather you choose to not steal or lie but I can't be the one to make the decision for you."

"Why not?"

"Because you're your own man, Oliver. Why didn't you leave like you said you were going to?"

"Because I figured you worked so hard on dinner, that the least I can do is stay the full night."

She smiled and stood up with the Bible still in hand. She noticed his tough-guy demeanor had slightly softened through their conversation and he now sat there with his shoulders lowered, eyes focused, and what resembled a smile.

"Thank you for gracing me with your presence for a full night or, as my father would say, 'Medase me adamfo,' she joked.

"Meh what?"

"Medase me adamfo. It means 'Thank you, my friend' in Twi. My Stepfather worked for the United Nations, and we used to travel a lot when I was much younger. Out of all of the places I've lived, Ghana was by far the most beautiful. As a fifteen-year-old white girl from New York, they were incredibly accepting, hospitable and friendly. The food was spicy, but the flavor was out of the world. Oh, how I miss it there."

"Is that in Africa?"

"Yes, it is. I think it's time for you to get to bed young man. You're probably exhausted, and we could spend all night talking about this."

She walked Oliver back upstairs to his room and told him to sleep in. It was now Saturday morning, which meant they would all eat breakfast together after everyone woke up. Oliver did not know exactly what this meant but figured if it was anything like dinner, he would enjoy it. When they arrived at the room, Ms. Mabel-Ara tucked him in and wished him a good night.

"I'm happy you decided not to leave.

Before walking out of the room, she placed the Bible on the table beside his bed and gave one final smile before departing.

As he lay there, he thought about how properly she spoke.

She's smart and speaks so well. She must be English or something. I want to sound smart like that.

CHAPTER 14:

SING THE WORDS YOU CAN'T SAY

Oliver Mahlah

By the time morning had rolled around, Oliver was awoken by a scent he had never smelled before. He thought it smelled like a sweeter version of cornbread or the biscuits they served at PACC, but wasn't entirely sure. When he looked over, he noticed the two others he shared a room with were gone and had left their beds unprepared and messy. He found this unusual because every morning for the last two years, the guards did not allow inmates to leave their cells unless bunks were made. He knew he wasn't in prison any longer, but could not escape some of the strict policies he had become accustomed to.

When he finished making his bed, Oliver walked over to the same bathroom he showered in the night prior and proceeded to open the closed door. Just as he cracked it, there was a female screech that frightened him and caused him to slam the door shut.

He still didn't know his way around the house and wasn't entirely sure which rooms belonged to who, so he proceeded downstairs toward the kitchen without brushing his teeth or washing his face. When he arrived, he saw Ms. Mabel-Ara with one of the young female residents, Evie, cooking breakfast. When he entered the kitchen, he was wished a good morning by the two of them, then Ms. Mabel-Ara walked over to him with a piece of bacon in hand. She handed it to him and told him breakfast would be ready soon, which brought him joy because he was starving.

As he chomped on the warm piece of bacon, Oliver saw Jeremiah sitting in the living room watching television. He felt so lost in the house and did not know where else to go, so Oliver decided to join his roommate.

"Does she always cook like this?" questioned Oliver. "Or is it just when she's trying to get new people like me to stay?"

"She cooks *all* the time," replied Jeremiah with a smirk displaying his satisfaction.

Jeremiah was a short, stocky African American boy with a big afro that stretched a foot above his scalp. He had an intimidating frame because of his size but a very friendly face.

"Every Saturday, she makes her blueberry pancakes with bacon, eggs, and grits. Honestly, I look forward to the weekends because of it."

"How long have you been here?"

"I've been here for about a year and a half," replied Jeremiah. "Not long after I turned fifteen, I came here because my mother became addicted to heroin and could no longer take care of me. My father was murdered in prison when I was a baby, so I didn't know him. The two officers who brought you here last night are the ones who helped me get here also. They have been with the police force for years and I've learned that they've known Ma a long while now."

"They helped you get here as in where? To this house or into the program? And who is Ma? Is that Ms. Mabel-Ara?"

"You sure you're from Brooklyn, man?" joked Jeremiah. "Yes, Ma is Ms. Mabel-Ara. Ma's what most people call her. Rumor has it, she built this house from the ground up more than ten years ago. She apparently used to be a big-time activist and gave up everything she was doing to build this. It's ironic, or something, man. Her name is Mabel-Ara, and her nickname is Ma. Sometimes I feel like it's because she's like a mother to this community."

"Wait, so all of you actually do live here?"

"Yeah, man. She took each of us in. She's like our mother. Where are you from?"

"She's like your foster mother?"

"No man, this ain't a foster house. She adopted each of us."

"She's not my mom so I won't call her Ma. I'll call her Ma'am and I'm from the other side of town."

"I know that, but what brought you here? Did something happen to your actual mom or dad also?"

"I don't know. I never knew my mom or my dad. The two officers randomly found me one day and long story short, they brought me here also."

"Things like that don't randomly happen. If you're here, it's because someone was looking out for you just like they looked out for me. Did you come from a foster home?"

"Yeah, I did. I came from Dunbar House."

"Oh wow, you were at Dunbar? I hear that place is a shit show and on the rougher side of town. I heard there was a police raid on that house a few years ago and they found guns, money, and drugs. I'm glad I didn't have to live there. Did the cops bring you here from there?"

"Something like that," Oliver replied shortly avoiding sharing any details about PACC.

"Wow, so I was right. Things like that don't happen at random. They saved you from a path that living in Dunbar would have taken you. You're going to see that life here is so much better because—"

Just as he was about to finish his statement, Ms. Mabel-Ara came into the living room and announced breakfast was ready. Jeremiah jumped up and excitedly trailed her into the kitchen. Oliver sat for a moment absorbing everything he was just told. As he got up and walked into the kitchen, he assumed the story Jeremiah heard about Dunbar was referring to him and his arrest. He also admired how well-spoken Jeremiah was.

After thinking about it for a moment, he was relieved to hear Jeremiah talk about his arrest as just a rumor. He was glad no one knew it was him arrested that night. It meant that he could really start over. He was over trying to live the street life and play a character he knew he didn't want to be. He wasn't like Rahzmel and knew that was not the type of person he cared to eventually become. In this new space, he had a chance to be someone different. This was his chance to be something different, which excited him.

*****

When they finished breakfast, the group of teens collectively expressed their gratitude for the meal. Ms. Mabel-Ara graciously accepted the thanks and joked that they should "not get too comfortable because there is work to do." She went back to the kitchen to grab her whiteboard calendar and when she came back, there were chore assignments already listed with names beside them. The three girls, Evie, Lillian, and Tonisha, were assigned to wash the dishes, vacuum the floors, and clean the windows while Jeremiah and Isaac were assigned to clean the three bathrooms. She verbally confirmed with the group of teens and after sharing these assigned duties, she looked at Oliver and smiled. She queued for the others to get to work and moved toward the kitchen.

Oliver saw the haste of the other housemates as they went to begin their chores and became curious about why he was left out. He knew he did not officially live there with everyone else, but he still wanted to feel needed and included. After everyone left the dining room, he approached Ms. Mabel-Ara with his inquiry.

"Hi, Ma'am. Thank you for breakfast."

"You're welcome, Oliver. Did you enjoy it?"

"Yeah, it was good. I was just wondering if you had anything else you needed help with?"

"Anything else like a chore?"

"Yeah… I mean… I see everyone else doing something. I figured I might as well help too."

"I appreciate that, Oliver. The others do chores to sort of earn their keep. I give them a roof over their heads, and they help me maintain the house. This is the home that I built but together we… as a family, work to maintain it."

"I understand. So…is there anything I can help you with?"

At that moment, Ms. Mabel-Ara smiled and reached underneath the counter for the garbage. She handed the full garbage bag to the teen.

"Drop it off in the basement. It will not be picked up from the curb until Tuesday morning." He quickly turned to start before she could get another word in.

"Wait!... The basement door locks from the outside so take the key with you or prop the door open while you go down."

"Okay." Without any hesitation, Oliver tied the trash up and followed Ms. Mabel-Ara's instructions for disposal. When he came back upstairs, he went right back to the kitchen and inquired if there was anything additional needed.

"Thank you, Oliver. That should be it for now, but I may call you later to help me with the laundry."

"Okay...I have a question for you, Ma'am."

"Go ahead, child."

"This is your home, right?

"Correct."

"Is this your foster home?"

"This is my *home*. I don't consider this a foster home because foster homes are for neglected and delinquent children. Everyone here is a part of my family and as a family, we stick together."

"So, these other kids here are your family?"

"Yes, even though they may not be aware, I've done my research on each child that lives here. I need to know I can trust them, and they need to know they can trust me."

"But how do you know you can trust them? Do they come from good homes?"

"Most don't come from good homes. Like yourself, most of the others came from unfortunate circumstances. The thing about a home though, is it isn't simply four walls and a roof. A home can be anywhere that your heart beats."

"That makes sense… What do you mean like me?" replied Oliver. "What do you know about me?"

"I know a lot more about you than you may know. As we begin to learn more about each other, everything will be revealed. Let's continue getting to know each other and hopefully, you'll decide to stay here with us. I need to run some errands but see if you can help any of the others with their chores."

*****

The next day was Sunday and Oliver was woken up by Ms. Mabel-Ara, who was wearing a beautiful cream-colored dress with a matching hat on her head. As his eyes forced themselves open, she told him that it was "time to get up for church." Oliver had never been to church before, so he was unsure exactly how to respond to her command. The extent of his "church" came from his regular conversations with Preacher at PACC.

"It's okay. I'll just stay here till y'all get back," he said in a voice only seconds removed from sleep.

"No. This house and its residents are protected by the love and will of the Lord. We honor Him every Sunday. The others are already downstairs and ready. We are just waiting on you. Now get up and get ready. We leave in 30 minutes. The church is in Greenpoint so we have quite the drive ahead of us."

"But I don't have nothin' to wear."

"That's okay, Oliver. Like I said before, we all take care of each other. In the closet, there are a few suits that I picked up for the other boys. Try them on and see what fits. Don't forget a shirt and tie."

"Okay, I will," he replied in the same groggy manner.

Ms. Mabel-Ara then began to leave the room and when she hit the bedroom door, she turned around and gave one look back. Oliver looked at her after wiping the sleep from his eyes.

"Thank you. Who's Ma?"

She smiled then walked back over and sat beside Oliver on the bed.

"Why do you ask?"

"I'm sorry, Ma'am. Jeremiah mentioned it was your name but said you weren't his mother, so I was confused. I didn't mean anything by it."

"Oh no...please don't apologize. I was just surprised to hear you say it. Since you arrived, you've been calling me Ma'am and Ms. Mabel-Ara. I was a little curious."

"But why do others call you Ma?"

"It's just a nickname I received growing up. My parents gave me the name Mabel-Ara which was a combination of my grandfather's and grandmother's first names. Let's just say the name Mabel aged me too much, so I took on the nickname 'Ma.' It was easier to remember and had a dual meaning which was good. As I grew older, I began to take on the motherly figure to my friends and younger brother, which made the nickname even more appropriate. You can call me Ma if you want. Everyone else does."

"I won't call you that since you're not my mother. Anyways, is that why you opened this house?"

"I think somewhere deep down inside of me, I opened this house to give children a safe place to turn to when their lives weren't going okay. A safe home should be a basic expectation for an innocent child who doesn't know what demons exist in the world. There were a few other things that really inspired me to open this house, which I call home, but others outside of our home call it the Burke House. This is due to my last name. Mabel-Ara Burke. There is so much I want to tell you when you're ready, but for now, we're late. We can get into those details later. Just get ready so we can go."

*****

During the church service, Oliver sat stone-faced as Ms. Mabel-Ara and the others yelled their praise during the morning's service. Based on their expressions, he could sense they were moved by the word but could not feel it himself. From his seat, he observed as some cried tears of joy while others shared tears of pain, which he assumed came from the powerful message being delivered. To him, it was just a show and he was ready to go.

Why are they all crying like this? Can't wait to get out of here.

When the choir began Ms. Mabel-Ara looked over and saw Oliver sitting and staring with an enthusiastic brightness from his seat. He was silently singing along and she playfully tapped him on the shoulder and then smiled. He smiled back and turned his attention back as they sang.

"Hosanna…

Hosanna…
Hosanna in the highest."

At that moment, he'd exposed himself. She finally saw where his heart and mind were, and watched as he continued. Although he'd been hiding himself since he arrived, his interest was now obvious to her.

After the service, Ms. Mabel-Ara escorted Oliver to the front of the church and introduced him to the choir who watched as he stood shyly beside her. They gave a basic inquiry on him and his thoughts on the message then asked him to sing something for them which he bashfully, but respectfully, declined. Ma looked at him and nudged him forward to get over his fear. He looked back at her and realized he did not want to disappoint her and may not have had a choice.

He stood there, legs and hands shaking as his palms became moist. Fear rushed through his body as he peered into the eyes of his audience, who all had looks of anticipation and excitement. He then looked at Ma and sang.

She watched as his once bashful demeanor softened and the fear dissipated. He looked back at her and saw a big smile on her face, which brought him joy. The words rolled off his lips as if he had sung that version of "Amazing Grace" over a thousand times before. The crowd watched mystified at Oliver's angelic voice as he sang the hymn.

Amazing Grace, How sweet the sound
That saved a wretch like me
I once was lost, but now am found
T'was blind but now I see

T'was Grace that taught my heart to fear
And Grace, my fears relieved
How precious did that grace appear
The hour I first believed

The group stood there and reveled at what they had just heard. A voice so beautiful, with an obvious painful undertone, created a moment so breathtaking that they had lost themselves to the concept of time. Without any consultation with the others, the choir leader motioned to the front of the group and asked, "Young man, that was beautiful. How about you join us and sing like that on Sundays?"

Ms. Mabel-Ara quickly interjected before Oliver had a chance to. "He's interested! He's looking forward to joining you."

She looked at Oliver who forced a smile. *She really thinks I can do it?* Oliver stood there content and shocked that he actually sang in front of these strangers and nodded.

While making their way back to the others, who were in the back of the church speaking with other members, Mabel-Ara asked Oliver where he learned to sing like that.

"I just like to sing. Before coming to your home, I had a friend named Preacher who used to sing all the time. Preacher used to jokingly sing about our miserable life which made me laugh. After a while, I began to pick up on his melodies but kept them under wraps. His approach was a good way to bring some relief to our unfortunate predicament and we would often exchange freestyled lyrics we made up. I've even found myself humming some of those songs in my mind during my idle moments."

Ms. Mabel-Ara stood impressed.

That afternoon, as Mabel-Ara and the six teens left the church to head back to the house, they were stopped by the church photographer. He gathered Ma and the children together and took a group photo before the family departed for the parking lot.

When they arrived at the car, one of the female residents, Lillian, asked what they were going to prepare for dinner that night. Ms. Mabel-Ara realized that in speaking with Oliver that morning, she forgot to do a quick inventory of what they needed. Despite that, she still decided to stop by a grocery store to pick up a few small groceries for the week. Normally, Ma would do this grocery shopping closer to their home, but since the weather was nice that early afternoon, she decided to do her shopping in Greenpoint.

*****

When she walked into the market, she noticed all eyes turned in their direction. The store, which was historically a shopping ground for only whites, had been one of the slower establishments to transition after the Civil Rights Act of 1964. Many of the employees who worked at the grocery store were white, outside of their one African American cashier, Wilson, who was an elderly gentleman.

As they perused the aisles for items, Oliver noticed they were being followed. It seemed that with every aisle they turned into there was a store employee there looking to address something on the shelves.

Jeremiah noticed the stunned look on Oliver's face and told him how this was a regular occurrence for their blended family. He then leaned in and whispered in Oliver's ear so the others could not hear.

"Don't worry about them, man. Ma is a beautiful, joyful white woman, and she's walking around this grocery store with her four black and two white teenagers. People aren't used to seeing that in a place like this. Or anywhere, really."

Oliver looked at Isaac and Lillian who were both white then turned his attention to Tonisha and Evie, who were both black. He then looked back at Jeremiah. "Why are they following us?"

"Because we're different. You don't usually see this type of arrangement for a family. People here are uneasy because of how we look. If they don't bother us, we won't bother them."

Oliver remembered seeing this type of segregation in PACC, but because of his connections through Rahzmel, he was not fully affected. The only directed racism he had encountered came at the hands of Officer Kellerman and Hagan.

Additionally, Dunbar House was in a primarily black neighborhood, so many of the people he interacted with looked like him. For the first time in his life, he felt he was being looked down on because of the color of his skin and he did not like it. He had zero tolerance for this type of treatment and became angry.

Jeremiah watched as Oliver's forehead glistened from the slow perspiration that had formed. It was clear that Oliver was upset, but he assumed his new roommate would be able to control his emotions. Unfortunately, he was wrong.

When they arrived at one of the available cashiers, Oliver watched as the young white woman dismissively told Ma that she could not ring them up because her cash register was not working properly. Oliver was skeptical because she had just finished with another customer but disregarded it. He watched as Ma shook her head to signal her understanding and asked which registers were working.

As expected, the young woman told Ma that Wilson's register was available, which was located all the way at the end of the line of cashiers. Ma smiled and began wheeling her cart toward Wilson's direction.

As they walked, Oliver looked back and saw another white customer walk into the same woman's line for service without incident. He tapped Ma's shoulder to tell her what he saw, but without turning around, she kept her eyes straight and simply stated, "I know."

By the time they arrived at Wilson's line, there was a handful of other black shoppers in his line. Ms. Mabel-Ara still stood in the back of the line with the six teens behind her.

She attempted to lighten the mood by mentioning how powerful the morning's message was.

"It put me in such a good mood!"

As she spoke, Oliver continued to look around and noticed they were being looked at now by both black and white customers. When they finally got to the front of the line, Ma greeted Wilson with a smile and asked how he was doing.

Wilson, who was a shy older man, replied, "I'm well."

She looked around at the other cashiers then back at Wilson, and leaned in.

"Young man, are you okay here?"

Wilson dropped his head in shame.

"I started the job as a janitor, but the owner allowed me to work the register to earn more income when I asked." He peered over at the other cashiers then dropped his voice to a whisper. "I understand that there really ain't no love for me or folk who look like me here. I can't worry 'bout that. This how I provide for my family."

Ma and the six teens listened carefully as he spoke before she interjected. "Raise your head, young man. You have nothing to be ashamed of. You come here every day to provide for your family. Others should take notes from you."

"Thank you, ma'am. I receive poor treatment and name-calling every day," claimed Wilson. "I do what I can."

Ma nodded her head in agreement and smiled. She used her free hand to raise Wilson's head high as he bagged her items.

"Young man, you're a beautiful soul and you have nothing to be ashamed of. Good for you."

"Thank you, ma'am. This is bigger than me."

She mustered up all the compassion that she could find.

"I'm so proud of you. Continue pushing forward. I wish you all the best."

As they walked toward the exit, which was back in the direction of the young female cashier, Oliver saw her staring at them while assisting another white couple. She smirked at him, and he instantly got triggered.

"You fuckin' racist bitch. I thought your register wasn't working, huh? You lyin' bitch."

The woman smiled at his truculent response which infuriated him further. He started walking closer to her, but before he could reach her, Ma grabbed Oliver by the shoulder and escorted him outside. In an assertive tone, she instructed him to get in the van.

"Don't say a word until we get back home," she demanded with conviction. She also wore an expression that he could not decipher in his rage, a warning in a foreign tongue that up until that point, he hadn't seen.

At first, he looked confused at why he was being punished but decided Ma was not the enemy, so he sat quietly in the backseat as instructed and calmed himself down. The ride home successfully softened his rage and when they arrived, she instructed Oliver to help the others put the groceries away and then meet her in the study.

CHAPTER 15:

MA

Oliver Mahlah

After assisting with putting the groceries away, Oliver made his way to the study as instructed. When he arrived, Ma was sitting in silence in her favorite chair with her glasses perched on the edge of her nose. Her Bible was in its normal position on the coffee table beside her and in her lap were cut-out newspaper articles.

When he entered the room, she did not acknowledge his arrival, so Oliver went to sit on the adjacent couch. He knew she was upset, but like any proud teenage boy, he assumed his actions were justified and he was prepared to stand by them. He sat there, also in silence, waiting for Ma to acknowledge his presence and after a few moments of silence, she spoke.

"December 1, 1955… Rosa Parks entered a bus in Montgomery, Alabama after getting off from a long day of work. She paid her fare like anyone else on that bus and sat in the front row of the 'colored' section. After the rest of the bus had filled up, the white bus driver demanded she give up her seat for newly boarded white riders who were standing. She gracefully denied the request and refused to give up the seat. She was then arrested for refusing to surrender her seat."

Oliver could hear the emotion rushing out in her cracking voice.

"November 1960… Ruby Bridges was the first African American to be integrated into a primarily white elementary school. Despite the treatment, hostility, and animosity she received, six-year-old Ruby took a brave first step on behalf of herself, her family, and all the other African American children to follow behind her. After *Brown v. Board of Education,* which deemed it unconstitutional to have separate black and white schools, the hostility between both races grew. The race wars were so bad at one point, that on Ruby's first day, she needed to be escorted into the new school by four US Marshals. Imagine that, a six-year-old child took a brave first step for the liberties we take for granted today."

Ms. Mabel-Ara's head dropped as she wiped away the tears that began to flood her eyes. She had fought them back while speaking on Ruby Bridges and Rosa Parks but could no longer hold them as she began her third story.

"August 28, 1963…Dr. Martin Luther King Jr. marched on Washington, DC to advocate for civil and economic rights for African Americans. For yea-"

She paused as her voice choked up.

"For years, he fought for… he fought for equality and equal rights for people who look like you, who look like me, who look like us."

"Like me and you?"

"Yes, like human beings. He was inspired by Mahatma Gandhi and after studying Gandhi's principles, practices and beliefs, Dr. King vowed to never use arms in his fight for equality."

"Who's Mahatma Gandhi?"

"He was another great man. As you can imagine, this was a crucial turning point in that period. Unlike many others at that time, his approach was nonviolent and peaceful, which was shocking because of the violent and aggressive treatment he received. They arrested him, threatened him, spit on him, and even bombed his home for what he fought for. He took their treatment and still found ways to take a peaceful approach towards a resolution."

Ms. Mabel-Ara once again stopped speaking and dropped her head back down, but this time she placed her hands over her eyes to hide her sorrow. After she finished the story, a silence grew between them. Oliver sat for a while longer, lost for words and embarrassed. He was sorry that his thoughtless action had been the source of such distress. He made no sound and simply reached in and took her hands in his. Although the shared silence between these two strangers was foreign, they both found solace in this ancient form of comfort. She returned back to her recount of the good and bad memories of her past. In doing so, Mabel-Ara discovered a guide in Oliver's presence. He did not know it, but that was the day that the mysterious brown baby Ma was introduced to by the officers over a decade ago became her beacon. That was the day that Oliver became Ma's reason and hope that everything would be okay. She continued.

"They killed Dr. King… for what he fought for. And now we—you, me, Wilson, and even the young white cashier, are a result of what he died for. Our future will be determined by the decisions we make today. The reason it's painful for me to tell his story is because I marched with Dr. King in DC that day. As a white woman, I certainly felt out of place and overwhelmed. Dr. King and others with him welcomed me and people who looked like me as if we were bound by more than just blood. Their goal for a unified country is one I still believe in today and we will never move forward as a country if we don't learn from the past. His legacy will always remain a reminder of why being different doesn't necessarily mean a bad thing."

Oliver stood impressed by her resolve.

"What happened at the grocery store was an unfortunate example of the rules being different for us. Yes, the playing field isn't fair, but we must never succumb to the level of hate that is bestowed upon us as people. An eye for an eye will leave everyone blind. That will always be a losing battle for both sides even if it doesn't always seem that way at first. The treatment we received was nothing compared to what I'm sure Wilson deals with every single day. Despite that, he clocks in and out for his shift because he understands the greater purpose of why he does it. What was very impressive about him was the fact that despite being around so much hate, he still finds it in his heart to work for something he loves—his family. That was my biggest takeaway from that occurrence. For you to react like a rabid animal only gives *hate* the reaction it wants. Yes, you're black, and yes, I'm white…we get it. That is not an excuse, but it's the situation we're in. We must be better if we ever hope to change the world."

Ma got up and sat beside Oliver. She grabbed his hand and placed it over his heart.

"Doesn't it beat like mine?"

"Yes, it does," Oliver replied shamefully.

"And don't we breathe the same, laugh the same, cry the same?" she questioned, wiping the tears from his eyes.

"Yes, we do," replied Oliver as he defended his position. "I get it, we're the same. But that's no reason for her to disrespect us like that. We didn't do anything to her or any of them and they treated us like second-class citizens. Why do they hate us so much? They speak hatred into the world like it's normal. This is not normal!" screamed Oliver in an emotional plea.

"They hate us because we're different. One thing I learned marching with Dr. King is that hate cannot drive out hate, only love can do that. We've all had years to better ourselves and some don't take the time provided to do so. I don't want that for you. I want you to be better than all of us. I want you to change the world."

"Why do you care so much about me?"

"To be honest, I've been watching you for some time. Trust me when I tell you that I plan to one day tell you everything, but right now is not the time."

"What do you know about my past?" questioned Oliver. "You mean you have information about Dunbar House?"

"Trust me, Oliver, I will tell you everything, but I can only commit to telling you everything if you can commit to staying here with us. I think you will make an excellent addition to our little family here," she offered.

"Like you want to be my mom?"

"No, I could never replace your mother. Those are shoes that aren't easy for a stranger to fill. The night you arrived, you said you were only planning to stay one night. Two days later, here we are. I really would like you to stay and join us here. I think this is the type of environment you need right now.

"If you stay, I cannot promise you won't receive racism again. I cannot promise you won't be looked down upon for being a young black man living in a world that wasn't built for you. Despite that, I can promise you a few things. I can promise respect in this household, I can promise you care and attention, a bed to sleep in, and a roof over your head. I can promise that if you live here with us, you will never go hungry. I can never change anything that happened in your past, but I think we can make the future a little brighter. I promise you that."

Oliver watched as Ma spoke. Her conversation with Wilson continued to play in his mind. If he could, he would listen to her speak forever. As he listened to her wrap up her lecture, the same question continued to plague his mind—*why me?*

For as long as he could remember, no one ever cared enough about him to worry if he went to bed hungry or had a roof over his head. From the moment he arrived at her home, he knew something was different about Ma. He could tell that, unlike Ms. Janet, Ma built her house on care and love. He was tired of sleeping with one eye open in fear of someone stealing his personal items or attacking him. Oliver also knew that he had nowhere else to go, so he lowered his pride and raised his trust. He told Ma that he wanted to stay with them longer. She smiled when she heard this.

"I'm happy to hear you say this."

*****

He began attending a new school, made new friends, and committed himself to doing much better this time around. Although he was committed to bettering himself, Oliver would often stay up in bed for hours. On the nights he was able to go to sleep, he would wake up frightened in a pool of his own sweat and tears. The same nightmares that had previously visited him at PACC had now made their way to his new home.

He regularly experienced the same recurring nightmare about his last night of freedom before his incarceration. In this same chilling vision, he was standing in the warehouse on the night they ambushed the Jamaicans. He was pointing the gun at the two men who stood with their hands up while he peered into their terrified eyes. He could feel the pit of his stomach sitting in the palm of his grip as it begged to turn at any second. In every nightmare, he glanced over at Rahzmel for confirmation, and when he saw the same pride on the drug lord's face that he once wore, he swallowed his doubt and pulled the trigger, unloading on the two men. In this vision, he was the one who pulled the trigger, not Rahzmel. Then he saw the bodies. The lifeless bodies that laid on the ground in puddles of blood.

When he first experienced the dream while in PACC, he thought it was just random because of his situation, but after experiencing the same nightmare a few more times, he realized this was no random occurrence at all.

As time went on, he realized that the most frightening part of the dream was not the actual murder or the bodies, but rather, his lack of remorse each time he took the life of another. He worried that every time the vision visited him, his subconscious changed its narrative and softened its effect. It was almost as if his conscience was telling him what should have happened.

*****

After leaving school exhausted from his lack of sleep the night before, Oliver knew he needed to do something about the nightmares. They were beginning to affect him at school, and he was determined not to disappoint Ms. Mabel-Ara. He confided in Jeremiah and told him about the nightmares he was having in hopes that his roommate would have a suggestion on how to address them. Fortunately, Jeremiah did and explained how he also experienced similar hallucinations when he first arrived at the new home, but with Ma's help, he overcame them.

"Speak with Ma. Tell her what's on your mind. She helped me and I think she can help you too."

At first, Oliver was reluctant because he did not want her to view him as a troubled individual. He was enjoying spending time with his new housemates and did not want to jeopardize his position as a member of her home. He attempted to think about all the positive memories, which mostly came from after he'd gotten out of PACC.

I don't think I should say anything. Things are going so well here and for the first time in a while, I feel comfortable.

He thought back to the countless positive memories they'd shared. His first thought was a recent memory from the local park. In it, he remembered how Ma noticed he had a talent for basketball and frequently accompanied the children to the park to watch the boys shoot hoops together, while the girls bolstered their expertise in double dutch. He recalled how she attempted to shoot around with them but could barely keep up after their first few shots. He laughed.

As time went on, Oliver began sleeping through the night and assumed these positive memories had finally entirely overshadowed the fog in his mind formed by his nightmares. Unfortunately, his assumption was wrong, and the nightmare returned about a week after confiding in Jeremiah. This was the day he finally decided to speak with Ma.

When he woke up that morning, he found her in the kitchen preparing breakfast for everyone and told her he was not feeling well.

"Do you think I could stay home today?"

She placed her warm hand on his forehead and then on his cheek. She noticed he did not have a fever but was a little warm, so she told Oliver to go back to bed to rest and that she would check on him in a bit.

About two hours later, Ms. Mabel-Ara came to the room to check on Oliver, as promised. She entered the room with a cup of tea and when she went to sit at his bedside, he sprung up.

"Hi Ma'am. Thank you for letting me stay home. I don't think I'm feeling well."

"Are you okay, Oliver?" questioned Ms. Mabel-Ara. "When I felt your forehead, it didn't feel like you had a fever. What's really going on?"

"I think I'm just tired. I haven't been able to sleep for a while…mostly since I got here."

"Do you think it's the new setting that's preventing you from resting?"

"I don't know… I think it may be something else because before I came here, I was somewhere else, and I slept okay."

"By somewhere else, you mean the corrections center?"

"Ummm… yes. I was there. How did you know?"

"Like I said when you first came, I've been watching you for some time. The day you first arrived at my home; I knew that was also the day you were released from PACC. Technically as a minor, you would not have been released of your own accord. How do you think the judge allowed for your release back into the normal world?"

"Ummm… because of Officer Smith and Officer Jefferson?"

"Yes. The three of us have watched you grow for some time and when you were released, we knew the first place you needed to come was here. We told the judge and Child Protective Services that after your release you would move into my home."

"But when I came on that day, you asked me if I wanted to stay. How did you know I would say yes?"

"I guess I didn't know. I kinda just hoped you would and took a chance. Now tell me, what's going on? Why can't you sleep?"

"I think I can't sleep because my mind is running all over the place."

Oliver was hesitant to reveal any details about the nightmare because he did not want to incriminate himself or Rahzmel in his testimony. He considered lying, but also knew that would not address the issue he was dealing with.

"Truth is, there are some things I did in my past that keep me up at night. My mind doesn't want to go to bed because of the nightmares and when I do fall asleep, I am awoken by the same nightmare."

"What's the nightmare of?"

"Well, before I went to the correction center, I used to hang out with some people in East New York. They were dangerous drug dealers and I thought I wanted to be one of them. One night, they attacked a rival gang, and my nightmares began."

"When you say 'they' I assume you mean "we?"

"Ummm…yeah, I was there, but I didn't attack anyone."

"I believe you. You don't have to worry, young man. I'm not here to get you in trouble. You've done your time and at this point, it isn't for me to judge you. You can tell me the truth."

"I know. I am telling the truth," exclaimed Oliver. "That night, the people I was with told me to kill people, but I just couldn't, so they killed the men themselves right in front of me. Now, when I sleep, I dream that I am back there during the attack, but I am the one who kills the men. I take their life and don't feel a thing after doing so."

His head lowered in shame.

"It sounds like you feel regret. My question to you is, did you do anything to try to stop them from being killed?"

"No, and what's worse, they were killed because of me. They robbed me, so the gang I was with killed them."

"Oh, I see, I see. Do you think it should have been you who took their lives?"

"No, I couldn't do it. I wasn't like those guys."

"So, then what do you regret the most about that night?"

"I'm not sure. I think I regret even going there that night because if we hadn't gone, they would still be alive."

"Yes, that's true. From the sounds of it, it seems like you've taken responsibility for the actions of others and haven't forgiven yourself for the death of those men."

"I don't know. I guess I shouldn't have allowed the gang to react the way they did."

"What could you have done?" replied Ms. Mabel-Ara. "You did not kill those men. The pressure you put on yourself for their deaths is something that will drag you down unless you forgive yourself. We all make decisions in our lives and those men made theirs."

She then picked up the Bible, which remained untouched since she gave it to him the night he arrived. She wiped the slight coat of dust that began to form and opened it.

"I can tell you haven't opened this since I gave it to you," she admitted with a giggle. She turned to

Luke, chapter six verse thirty-seven, then handed the Bible to Oliver and asked him to read what he saw.

"*Judge not, and you shall not be judged. Condemn not, and you shall not be condemned. Forgive, and you will be forgiven.*"

"Do you understand what that means, Oliver? It means you must not condemn or judge yourself for the actions of others. Judgment is between each of those men and their god. What happened that night was a result of some gangsters being gangsters. You were wise enough not to allow yourself to take part in those actions. The blood is on their hands. The second part is about forgiveness. 'Forgive and you will be forgiven.' This is speaking about you."

Oliver was shocked to hear her speak about forgiveness like this. It reminded him of the conversation he had with Salena about forgiving others and letting go. He found comfort in her reassurance that he was forgiven. He realized he couldn't forgive others until he first learned to forgive himself.

"That reminds me of something an old friend told me. She told me that when we don't forgive, it produces a black cloud that we carry atop our heads. The cloud can't be seen by others, but it slowly eats away at us."

"Yes. Your friend is very wise. That's very good advice."

"*Was.*"

"What?" replied Mabel-Ara with a surprised look on her face.

"She *was* very wise," he emphasized. "She was killed last year."

"I'm sorry to hear that. She *was* very wise and I'm sure she would give you very similar advice. You cannot change or take back what happened that night, but you can change what happens from it."

"How can I forgive myself?"

"Tonight, when you go to bed, read Luke chapter seven verses forty-seven and forty-eight. After that, say your prayers then go to bed. In the morning, come and find me."

"Will that allow me to sleep?"

"Just do it and come find me in the morning."

"Okay, I will... Thank you."

*****

That night, Oliver did as instructed and for the first time in months, he slept through the night. When he woke up fully rested in the morning, he immediately went to go see Ms. Mabel-Ara and told her of his full night's rest and absence of any nightmares. She was pleased to hear this and smiled at his joy. She embraced him with a tight hug and at first, he stood there, scared to fully accept her warmth. He wasn't used to this type of affection and was closed off.

She really cares.

He was getting emotional at her embrace and finally opened his arms to reciprocate the feeling. He found himself melting in her presence. *I never want to let go of her.*

"The nightmares came but didn't come often in PACC. They didn't truly get bad until I arrived here."

"Hmmm…I can't say why," she began. "My assumption is that maybe because at PACC, you were around a bunch of people who were very similar to the gang you were running with. Being around those types of individuals probably didn't bring out the person who stands in front of me today. It sounds like coming here was great for you because the *real* Oliver has come out. You're such a sweet and caring young man."

He continued to stare intently and blushed at her praise.

"Your conscience was probably fighting itself when you arrived here because of the person you were and the person you thought you wanted to be. My advice for you is to continue to let the person you truly want to be take full control. Trust me when I say that story will always end up better. Also, continue to read at least one Bible verse and one chapter before bed. I've been doing it since I was young, and it has made a tremendous impact on my life. You're a very special young man Oliver and I'm happy you're here."

For the first time in his life, Oliver felt like someone cared about him. Ma's advice was exactly what he needed, and he was excited to use it.

"Now go get ready for breakfast."

As he walked out of the kitchen, Oliver looked back with a heavy heart and admiration in his eyes.

"Thank you, Ma."

CHAPTER 16:

EIGHTEEN

Oliver Mahlah

Over the next twenty months, Oliver continued with his growth, maturity, and development. He continued to help Ma around the house with various chores and responsibilities. He had never lived in this type of environment before coming to Mabel-Ara's home and as time went on, he realized he loved the feeling of inclusion. The feeling of being needed was something he hadn't experienced since he ran with Rahzmel's crew, but he knew this was different. There was no cost to him being wanted, but he still sought to seek any opportunity he could to feel valuable.

He made it a point to have the chores completed even before he was asked and developed himself as a leader amongst the others. He would assist with homework, champion their group efforts, and ensure there was always unity amongst the six teenagers. His intention was for Ma to always see his value. He didn't ever want to go back to the life he led before.

Ma encouraged independence and free-thinking but also strived for a unified home. She saw how strong the bond was becoming between the six teenagers she cared for and regularly held family dinners and family breakfast on Saturday mornings. She wanted them to maintain that trust and comfort with each other. Her goal was also to ensure she offered the children less of a house and more of a home where they could one day view each other as family—even after she was gone.

Over that course of time, Oliver connected more with his housemates and grew hopeful after hearing their stories. He learned that despite their tough backgrounds, each of them had been adopted by Ma and now viewed her as their mother. He was determined to stay in her care for as long as he could and hoped he could also find a permanent place by her side.

There were several reasons for his desire to remain in her care but the top of the list included fear. He feared going back to his life before coming to Ma's home. It was filled with isolation, corruption, violence, and manipulation. As an orphan growing up on the streets of Brooklyn, he knew there was no place for him to be weak. He tried to be tougher than he really was and placed himself into a life he didn't understand. He didn't want to force this anymore.

*****

On Oliver's eighteenth birthday he woke up and prepared for school just like he did any other day. His normal routine was to wake up, shower, head to breakfast then finish getting ready before heading out the door. Today was no different and his routine was off to its normal start. As he returned to his room from the shower, he noticed his bedroom was unusually quiet and the beds of his roommates were both made to perfection. This was strange, but he didn't think too much about it because it was so early in the morning, and he was still very tired. He wasn't sure if anyone else knew it was his birthday, but he also did not care for it to be known. He was not hoping for anything besides another one of Ma's uplifting messages, and maybe also her pancakes, which he grew to love equally as much as her meatloaf.

After getting dressed, he excitedly made his way downstairs to the kitchen expecting to see everyone but found no one. When he arrived, he noticed the stovetop was spotless, dishes were put away and the dining room table was empty.

Where is everyone? Why isn't anyone here for breakfast? Did they all leave without me?

His annoyance slowly grew on his face which began to mirror his confusion. He found it unusual and began to worry that everyone had gone without him. He looked around once more then slowly made his way back upstairs to finish getting ready in disappointment. When he was done, the annoyance had left and he was left with sadness. He felt a heaviness in his chest that he hadn't felt in a long time and made his way downstairs.

They left without me.

Saddened and confused, Oliver walked downstairs to head out, but when he hit the bottom floor, there was a loud cheer from the dining room which startled him.

There, in front of him, was Ma, Officer Jefferson, Officer Smith, and the five other teens who shared residency with him, all standing around a birthday banner that read, "Happy Birthday Oliver Burke!" The heaviness he felt in his chest now felt like an overwhelming sense of emotion and he looked around as he fought back his tears.

Ma, who now walked with the help of a cane due to a minor knee injury she experienced while attempting to keep up with the boys on the basketball court, approached Oliver and gave him a big embrace. He melted at the surprise and for the few moments he was in Mabel-Ara's arms, nothing else mattered. She finally let go and gave him a kiss on the cheek, wishing him a happy eighteenth birthday.

"In the short time you've been with us, we've seen so much growth and maturity. You came to my home as Oliver Mahlah: a scared, battered, aggressive teenage boy with little trust, no manners, and probably a small chance of seeing your post-teen years. From the first moment I laid eyes on you, I saw your potential and still see it to this day. I'm excited for what the future holds for you, young man, and cannot wait to help get you there. You've become such a beautiful, respectful, outgoing, and courteous young adult. You came in a boy, but now you're a man. As a man, you now have the choice to go into the world and pursue the life you have envisioned for yourself. You'll have the freedom to make your own decisions, you'll have the choice to correct your own mistakes and you will have the power to foster your own future. The other option is for you to open this letter from all of us."

She handed the unsealed envelope to the eighteen-year-old Oliver, who began to slowly open it as he traded glances between the envelope and Ma. He saw the giddy look everyone had in anticipation and too became excited. He had no idea what the letter was but was hopeful it was what he had wished for.

When he finally unfolded the letter, he dropped to his knees, lowered his head, and instantly broke down in tears. In the envelope were adoption papers, filled out by Ma, and a copy of the family picture they took after church a few days after he first arrived, almost two years prior. When he read the adoption papers, he noticed it read **Ms. Mabel-Ara Burke** in the "Adopting Parent(s)" column. In the "child's name after adoption" column, it read **Mr. Oliver Burke**, which confirmed Oliver's wish had finally come true. For the longest time, he had wanted to know what it felt like to have a family. Since he arrived to her home on the day of his release from PACC, Ma showed him more love and genuine kindness than he had ever received before. She respected him as an individual and treated him as one of her own from day one. His hysterical crying mixed with his running nose caused him to fumble over the words of appreciation he was attempting to share.

"Does this mean you're officially my guardian?" questioned Oliver as he wiped away tears.

"Yes! That's exactly what it means. I'd like to invite you to officially join our family, Oliver. I can never replace your mother. That isn't my intention. My wish is to be there for you and nurture you. I can't promise life will get any easier, but I can promise that I will ensure you receive the same level of love that any child should receive from their mother. I promise to protect you. I'd like to ask to officially become your guardian. My Obie," she smiled.

"Obie?"

"Yes, honey," replied Ms. Mabel-Ara, glowing with pride. "I've been waiting a while to give you that nickname. Oliver Burke. My sweet Obie."

"You wouldn't be replacing my mom," he disappointingly admitted as he wiped away the tears still rolling down his face. "I've never had a mom."

The group came together for a hug and Oliver melted in their embrace. He was having a difficult time forming full words and as the others continued to issue their congratulations, his jaw muscles began to cramp up from the smile that was still painted on his face.

"I can finally and officially call you brother," Jeremiah exclaimed loudly and proudly. "I waited so long and knew you would fit in the first day you told me to make my bed. Just like an overbearing brother would."

The entire room erupted in laughter and Ma just smiled. She was glowing as she watched all her children embracing. She then looked at the time.

"Okay…okay…we have more celebrating to do later but for now, you all need to go to school. You don't want to miss the bus. I'll come by later to pick you up."

*****

At 3 o'clock p.m., the final bell let out and the students leaving through the main exit dispersed in various directions as if they were a sea of ants guided by the smell of food.

It was very difficult for Oliver to concentrate in class that day because it seemed like every second, he was replaying the morning in his mind. In this daydream, every time he opened the envelope, the surprise of its contents shot chills up his arms and spine.

As he made his way out of the school that afternoon, he saw Ma's minivan was parked right in front of the building which was her usual spot when she picked them up. The others were already in the van by the time he'd arrived so he sat in his usual seat in the back.

"I ordered your favorite birthday cake from that small bakery in East Flatbush. Should be ready soon. Then we can go back home to continue to celebrate."

*****

When they parked next to the bakery, Oliver noticed a group of young black teens idly standing on the adjacent corner. They weren't bothering anyone, and they all looked like they were bored out of their minds. Although the others seemed oblivious, Oliver knew exactly what they were there for. He had not been back to this side of town in close to half a decade but seeing this reminded him of the dark underworld he once ran in with Rahzmel as its king.

Ma looked so excited to bring them to the bakery, that he did not want to ruin her joy with any talks of the local drug dealers or rough neighborhoods. She was not afraid so he knew he couldn't be either.

"I'm going to run in and pick up the cake," Ma stated. "Who wants to join?"

Oliver quickly shot his hand up which was followed by the others doing the same. He knew they weren't in the best neighborhood and didn't want to leave her side.

Just as he exited the minivan, he noticed a car with tinted windows, a loud base, and spinning rims pulled up to the group of bored teenage dealers. He hadn't seen a vehicle with this much flair since he ran with Rahzmel's gang but figured there were enough drug dealers in Brooklyn.

What are the chances that I know this drug dealer?

As the car came to a stop, the driver's side door opened first, then the passenger side. His eyes widened and he grew anxious. There, roughly twenty-five feet away, was Chino exiting the passenger side of the car followed by Rio, who exited the driver's side.

Without thinking twice, Oliver rushed the group inside to avoid them being seen.

Although he appreciated the protection the gang leader provided him inside the prison, Oliver knew he had no intention of paying back that "kindness" with sweat, which he knew Rahzmel was expecting. He did not want Rahzmel to know where he was and began to worry.

From inside the bakery, he peered outside of the front windows and noticed Rio yelling at the teenage drug dealers. Rio seemed more concentrated on yelling at the young dealers than on the random van that was parked across the street, so Oliver assumed he wasn't seen.

Jeremiah noticed Oliver pacing back and forth near the entrance and saw the concern he wore on his face.

"Yo, Oliver. Everything okay?"

"Yeah, everything's good. I'm good."

Oliver had become very close with Jeremiah in their two years together and now trusted him like a brother. Although their bond was strong, he still did not want to reveal what was going on in fear of Ma finding out.

"Don't worry, Jeremiah, I'm just watching to make sure no one steals our ride home," he lied with an accompanying smirk to emphasize his humor. Jeremiah accepted this and went back to studying the assortment of available ice cream flavors with the others.

After they finished paying for the cake, the group made their way back to the van. Jeremiah was first out of the door followed by Mabel-Ara and the other teens. Oliver was the last to leave and before walking out, he peered across the street one more time. Once he saw the others had arrived at the van, he knew he could not wait any longer or it would become suspicious. He quickly made his way to the van, using his hands to cover his eyes as if the sun's rays were blinding him.

With his head lowered, he entered the van and looked back to see if he had been seen. He noticed Chino looking in the direction of Ma's van, so he sank down into the bottom of his seat. He was sitting in the back with Jeremiah who once again asked if everything was okay. Oliver motioned for him to also sink down.

"I think I saw some guys from my old life."

"Who?"

"Just some guys. Look, man. Do me a favor. Slowly look up to see if anyone's looking at us."

At this time, Ma had finished packing up the cake and was starting the van for their departure. Jeremiah quickly and very discreetly looked through the back window and shot back down to the bottom of his seat. As Ma began to drive away, she turned on her jams which gave Oliver the distraction he needed. Since the others in the car were swaying and dancing to the music, they did not even see the two boys in the back seat crouching and whispering.

Jeremiah whispered to Oliver that there were two men talking and staring at their van. When they pulled around the corner, the two of them sat back up and Jeremiah asked Oliver to tell him what was going on.

"Those two are with the drug lords I used to run with. They're very dangerous and I didn't want them to see me. Before I went to prison, I used to hang with them and they were expecting me to go back after but I never did. I never can."

For the remainder of the car ride, the two teens discreetly discussed Oliver's past. The only other person in the house whom he had told about this in detail was Ma, so he whispered so the others wouldn't hear them speaking. He was not yet ready to reveal this piece in his story.

When they arrived back at the house, they excitedly made their way toward the door to finish their celebration. Oliver felt good because he assumed he had escaped a reminder of his dark past that once again attempted to disrupt his new life.

His joy was accompanied by his melodic recitation of Whitney Houston's "I Want to Dance with Somebody," which was released only a year before, but he knew it word for word. Like they did normally, Ma and the others joined the playful moment.

*****

Almost one hour after returning back to the house, Ma and the kids continued celebrating. She prepared a special birthday dinner, which would consist of all of Oliver's favorite items, while the kids gathered in the living room to play Monopoly. As they began, there was a loud knock at the front door which Lillian responded to. A few moments later, she came back to the living room and called Oliver.

"There are some guys at the door asking for you," she remarked nervously.

Based on his facial expressions, Oliver's confusion was also obvious, but the others just disregarded it, assuming he simply had visitors coming by to wish him a happy birthday. Oliver did not assume the same.

He knew that the only other people who would have visited, who didn't live in the house, were Officer Smith and Officer Jefferson. Being that Lillian didn't introduce the visitors as either of them, he feared this was not a friendly visit.

When Oliver walked out of the living room and turned the corner toward the front door, his jaw dropped, and he froze in his place at what he saw. There at the front door stood Rahzmel, with a big smile on his face, exposing his yellow teeth. He had aged significantly since Oliver last saw him and now carried more black spots on his face and bags under his eyes. He was standing beside Croc, Chino, and Rio, who all wore the same look of shock with slight relief that they were at the right place.

When Oliver looked at Rahzmel's face, his own face became pale, almost diaphanous from his surprise. His hands and legs shook as he attempted to walk towards the door. It was as if he was staring at a ghost from his past.

"Surprise!" yelled Rahzmel as he looked up at the banner still hanging in the foyer. "You know you couldn't celebrate your birthday without your oldest friends, right? We've missed you, Oliver. After you left, it was almost like you just disappeared into thin air."

On Oliver's face was pure fear and shock. He could hear the underlying coldness in Rahzmel's tone and quickly began to worry. *How did they find me? Chino and Rio must have seen us and followed us back to the house. I'm so stupid. How could I be so careless?*

He knew Rahzmel was an emotionless killer who didn't like to be made a fool of. In an effort not to make it seem like he did something wrong, Oliver quickly forced a smile on his face and stood up straight.

"Hey, Rahzmel. Hey guys," remarked Oliver who struggled to still the shaking in his tone. He forced as much confidence as he could into his words but struggled with its authenticity. "How have you been?"

"We've been good, man. It looks like you've been doing a little better. Is this where you've been hiding…I mean staying?" Chino chuckled.

"Yeah, I've been laying low after the whole thing with the Jamaicans like you said. Found this place after I got out and have just been hanging here. I tried to find you when I got out but couldn't seem to find you anywhere."

"You sure?" replied Rahzmel in a passive-aggressive tone as he clicked his tongue. "Because you know me, and you know a lot of motherfuckers in Brooklyn who know me. If you was really looking for me, one of those motherfuckers would have found me. I heard you got out and just disappeared." His tone grew louder so Jeremiah came around the corner and saw what was going on. He recognized Rio and Chino from the bakery and walked up to the front door and nervously stood beside Oliver while keeping his attention on their visitors.

"Yeah, I checked with some people on the street, and they said you were laying low too," he remarked, turning to see Jeremiah approach. "After that, I thought it was best to just stop asking around. Didn't want to put your name out there too much so the wrong people could get wind."

"All good man. Who this?"

"I'm his brother," interjected Jeremiah, forcing confidence. "Who the fuck are you?"

"I'm his real brother, nigga. I'm the motherfucker who raised this youngin'. Watch your mouth, young man. No one taught you to be respectful to your elders?"

Oliver placed one hand on Jeremiah's shoulder to pacify him. Despite his silence, he wanted Jeremiah to feel his fear through his touch and calm down. He wanted to handle this his own way.

"Well, we're about to have dinner so I'm going to have to ask you to leave," remarked Jeremiah in a tone that grew bolder with every word. He disregarded Rahzmel's previous comment. Jeremiah had heard stories about Rahzmel and his crew from Oliver and did not want to come off as weak during this first encounter with the kingpin.

"Oh perfect. We didn't eat yet. Hope there's room for four more," interjected Croc sarcastically.

Rahzmel then attempted to take a step into the house, but Oliver put his hand up to his chest to stop the kingpin from entering the home. Rahzmel looked down at this then looked up at Oliver. His nostrils flared in anger. Jeremiah saw what was happening and rushed back to the kitchen to notify Ma.

"Sorry, Rahzmel. I don't think there will be any extra. We weren't expecting you guys so there won't be enough food for everyone. How did you find me?"

"Well funny story about that. Chino thought he saw you or a nigga who looked like you this afternoon, so he called me. He then asked the cashier at some bakery for this address and after a little bribe, we were given this location. I wasn't sure what I was going to find, but here you are. Now…. had you just found me like I would have thought you would have done, we would all be a few hundred dollars richer," said Rahzmel in a chilling tone that Oliver had become familiar with. "Do you have a couple of hundred dollars to give me for me having to search for your ass?"

"No, I don't. Listen Rahzmel, I don't want any trouble. These are good people. You guys should just leave."

"Oh, we'll leave, but you're coming with us. Don't you miss us? You were like my right-hand man. I paid quite a bit of money to keep you alive after your little incident in the club and even more to keep you protected in jail after your little scuffle. Ha! Heard you even got your gangster on in jail. Let's not forget a certain guard who was giving you problems. What do you think happened to him? Do you think that just took care of itself? No need to repay the money though. We will just hit the streets harder to repay everything."

"No, Rahzmel. I don't want to do that anymore. You guys really should leave before the owner of the house comes and calls the police."

"We're not leaving without you. Now go get your bags and let's go," demanded Rahzmel in a stern, aggressive tone.

"The young man nicely asked you to leave and now this is me demanding you get off of my property," interjected Ma as she approached the front door with Jeremiah trailing at her side.

"Who are you, lady? I'm talking to my little brother, Oliver."

"Oliver is no brother to you. Now leave my property before I call the police."

"Listen, lady. Like I said before. We don't want any problems either. We'll just take little Oliver and be on our way."

"He's not going anywhere with you," remarked Ma in a bolder tone as she reached for her phone.

"No need to call the police. This is a friendly visit. I'm sorry *you've* made this so difficult. We'll leave and wish you all a *safe* evening," Rahzmel emphasized with a crooked smile.

The four men then proceeded down the front steps. Ma stood in the doorway and waited for them to drive away before closing the door. When she turned around, she saw Oliver was shaking in fear and had urinated in his pants. The other teens were standing in the doorway to the living room located behind where Oliver was standing so they did not notice. Ma saw this and demanded that they go back to playing their game, then she took Oliver upstairs.

She walked him to the bathroom and sat him on the toilet until he calmed down.

"It's okay. They're gone now."

"How could I have allowed them to find me? That was him. That was Rahzmel. It *won't* be the last time we see him."

"If he comes around here again, I will call the police. I will call Calvin and Jalacie. If he comes near this house again or touches you, I will kill him myself. I promise. Stay away from him. He's the devil."

Oliver continued to stare blankly so Ma wiped the perspiration from his forehead.

"Don't worry, Oliver. It's okay now. Just clean up and come eat. We can't let them ruin your birthday. I'm going to call Calvin and have him do a few laps around to make sure they're gone."

As he began to clean himself up, Oliver's trepidation grew. He knew Rahzmel was very proud and did not like to be embarrassed. Ma had not only embarrassed him, but she did so in front of his crew, which made it worse. He knew Rahzmel was not one to stand for that. Everyone had feared him, so no one ever questioned or disputed his commands the way she did. It was this fear that made the kingpin seemingly untouchable.

At that moment, Oliver realized how much he loathed Rahzmel. As he stood there, he felt a heavy ball of uncertainty form in his throat. He considered leaving things as they were but feared what would happen if he did not act.

I need to do something. I can't let this stand. I need to protect her.

He did not want any trouble to come to Ma, Jeremiah, and the others, and feared any disruption to his new way of life.

I need to find a way to pay them back. That may be my only way out because I can never go back.

CHAPTER 17:

EVERYONE WE LOST IN THE FIRE PT. 1

Oliver Burke

Oliver spent the remainder of the weekend brainstorming ways to approach Rahzmel with an offer that would be enticing enough to let him go without committing himself to the kingpin's reach any longer. He knew he did not have the money to pay back his debt and did not want to ask Ma for it because it was not her burden to bear.

I need to handle this alone. I can't ask her for any more than she's already done for me.

On the night of his eighteenth birthday, she showed her true strength as a parent in protecting her child and Oliver knew he couldn't have asked her for any more than she had already given him. He knew the guys he was dealing with and wanted to leave her out of any further dealings for her safety.

By Monday morning, he woke up much earlier than usual and went straight to Ma's bedroom. He woke her up to tell her he still wasn't feeling well.

"Do you think I can stay home today? I think the rest will help."

"Do you need a doctor?"

"Oh no…no… some sleep should help. I think that should be enough."

"You sure?"

"Yes. This old age is catching up to me much quicker than I thought it would," he joked.

She laughed and began to get up to make him ginger tea with honey.

"Wait… you don't have to get up."

"I was getting up already, my love," she lied while pulling her covers back.

After the others had left for school, Ma came back to Oliver's room with the tea and rested her soft hand on his head, feeling the curve of his forehead. It did not feel unusually warm, but she was okay with him resting at home. He had a long, exciting weekend and she knew he could benefit from a day of rest.

After dropping off the tea, Ma began to walk out of the room, but Oliver stopped her.

"Can you tell me a story?"

"There's one particular story I've been meaning to tell you, Oliver," she paused, swallowing the saliva in her throat. "When you first came here, I told you that I had watched you for some time and there were things about your past that I've been meaning to tell you. I think now is a good time for us to talk."

"What things about my past do you want to talk about? Is this about Rahzmel? He shouldn't be bothering us anymore."

"He actually is a part of this story, but it's not about him. This story is actually about… your mother."

"I never knew my mother. I was told she left when I was younger. I never even cared to ask about my father… that ingrate. What do you have to tell me about her?"

"Back before I started this home, I worked very closely with various communities within Brooklyn. I told you that I marched with Dr. King, but my involvement with Brooklyn went deeper than just Civil Rights. Roughly eighteen or nineteen years ago, I worked as a community organizer and activist in Brooklyn. I fought for equal rights but also against drugs, guns, and prostitution. At that time, it was like the wild wild west in Brooklyn. There were a lot more gangs and even more regular violence in the streets. Prostitution was the worst of them all because most of the time, the women forced into this career choice were too young to know any better. Most were victims of their circumstances and became a product of their environment.

"This was also around the time I first began to work with Officers Jefferson, Smith, and Moran who you didn't know. One day, they reached out to me about an interesting situation they found themselves in. When they called me, they told me they had picked up a lady with a baby in an alley while on patrol. They claimed to have found the lady holding the baby beside a dumpster. They described how they had questioned the lady that day and were told that she had found the baby. They assumed she was lying."

"Wait…are you telling me that was my mother?"

"Stay with me. Let me finish… After investigating further, we learned that this lady was not lying. She was *only* the person who found the baby. She was not the baby's mother.

"Not long after the baby was found, Officers Smith and Moran called me to a crime scene of what looked like a homicide. I was not a police officer, but because of my continued fight against crime and prostitution, they regularly kept me plugged into these types of occurrences because of my connection with the people within the communities.

"When I arrived on the scene that afternoon, I saw a young black girl laid dead in the middle of the street. She was shot in the head," her head lowered. "After Officer Smith walked me through the scene, we saw she had a pink backpack with a baby's bib in it. *That* was your mother, Oliver. She was killed that day in the middle of the street."

"How did you know it was my mother?" he questioned. "That could have been anyone."

"No, Oliver. That was your mother. After the coroner inspected the body, he confirmed that she was fourteen years old and had recently given birth. There were many signs that all pointed to the same conclusion. That you were her child."

"But.....*how* do you know it was her? What else did she have on her?"

"She had a few other items in the bag which unfortunately included some drugs. There was a big cocaine circuit growing at the time so she had a few packs of the popular drug 'creedo,' which is identified with the letter 'c' in cursive and red font. With the amount that was found in her bag, my assumption is that she was selling it."

Oliver's face changed as he slowly slid up in his bed. He remembered Minnie had a drug like this with her the night they had sex. He also recalled seeing it all over Angela's club the night he visited with Rahzmel and Croc.

"When I used to run with Rahzmel, they used to have a lot of that around, that drug with the letter 'c.' It was always around."

"Yes. Creedo has destroyed lives and if it was around Rahzmel, chances are he was involved with its distribution. Anyways, after surveying the scene, Officers Smith and Moran investigated further and we learned that your mother was also involved in that business. Shortly after that, the FBI made one of the biggest busts Brooklyn had seen in a while and took down one of the main street crews selling creedo. The leader, Lefty, ended up dying in jail and we thought that was it but were wrong.

"I didn't want to assume anything, but from the looks of it, your mother was dealing creedo. It was so unfortunate because she was so young and so beautiful. When I first laid eyes on you, my heart broke into so many pieces. There you were, so innocent, not knowing what kind of a world you were coming into. On that day, I knew we needed each other. Unfortunately, I was deeply involved with my activism and I felt that stepping away would have undone everything I had worked so hard for. That was the day I told Officers Smith and Moran that we needed to watch you until I was ready to give up the activism and open this home. We did not want you to fall victim the way she did.

"Unfortunately, we lost you for a short time during your time at Dunbar House. Going to PACC may have been tough for you, but I think it was one of the best things to happen to you because it allowed you to hit the reset button and gave me the time I needed to finalize my home. Now we've been reunited, almost two decades after that first day I was introduced to you."

"Thank you for telling me this," he lowered his head. "What involvement did Rahzmel have in all of this?"

"To be honest, that's been questionable for some time. From what Officers Jefferson and Smith tell me, Rahzmel was a member of a street crew the FBI dismantled when Lefty was arrested. That street crew was the first to flood the streets with 'creedo' and they think Rahzmel continued even after the original crew was disassembled. When they later learned that Rahzmel was back and had built a new operation, they knew he was the source of the drug. Unfortunately, because of the support he was receiving from corrupt cops and politicians, their hands were tied, and they were very limited in what they could do to stop it. They stayed within the department because they wanted to be the last piece of integrity and honor for the police department. They also wanted to continue to stay plugged in with their resources.

"To be honest, it wasn't until you told me about your involvement with Rahzmel that I was able to piece everything in the puzzle together. I never knew how deeply connected all of this was. Not until recently at least."

"He's the reason I went to jail."

"I'm sure…listen, Oliver, I've seen guys like Rahzmel all my life. They are dangerous because they are manipulative, and their power comes from fear. They can talk their way through anything. People like that are dangerous because they are afraid to lose everything they've built. They say if you know a man's fear, you can conquer him. That's why Rahzmel is threatened by you. It's because he's afraid of you. You were once close to him and the things he loves so he doesn't want to lose you."

"But I won't ever go back to him."

"I know. I've never met him or spoken to him until he showed up at my door on the night of your birthday. I don't fear him, but I want you to promise me you will stay away from him and everyone else associated with him. As a member of this household, I want you to promise me that."

"I promise."

Oliver had so many questions and knew Rahzmel may have been the only one who could answer them. Although he lied and promised Ma that he would stay away from the drug kingpin, he knew there was one more conversation he needed to have with him. He needed to break away from Rahzmel completely and needed to know the truth about who killed his mother and why. He looked at Ma with a face filled with hope.

"I have one more question for you. Do you wish I never came into your life?"

"No, Oliver. You are one of the best things that I could've ever asked for. Who else would keep me entertained in my old age?" she giggled. "Why do you ask?"

"Just something I was told at the old house. I was told that no one will ever love me."

"Whoever told you that was a fool. I love you like I birthed you."

"But why? You didn't birth me…"

"Blood doesn't define who we are to each other. It's what's in our hearts that truly defines us. Our hearts beat for the same things and that is what makes us family. I love you more than you may ever know. My sweet Obie."

*****

After their discussion, Oliver told Ma that he was feeling better but was hit with sudden fatigue and wanted to get some rest. He wasn't actually tired but figured this was a good enough excuse to buy him a few hours. She smiled while staring into his eyes and said nothing. She simply kissed him on the forehead and made her way out.

After Ma left the room, Oliver crept to the door to ensure he heard her hit the bottom step of the hardwood staircase. He then grabbed a few pillows from his roommates' beds and stuck them under his covers to make it seem like he was still sleeping. This was just in case Ma came back into his bedroom to check on him. He had never snuck out of his bedroom window at Ma's home but knew he needed to make it happen. There was one more conversation that needed to happen.

It was now 10 a.m. and he thought back to Rahzmel's routines. He knew Rahzmel was fairly mobile and he wasn't entirely sure where he may have been at that moment but figured it was best to make his first stop the clubhouse.

When he arrived, he did not see any of the usual vehicles parked out front but still proceeded to the front door. After knocking, one of the girls from Angela's club opened and motioned for him to come in. Oliver remembered her as one of the girls he saw when he used to run with the crew and was unsure if she knew about him and his situation. She looked impaired and he figured she was probably on one of the many vices that floated around the clubhouse on a regular basis.

"Is Rahzmel here?"

"Nah, baby. Think he's at the club. You want to come in for some *fun?*"

"No, thank you. Take care of yourself," he remarked, turning around.

She looks like Minnie, he thought as he shook his head in regret.

While commuting to the club he thought about the woman's offer and began to also think about his biological mother. *I wonder if that's how my mother acted. Was she offering sex to people just like that? Was she too under Angela's spell?*

When Oliver arrived at the club, he went straight to the VIP section where he found Rahzmel and Croc sitting with a bunch of women, alcohol, and drugs around. When he looked at the table, he saw there were multiple packs of creedo sitting next to rolled-up marijuana joints and several bottles of champagne sitting in ice baths. It was as if they were celebrating but he knew this was just a regular Monday for them. Rahzmel looked up from rolling his joint and smiled when he saw Oliver approaching. He demanded the girls leave, then stood up to embrace Oliver with a big hug.

"Where have you been, Oliver?" Rahzmel said, trying to mask his anger. Oliver stared at his words as they spewed out of the kingpin's mouth. He stood silent and watched Rahzmel's facial expression lighten as he forced a smile.

"I'm happy you decided to come back home. I didn't mean to make a scene the other day. You know me, that was very out of character for me. I will admit though, I was surprised at how much resistance you gave us that night. I mean… we're family, right?" remarked Rahzmel who continued before Oliver had a chance to reply. "No matter… Regardless, now you're home with us. Grab a drink and get comfortable. I'll get the girls back over here to show you a good time."

"I didn't come for that, Rahzmel. What happened to your cousin? What happened to Lenny?"

"Lenny…? Lenny…? I heard Lenny was killed in prison. Didn't I tell you that?"

"No, you didn't! Why didn't you protect him like you did me."

"It's complicated, man. From what I hear, when Lenny got to PACC, he was doing a lot of talking about things he shouldn't have been talking about. He had my protection, but I couldn't protect him from running his mouth. I heard he was killed before you got there. It was sad what happened to my cousin. He was weak anyway and talked about things that were bigger than him. He probably would have gotten killed on the streets. Why are we talking about Lenny?"

"Because he was my friend and you never told me what happened to him. Maybe I could have saved him."

"Listen, Oliver, Lenny wasn't built like you. He was weak, loud, and thought he was a real gangster. He was constantly running his mouth about things that didn't concern him and I guess his talking caught up with him. You were quiet and knew when to talk. That's what I like about you. You know your place. You both had my protection, but you used it better than he did.

I will say, your little stunt on the basketball court cost me *a lot* of money to clean up. I couldn't prevent your isolation but I was able to make sure that nothing else came from it."

"You had to pay for that?" questioned Oliver in surprise.

"Of course! Do you think that just went away? I paid a lot more than you think for you. Like I said before, who do you think took care of that situation with that guard? The OGs from the prison called me and I took care of that for you. It was OUR problem to deal with and I dealt with it. I expected you to be more grateful and to come to find me when you got out, but you didn't. I trusted you…"

Oliver stood there surprised to learn all of this. He didn't know the punishment of Kellerman would make it back to Rahzmel but this was a reminder of just how far the kingpin's reach went. He then reached onto the table and grabbed one of the small packs of creedo and threw it to Rahzmel.

"I need to know, where did creedo come from?"

"Oliver…why are you asking all of these questions?"

"I need to know where it came from!" repeated Oliver in a bolder tone. "Did you know my mother?"

"Your mother? Why would I know your fuckin' mother? What's with all these questions? You better remember who you're talking to, young man."

Rahzmel's face then changed as he grew silent. His body stiffened, and the veins in his neck protruded. He looked at Oliver with cynicism, then back at Croc. He motioned for Croc to check Oliver for any wires or recording devices. When Croc finished his search he shook his head, confirming Oliver was not recording their conversation.

"I just need answers! She was killed eighteen years ago and had multiple packs of this drug creedo on her. I need to know where it came from and why she had it on her."

"Listen, Angela and I been pumping the streets with this for years," he emphasized. "You knew that. I'm not sure who your mother was but if she had it on her, she very well may have been selling it or buying it. I won't lie to you, I wouldn't remember her if she was sitting right next to you right now."

"I don't believe you! For someone who always claims to be the smartest person in every room, I find it surprising that you cannot remember someone who had a pink backpack."

Rahzmel's face dropped as he began to scratch his head. It was as if he had just remembered something obvious but not obvious enough for him to figure out without the teen's inquiry. Oliver quickly noticed a shift in the kingpin's facial expression.

"Your mother had the pink backpack?" About eighteen years ago? That was her?"

"Yes, Rahzmel. That was my biological mother. What happened to her?"

"Listen, man. She was young. She was a kid. She worked here at the club and Angela found out she was stealing. I wasn't there so I'm not sure exactly what happened, but my assumption is that your mother tried to run or lie when confronted."

"You weren't there? You probably gave the order!"

"Listen, Oliver," replied Rahzmel very aggressively as he repositioned himself to stare Oliver directly in the eyes. "You better remember who you're talking to. If your mother or anyone else stole from us, she deserved to die. Actually, now that I think about it, I do remember her. She was a little brat who stole drugs and money from us. We made an example of her that day and none of these girls ever stole from us again. She was a nobody anyway. You're doing well for yourself without her. Just get a drink and let's have some fun."

"No!" he yelled. "I don't want to go back to that life. I don't want to run with you guys anymore. This is the last time you'll see me."

Rahzmel burst out into such boisterous laughter that Oliver had to knock a bucket of champagne off the table to regain his attention. Croc stood to his feet, but Rahzmel queued for him to sit.

"Who the fuck are you? I remember the first day you walked into my clubhouse with your hands shaking, looking like a little bitch. Now what? You're some big shot who suddenly isn't afraid to die?"

"I don't want any problems, Rah. I just want to leave and be done with all of this."

"You're leaving the family?" questioned Rahzmel with a doleful look on his face. "Stop playing around and take a seat. Sit down *now* and I'll pretend we didn't have this conversation. I'll bring the girls back and they'll make you feel better."

"No! I'm not doing this anymore. I don't have any money and can't pay you back for anything but I'm out. Thank you for everything you did to protect me but my appreciation will have to be enough. I'm leaving."

"You ungrateful little bitch. You don't quit this," his tone grew louder and more direct as he stood to his feet. "You're in it for life like the rest of us. It's either jail or death. There is no other ending."

"I'm not like you, Rahzmel. You have everything you could ever need. You have money, power, and respect. You don't need me anymore."

"There's no quitting this, kid. There's a saying about guys like us. 'A gangster is nothing more than an hourly employee to the streets. They punch in, they punch out, and report to one of two makers: the judge or God.' You already met the judge once. I cannot guarantee you will see him next time," threatened Rahzmel in a direct tone void of any sarcasm.

"I don't care. I'm done."

Oliver then turned around and began to walk away. Before leaving the end of the VIP section, he turned back around and walked back toward Rahzmel.

"Also, don't ever come to my home again. You aren't welcome. If I see you there or hear you bothering any of us again…I'll kill you myself."

"You promise?" replied Rahzmel in a chilling tone while looking the teen dead in his eyes.

Oliver then turned away and once again began to leave.

As he walked away, Croc yelled after him: "Don't sleep, Oliver! Don't sleep!"

Oliver heard the enforcer's threat but continued motioning through the exit till the door slammed shut behind him. When he was out, he exhaled a deep breath of relief and wiped the fear-filled tears that began falling.

What did I do? Am I free?

Hearing Rahzmel's confession about his mother and the disdain he held in his voice as he spoke about Lenny gave Oliver the confidence he needed to finally take a stand. He knew this was fueled by anger but deep down inside he could sense it was his terror driving his plea. He was scared of remaining tethered to the gang life for the rest of his life and losing everything he'd built in Mabel-Ara's care. For the first time in a long time, he felt like he was finally rid of Rahzmel.

CHAPTER 18:

EVERYONE WE LOST IN THE FIRE PT. 2

Oliver Burke

When Oliver arrived back at the house early that afternoon, he climbed up onto the garage then made his way back into his bedroom window. This was his first time having to climb back into the house and he did not feel proud about it. He realized this was what he needed to do to end things once and for all with his past life and knew this was his means to an end.

He had never asked questions about his biological mother, but subconsciously, he'd always held resentment toward her for abandoning him to a world that wasn't built for him. He attributed his issues with confidence, anxiety, and his childhood anger to this.

It was 2 p.m. when he arrived back at the house. When he got into his bedroom, he saw everything was exactly as he'd left it, which was his confirmation that he made it out okay. He threw his pajamas back on and then walked downstairs to see Ma sitting in her regular spot in the living room watching TV while knitting a sweater. He sat beside her and kissed her on the cheek and thanked her. She closed her eyes and placed her hand on his shoulder to embrace his gesture.

"What was that for?"

"That was for being you and for telling me the truth," replied Oliver. "I just wanted to show my appreciation for you and everything you've done for me. You helped me at a time when I didn't think a better life existed."

"Thank you, Oliver. I felt you were ready, and it was a good time to share a little more of your story. I'm sure you had so many questions growing up. How did you rest?"

"I rested fine. I guess I wasn't as sick and tired as I thought."

Oliver then started walking toward the kitchen for a snack, but before leaving the living room, Ma made one last statement.

"Did you find the closure you were looking for?"

He froze. "What do you mean?"

"You left the house, didn't you? Did you find the closure you were looking for when you left the house?"

Oliver's face dropped.

"I think I did. There were things and people in my past that anchored me down. How did you know I left the house?"

"This is our home, Obie. The home that I built. You can't think I wouldn't know when someone sneaks out of their bedroom window. I've been doing this for some time, honey."

"Why didn't you try to stop me?"

"Like I said the first night you came, you are free to make your own decisions. I know they're things in your past that you're running from and knew you may have acted on those things. I mean, you sneak out right after I tell you the truth about your mother. I figured you weren't going for a walk."

Oliver stood bashfully looking down at his hands, his left wringing his right.

"I'm happy we spoke this morning. I'm getting old, Obie, and I would've hated myself if I never told you more about your past before something happened to me."

"Something happened to you? What do you mean?"

"Oh no! I'm sorry. I don't mean to scare you. I'm just talking, honey. Now go clean up so I can make you some lunch."

*****

By 7 p.m., Ma had finished dinner and called the children downstairs to come together to eat. Since it was Monday and the start of the school week, she decided to make grilled chicken with vegetables and savory mashed sweet potatoes for dinner. She liked starting the week off with a lighter meal so everyone could remain focused throughout the week.

During dinner that night, they each spoke about something they were grateful for. After the children spoke, Ma then shared what she was most grateful for.

"Although I was not blessed with the ability to have children like many women, I'm grateful for the six of you and the roles each of you plays in my life. I love how close all of you have become. You complete me and remind me every day why I fight for equality. Our small, beautiful, blended family is something I am very proud of and each of you brings something special to it. It doesn't matter who you were before you came through these doors. It's the people whom you've allowed yourselves to become that has made the biggest impact on me."

Oliver sat and watched in astonishment as the others wore the same look of admiration on their faces that he bore that evening.

"Our past is something that many people dwell on which causes them to lose sight of the exciting opportunities the future holds. As you've shared, each of you has a past that you may not be proud of. I mean, there are things in my past I'm not proud of too."

She looked around and placed Tonisha's hand in one hand and Isaac's hand in the other.

"Despite that fact, I'm thankful that you've allowed me to come into your lives and influence your future, hopefully for the better. If I've never said it before, remember it this day. I thank each of you for changing my life for the better. I love you. Now let's clean up so we can watch a film before bed."

All six children got up and crowded Ma for a group hug as they thanked her. The children then went to review the chore board, so they'd know what had to be done and by whom. Oliver saw he was on dishes this evening which he was happy about.

"I feel like I've been on garbage duty for like a month straight," he joked. "I don't mind it when I can take it to the curb but that damn basement is scary."

"You scared?" Jeremiah traded with a good-natured shove.

"Yeah! It's big, dark, and we haven't gotten that stupid door fixed. Why does it have to lock from the outside?"

"Great question. Guess it's Tonisha's problem today."

Oliver laughed and began his chores while Jeremiah returned to his own.

While washing the dishes, Oliver heard Tonisha shriek.

What was that? Maybe she saw a rat or something. My hands are wet. Jeremiah will have to deal with it.

He ignored the yell and returned back to the full sink of dishes in front of him.

Moments later, Oliver heard Tonisha run into the dining room where Ma was sitting and tell her that she thought she saw someone walking around the house through the living room window. He could hear the panic in her tone and from Ma's response, sensed their adoptive mother could hear it also. Ma didn't know any of the kids to be frightened by much, so she followed Tonisha to the same window and peered outside. She looked around carefully and informed Tonisha that she could not see anything. Oliver listened as she explained how the darkness made it very difficult to see anything besides things she already knew were in place.

"Isaac," she called. "Come look. Do you see anyone?"

When Isaac peered out through the front window, he too thought he saw a figure but wasn't sure, so he ignored it.

Just as they both were about to turn around, Isaac thought he saw the shadow move and yelled. "Wait! I think I saw something. Do you see it?"

Ma squinted to focus closely. "I don't see anything."

"Okay, maybe I'm mistaken."

Tonisha was still a little shaken up because she was confident that she saw someone. So, before taking the trash outside, she asked Isaac to join her. Ma didn't hear this exchange and went back to the dining room to continue clipping coupons while drinking her chamomile tea. Oliver and Jeremiah were still doing their chores, but when Isaac finished his chores, he assisted Tonisha.

Moments after the door closed behind the two teens taking out the trash, Ma heard a female's voice yell, followed by what sounded like two gunshots. Everyone in the house looked at each other in confusion. Ma knew what gunshots sounded like, so despite her poor knee, she ran to the front door and when she looked outside, she froze. She saw there in the dark, a man with a cigarette in his mouth standing beside two other men in the driveway. One of the men had something in his hand which appeared to be a gun. They didn't make any moves and simply stared back in the darkness. She then saw two bodies laid on the ground in front of the men and instantly knew what had occurred.

Ma quickly slammed the door shut and locked it up to the deadbolt. She then yelled for the children to stop what they were doing and head to her. She did not give any other directions, but from the urgency in her voice, Oliver could sense something was wrong. He turned the sink off and rushed over to her location with the others. When he'd arrived, he saw a look on her face he'd never seen before. For the first time since he'd arrived, he saw nervousness and terror. Without her saying another word, Oliver knew what was going on.

Jeremiah counted only four other children and turned to Ma.

"Where are the others? Where's Tonisha and Isaac?"

Evie responded, "They're outside taking the trash out. We need to let them in!"

"We need to go get them," he implored but Ma interrupted him midsentence and replied in a stern, yet sad voice.

"No. There are some people who are outside of our home right now. I don't exactly know why they're here, but I have reason to believe they've shot Tonisha and Isaac. I believe they're here to cause us harm. I need each of you to do exactly as instructed if we want to make it through this."

She placed one hand on Oliver's shoulder and the other on Lillian's.

"Lock all doors and windows and turn off all lights." She then turned to Evie, who was shaking. "I know you're scared but focus! Grab the key from the basement door and call 911. Call Officer Smith to tell him what's going on while I go upstairs for my father's revolver from my bedroom."

She finally turned to Jeremiah. "Grab any weapons you can find."

She wasn't entirely sure who was in front of her house but knew that Officers Jefferson and Smith may have been the only two people not living in the house that she trusted. When she returned downstairs with her gun, she peered out through the front window again and saw that the shadows of the three men had moved closer to their front door. The kids were still scattered to complete their assigned responsibilities, so she yelled.

"Let's all go down to the back room of the basement and hide while we wait for the police to arrive."

Not even a second later, there was a banging at the front door. The two girls were frightened by this and crept backward. In the melee of it all, they mistakenly thought they heard Ma instruct them to go "to the bathroom" and unknowingly made their way upstairs to the bathroom in her bedroom, while Ma made her way to the foyer with Jeremiah and Oliver in tow.

They hadn't noticed the two girls had gone upstairs instead of downstairs, and just positioned themselves to take on anyone who came through the front door.

She saw the boys had moved forward and urged them to also "go downstairs to hide," but they ignored her command. They both had household items in their hands that they were planning on using as weapons. In this case, their weapons of choice were kitchen knives. Both Jeremiah and Oliver told her that they would never leave her alone and repositioned themselves to stand firm by her side.

The banging continued, but instead of sounding like it was to get someone's attention, it now sounded as if someone was attempting to break down the door. Ma motioned for the three of them to make their way to the nearby coat closet which was in the foyer beside the main door.

They entered and slowly closed the door behind them. While they stood there, Ma whispered to the boys. "Keep quiet, boys." Oliver could hear shaking in her voice. "If anyone enters our home, it's because they're here to harm us and we need to be ready to defend ourselves."

"We are, Ma."

"Did your sisters make it?"

Both Oliver and Jeremiah looked at each other and shook their heads.

"Okay. Are you both ready to do what you need to do to protect our family?"

Oliver quickly thought back to the night at the warehouse and how he was unable to take a life. *What will I need to do?* He pondered to himself. *I couldn't take a life back when we attacked the Jamaicans. Can I take one now?*

He then looked at the terror still painted on Ma's face and knew he needed to be brave. *If they come to hurt her, I need to do what needs to be done.*

He could never forgive anyone who harmed Ma. She was the only person who saw through his rebellious shell and helped this sad teen searching for belonging. He looked back at Ma and Jeremiah, then nodded. "We won't let anything happen to our family."

Jeremiah and Oliver, both positioned themselves in front of Ma. "You have the gun so you have a better vantage point if you stand behind us."

"Thank you, boys. We don't know how many people are out there."

"Exactly. We'll need every advantage we can get."

Their plan was set. They would wait for the men to enter the home and then attack once they got close enough.

The main door finally busted open and from their position in the front closet, they saw two men slowly enter the home with handguns drawn. The two men crept into the foyer while looking around shiftily. They approached the closet door and Jeremiah looked back at Ma. From the look on his face, Oliver sensed he was about to do something stupid and before he could say something, Jeremiah placed his index finger over his mouth advising them to be as quiet as possible. When he dropped his hand, he looked Ma square in her eyes and whispered, "Thank you."

He then turned around and busted out of the closet and tackled one of the two men to the ground. As the two of them wrestled, Jeremiah repeatedly stabbed the unmasked man in his chest several times. The man dropped his gun when he was tackled, which fell toward Oliver's feet. The other man quickly turned around and then unloaded four gunshots into Jeremiah's body until he fell lifeless on top of his partner's bleeding body. He saw Oliver motion and when he turned his aim in the teen's direction, he was quickly shot down by Ma, who emptied her gun into the man's falling body. She knew she saw three men out front which meant there was at least one more coming through the front door. From their position in the main foyer, they also now heard someone banging on the back door, attempting to break it down. Ma pushed the front door shut and then urged Oliver to grab the gun and follow her downstairs to hide.

She assumed the two girls were down there when she saw the basement key missing, but when she called out for the girls, she realized there was no one there. She worried for them but was hopeful that they had found a safe hiding place somewhere. She also realized she had no more bullets in her gun and quickly devised a plan to trap the men. Her plan was to lure the preparators into her basement and then lock them down there until the officers arrived. She knew there was a window down there and she was planning on escaping with her remaining children.

By now, she could not hear if the back door had been busted open but assumed so because it sounded like there were multiple men walking and talking on the main level. She could hear the sound of heavy boots clicking across the hardwood floors, growing louder as each click grew closer to the entrance.

"Stay quiet," she remarked. "We don't know how many more there are at this point. We cannot fight them all and should be prepared to run. From here, the only place for us to escape is through that small window in the back corner. Let's just stay quiet. They may not even come down here." He could hear hope in her voice.

Moments later, the basement door swung open, and Oliver could hear Rahzmel's voice whispering to another person. He and Ma knew they did not have enough time to get through the window and went to hide in a small closet in the back where he had repositioned a large bookcase in front of. He then heard the two men making their way downstairs allowing the door to slam shut behind them.

"Oh, Oliver…where are you hiding? You didn't think you could just walk away like that did you? I own you, bitch, and now I've come to send you to be with your mom," yelled Rahzmel in a snarky tone as he slowly made his way down the stairs. "I would have stayed back but wanted to see the life I gave you leave your eyes as I take it from you."

In front of Rahzmel was Croc with two gas containers in hand. When the two men reached the bottom of the steps, Rahzmel again whispered something in Croc's ear, which resulted in him uncapping the two containers and begin pouring gasoline on the ground.

"I don't know how many people you keep in this place, but I am sure by now you've called the cops, old lady. Two of your little children are laying on your front lawn waiting for you. Don't you want to go be with them? Can I help you get there?

"Anyways…. I'm not going to waste any time looking for you or that fuckin' ingrate. You have two options. You can come out now and talk to us or you can burn in hell with this house…your choice."

When there was no response, Rahzmel motioned for Croc to pour more gasoline, which he obliged. Croc walked around pouring and when he stood in front of the bookcase, Oliver was tempted to jump out and give himself up in hopes of saving Ma's life. Before he could do anything, he felt Ma's weak hands grip his arm. He took this as his reminder to remain still and quiet. He knew she, too, was hopeful that the officers would arrive in time.

When the gasoline canisters were empty, Croc made his way back to the stairs and informed Rahzmel that he could not find them. The smell of gasoline filled the dimly lit basement. Rahzmel was now frustrated because he wanted to look Oliver in the eyes to see the pain as he took everything from him. Oliver had not only disrespected Rahzmel in front of the others, but he broke the trust that the drug lord did not normally extend to others. Although this angered him, Rahzmel knew he did not have any more time, so he made one last statement before walking back up the steps towards the basement door.

"Oliver…die."

From the top of the stairs, Rahzmel threw his cigarette down and when it hit the basement floor, the fire quickly began to spread, attaching itself to everything covered in gasoline. Rahzmel waited a few seconds to ensure it spread, then smiled and turned around to leave. When he turned the door handle to exit, he noticed it was locked. He looked down at Croc, who stood a few steps below him, and again attempted to forcibly turn the handle but was again unsuccessful.

He continued to jiggle the door handle, expecting different results, but each time his force grew, so did his doubt, fear, and panic.

Rahzmel then started banging on the door hoping someone would hear his cries. He knew there was no one on the other side of the door but his banging continued. He saw this was to no avail and looked back at Croc. "Go find another way out," he yelled.

Croc looked down at the fire that quickly spread then looked back at Rahzmel with a face of confusion.

"Rah, let me try the door."

The kingpin again yelled his demand and shoved Croc back downstairs. "Go find somewhere else!"

He was beginning to panic, and it became obvious to the enforcer. Croc slowly made his way back down the steps to analyze how much the fire had spread and look for another exit. When he reached the bottom steps, he crouched down to stay beneath the thick blanket of smoke but was having a difficult time seeing. All he could see was smoke and saw that the fire had fully engulfed the large room.

Croc walked back up the stairs. "Move out of the way, Rah. Let me break this door down."

In Rahzmel's panic, he did not hear Croc's statement. He simply saw the enforcer making his way back up the stairs, and assumed he purposely disregarded his command to find them another way out. His authority had already been tested, and the cocktail of anger and panic that had been formed caused him to react without thinking.

When Croc reached Rahzmel, the two of them once again locked eyes. The last thing Croc saw was the kingpin reaching in to push him back down the stairs. Rahzmel did not care for anyone else but himself and this was obvious when instead of helping his friend, he quickly turned back around and continued slamming his body into the basement door attempting to get it opened.

Croc tumbled backward down the steps until he reached the bottom and when he hit the basement floor, the flames quickly attached themselves to him and began burning the large enforcer. He attempted to roll around the ground but was unsuccessful because of the amount of gasoline poured around the bottom of the stairs. He shrieked until his body laid still and lifeless. The smell of burning flesh began to mix in with the smell of gasoline and burning wood.

At the same time this was going on, Ma and Oliver were still in the backroom closet and noticed smoke beginning to fill most of the room.

"I know we're locked in because I heard them slam the door shut," explained Ma. "He doesn't have the key, so he's trapped in here with us. We need to get out through the window in the back of the room. It's the only way. We have to go now!"

"Okay," replied Oliver in a short manner while trying to reserve the small amount of clean air they had left.

"The window is located behind a large refrigerator, so its location isn't obvious to anyone who doesn't already know it's there. That's our only way out."

Oliver saw nothing but strength in Ma's face as she spoke. He, himself, was petrified of the fire, but also of Rahzmel and Croc finding them. He was shocked and impressed to see how Ma remained somewhat poised and level-headed throughout the ordeal. He forced confidence on his face as he agreed to her command.

He slowly made his way out of the closet and saw the flames tearing through the items in the room. By now, it was all over the basement, and he could not see even a few feet in front of him because of the thick cloud of black smoke. Fortunately for him, Mabel-Ara knew the way.

He assisted Ma, who had lost her cane in the melee and now simply hobbled with a slight limp. She still had her gun but realized she had used up all six of her bullets.

When they were both out of the closet, they looked in the direction of the stairs and heard something tumbling downstairs.

"Stay low, Oliver, and follow me," she whispered, while also coughing to breathe.

They made their way around several stacked-up wooden containers, which were placed between them and the stairs. The containers were burning from the heat and provided a path straight to the fridge, which was on the other end of the room. There was a distance between the containers and the refrigerator, and Oliver knew they needed to get around a few other miscellaneous items to reach their destination.

They moved in the direction of the refrigerator, and both craned their necks simultaneously when they heard Croc's body hit the ground and his screeching. The sound was loud and it frightened Oliver, who had always seen Croc as seemingly invincible. The sound was lurid until it was gone, and Oliver knew even the large enforcer wasn't immune to the temperamental flames which held no allegiance to anyone or anything but oxygen. Even the invincible enforcer was no match.

As they continued toward the window, Ma wrapped her arms around Oliver as cover. She stood between him and the flames, which had now penetrated past most of the wooden containers. She used herself to add another barrier between him and the fire to protect him. He didn't realize what she was doing and saw her cover as a means to remain close. On the outside, he was trying to display as much bravery as what he saw from her, but on the inside, he was petrified.

They continued to creep to the other side of the room, and Oliver noticed tears and sweat running down her face. He admired how she had always been so strong. Even though this ordeal was terrifying, he knew she was doing her best to remain strong for him. Her tears were his confirmation that he needed to get her out. He needed to save his mother.

When they finally reached the fridge, Oliver attempted to move it himself to make enough room to crawl through the window, but because of its size and weight, he barely budged it. He continued using all the strength he could muster and when he looked by his side, he saw Ma, in her old age, also attempting to move the refrigerator. When he looked closer, he noticed she had been severely burned on most of her back and on the side of her right arm, and he gasped in shock at what he saw. That was the moment he realized that in her wrapping herself around him, she was actually shielding him from the flames by taking its infliction and burning herself.

This must have been why she was sweating and crying. She was hiding her pain.

Something about the sight of this further motivated him to get her out. The sight of her aching gave him the strength he needed. He forced all the pressure he could, and they were finally able to move the large fridge together, making enough space to fit one person through the window at a time.

Although she did not speak about it, Oliver knew Ma was in excruciating discomfort so he told her that she should go out first.

"I see the burns on your back, Ma. You need help and should go out of the window first. I will lift you up."

She reassured him with a smile.

"Don't worry, Obie. I'm okay. I don't even feel it," she lied craning her neck to see the approaching flames. "You go first, and I will be right behind you."

His shock and confusion were glaring, but she used the same convincing smile. "The window's high and it would be easier for you to pull me up. I don't have the strength to pull you up."

He nodded and jumped up, attempting to grab the frame of the window, but realized he wasn't tall enough to reach it. Ma saw this and crouched down on one knee and told Oliver to use her other knee to propel himself up. She was crouching down on her bad knee, and he could see she was still attempting to fight the pain which was glaring in her face. She urged him to "hurry!"

With the strength only a mother saving her child could gather, Ma took Oliver's weight on her knee and helped give him enough height to reach the window.

She held him there until he unlatched it and climbed through.

Just as he finished sliding his body out, he turned around and attempted to reach his arm back for her. Before he could do so, a bullet whizzed past him, hitting the adjacent wall. He looked up and saw Rahzmel crouching down on the stairs, shooting a few more shots in their direction. Unfortunately, Oliver no longer had the gun he picked up earlier and realized he must have dropped it during their scramble. The fire was also now quickly making its way towards the window, and he knew they needed to act quickly.

Ma ducked down and craned her neck to see Rahzmel looking in their direction with his gun pointed. She withdrew her arms from the window. Rahzmel ducked back up the stairs to escape the rising smoke and when he got back to the door, the fire jumped from the bottom of the stairs toward the top. He continued to yell for help while banging on the basement door.

Oliver started yelling for Ma to come back but when she came back towards the window, Oliver noticed she was bleeding from a gunshot to the shoulder.

"Ma, reach for my arm," begged Oliver. "Please reach for my arm. We need to go now."

She attempted to lift her arms to climb out, but the pain was too much and her body was too weak. She was injured and knew she did not have the strength to get out. Oliver saw her wince for the first time all night and finally asked, "You're hurt, aren't you? She had a forced smile on her face but didn't look scared. She now wore an unusual calmness to her and Oliver could sense she was no longer as afraid as he was. The smoke was making its way out of the small window and pulled the little bit of fresh air Oliver had.

"My sweet boy," remarked Ma as she choked on the black smoke. "You need to get out of here. We both won't make it. You need to go. Now!"

"No! I'm not leaving you here. We both need to get out of here. Together! Let's go!"

"I won't make it. You need to go. I don't have the strength to continue."

With tears pouring down his face, Oliver pleaded for her to reach for his arm. He begged her to reconsider.

"Ma…I'm so sorry. I'm so sorry I brought all this trouble to you. Please don't do this. Please reach for my arm. We need to go. Please grab my arm."

"I want you to listen to me and hear my voice, my sweet Obie. You are the best thing that has ever happened to me, young man. I couldn't save your mother eighteen years ago and I will not allow you to also die at the hands of these monsters. Rahzmel and everyone else involved with your mother's death is gone. This is the last thing I want to leave you with. Peace of mind to know these monsters are gone and you're safe."

There was then another explosion at the staircase causing it to collapse. Rahzmel fell through it and hit the ground. He slowly stood up, picked up his gun from the ground, and again started firing in Oliver's direction. Ma ducked down and yelled, Go!"

She knew she was the only person capable of saving him from this last piece of his past. She knew Rahzmel wouldn't stop chasing him unless she put an end to it. She connected eyes with Oliver and smiled.

"I love you, my son. Now go!"

She then turned around and with the little strength she had left, she hobbled through the roaring flames and straight into Rahzmel, tackling him to the ground. It was hard to see through the thick black smoke, but Oliver could hear the thump from their collision. He then heard Rahzmel screaming from the pain of the fire melting his skin but heard nothing from Ma.

What is she doing? Where is she? Is she okay? Maybe Rahzmel is the only one who fell into the fire.

From his perch at the window, Oliver watched as the only parental figure he had ever known was taken from him as quickly as she came into his life. With the flames still tearing through the basement, Oliver quickly convinced himself that he could save her. The fact that Rahzmel was the only one screaming gave him a shred of hope that she was still alive. He didn't think twice. I need to do something.

Just as he was attempting to climb back through the window into the basement, he felt hands on his legs and thighs pulling him back out away from the basement window. When he frantically turned around and looked up, he saw two officers he'd never seen before. He realized they were the ones who had pulled him away from the roaring flames.

From the lawn, Oliver watched as fire engulfed the house from all sides. There were flames everywhere and from their position, the three men could feel the blistering heat, which was accompanied by the smell of burning wood, plastic, and dust. It was searching for air and tore through any and everything that stood in its way. This was a one-sided relationship that cost many lives to achieve its one goal…to live.

Oliver, who was still in disbelief, watched as the deep red and amber flames tore down the only house he had ever called home. He could not believe that the fire Rahzmel started had traveled so quickly and had taken over the entire house. His doubt that Ma was gone made him hopeful that there was more that could be done. The officers did not share his optimism.

"We need to get out of here now," remarked one of the officers as he went to grab Oliver's shoulder. "We need to leave now!"

Oliver attempted to shake their grip and when he realized he couldn't, he begged for them to release their hold on him.

"Let me go! I need to get her!"

Despite his fighting, the officers forcibly pulled Oliver away from the burning house until he was at one of the police cruisers. They were about to place him in the back when they heard a voice yell in the distance.

"Hey, don't touch that boy," Oliver Smith yelled as he ran over in his jeans and tennis shoes. His sweater looked as if he'd hastily put it on and his hair was disheveled.

"Why are you putting this young man in the back of the cruiser instead of an ambulance? Can't you see he's burned?"

The two officers looked dumbfounded so Officer Smith pulled Oliver away as he flashed his badge. "I'll take it from here. I'll get him to the hospital. Get out of here before I get the Chief of Police on the phone and explain your negligence."

Before the officers could say anything else, Officer Smith yanked Oliver away and walked him towards his car. His radio was still glaring with details coming in about the house fire.

"She's still there," Oliver remarked as he wiped the sweat and tears from his face. "Ma's still in the basement, and I need to save her."

"Where are the others?" questioned Officer Smith. "Where are the other children?"

"He killed them. Rahzmel killed them all."

Officer Smith listened as Oliver spoke and this also gave him a shred of hope. He became optimistic that Mabel-Ara was still alive and looked back towards the open window. At the same moment he motioned forward, there was another explosion that spewed fire out through the basement window, causing him to grab Oliver. He noticed the teen had been severely burned on his right tricep and knew he required medical attention as soon as possible.

Oliver barked in disagreement and pleaded for someone to do something.

"Please save her," begged the desperate teen with tears and sweat furiously running down his face. "She's in the basement and she's still alive. I know she's still alive and she needs help. Please, someone, help her. I can't lose her. Please-"

As they stood speechless in the shrill silent aftermath of her sacrifice, Officer Smith stood there staring at the young man. He was at a loss for words. What could he say? Everything would be okay? How did he know? What could he say to comfort the lost teen in his greatest moment of despair?

Soon two fire trucks pulled up to the house and analyzed the full-blown inferno that was in front of them. There was a putrid smell that took over the entire neighborhood. The fire department's first priority was to create a perimeter that allowed some distance for all the neighborhood residents watching the incident. The entire house was now going up in flames and collapsing section by section. They knew they would not be able to perform a search and rescue because of the house's condition. They quickly began shooting their water cannons at the burning structure to extinguish the fire.

After twenty-five minutes of fighting the flames, the fire department was finally able to put it out. They went to assess the damage and when they came out, they stated that they were barely able to confirm anything because of the rubble.

"Everything's gone and the fire's out, but it appears there were several casualties. Multiple bodies in the basement and it looks like two more which may have fallen from the second floor."

Oliver could not believe it.

She told me my life would be better.

PART IV
HELP ME HEAL

WILL APPIAH

CHAPTER 19:

STRANGER IN A STRANGE LAND

Oliver Burke   *Manhattan, 1988*

That night, Officer Smith accompanied Oliver to the hospital where they met Officer Jefferson. They intended to have a well-being check completed on the teen and knew they also needed to treat the burn. To the two officers, he did not seem injured, physically, besides the burn on his tricep, but knew that he must have been going through something deeply painful, internally, which he was not communicating with them. They'd remained close during his developmental years which allowed them to be intimately aware of the many challenges he'd faced over the course of his life. Now, after all that time of growth and healing, he was presented with another tribulation intended to cripple him.

A person who saw through his antagonistic cloud of armor and gave him a chance was taken from the eighteen-year-old right in front of his eyes. She was the only person who had ever told him that he mattered and was loved. She was gone just as quickly as she came into his life and they worried for him. They were at a loss at what could be done to find solace at the loss of one of the greatest people any of them had ever known.

Because of their relationship with Ma, the two officers were also saddened by her passing but were trying their best not to show their pain in front of the teen. They knew of his constant battle with his self-confidence and believed they needed to be strong for him.

When they arrived at the hospital, the nurse did a quick check on Oliver to look for any physical injuries. She scanned his body and then peered into his eyes with a flashlight. She then asked Oliver a few questions which were answered with a simple "yes" or "no." After completing the exam, she stepped out of the room with the officers and pulled them to the side.

"From my initial observation, there are minor physical scratches, various bruises around his body, and a pretty serious burn that requires immediate attention. There's nothing to worry about on that front but we should treat that burn quickly. It's going to leave a permanent scar but he'll live."

The officers continued to stare intently, wiping their eyes every few seconds as she spoke.

"The only other thing I'm worried about at this moment is his shock. When I flashed the light in his eyes, he barely even flinched. I think he may have still been processing everything from his house burning down."

Officer Smith used his sleeve to wipe the corner of his eyes then cleared his throat. "He also lost his mother tonight." He paused.

Officer Jefferson patted his partner on the back and continued with the words he knew he could not finish. "He just watched his mother and home go up in flames. He lost everything tonight. We all did."

"It makes sense. I can't imagine how any of you are feeling right now. I'm very sorry. Are you two family?"

"Yes. We're the closest thing he has to family right now," replied Officer Smith.

"Okay, good. You'll need each other. Going back to Oliver, you'll need to stay close and remind him that there are still people who care for him. People he can count on."

"We're not going anywhere. It's what Mabel-Ara would want."

Even though both officers were also grieving, they returned to the room and painfully hid their hurt as they stood by Oliver's bedside in support.

"Oliver…I am so sorry," remarked Officer Jefferson. "Are you okay?"

Oliver sat there silently. His stomach was in knots, and he could barely move. The pace of his breaths was rapid, and he sat with his knees hugging his chest. Tears were still running down his eyes and, on his face, he wore a look of surprise. He looked up toward the officers.

"One of the last things she said to me was that she loved me and her final gift to me was the peace of mind to know the monsters that haunted me were gone," revealed the teen as he lowered his head back with cracking in his voice. "This life that I built over the last two years was purely based on the lessons she taught me. I thought I left my demons in the past and moved forward. I don't understand… I read my Bible every day. I prayed every…single…day. I even opened myself up to loving others, but she was still taken. She was willing to give her life to save mine. I'm the reason she's dead. It doesn't make sense. The one thing I cannot stop thinking about is why do I deserve to be here, and she doesn't?"

Both Officers stood in silence as they held back their own tears. Officer Smith then placed one hand on Oliver's shoulder.

"You aren't the reason she's dead, young man," Officer Smith spoke, also with shakiness in his voice. It was obvious he was trying to be brave, and Oliver appreciated him for that as the officer continued. "Mabel-Ara was a tough lady who never did anything she didn't want to do. Whatever she did or said in her final moments with you was done because she wanted to do it. You were one of the best things that has ever happened to her, and she would have traded ten of her lives to ensure you could live. I know this because of how much she used to brag about you."

There was then a cold silence in the room. The two officers stood there still fighting back tears and stared at each other. They then turned and watched Oliver who still had his head lowered.

"Then I heard the voice of the Lord saying, 'Whom shall I send? And who will go for us?' And I said, 'Here am I. Send me.'"

He looked up.

"This is a Bible verse from the book of Isaiah, chapter 6. It was the Bible verse we read together yesterday morning. She purposely selected this verse and told me that she was not going to let anything from my past hurt me in the present or future. She was killed for the sins of the life I led in the past. I don't want to talk anymore."

He laid back down as the questions flooded him.

Why? Why had she done it? Why did she sacrifice her life for me? Was my life any more valuable than hers was? What makes me so special?

In his shame, he covered both eyes with his palms and sobbed silently. Officer Smith had known Ma longest, so the sight of this and the emotion he'd carried since the fire forced him to run out of the room sobbing. Oliver could hear, not see, him hyperventilating, and knew the officer didn't want him or his partner to see him like this.

Officer Jefferson remained in the room, knowing he needed to be tough for Oliver and for his grieving partner whom he'd never seen like this before. He sat back down in the chair beside the bed and patted Oliver's back as the teen just laid.

"We're all here for you," he whispered.

When Officer Smith returned to the room about forty-five minutes later, Oliver had fallen asleep so Officer Jefferson told him that he would stay at the hospital and watch him. He saw his partner's swollen eyes and advised him to go home and rest.

He knew that they needed to figure out a plan for Oliver, but that night, they all needed to rest. He asked Officer Smith to look into a plan for the following day, which he agreed to while embracing his partner for support. Neither wanted to minimize their enormous loss but knew their healing needed to first begin with acceptance of the things they could not control.

*****

The next day, Officer Smith arrived back at the hospital early in the morning. Oliver was still sleeping but Officer Jefferson was not. He told Officer Jefferson that he had connected with their mutual friend in Chicago. He explained that he spoke with this acquaintance the previous night about everything that had occurred and about Oliver.

The friend was a priest and was also a friend of Mabel-Ara's. In hearing about Oliver's struggles and connection to the Bible through Ma, he invited them to Chicago. The unfortunate events of the nights had created an opening and he was eager to finally meet the teen.

Since Oliver was now eighteen, the officers also knew he could make his own life choices, but did not want that for him at this time. After Mabel-Ara's passing, the last thing he needed was to be alone.

When Oliver woke up that morning, they told him of the plan to go to Chicago for a bit.

"We have a friend in Chicago who wants to meet with you. What you experienced last night is not something anyone should go through. None of us believe you should deal with this alone and want to help. Later this morning, the three of us will be driving to Chicago to meet with some good people. Please don't fight us on this."

Oliver remained silent. He was mentally and physically fatigued and no longer cared to fight or argue with the two officers. With a pang of sadness in his voice, he responded. "I don't care. We can leave."

"We'll head out in about an hour," Officer Jefferson began. "I'm going to make a quick trip home then we can go."

About an hour and a half later, he returned to the hospital and the three men were off. They spent the next thirteen hours driving from Brooklyn to Chicago. For the entire ride, the officers traded driving responsibilities while Oliver laid in the back seat and did not say one word.

*****

When they finally arrived in Chicago, they pulled up to a large two-level brownstone house that sat beside a church. When they parked, an elderly African American man wearing all black with a white collar walked out. He approached the car and opened the backseat door for Oliver, who did not know they had arrived.

"Hello, Oliver. Welcome to Chicago," remarked the man as he shook the two officers' hands through the passenger side window. "How was your trip?"

"Okay," he replied shortly.

"Oliver…this is Father Nana," explained Officer Smith who was still wretched but now seemed more exultant than the night before. "He's a priest in this church and also a good friend of ours and Mabel-Ara's. He used to live in New York but moved to Chicago sometime back."

"Hi Oliver, I'm so happy to finally meet you. I wish the circumstances could have been different. Please, everyone, come inside for some supper."

Oliver had a deadpan expression on his face which led the others to believe he was still struggling in ways he was not communicating. His mind was held hostage by the thoughts of what could have been if they all had lived, and they sensed it.

When they arrived inside, Father Nana introduced Oliver to his wife, Amma, who had just finished preparing supper for the group, and their sixteen-year-old son, Reginald. They all sat and ate together, during which the officers did most of the talking.

They explained the trip, how much New York had changed over the years, and spoke about how corrupt the police department had become in New York. They tried their best not to talk too much about Mabel-Ara because they wanted to wait until Oliver felt comfortable. Oliver also did not say a word during dinner and after finishing up his food, he finally spoke.

"Thank you for the meal. I'm tired. Is there a place I can lay down?

"Yes, of course," Amma responded as she got up and escorted the teen to one of three guest bedrooms.

After a few hours had passed, Oliver lay there sad and distraught. He was exhausted and wanted to sleep, but could not bring his racing mind to stop or slow down. He could not find even a moment's reprieve from his grief. He stayed restless in bed for a bit, thinking.

Just a few days ago, we were all celebrating my eighteenth birthday and now my entire family is gone. How did things go so wrong? How did I allow that monster to hurt her? I'm so stupid. I knew I was too happy for this to be real.

The door cracked open, and Officer Smith popped his head in to check on Oliver. The teen laid in bed with his eyes shut pretending to be asleep because he was not in the mood to converse, so the officer left.

After another hour had passed, Oliver still could not fall asleep, but also could not lay restless any longer. He had always used his strolls as a coping mechanism for dealing with things and decided he needed to go for a walk to clear his racing mind.

He looked over at the clock and saw it was about 1 a.m.

I don't know where I'm going but I need to go.

Oliver threw on his hoody and left the guestroom towards the stairs. As he made his way down, he noticed the entire house was dark and quiet and figured everyone was sleeping. His destination was unknown, but he felt compelled to walk until his legs felt weak. When he exited the house, he made a left and glared at the large castle-like church next door. It was double the size of Father Nana's home with more of a devout feel to it. On the front was a cross like the one he'd seen at their church in Brooklyn.

Oliver continued past it and walked until he could no longer see the house or church. As he moved forward, he once again thought back to the things that led up to his last moments with Ma and her final words. He broke down again and dropped to his knees. His tears began to blind him and his breathing had intensified.

"*I love you son.*" Her words repeated in his mind like an orchestra extending its final score.

He felt the weight of his burden holding him down as he walked aimlessly. On his shoulders rested the heavy cargo of regret, which had begun to replace his sorrow, and he felt his legs growing heavier and heavier with each step he took. He regretted going to the clubhouse that day he went looking for Lenny. He regretted accusing Rahzmel of killing his mom and embarrassing him. Most of all, he regretted even meeting Rahzmel in the first place.

While walking back to Father Nana's house, Oliver passed by the church once again. This time, however, there was a light on behind the colorful window, hinting that someone might be inside.

During his time with Ma, Oliver had associated the church with being a safe space—a space where he didn't need to be afraid and could leave his wellness to a higher being. After her passing, he began to feel doubt in his belief and whether there was even a higher being looking out for them. *How could any higher being allow her to be killed?*

Although he began to question his faith, Oliver still felt somewhat comfortable in churches because of how Ma had described their impact on her own life. Its impact had made for the most cherished memories— a few of which he thought back to at that moment.

He thought back to how Ma loved to watch him sing with the choir and he enjoyed seeing her radiant with pride. Every time he would finish a verse of a song, he would find his eyes wandering back to her for confirmation that she was still paying attention. Their eyes connected every time. He also smiled when he thought back on another cherished memory of when the AC in the church went out and he and his siblings all used their paper fans to cool Ma down. They had all worked extra hard that day to keep her cool while others in the church had sweated off their breakfast because of the heat. These were the moments he never wanted to lose.

When he entered through the church's double doors on this night, he proceeded slowly into the foyer area. As he stood, he heard someone speaking and noticed a figure at the end of the church doing what looked like praying. This person was on their knees facing the large cross and had their back toward Oliver. He proceeded forward and when he grew closer, he saw it was Father Nana and froze. *What's he doing here in the middle of the night? I hope he didn't see me come in. I should leave. I just want to be alone.*

Just as he was trying to turn his body back toward the exit, he felt his legs once again get heavy and then go slightly numb, resulting in him freezing in his place. *Why can't I leave? Why can't I move?* He was frightened and turned his attention away from him leaving and towards the priest seeing him. In doing so, he noticed himself calming down.

This must be a message from Ma. She's still giving me orders to stay, he smiled. Despite his growing lack of faith, Oliver saw this as his reminder that he was exactly where he needed to be at that moment. He decided he needed to listen and proceeded toward the front.

When he arrived, Oliver knelt right beside Father Nana, who did not motion toward or acknowledge the teen's arrival. The two of them simply remained silent with their eyes shut and each of their warm palms held together.

"Come to me, all of you who are weary and carry heavy burdens, and I will give you rest. Take my yoke upon you. Let me teach you, because I am humble and gentle at heart, and you will find rest for your souls."

Without opening his eyes, Father Nana lifted his right arm and placed his hand on Oliver's left shoulder.

"Father…tonight we are joined by Oliver Burke, son of your latest addition to the kingdom of Heaven, Mabel-Ara Burke. She was recently called home and now her child seeks deliverance. We come to You together, as Your children and servants, to ask You to share the same love with Mabel-Ara, also known as Ma. The same love that she shared with Oliver, she shared with me and countless others when she was with us.

The world collectively grieves for this excruciating loss, but we smile at the peace she can now finally achieve by Your side. We ask that You thank Mabel-Ara on behalf of each of us for all the lives she helped shape while serving as Your servant on earth. In Your name, we thank You. Amen."

After Father Nana's prayer, he opened his eyes and wiped away the droplets of tears that had begun running down his face. When he looked over, he saw Oliver's eyes were still closed and he too had tears running down his cheeks. He used his right hand to squeeze Oliver's shoulder to comfort the teen and show his support and understanding of what he was dealing with. Something in the message of the prayer that was delivered showed Oliver that Father Nana was someone who may understand him.

He seems like someone who knows how I feel. Maybe I can talk to him.

"My child," the priest began. "I could never understand what you're going through, but I would like you to know that we're all here for you. If I may, I'd like to ask if you want to talk about anything in particular?"

"To be honest, I wouldn't even know where to start. I'm in so much pain and I can't even find the words to describe the emptiness I feel right now. Everything hurts and nothing makes sense."

"In your voice, I hear a battered and weakened soul. As I stare, I see your eyes display the broken heart that I bore when I looked in the mirror this evening. I know you're grieving, and I can't even imagine your troubles right now."

"It troubles me to know that she's dead but even worse that she's dead because of me," Oliver admitted. "Everyone's dead because of me."

He paused and wiped his eyes. "Everything was my fault. If I never even came into her life, she would still be alive. I brought strife and sin into the life of the purest person either of us may ever know. Why would this so-called *heavenly father* take her?"

"Trust me when I say, everything happens for a reason. Even this."

Up until that moment, Oliver could not bring himself to look Father Nana in the eyes. He spoke with his head lowered as if there were a weight on his shoulders holding them down. It wasn't until this moment that he turned his head and looked the priest square in his eyes.

"If there is a God, how will He punish me?"

Father Nana had a look of surprise with a mixture of compassion and disappointment. He wiped the tears from his own eyes and then looked back at Oliver with a strange and confused glare.

"How will He punish you? God doesn't punish. He forgives, teaches, sacrifices, and loves. He does not punish."

"I don't deserve anyone's love or forgiveness. If He exists, He shouldn't waste His forgiveness on me. I could have prevented all of this. It's all because of me."

"My son…You're grieving. The regret in your tone and the doubt I hear in your words is a clear indication of the pain you're going through. Mabel-Ara was truly a blessing to this world. You've immersed yourself into this feeling of shame because you think you let down the people you care about. Mabel-Ara would think differently. Her absence from us is a terrible loss. Although she isn't with us any longer, I'm confident she would have said that the true blessings in her life were the lives she affected for the better. That is what she strived for. Would you say your life is one of those that was affected for the better?"

"Absolutely. She changed everything. Everything I am is because of her."

"So, what is it that you regret?"

"Well, I regret the fact that she was killed trying to protect me. I regret not being able to save her. I regret coming into her life in the first place. I regret the fact that because of everything now I'm alo-"

Oliver caught himself before he finished his sentence and lowered his head at the thought of the word he left unfinished.

It pained the priest to see the agony Oliver could not express through his words. He knew where Oliver was going in his statement and realized it was a much deeper wound than simply the forthcoming absence of his mother.

"Now you're alone. You feel like you're alone now, don't you?"

"I don't want to ever be alone again," admitted Oliver as he broke out silently sobbing.

"You're not alone, Oliver. We're all here for you. We just met, but you should know we all care about you. We love you, son, and will never leave you to be alone again."

"But we just met."

"Time doesn't always determine love. I will care for you just like Mabel-Ara did."

"I don't deserve your love. I don't deserve anything."

"That's your shame rearing its ugly head again. Don't memorialize your pain in a place of punishment because you think you need to. This is not your fault. The one thing that has helped me cope with my regret surrounding the death of loved ones was knowing that their memory and life would carry on through me. Your situation is very similar. Ma died protecting someone she cared about. She left behind an amazing life with an amazing son to keep her name and memory alive. You must not judge or condemn yourself for the actions of others. This wasn't your fault in any way."

Oliver was shocked to hear this because this was the same piece of advice that Ma gave him when they spoke about forgiving himself back when he was having a difficult time sleeping.

"That sounds like something Ma told me. She told me to forgive myself and accept the things I cannot change because what happened in the past was not any direct result of anything I could've controlled. Our stories are written long before we're born. She told me to learn to forgive myself so I could, in turn, learn to forgive others. The only thing is, how can I forgive myself for not doing more to save her?"

"What could you have done?"

"I could have run back into the house and saved her. I could have saved everyone. I could have never come into her life in the first place."

"You not coming into her life would not have made her life better. Her last days were beautiful. Actually, a few days ago, she called me and told me she was planning something special for your birthday. She was so excited to tell me about her plans to adopt you. I'd known her a very long time and had never heard that type of excitement before."

"Really?"

"Yes, Oliver. She was so excited to have you join her family because you reminded her of herself. She had always been a fighter. An advocate trying to do right despite the temptations of the environment. You were her reminder of why she started fighting in the first place. She said you were like an angel who came into her life the moment she laid eyes on you."

Oliver had never heard this type of testimony before. He was surprised to hear the impact he played in her life because *she* was always the one impacting the lives of others.

"I am far from an angel. I've done some horrible things in my life."

"Angels don't always wear wings, sport a halo, or fly around heaven. Ma told me that," Father Nana replied.

"Did she really say all of that?" questioned Oliver, with a newfound interest glaring all over his face. He had stopped crying and his facial expression had softened.

"Yes, she did. She also said you had taken to the Bible during your time there. How has that been for you?"

"It's been good. I feel that I learn more about myself through it. I still want to believe because I know that's what she would want."

"Very good," replied Father Nana with a compassionate smile. "It's what she would want for you. It's getting late, so we should head back. You're an adult and free to make your own choice. If you'd like, there will always be a room for you in our home, shall you need one."

"Thank you, Father Nana."

As the pair walked down the aisle toward the exit, Father Nana grabbed Oliver's shoulder to stop him. Oliver turned back in surprise and with the look of hope beaming on his face, Father Nana made one last plea.

"Anytime you're feeling low and need a reminder why you should push through, remember it's Ma who showed us what love meant. Don't ever forget that."

Oliver smiled and they made their way out of the church and back to the house. To his surprise, Oliver found comfort in his conversation with Father Nana. He hadn't thought it possible but felt slightly better because he believed everything the priest had told him.

When they arrived at the house, they went to their respective rooms and Oliver fell asleep right away. That night, he dreamed Ma had come to see him while he was at Dunbar. In the dream, she didn't say a word at first, the two of them simply embraced for what seemed like an eternity. Despite her weak and gentle touch, Oliver sank in her embrace. He missed the firmness of her light touch, which made him feel like the whole world was between them and nothing else mattered.

Just as the dream was wrapping up, Ma whispered something in Oliver's ear.

"My son…if tomorrow wasn't promised, what would you give for today?"

Oliver retracted himself from her body and stared into her eyes. "I would give everything… I would give it all for one more day with you. I miss you so much."

"I want you to go live your life and go be great. Live each day like it's your last and as long as you keep your heart pure, I will always be with you."

He kissed her on her forehead and woke up right after that, and sank in her love until the sun came up the next morning. Her command replayed in his mind.

*****

Oliver took Father Nana up on his offer and the next day, he told Officers Smith and Jefferson that he was going to be staying in Chicago. He had no particular ties to New York and was looking for a new start. The conversation with Father Nana really helped him begin to address Ma's passing and he knew there was a lot more healing he needed. He knew that by Father Nana's side is where he needed to begin.

Like Ma, Father Nana was a very empathetic and caring individual who always acted in the interest of others before himself. Oliver knew he was impressionable and needed this type of figure around.

The officers agreed and left around midday the day after they arrived. They told Oliver that they were going to take care of all the investigation surrounding the house fire and the death of his family. They reassured him that there was nothing to worry about.

After they had gone, Oliver told Father Nana that he would stay as long as he could and planned to support them in the church. He promised he was going to get a job and assist with paying bills.

There was a memorial held in New York a few days later that Oliver could not bring himself to attend. He was not ready to return to New York and told Father Nana he preferred to do something small and intimate.

The priest obliged his request and held a small service in Chicago to pay his final respects to his fallen friend and her children.

*****

Oliver spent the next seventeen years in Chicago. He was given the nickname "O" by Reginald. They grew close but their relationship was nothing like the relationship he had with Jeremiah. Reginald had become more of a friend while Jeremiah, who was also once a stranger, was more like a brother. Although he lived with Father Nana, he was attached to the name Oliver Burke because of what it meant. It was one of the last things Mabel-Ara left him with before her untimely death and he didn't want to lose any memory of her.

Because of his circumstances, he chose to live with Father Nana, Amma, and Reginald for the first five years to get himself situated. He needed to mend the broken pieces of his heart and become whole again and knew this was the place he needed to do it. He was a man now and although knew he could not depend on anyone to pay his way through life, he welcomed the guidance.

Fortunately for him, Father Nana had many connections in Chicago which made the adjustment easier for Oliver. Less than three months after he arrived in Chicago, Father Nana was able to help Oliver secure a job with a national staffing company called Singular Staffing, which was based in New York City but had remote offices across the country.

He used this opening to prove himself to the company and with Father Nana's support, he continued investing in his development. He attended church regularly with Father Nana and even joined their choir. Ma had always encouraged him to sing, and he knew she would have wanted this for him. He had a very soft singing voice that allowed him to take on the role of a cantor. Every time he sang a solo, he thought back to the first day Mabel-Ara made him sing in front of others and smiled inside as if she was sitting in her normal seat beaming with pride.

In 2002, at the age of 32, Oliver obtained his commercial driver's license which helped him land a job through Singular Staffing as a bus driver in Chicago.

CHAPTER 20:

THE MAGNIFICENT MILE

Oliver Burke *Chicago, 2010*

Eight years had now passed since he received his commercial driver's license and Oliver was very happy with where life had taken him. At forty, he was getting a bit too stiff for basketball and his black hair had now been peppered with grays, which began at his temples. With age also came gravitas and wisdom.

Over the years, he attached himself to Father Nana and the many lessons the priest had to share. These lessons helped raise his confidence, understand his value, and even helped him find different ways to connect with people. He had been so closed off for so long, he loved this new change in himself. He was paying his own bills, living on his own and he even began placing money in a savings account. *Ma would be proud*, he often thought to himself.

Oliver was happy to have a job that he felt proud of. Although some days were tougher than others, he did not see himself as simply a bus driver. He knew his responsibility was to be more than that. He had to be someone whom others could look at and depend on. Someone they could trust.

In the forty years he had been alive, he had experienced so much. From the low moments he spent in the darkest corners of a cold jail cell to the high moments he spent with Ma, Jeremiah, and the others, he knew he had a lot of insight that others dealing with similar challenges could benefit from.

The streets of Chicago closely resembled the Brooklyn streets he grew up in and it frightened him to know that somewhere, there was a kid just like him looking for love. The gangs in Chicago were very bad at this time. Gun violence was all over the news, and it seemed like every day he watched a mother cry on the television about her child's life being selfishly taken by outlaw gangsters who lived by no code. Because of everything he had seen over the course of his life, he knew the pain these mothers were feeling and deeply sympathized with them. It saddened him to see others falling into the same downward spiral that he once found himself in.

*****

One Monday morning, when he clocked in for his 11 o'clock shift, his supervisor called him into the breakroom for an unscheduled team meeting. He told Oliver that there was something important they needed to discuss which worried Oliver because this was unusual. He thought he was doing well as a driver and was hopeful this surprise meeting was nothing to worry about.

When he arrived in the breakroom, he realized he was fortunately mistaken. When he walked into the room, he saw all the other drivers, sitting, waiting to find out what was going on. Like himself, he could see the worry on each of their faces and when his supervisor walked in, all eyes turned in his direction.

The worry on people's faces turned to trepidation when they saw a police detective in plain clothes enter.

Oliver's supervisor announced that one of the bus drivers from the overnight shift had been killed the night before which resulted in a collective gasp from the group. The detective then interjected.

"We don't have any suspects yet but believe it's attributed to the growing gang violence issues we all see every day. We simply want to remind you to always ensure your safety is prioritized first and never attempt to fight anyone off."

The room sat nervously and continued to watch as panic on their faces grew.

"We don't want to scare you, but this is a serious problem right now. We recommend taking longer routes to avoid certain neighborhoods that are known to have heavy gang activity. We're going around to public benefit corporations and issuing emergency mobile devices that can be used to dial directly to our public safety unit dispatch. I repeat…these phones should only be used for emergencies on buses, trains, etc. I can't emphasize how important it is for this to go right. There are several young punk kids looking to make names for themselves as gangsters. Don't try to be a hero."

After the detective finished his safety reminder, he left the room and Oliver's supervisor stepped up to hand out the phones.

"I probably shouldn't say this," he started as he looked back to ensure the officer was gone. "But I overheard the cops talking about the murder rate in Chicago and they mentioned we're not even halfway through the year, but it already looked like the city's pacing toward its worst year yet."

There was another collective gasp from the room.

"I don't mean to scare you. Just saying, the officers are the ones who get paid to fight crime, we just get paid to drive— remember that."

He concluded the meeting with a twenty-five-minute video on building business relationships, which the company put into place to protect their drivers. The video emphasized and encouraged their drivers to use the 5-10 seconds while riders are boarding the bus to find a connection point with them to observe and report any concerning individuals.

As a bus driver, this was not an issue for Oliver. Fortunately for him, he hadn't been involved with any situations during the time he was in Chicago. When he thought about it, Oliver found the people to be more friendly than people in New York. He wasn't sure if that was attributed to his maturity or the fact that people in Chicago cared more, but he loved it. He was proud to drive a bus and loved the many different characters he met daily. Some were loud, some were quiet, some dressed conservatively while others wore bright, loud colors. He loved meeting people and most riders loved riding on his bus.

There were many individuals he grew to know, but his favorite riders were two teenagers, Tremaine and Mike, who rode his bus twice every weekday. When he met them earlier that year as they boarded his bus, he overheard them talking about something he had just seen in a book he was reading. At first, he felt a little uneasy around them because they had the carefree swagger of most other young teens in Chicago. Because of the growing violence, he didn't want to take any chances. It wasn't until he heard them speak that he knew he was wrong. They weren't like the other young outlaws running rampant in Chicago. These boys wanted more.

He loved the fact that he was transporting the teens to and from school which made him feel like he had a special purpose when driving them. They were young and immature but seemed very focused for individuals their age, which made building a relationship with them very easy. After a few bus rides, the three of them had become fast friends. When they would board his bus, they typically sat in one of the first seats so they could chat with him during their commute.

Both young men had a boldness and confidence in the way they carried themselves which impressed Oliver. Their candor reminded him of Jeremiah.

*****

On the second Thursday of May, Oliver pulled into the bus station and saw Mike and Tremaine laughing while waiting for him. As the bus came to a halt, he received a chill up his arms from the rush of joy that sprung upon him. He remembered being their age and how different life was for him. He loved seeing their pure joy. They still had a chance to be better.

Once the bus finally stopped, the boys ran on, and Oliver greeted them with a wave and then turned his head back toward the front. He did not notice but Tremaine assumed Oliver's wave was the preface of a handshake and extended his hand to the driver. When he saw Oliver did not see his hand, he suggested they create a handshake that would signify an exclusivity that only their friendship had. Oliver laughed in agreement. He played off this invite as if he had received requests for private handshakes often, but deep down, he was ecstatic. He saw this as his chance to be what Rahzmel never was for him: a positive influence.

Before pulling off to the next stop, Oliver and the two teens quickly created a handshake that they would use as their greeting whenever they met. Tremaine made it up and Oliver admired his creativity.

On the very next day, Tremaine boarded the bus alone. Oliver looked surprised that the duo was separated and gave Tremaine a confused look. The teen mentioned Mike's allergies were very bad that morning so his mother said he could stay home.

"Is he okay?"

"Yeah, he's fine," replied Tremaine. "He just woke up this morning and I don't think he had any Claritin so his mom said he could stay home. We graduate next month, and I believe he has a few extra sick days so I don't think it was an issue."

"Well, that's good."

"Yo, O, I have a question for you. Why did you become a bus driver?"

"Why do you ask?"

"Because I graduate from high school next month and need to get an idea of what I want to be. For the longest time, I wanted to become a politician but I'm not sure I still want that."

"Why not?"

"Because there are really no other black politicians who stand for anything besides Barack Obama. I want to be like him when I get older, but it seems unlikely. Is it hard to become a bus driver?"

"Why? Do you want to become a bus driver?" Oliver remarked in a sarcastic tone while chuckling. He was proud of his job but also knew he would be doing something else if he could. He didn't want Tremaine to get that message and simply glared at the teen to display his comprehension.

"I mean, I wouldn't be against it. You're cool as hell and seem to be doing okay."

"Listen, Tremaine, I'm very happy to be a bus driver and really enjoy the conversations I get to have with people like you and Mike. Don't get me wrong, I'm happy. But if I could, I would've taken another route. I had a rough childhood which led me to where I am now. You're in such a great position to change the world and I don't want you to sell yourself short. If you want to be a politician, go be a politician. Don't aim to be Barack Obama, aim higher."

"That's actually some advice I got before," replied Tremaine. "There's this guy from my neighborhood, Roland, I know. Back a few years ago, I stupidly wanted to join a street gang because I saw that's what everyone else was doing. I dressed the part, hung around some gang members from my school, and even went as far as trying to buy a gun because I thought that's what I needed to do. What I didn't know was I was buying a gun from a member of Roland's street gang.

"Roland was a big-time gangbanger in Chicago. From what I hear, he had some hard times and changed his life around. When Roland walked in on me making the purchase, he yelled at the gun dealer and then asked me what I was doing. He saw how young I was and refused me from making the purchase. He demanded I go home, look my mom in the eye, and apologize for almost making the worst decision of my life. He told me I was the future and not to sell myself short to become another statistic on these rough Chicago streets.

"When I got home that day, I told my mom what had happened and what he said. She didn't know him well but knew of him because he lived in the neighborhood. She cried so hard that day because she was so disappointed in me. Watching the pain on her face was one of the hardest things I think I've ever had to deal with. That was the day I told myself I was never going to break her heart like that again."

"That's amazing. I'm so proud of you, T. I had someone similar in my life when I was younger. They were older but did not lead me to anything good like what Roland did for you. If anything, he tried to steer me farther in the wrong direction. What Roland did for you that day is invaluable. Don't strive to be a bus driver, strive for bigger and better. You graduate next month, and college should be the next thing you do. After that, go be successful and come back and change the world."

After that, the two exchanged their handshake and Tremaine left the bus. As Oliver pulled away, he realized that Tremaine was one of the people he was meant to help. Like what Roland told him, he too had the tools and experience to change Tremaine's life. He was excited to continue having regular conversations with the teen and to serve as a mentor for him.

Oliver felt like his goals as a driver were finally coming to fruition after seeing this. With so many young, black men turning to the street life, he was happy to see Tremaine turn out different. He was finally settling into the role he'd hoped for. The role Mabel-Ara played to him.

Over the next few weeks, Oliver continued with his day-to-day duties and when graduation day finally came, Oliver was overjoyed. He gave the boys their secret handshake and wished them the best of luck on their last day of school.

"I'm so proud of you both. Can you believe it? Next time I see you, you'll be high school graduates."

"I'm so excited!" Mike exclaimed. "We'll bring some pictures from graduation. This way you actually will believe we graduated!"

*****

A week had now gone by since the boys' graduation and Oliver had not seen either Tremaine or Mike. He didn't find this unusual because he figured they did not have to attend school any longer so there was no regular cadence on when they were going to ride the bus. After another week had gone by, Mike finally boarded his bus alone.

"Hey, Mike. You okay? Where's Tremaine?"

Mike instantly broke down in tears so Oliver walked him over to the first available seat behind him.

"Tre…Tre…Tremaine is dead, man." He attempted to catch his breath as he spoke but struggled. Oliver wore his shock as he tried to calm Mike down. After a few minutes of hyperventilating, his young friend was able to settle down and continue.

"Someone killed Tremaine on the night we graduated."

"What?!?"

"Yeah, some lady. Just shot him because she thought he was someone else. He's gone, O. She killed him."

Oliver was shaken and saddened by the news. He expressed his deepest condolences to Mike and told him to keep his head up. He shared his contact information with Mike.

"Please call me if you ever need someone to talk to. I will always pick up."

He was shaken by the news. He hadn't lost anyone close to him in years and cursed Chicago for taking another one of the good ones.

After completing his shift that evening, Oliver parked his bus and sat in silence as he recited a prayer for Tremaine. He saw so much potential in the young man and wished he could have done more to save him.

Despite Tremaine no longer being able to be there with his mother, Oliver knew he was in a better place. He recited the same prayer Father Nana recited the night he came to Chicago. In his prayer, he asked Ma to watch over his young friend and asked that she give his mother strength in her grieving period. He continued with his life and was honored when Mike introduced him to Tremaine's mother as their friend, "O."

*****

Five years after learning about Tremaine's passing, Oliver received a call from a number with a 917 area code. The last time he saw a number like this was when he was in New York. He knew there were only a handful of people in New York whom he kept in contact with. Outside of them, he didn't know this number and decided to ignore the call. His life was so good, he did not want any issues, so he declined the call and proceeded as normal. Moments later, the same number called back and left a voicemail.

On the voicemail, there was an elderly woman's voice asking Oliver to call her back. When he finally called the number back, the same woman's voice introduced herself as Calvin Smith's wife and claimed to be calling because the retired officer had passed away. She mentioned that he went peacefully in the night, and they were planning on holding a memorial that weekend. She claimed that Calvin spoke very highly of Oliver for a long time and that she would love it if he could make it. Oliver agreed and shared similar sentiments about Officer Smith.

"I will see you in a few days."

CHAPTER 21:

WHAT GREW IN THE ASHES

Oliver Burke   *Manhattan, 2016*

That first weekend in January, Oliver arrived at the church with Father Nana, Amma & Reginald. They had traveled to New York together to pay their respects for the now-deceased police officer, whom they had all known.

As they proceeded inside, Officer Smith's wife, Rachel, greeted them at the door with a hug and kiss on the cheek. She had met Father Nana previously and displayed her joy to see him and his family again through a faint smile that hid her hurt.

Beside her stood Officer Jalacie Jefferson who had also aged significantly since the last time Oliver had seen him. His age was displayed through the salt and pepper hair and sluggish body frame that now demarcated him. Oliver hadn't aged like Jalacie, but he had grown a few of his own gray hairs. They hadn't spoken on the phone in some time and hadn't seen each other in over a decade.

When Oliver walked in, the two of them stood there and just stared at each other until Oliver found his voice. He rushed up to the officer and whispered in his ear, "I am so sorry," as they shared a heartfelt embrace.

"Thank you for coming back, Oliver. I know it means a lot to Rachel that you're here. It means a lot to me also."

"I would have never missed my opportunity to pay my respects to Calvin. The two of you were there for me when no one else was and now it's my turn to be here for you. How were his last days?"

"They were good. He went peacefully. He was much older than me, but he lived a wonderful life filled with love and care. It was his time."

The two men ended their embrace, and Oliver and his company proceeded inside to their seats.

During the memorial, the priest shared some stories about Calvin Smith and then said a prayer for him. Officer Smith's wife and son then spoke about him and how he was as a father and husband. Last to head to the podium was Jalacie Jefferson who spoke about who Calvin Smith was as a police officer, a partner, and a brother, with or without the badge. In his message, he mentioned how much Calvin had shown him when he first came into the department.

"Calvin took me under his wing because that was the type of person he was. He always saw the best in people, and it made this young, once baby-faced officer very comfortable joining the police force during a very scary time in Brooklyn."

While Officer Jefferson spoke, Oliver looked around the room and saw a beautiful middle-aged white woman with brunette hair staring at him from two isles back. They exchanged the occasional glance and every time they caught eyes, he saw her smiling. He saw her wide smile and compared it to the bright smile his adoptive mother used to display when she was happy with him.

After the service, Oliver saw Jalacie standing by the entrance thanking guests for coming. Jalacie pulled Oliver to the side.

"What are your plans back in Chicago?"

"To be honest, I'm really enjoying my life there," replied Oliver in a tone that sounded like he was convincing himself. "I have a job, my own apartment, and I'm only a short ride from people I care about. What more could I want?"

"You could want more," Jalacie countered.

"What else do I need?"

Jalacie saw how well Chicago had treated Oliver and was happy he found a future there.

"After you left New York, Calvin and I came back to Brooklyn and took over the youth development program that Ma used to run. We didn't want her memory and impact on the community to disappear with her passing. We signed up to take over the program she created at the youth center to help move it forward. Calvin retired before me and even after his retirement, he helped me run the program. Now that he's gone, I'd like to ask if you'd be interested in working with me on this?"

"Are you offering me a job?"

"No, not a job. This is something we did outside of our normal work. We don't get paid for the work we do. It was important to Mabel-Ara and so it was also important to the two of us."

"Ma loved being there for kids who needed a better way. I am a result of her efforts and think I may be able to help. It may also be a nice change to come back home."

Just as they were wrapping up their conversation, the beautiful brunette from earlier walked out of the church and approached Jalacie.

"Hi, Amerie. Thank you again for coming."

"Hi, Jalacie. Again, I'm so sorry about your loss. I'm happy I could be here."

"Thank you." He then looked over to Oliver, who stood beside him with a bashful smile.

"Amerie, have you met Oliver?"

"No, I don't believe we've met yet, but he did catch me staring at him a few times inside," she joked, again exposing her beautiful smile. Her dark eyes stared as she extended her hand. "Hi, Oliver. Nice to officially meet you. Didn't mean to stare you down inside. How did you know Calvin?"

"He and Officer Jefferson …I mean Jalacie were friends with my father."

Jalacie laughed. "Do you still refer to Mabel-Ara as your father?"

"Yeah, I do. It's a bad habit," he joked. "She was really my adoptive mother. I got into this habit of referring to her as my father depending on the context of the conversation. You know it was always easier to just say my father to avoid the judgment that came when I told people I didn't have a father. But yes, Jalacie and Calvin were friends with my mother, Mabel-Ara Burke, so I've known them for a while."

"Oh, that's nice. I'm sure she's a sweet lady if she's friends with these two characters."

"She actually passed away some time ago, but yes, she was very special."

"Oh, I'm so sorry for that."

"It's okay," replied Oliver with a smile. "The three of us have quite the history. Hopefully, I can tell you about it sometime."

"Yeah, I'd like that. Well, I should be heading out. It was so nice to see you again, Jalacie. Oliver, it was very nice to meet you. Hopefully, I'll see you around more."

She then departed the church and Oliver looked at Jalacie with a smile.

"I know what you're thinking Oliver and yes, she's single. She works as a nurse at New York-Presbyterian in lower Manhattan. She was married before and was divorced a few years ago. Want me to set it up?"

Oliver smiled at Jalacie, "It would definitely give me more incentive to move back to New York."

"Perfect! I'll set it up! I'm glad you're deciding to stay!"

*****

Shortly after the memorial, Oliver moved back to New York, as promised. The city he left behind close to two decades ago had changed so much since he was last there and he was excited to fully immerse himself back into it. The trains and streets were cleaner, the once-popular oversized clothing trend had been taken over by tight jeans, polo t-shirts, and man buns. Even the drug trade was different. The once-revered drug dealers had become irrelevant in comparison to the drug users and musicians who glorified them.

Chicago didn't grow as quickly as New York. Oliver saw some of these trends occurring during his time in the Windy City but assumed they were nothing more than one-off fads that would die as quickly as they started. Despite the major differences, Oliver found this version of New York to be much better than the city he grew up in. Violence was down and people seemed generally happier.

When he arrived back in New York City, Oliver quickly found a place in Brooklyn with Jalacie's help. His small studio apartment was a short train ride away from the youth center and an even shorter ride from Manhattan. This was perfect for him because he had quickly found a job in the city through Singular Staffing. Their main office was in Manhattan, and they were able to quickly assign him to work in Lower Manhattan.

His role was as a building security guard at a large edifice called the Triage Tower. When he first started working there, Oliver was uneasy about his job. He loved his new role with Singular but was very intimidated by the "clients" he would be serving. He did not fear the security aspect of the job. His fear was derived from the fact that he knew there were very high-level executives who were moving throughout the building regularly. He felt, compared to them, he was minuscule and not as educated which meant he was immaterial. He assumed this was enough of a reason for them to look down on him and treat him differently. What also made it worse was the fact that his shift supervisor, who had worked in the building for a few years, advised him not to look any of the brokers or executives in the eye and not to speak to them unless spoken to first.

"The executives are very proud people. They think they run New York City because of their expensive education and huge salaries. I would avoid making any eye contact if I were you. Just keep your head down, make your money and go home."

Oliver understood this and started his time off very quietly. He completed his daily rounds and when he was not walking the grounds, he was positioned in the security booth which was in the parking garage beneath the building. He assumed all days would be quiet and he could remain under the radar and get paid. It wasn't until he met one of these executives that his perspective on everything changed.

*****

One morning, about a month after starting his new role, Oliver was sitting in the booth watching the cameras on the floors when he was approached by a heavyset black man with a dark Caesar haircut, tailored gray pinstriped suit, and a big smile on his face. The man stated he misplaced his ID badge and was hoping Oliver could assist him with securing a new one. Oliver thought he had seen this man before and knew he worked in the building, but he still followed protocol and asked for his driver's license to confirm his identity. The heavyset man reached into his wallet but before handing over his identification, he extended his hand.

"Hi man. I'm Eugene Garry. There you go, here's my license."

"Thank you, Mr. Garry, I will confirm your identity now."

"Thank you....um...what's your name?"

"My name is Oliver, sir. Oliver Burke."

"Nice to meet you, Oliver. You're new here, aren't you? What happened to Rodney?"

"I'm not too sure about Rodney, sir, and yes I started about a month ago."

"No need to call me sir. We're both men," replied Eugene again with a big smile. "You can call me Eugene and I will call you Oliver unless you prefer to go by another name?"

"Ummm… some people call me "O" or Obie."

"Great! I like that. I'll call you OB for Oliver Burke. Clever," he remarked as if he had come up with the name himself. "I like that nickname."

"Thank you, Eugene. That works for me. Here's your new badge."

"Thanks, OB. I'll see you around."

"See you around as well, Eugene."

Oliver left that conversation very happy. He did not know who Eugene was but knew he may have been someone important because of his proper vernacular, eye contact, and body language. He was impressed by how he carried himself. He also wore a certain confidence that was high enough to inspire others, but low enough that it wasn't mistaken for conceit. Oliver was impressed.

On his way home that night, Amerie called Oliver on the phone.

"Hi, Oliver. How are you? How was your day?" she said. Her voice was emphatic—she really wanted to know.

Oliver was hesitant. People as beautiful as Amerie didn't usually care how he was. "Good. It was good, I guess."

Amerie was undeterred. "Great! I'm so glad it was a good day! Why don't you come over to my apartment for dinner and a glass of wine tonight?" Oliver accepted her invitation, but he was nervous.

When he arrived, she opened a bottle of wine. Soon, a big meal of Italian takeout arrived. They sat down to talk and eat.

"Tell me all about your day," Amerie said. "What was good about it?"

Oliver didn't say much, though. He chewed his food and gave vague answers, saying only "yes" or "no" whenever he could. He liked Amerie a lot but feeling attached to a woman made him uncomfortable. He had not been with a woman in this way in many years, which played into his hesitation. Amerie sensed a disconnect in him.

"You're very quiet tonight."

"Oh yeah?"

"Yeah, seems like I'm asking all of the questions," she remarked. "Is everything okay?"

I really like her. Stop being stupid Oliver.

"Yeah, everything is fine," Oliver lied. "I'm sorry I just have a lot on my mind."

But he could not bring himself to have a real conversation, and the rest of the meal passed awkwardly. He went home after the meal and let the night replay in his mind until he finally fell asleep.

*****

Days passed and Oliver still had not spoken with Amerie since their dinner. He was very conflicted and upset with himself. *Why couldn't I just be more friendly? I really like her. I think she likes me. At least, she used to. There's no reason to distrust her.* He stewed over it for days.

Eventually, he decided to be better and try again. He thought of Ma. She never hid herself. He knew she would tell him not to hide himself. She would tell him to shine his light.

*****

Roughly a week after their dinner, he finally mustered his courage and called Amerie on the phone. It was now the day before Valentine's Day, and he was determined to make amends for his thoughtlessness.

"Amerie? It's Oliver. Look, I'm sorry. I was not very nice to be around when we had dinner. I'd like to try again. Would you join me for dinner tomorrow?"

He was ecstatic when she said yes and now, he was left with the task of planning Valentine's Day dinner.

I need to make it special to make up for being dumb.

*****

Around 4:30 p.m. on Valentine's Day, Oliver found himself sitting at his desk jotting down a few of the most popular chocolates and the stores he knew would be carrying them. He never celebrated the holiday and wanted to make sure he did it right. When he looked up from his scratchpad, he saw Eugene standing in front of him with the same jovial presence he had during their previous encounter.

"Hey, OB! What's up, man. How's it going?"

"Hi, Mr. Ga…. Eugene. I'm doing well."

"What you got there?" remarked Eugene peering over Oliver's desk.

"Well since it's Valentine's Day, I'm making a list of stores that carry popular, expensive chocolates. The woman I really like has pretty good taste and I want to impress her. I want to get her something she might like."

"Might like?" replied Eugene with an accompanying laugh. "What's the point of getting her something she may not like?"

"To be honest, I've never really celebrated Valentine's Day like that so I'm not sure what to get her."

"Well for me, my wife is taking my two daughters to see a film right now, which is why I'm leaving the office a little early. I told her not to eat dinner and to come straight home after the film. I didn't give her any other details besides that, but I'm planning on picking up a family photo that I had framed and cooking dinner. It won't be just any dinner. My daughters love spaghetti and meatballs so I'm going to prepare everything so that when they get home, we can finish cooking it together. I'm doing this because I know my three girls will love the thought behind it. It's one thing to spend a lot of money to make your girl happy. It's another thing when you spend time. I like to spend time with my girls.

"I tell you all of this because it doesn't matter how much you spend, if your heart is in the right place. I don't think there's a right or wrong gift. As long as it comes from the heart, I'm sure she'll love it."

"Thank you, Eugene. That's great advice!"

"Where you from Oliver?"

"I actually just moved here from Chicago a little over a month ago. I grew up in New York but moved to Chicago when I was a teenager."

"What made you come back after being gone for so long?"

"Um, my uncle passed away, so I came home for the memorial and decided to stay."

Calling Calvin his uncle might have been a white lie, but he realized at that moment he really did feel like Calvin and Jalacie were family. They were the bridge that connected him with the positive pieces of his past. Similar to how he told people that Ma was his mother and father, he wanted to limit the additional questions he may have received into his childhood.

"Nice. Well, I should be getting home to start prepping."

"Wait...I have one question for you before you leave. Why did you stop by today?"

"Why not?" replied Eugene in a very ebullient manner. "I saw you were working and decided to come in to say hello."

"Not many people would have stopped," remarked Oliver in a reticent tone. "Most people usually just walk by as if we aren't here. One thing I noticed about people here is that everyone's in a rush, which makes me assume they're important."

"Don't let everyone's haste and unfriendly demeanor fool you. This place is filled with a bunch of people like that. I think that's what's wrong with the world. People don't always stop to smell the roses. I'd rather stop and say hi now, while you're here, rather than wait till something happens. Just remember that people will not always remember what you told them, but they will always remember how you made them feel."

Eugene chuckled and then walked toward his car. Oliver watched in amazement as this Wall Street bigshot casually walked away after going out of his way to make conversation. He couldn't wait for their paths to cross again.

Instead of picking up the expensive chocolates for Amerie that evening, he attempted to emulate what Eugene told him and instead picked up some groceries. She was Italian and loved to eat. That night, he prepared fresh rigatoni with a Bolognese sauce that she fell in love with. She adored him and his effort and that night, they made love like it was their first time and they were both trying to make the right first impression.

*****

In May of that same year, they began a formal relationship which moved very quickly because they both had grown such strong feelings. The speed of their relationship made him uneasy at first. It reminded Oliver of his past on the streets, when a woman's affection was used to pull him into a hellish life. But he knew this was not that. He always reminded himself to trust. Amerie was different. She was simply trying to be an equal partner looking to support him through love and attention.

They did everything together and finally moved in together that August. She had a cozy one-bedroom apartment in Tribeca which she had inherited from her parents. The location was perfect because it was still just a train ride away from the hospital, his job, and the youth center in Brooklyn. Similar to his former studio apartment, Oliver's new home still allowed him the convenience of the MTA.

When they finally moved in together, Oliver confided in Amerie and informed her of the occasional nightmares he still experienced. This was the first time they would be sharing a bed for more than a few days at a time, and he knew it was best to be honest up front. He revealed everything.

"The nightmares wake me up and usually I'm confused and frightened. They aren't similar nightmares to what I experienced as a child, but in every one, I feel Ma is there. It's hard to explain, but she played a very large role in my life, and I can just feel her presence. She saved me."

It was at this moment that Oliver felt most connected with Amerie. He trusted her so much and decided to reveal the pieces of his horrible past, leaving no detail out. When he finished, she found herself embracing him to comfort him. She wasn't sure how to fully provide comfort but knew he needed it.

CHAPTER 22:

GREATER THE LOSS, DEEPER THE WOUND

Oliver Burke   *Manhattan, 2016*

On New Year's Eve that year, Oliver decided he wanted to do something special for Amerie because of how hard she had worked toward their relationship. 2016 was a good year for them both and Oliver wanted to carry that positivity into 2017.

This would be the couple's first New Year's Eve together and he wanted to make sure it was one to remember. Both were fairly conservative when it came to money and enjoyed any time they could get together. They regularly read together, watched TV together, and cooked together. One thing that really impressed her was how Oliver loved to randomly grab her to dance. She especially loved how every time they would slow-dance, he would serenade her with his singing.

Oliver had learned to cook from Amma when he lived in Chicago. He enjoyed making a few traditional Ghanaian dishes for Amerie, and would regularly find himself making his favorite, jollof rice: a dish with rice, onion, tomato, and meat—often called a staple of Africa. He loved when Amma would make her jollof rice with smoked turkey because of the splash of flavor it provided the dish. Although he had to worry about the bones, this was a small price to pay for the pleasure.

She grew to love all dishes because of their flavor, but even more, because of the time they got to spend cooking together. Cooking together was one piece of advice Oliver learned from Eugene. It was one of the main lessons he could never forget about one of their best encounters.

Although his favorite dish to make was Jollof, her favorite dish to eat was garri and beans. Garri is a floury grain with a slightly fermented flavor. It takes the taste of its accompanying dish, which in most cases is some sort of bean stew. Oliver would make this on nights when they both wanted something heavy.

He loved her Italian heritage because she liked to eat. They also loved making homemade pasta together. He knew food was the key to her heart and took advantage of every chance he could to unlock it.

In the past, he normally did not celebrate New Year's by doing anything extravagant. He usually spent it with a bottle of red wine and friends or family when he was back in Chicago. This year needed to be different. He brainstormed ways he could surprise Amerie.

Prior to that day, Oliver had overheard her speaking with a coworker on the phone about the restaurant, Beauty & Essex. From what he was able to gather, her coworkers were explaining their positive experiences, and he could hear Amerie's delight and slight envy. This gave him some direction on his planning, and he quickly reserved a table overlooking the entire restaurant.

*****

When they arrived at the address around 8 p.m. that night, they were greeted by a brightly lit sign which read, "Beauty & Essex." The sign sat atop the remnants of what looked like a former furniture store signage.

The couple looked around confused, unsure if they were at the right place. In front of them was a pawnshop with what looked like a cashier on one end and a tall, brawny looking gentleman dressed in all black on the other end of the room. The shop was covered with black and gold decorations which was their indication that they were ready to celebrate the New Year's holiday.

While they proceeded toward the cashier, Oliver, and the brawny gentleman connected eyes, but Oliver quickly diverted his attention back toward the cashier, who looked like he could care less. Before he reached the register, the brawny gentleman announced, "Bar or restaurant?" Oliver looked over and saw the bouncer now had a smile so he proceeded toward him.

Oliver wore his favorite roasted-almond-colored wingtip oxford shoes and a navy blazer atop a white button-down. Amerie wore a beautiful black dress that complemented her curvy figure. The bouncer looked them both up and down and joked that he could tell they weren't there to purchase a fake Rolex. He peered over Oliver's shoulder to connect eyes with the cashier who looked puzzled at the bouncer's slight.

He welcomed them to the restaurant with a smile and handed them a ticket which was to be used later for a picture to capture their evening. Oliver smiled back and walked through the door. He was surprised to see how beautiful the restaurant looked inside. To his right was a gorgeous white marble staircase with a dark wood railing. To the left of the stairs was a hostess stand which had two beautiful young ladies who looked no more than twenty-five years old. They both wore big smiles on their faces as they greeted the couple with a warm welcome. They announced that the couple's table would be ready in about 30-45 minutes, which they understood because of how busy the restaurant appeared. They offered them a drink at the bar for the wait which Oliver and Amerie happily accepted.

Once they were finally seated around 9 p.m., Amerie commented how much she admired the beautifully lit room, which fed into Oliver's confidence. He had planned the night so diligently that this was his confirmation that his planning had panned out. The small bit of narcissist in him loved to hear her rave.

This is perfect.

He ordered a bottle of Argentinian Malbec, which Eugene told him was his favorite. He too wanted a favorite and hoped Amerie would like it as well. The pair knew the night would be long and wanted to ensure they were able to stay up to see the ball drop. From their table, which was on the second-floor balcony overlooking the entire restaurant, they could see the adjacent balcony directly across from them filling with partygoers. Oliver had never celebrated New Year at this level before, so he was particularly interested in seeing how others enjoyed the holiday.

As the evening went on, Oliver and Amerie dined, danced at their table, and laughed the night away. They shared stories of past holidays and as they watched the rest of the restaurant, they joked about how their previous experiences had never been anything as extravagant. Oliver was happy to see the big grin on her face as they spoke about her failed past experiences.

It also made him think back to Eugene's advice on the importance of how you make someone feel. He was happy to be able to share in such a wonderful memory. Amerie hadn't had this much fun in years and like Oliver, she was happy they spent the holiday together. She expressed how excited she was to get back to work and brag about her night with her coworkers. Oliver smiled.

In the moments that Oliver was not conversing, laughing, or dancing with Amerie, he found himself gazing across the restaurant at the various other patrons enjoying their evening. There was one group in particular that kept his attention for most of the night.

In the adjacent event area, he noticed a group of younger individuals who were enjoying themselves to the company of beverages, light fare, and conversation. By the time their own food had arrived, the adjacent balcony had now filled with so many beautiful men and women who all wore dashing outfits that could turn heads in any room they entered. He watched as the wait staff graciously approached each of the patrons with a refill on beverages and various hors d'oeuvres. Oliver smiled at the sight of joy on each of their young faces.

Since the group had arrived, Oliver noticed one particular patron who stood out from the others. He was a well-dressed, younger black man running around greeting guests and working with the staff to ensure accommodations were correct. Strangely, Oliver felt like he remembered the man from somewhere, but could not recall from where.

Where do I know him from? He thought.

Oliver admired from afar and continued to monitor as this man circled the room. He could tell that this man was the steward of the night by how he tended to the needs of the visitors before his own needs. Oliver assumed he must have been the party promoter or restaurant host.

After a while, he noticed the same individual had now begun drinking with the rest of the guests and was particularly focused on one young, caramel-skinned woman for most of the evening. He realized his initial assumption was wrong and this was just another one of the guests looking to have a good time.

By the time the clock had struck midnight, both Oliver and Amerie were exhausted and ready to head home. They were much older than most of the other patrons in the restaurant that evening and did not care to party until the sun came up. Their cheeks were strained from the excessive laughter they had shared, and their feet ached. They both were looking forward to ending their night by cuddling in their shared queen size bed.

As the night ended, Oliver was happy with how it had turned out. Everything went off better than planned, but his curiosity had now peaked. He was still curious about who the mysterious stranger from across the room was and where he recognized him from. He was not usually star-struck, but something seemed different about this individual.

On their way out, Oliver stopped by the host stand and asked them which celebrity was hosting the party on the second-floor event space.

"I couldn't recognize anyone at the party but it seemed like they were important people. I don't really know anyone famous in today's generation."

The hostess looked into the computer and replied, "I'm unsure if there were any celebrities there but it looks like it's some sort of coming home party."

Oliver shrugged it off as he locked hands with Amerie and they exited.

*****

For days following New Year's, the couple continued talking about how perfect their evening was. Neither was used to anything so profligate, and Oliver was happy to see everything had proceeded better than originally planned. He assumed his greatest delight came from Amerie's happiness, but deep down inside, he selfishly knew that he found the greatest joy in knowing this gave Amerie something to boast to her colleagues about. She was not a braggart, but he was certain that she enjoyed being a part of these types of conversations with her colleagues.

*****

One Sunday morning that January, Amerie was awoken by Oliver's body wildly shaking. He was not having a seizure, but his body jerked awake as if he was falling and trying to catch himself. She placed both hands on his clammy cheeks, which were covered in sweat. When he finally opened his eyes, she noticed they were bloodshot as if he had been crying. She cradled his head in her arms, and kissed his forehead, reassuring him that everything was okay.

"Honey…honey…you were having a bad dream. It's okay. You were just having a bad dream. Are you alright?"

"Yeah, I'm okay."

"Did you have another nightmare about your mother?"

"I don't think so to be honest," replied Oliver with uncertainty in his voice. "I didn't see Ma in this nightmare. I felt like she was there, but I couldn't see her."

"What do you mean? What do you mean she was there?"

"I don't know. It's so hard to explain. It was just different," he remarked as he wiped his eyes with his hands. "I was in a windowless room with no sound. It was just me laying on the floor and all I could feel was a rush of various emotions hitting me one at a time. It was overwhelming and I was having a difficult time understanding it. Joy, love, fear, frustration, hate. I could not see her, but I knew Ma was there. The dream started off so pleasant. I couldn't see her but strangely felt so happy to be where I was. Outside of meeting you, I hadn't been that happy since she told me she was adopting me, and I knew this may have been her. I could tell she was there with me. I could just feel it."

"Is that why you woke up in such a panic?"

"No, it's not. The dream changed which caused my panic, I think. As I lay there, that love, and joy turned to fear and pain. I began crying because I felt I had just lost something very special to me. It was like there was a huge gaping hole in my heart. I assumed it was Ma but it did not feel as painful as it felt when I lost her. It felt as if I lost someone else I cared for."

"That's awful. I'll call Dr. Novak to see if you can get a therapy session for today. You've made so much progress since you started seeing him last year."

"I agree. I'm off today so I can go see him this morning. Thank you for always being there. It means so much to me to have your love and support. More than I can ever explain in words."

*****

Only two days after the nightmare, Oliver was back at work doing his normal rounds. The building seemed quiet, and Oliver hadn't had lunch yet, so he headed back to the security booth to eat and talk NBA statistics with his colleagues. He enjoyed being in their company because all three of the other security guards who worked on the same shift knew their information. He looked forward to their regular debates about who was the greatest player of all time; Kobe Bryant, Lebron James, or Michael Jordan.

Just as he was wrapping up lunch, Oliver's colleagues decided to tour the grounds for their normal walkthrough. After they had gone, Oliver noticed they left their radios in the guard's booth but assumed they had their cellphones on them in case anything came up. He disregarded and continued with his day.

While Oliver was sitting at the desk by himself, he peered over and saw Eugene walking back to the office from the parking lot, so he waved at him. Eugene normally did not drive out for lunch, so it was a little unusual to see him coming back at this hour. The corporate bigshot lacked his normal cheerful resolve and walked with unusual haste. He did not respond the first time so Oliver waved again, but when Eugene did not wave back or acknowledge the gesture with a reciprocating smile or wave the second time, he figured something must be wrong.

He must be late for a meeting or something.

Roughly ten minutes later, Oliver felt his phone ringing and saw it was a call from his supervisor, who was at another site that day. In the call, his supervisor told Oliver that there was a situation on the trader floor and asked Oliver to rush over. He did not receive any other details but still rushed upstairs. He didn't know this was Eugene's floor and when he arrived, he had no idea where to go or whom to see. Everyone on the floor was working as normal so there was no indication of an issue.

He continued to walk around until he found someone who frantically begged for his help.

"There was a commotion in the office over there," he remarked pointing. "I just heard something slam to the ground."

When Oliver opened the door, he saw Eugene laying on the ground with three men around him. Two of the men had sweat on their foreheads and looked disheveled and the third, who was the manager, was standing by the desk with his phone in hand.

"What happened?" He asked looking over at the manager. He then looked over at the two younger men who were sitting on the ground besides Eugene's still body with a look of guilt on their faces. Oliver quickly pushed them aside and began to perform CPR on Eugene's lifeless body.

"Contact the paramedics. Call them now!"

"I already did," remarked the manager in a tone attempting to separate himself from blame. "I called them."

"How long has he been like this?"

"He just collapsed," replied one of the young traders who still sat in disbelief at what was happening.

"I asked how long has he been like this!" barked Oliver as he continued CPR. After about ten minutes of performing CPR, there was no change. Oliver, who was breathing heavily, dropped his head and wiped the sweat that was running down into his eyes. In a somber and sad tone, he remarked, "What have you done?"

The paramedics then came into the room moments later and asked the same questions Oliver had. There was a very weak pulse that they were able to locate so they rushed Eugene out of the building into the waiting ambulance.

As he watched the ambulance drive away, Oliver thought about how bad Eugene looked. He, so badly, wanted to accompany him to the hospital but knew it wasn't appropriate. He spent the remainder of his shift in worry.

Before his shift ended, Oliver made one final trip up to the trading floor. He spoke with the manager about what had occurred because he needed to collect all the details.

Just as their discussion began, Eugene's manager received a call from Eugene's wife who stated that her husband had passed away. She claimed that the doctors were certain that his death was from asphyxiation. Oliver could hear how frantic she was and listened as she demanded answers about what happened. He could see her pain through the manager's face and knew there were no answers he could provide that would make sense. The manager wore a look of disbelief which was Oliver's indication that this was a terrible mistake. When he hung up the phone, he released a loud sigh and looked back at Oliver, who resumed his questioning.

As his questions continued, Oliver could hear his voice growing louder so he forced himself to calm down.

"Why did it happen?"

Oliver knew it was inappropriate, but also felt as if he, too, had lost someone close to him. He attempted to mask his questioning as a part of his incident report, but deep down, he was hurt that his friend was killed senselessly. "Why was Eugene so upset?"

"Well, we had just terminated him, and he became incredibly aggressive."

"When you say 'we' you mean you and those two young men?"

"No, I don't know anything about that."

Oliver felt a ball of emotion forming in his throat and there was so much he wanted to say but instead, he stormed out of the room before he could do something he may have regretted.

He rushed to the hospital, which happened to also be where Amerie worked and he told her what he believed happened. Eugene's wife was still there so Oliver asked Amerie to introduce them. They both spent the next few hours speaking about Eugene and what he believed had happened that dreadful afternoon. She told him that she had plans to sue, and Oliver reassured her that he would support her in any way he could.

Eugene's passing was devastating and despite it not being a personal loss, Oliver shared the pain Eugene's family was feeling. He was more confused at why everything had occurred the way it did and struggled to find answers.

His regret once again assailed him, forcing him to question how different the results would have been had he gotten to the room earlier or even if he stopped Eugene when he saw him rushing into the building that early afternoon. He continued seeing his therapist who helped him with coping mechanisms for dealing with nightmares and all the loss he continued to see.

*****

One evening late that January, Oliver and Amerie were out to dinner in the NoHo neighborhood of Manhattan. That night, as they dined, Amerie informed him that she had received an urgent opportunity to aid a Baton Rouge hospital that had not fully recovered from a recent hurricane.

"I was presented this opportunity and they would need me for six months. It should run from the end of January through the end of July."

Oliver did not know how to react to the news at first. Six months was a long time to be away from Amerie but he did not want to prevent her from taking advantage of the opportunity. He knew how much it meant to her and wanted to do what he could to support her. Fortunately for him, there was some flexibility in his work through the staffing company.

"I'm going to call the office tomorrow to see if they have any work down there. I'd love to be down there with you if that's okay. With everything going on here, it would be a good distraction for me."

"Of course, that's okay, my love. That would mean so much to me. I was worried about how you'd respond but there you are, creatively finding new ways to my heart."

*****

As dinner wrapped up, they decided to walk home to take in the cold breeze. After turning from Houston St. onto Thompson St., Oliver thought he saw the same man from the New Year's party at Beauty and Essex. He was unsure if it was this individual at first, but as they approached closer, he confirmed it was him and what looked like his twin brother, because of the resemblance between them. They were casually talking outside as they walked out of the A-lister Italian restaurant, Carbone, toward their waiting SUV.

Oliver tapped Amerie and asked her if she too remembered seeing this younger man, which she confirmed she did. He considered introducing himself and telling the man of this unusual coincidence, but before he could do so, he watched as the man grabbed the two bags of leftovers and crossed to the adjacent alley.

Oliver and Amerie both stopped walking and watched as the man handed the bags full of leftovers to a man sitting on a cardboard box in the empty alley. The sight of this sent chills up Oliver's spine as he gripped Amerie's hand. He wasn't sure if the two men knew each other, but he still saw the gesture as meaningful. Before Oliver had a chance to introduce himself, the young man quickly jumped in the waiting vehicle, which already had his brother in the backseat, and pulled off. Everything happened so quickly.

As they drove away, Oliver and Amerie continued on their path home. Oliver was impressed by what he had just seen. He considered going back to the alley to speak with the man himself, but Amerie wanted to get him home. The gesture reminded him of the various people in his life who made a similar impact on others. From the officers finding him beaten and bloody on the side of the street to Ma welcoming him into her home, he smiled at the thought of the amazing efforts of someone who cared.

*****

The next day, Singular Staffing's Baton Rouge office confirmed that they did have a role available at a local elementary school. They informed Oliver that the role was maintenance, which wasn't his forte, but he was ready to take on this new task.

When he arrived for his first day on Thursday, February 1st, he learned the role was more janitorial than maintenance. He called the office to confirm if this was the correct role he was assigned. When they confirmed, he inquired if there was a more appropriate placement based on his skill set but was informed that there were no other short-term opportunities that met his parameters.

"There are no other roles for you at this time and you can take it or leave it," remarked the administrator in a tone absent of empathy. He decided he would work as a janitor at the school just so he could stay with Amerie. The one main benefit he found was the school year ended a month before Amerie's assignment was over so he could use that time to explore Baton Rouge with Amerie before heading back to the Big Apple.

327

CHAPTER 23:

SUGAR STATE

Oliver Burke   *Baton Rouge, 2017*

As his first day as a janitor came to a close, Oliver recapped his shift in his mind and was saddened by the thought that this would be his life for the next six months. He was grateful for the opportunity to make money and be in Louisiana with Amerie, but knew he would be unhappy with his job duties.

Just as he was making his way to clock out, he saw an African American man, who was much younger than him, speaking with an African American woman much older than both of them. The two of them were right beside the time clock and he knew he needed to get past them to officially end his day. As he approached, they both looked up and greeted him with a smile.

The elderly woman introduced herself as Mary Sillioux but said that most people called her "Ms. Mary." The younger gentleman introduced himself as Peter Castile and informed Oliver that they both were cooks at the school. Oliver introduced himself as Oliver Burke but informed them that most people called him Obie.

"I'm just starting here as a senior custodian," Oliver remarked in an effort to give his role some importance. "That's it for today."

They both joked and expressed their joy to see "another black man with a job," which confused Oliver at first, but he disregarded their playful comment. These were the first friends he had made at the school, so he began asking them various questions about the school, city, and students. Ms. Mary began explaining, but before she could finish describing the city, Peter interrupted and apologized because he needed to cut their conversation short.

"I have another part-time job at a diner which I'm running late for. See you both later!" He barely finished his last words before rushing through the exit door.

Ms. Mary stayed a little longer as she waited for her ride. She continued explaining everything to Oliver.

"The school is outdated, ya hear. We been complainin' fo' years, but the school distric' ain't get it togetha. I just keep my mouf shut and get my money, honey," she remarked in a manner displaying her heavy Creole accent.

"How are the students?" questioned Oliver.

"The students are nice fo' da most part. Dere are a lot of black students here and I feel da school don' invest in dem like dey should, ya hear? Dis cause dem not caring about nothin' roun' here. Don' get me wrong, not all students is bad, but I don' been roun' here a while and seen more students quit or fail out befo' dey graduation. It's so sad."

"How long have you worked here?"

"How old ya is, baby?" she questioned with a giggle.

"I'm forty-seven."

"Let's just say I started workin' here when you was runnin' around your mama's house in diapers wit' ya binky in your mouf," she joked as they exited the building. Oliver again smiled at her heavy accent as he attempted to decode her words.

As he watched her get into the waiting Chevy Buick, he thought to himself how nice she was.

Her accent was so heavy. She must have been born and raised out here.

Oliver made his way to the bus stop and caught the L490 bus back to the condo that he was staying in with Amerie.

*****

Over the course of the next few weeks, the relationship between the three colleagues grew quickly. They all worked the morning shift, so they became familiar with each other's routines and even created a regular system of picking up coffee for each other. Each of them functioned better with caffeine and because of their early shifts, they made it a priority to have a cup before starting their shifts. Unfortunately, the coffee provided at the school wasn't that great, so they would pick up a coffee from other places on their way in.

Ms. Mary was an elderly heavyset black woman with a heavy creole accent who loved to talk and laugh. Cooking was her favorite thing to do, and she used it as an outlet to keep busy. She was well over the retirement age but enjoyed working at the school to stay busy. She was very joyful and a proud mother to nine children and grandmother to five. This strong motherly figure carried into her work relationships as well which was why both Oliver and Peter loved being around her.

Peter Castile was much younger than Ms. Mary. He was a slim black man with braids in his hair, glasses over his eyes, and a phone always on his waist. He had worked at the school for some time, but every time Oliver spoke to him, Peter was full of enthusiasm and excitement for life. He didn't have as strong of an accent as Ms. Mary, but Oliver could tell he was also from there.

He regularly spoke about his girlfriend, Ramona, and her daughter Annalise, whom he called his own. During that period, Oliver learned about Peter's rough upbringing which helped the two of them to connect. Like Oliver, Peter had also been involved in the drug game in his early teen years. He too was able to make it out and fortunately for him, he was able to do a few years in college before having to drop out to come home to care for his ailing mother.

What Oliver admired the most about Peter was he did not allow himself to be a product of his environment. Oliver learned that Peter was working on opening a resource center for children who needed a place to go when they couldn't go home. He knew how different both of their lives would have been had something like this existed when they were children.

There were so many young black and brown kids like himself who needed a safe space that could separate them from the streets. Peter regularly spoke about how he saw a lot of people lose their lives to the drug trade and every death or arrest took a greater piece out of him. He knew the only way he could be whole again was to actualize this safe space.

*****

By the time April had arrived, Oliver had changed his views on his work situation. Ms. Mary and Peter made work enjoyable, and he looked forward to going in every day. Ms. Mary's ability to turn anything they were speaking about into a story that began with "back in my day" or "look here honey," made every story she told captivating. The way she brought her story to life through her storytelling was a skill Oliver admired. Despite his regular skepticism toward her details, he knew there was always some truth to every story she told. He appreciated her efforts to entertain.

Through Oliver's storytelling, Ms. Mary had learned about Reginald, Amma, and Father Nana. Since he moved out of Chicago, he kept in contact with them through group chats and the occasional phone call. With the huge revolution of smartphones and social media, staying connected was easy.

*****

One evening, Jalacie and Oliver were catching up over facetime about life when Jalacie told him about a horrible news broadcast he had just watched that detailed a brutal home invasion, resulting in a triple murder-suicide in Jersey City, New Jersey. Jalacie had moved to Hoboken a year prior and had developed a habit of informing Oliver on the happenings over the Hudson. He told Oliver that the news broadcast was airing again at 10 p.m. and Oliver told him he was going to log in through his computer to watch. Jalacie had always been one of the smartest people he knew, so if he suggested Oliver watch, it meant it was a story he didn't want to miss.

When he watched the broadcast that evening, Oliver was horrified at what he saw. He watched as the news reporter described a brutal home invasion in a luxury apartment building that left four people dead. He clung to every word and dropped his jaw at what he saw next.

There on the screen was the same young man who had partied in Beauty & Essex and handed the homeless man the bag of food. The same man who had previously seemed joyous and full of life stood beside the news reporter somber, sad and defeated.

He watched as the man, whom he learned was named Walter Benine, was interviewed about a neighbor, Santina Sanchez, who was killed in the attack. When they displayed a picture of the female victim, Oliver was sad to see it was the same woman who was with Walter on New Year's Eve. As the interview continued, Oliver noticed that Walter bore a resemblance to a pain he once wore after having his heartbroken.

I know that look.

Oliver knew the impact Father Nana had in his life and questioned if there was anyone there for Walter. He knew that when Ma died, his healing came from the many people who clung to him in his fragile state.

As the broadcast ended, Oliver began to think this was not just a coincidence. This was now the third time in less than six months that his path had crossed with Walter Benine's and he knew there had to be a greater meaning. Ma had always told him about the concept of "paying it forward" and it wasn't until this moment that he finally figured out how it applied to him.

He saw this unusual coincidence as his mother still guiding him, despite her absence.

This is Ma's message to be there for Walter. She's guiding me.

He looked over at Amerie, who was also watching the news broadcast, with both hands over her mouth to display her shock. He told her he needed to go back to New York at the end of the school year.

"I have a strange feeling that this coincidence is not just random. Do you ever think we're placed on this earth to change someone else's life for the better?"

"Yes, of course. I know we are."

"Well, I think this is my person... I believe I need to impact Walter's life for the better. I think he needs me."

She knew how much this meant to him and admired his big heart. She was in full support.

*****

Life continued as usual over the next few weeks. Oliver told Ms. Mary and Peter about the coincidences, and what he was planning to do when he arrived back in New York. They were sad to hear that he would be leaving them at the end of the school year but were happy to know he was leaving to do something so great. Their excitement inspired him.

Peter had also shared some exciting news about his plans for the resource center. He told them that the bank had agreed to assist with funding, and they wanted to meet with him to discuss specific details. Both Oliver and Ms. Mary were overjoyed to hear this because of how much they knew it meant to Peter.

They were happy to see Peter executing such a sizable dream.

*****

At 5 o'clock, one Thursday morning in late April, Oliver suddenly woke up from one of his nightmares, which were now not as frequent but still randomly occurred. Because Amerie was working the 7 p.m.-7 a.m. shift, he woke up alone in a pool of his own sweat. Feeling sick, he considered calling out that morning but felt compelled to make it to work because he knew it was simply another one of his nightmares. He called his supervisor to inform him that he would be in later than normal. His next call was to Dr. Novak.

Because he had arrived much later than normal, he didn't get a chance to sit down and chat with Ms. Mary or Peter as he normally did. He jumped right into his job duties when he arrived. By the time the workday had ended, Oliver found Ms. Mary in the breakroom grabbing her things and preparing to depart. They decided to depart together.

As they walked toward the school exit, Oliver began telling Ms. Mary about his nightmare from that morning.

"When I woke up this morning, I felt like something was missing. There was a gaping hole in my heart causing me to feel less than whole. It was like someone, or something was missing. Sort of like someone had left my life. I hadn't experienced anything like this in a while."

"Did ya recently lose someone, baby?" questioned Ms. Mary.

"No, I haven't lost anyone close to me recently but I have lost people in my life. It was so unusual. I felt this sudden feeling of loss and despair. I can vaguely remember details, but I do remember there was a highway or a car involved. Maybe a car crash?"

Ms. Mary looked intently into Oliver's eyes and when he commented on the car crash, she shut her eyes to hide her sudden sorrow. Oliver gave her a moment, then placed one hand on her shoulder to comfort her. She looked back at him, and he could see the anguish beaming in her glare, which was his indication that something about his nightmare was tormenting her.

When he apologized, all the fighting back she had done to hide her sadness stopped and her eyes flooded. She broke down in the middle of the hallway and he reached out in hopes of comforting her.

"I'm sorry, honey," remarked Ms. Mary as she wiped away the tears. "Four years back on dis day, my eldest grandson Jacobi was killed by a drunk driver wen drivin' home from a party at a frien's house. We called him 'Sugar' cause he was da sweetest little boy and so well-behaved. He was a good student and wantin' to atten' Penn State.

"On the night he was killed, I tol' him I didn't want him to go out. A mama's instinc' is so powerful and mines was talking to me dat night. He fought us so hard and we finally gave in. 'Don't worry, cher, I'll be back befo' curfew,' was his last words.

"He never made it back home dat night and I regret not fightin' harder for him to stay home. I was in a dark place fo' a long time, ya hear?"

"I'm so sorry, Ms. Mary," replied Oliver in a compassionate tone which displayed his empathy for her loss. "I also lost someone very close to me and fought regret for a long time after. I found peace in the company of my loved ones. I know how you feel and share your pain."

Oliver began to tear up as he thought about Ma and how much he missed her. Although different races, Ms. Mary reminded him so much of his deceased mother because of her presence and big heart.

As the pair stood there consoling each other, Peter approached. He was also on his way out of the building and saw his friends. Peter asked what was wrong, but both Oliver and Ms. Mary assured Peter that everything was okay. Oliver wiped away his tears and assumed his dream may have been aligned with Ms. Mary's grandson. This was unusual, but it was the only sense he could make of everything.

"You're bouf' beautiful young men," remarked Ms. Mary as she glared at Peter and Oliver, placing one hand on each of their cheeks. "I'm so excited to see you bouf' succeed at all ya dreams."

Oliver interjected with an accompanying smile. "I agree. Peter, you are an amazing person. I'm so grateful for our friendship and cannot wait to hear the good news about your meeting with the bank."

"Thanks, guys. I hope you're okay. I hate to see you crying like this, but I need to run. Let's talk about it later?"

"Don't worry Peter, we're okay," remarked Oliver as he stuck his hand out. "Thank you for everything."

"Okay, I have to run, but I will let you know how it goes." Then Peter quickly ran out through the exit.

*****

That weekend, both Oliver and Ms. Mary had reached out to Peter to inquire how the meeting went but they did not hear back from him. This was unusual since the only time he was unresponsive was when he was working. He was one of the only people they knew who still kept his phone holstered on his waist and knew it was no more than an arm's length away at all times.

That Sunday evening, Oliver finally received a call back from Peter's phone, and when he picked up, he heard a woman's voice that he did not recognize on the other end. The voice sounded despondent, and Oliver quickly knew something was wrong. As the woman whimpered while attempting to get her message out, she introduced herself as Peter's girlfriend, Ramona, and informed Oliver that Peter had been shot and killed on Friday after his meeting. Oliver couldn't believe it. She provided all the details of his murder and Oliver was shocked to hear Peter was killed by police officers during a traffic stop.

Oliver called off for his Monday shift and went to see his friend's deceased body one last time.

*****

Over the course of his life, Oliver had seen so much death and loss. From not knowing his real parents to the loss of his adoptive mother, he felt everyone around him was taken before their time. Even though he was still determined to regain control of the remainder of his story, Oliver realized this was the unfortunate truth of how his life's story was written. It was important now more than ever for him to go back to New York to meet with Walter Benine.

Something in Oliver told him they needed each other more than either of them may have known. He knew their meeting would be crucial for both of their healing.

After the school year had ended, Oliver said his goodbye to Ms. Mary. They agreed to keep in touch, and she promised to pay him a visit to the Big Apple with her entire family. She also prepared some of her jambalaya for his departure and they shared an emotional hug before parting ways.

Back at their shared temporary residence, Oliver and Amerie also shared a sad goodbye. Both of their eyes were brimming with tears as they shared their emotional farewell. She still had less than two months left in Louisiana and was saddened by the fact that she wouldn't see her man until she returned to New York.

Oliver knew how important Amerie's work was in the hospital and how much it meant to her. He loved her level of care and realized that he wanted to also affect something he cared about to make her just as proud of him as he was of her. As they embraced, he reminded her that she was his everything and he would make her proud.

"I'm already proud of you, my love. I can't wait to hear about your meaningful meeting with Walter." They ended their goodbye with a very long kiss before he boarded his plane home.

PART V
THE PURPOSEFUL OLIVER BURKE

CHAPTER 24:

LIVE IN YOUR LOVE

Oliver Burke   *Manhattan, 2017*

When Oliver arrived at John F. Kennedy International Airport late that June afternoon, he was welcomed by the extreme warmth from the glaring rays of the hot day. The blistering heat from the sunny summer sky beat down on his exposed neck while the humidity choked him. *I thought I was escaping the Louisiana heat*, he joked to himself as he herded with the crowd past a sign displaying DEPARTURES in capital letters. He traded the swamp, jambalaya, and southern hospitality for traffic, skyscrapers and a certain haste that only New Yorkers could get used to. He knew he was home.

As he exited the airport, he quickly decided it was in his best interest to flag down a taxi instead of waiting for an Uber. He could not stand to wait outside longer than he needed to.

While commuting home, he smiled at the thought of the warm summer days he used to spend causing well-intentioned mischief around Brooklyn with Jeremiah. The two of them used to race from one street to another as their sisters stood judge on who was the fastest. When he beat Jeremiah, he laughed at the facial expressions his brother made as he fought to hold back his embarrassment while attempting to regain his breath. He smiled.

As the taxi made a right onto the Belt Parkway, Oliver recalled another memory when he and his siblings were in church and Isaac had the bright idea to switch the lyrics for everyone in the choir, to throw them off. Like he had done many times before, Oliver agreed without incident and by the time the choir was singing their second song, Oliver could not help but laugh at the confusion. He blurted out in laughter at the knuckle-to-skull punishment Ma had given both boys as he scratched the same spot on his head to remember the pain. This was her go-to when she needed a quick reprimand for their mischievous behavior.

Oliver continued to chuckle until he felt himself being shaken. He opened his eyes and realized he had fallen asleep for the entire car ride and had actually dreamt about the summers back in Brooklyn. When he looked over at the driver, he saw the man sitting impatiently, as if his time could have been spent better elsewhere. After handing the driver his fare, plus a 25% tip for allowing him to sleep without disruption, Oliver smirked at his pleasure for the positive dreams.

When he walked into the house, he stood in their foyer just basking in the moment. As he stood, he remembered he had not called Singular Staffing to secure work. He had no interest in driving a bus in Manhattan nor did he want to work as a custodian ever again. He was hopeful that Singular's New York City department had some better placement opportunities for him. Fortunately for him, the staffing company had been very flexible with their assignments up until that point.

He first checked in with Amerie to let her know he had arrived safely, and he was thinking about her. His next call was to the Staffing's office. They placed him on hold and when the placement manager finally got back to him roughly twelve minutes later, they informed him that unfortunately there were no available assignments in the city at the time. This disappointed Oliver, but he knew he had been very lucky with securing assignments up until that point. This was the first time since he began working with them that they could not immediately place him, so he figured he should exercise some patience. He cordially agreed to be placed on a queue list and provided the manager with his contact information.

His plan was to use the duration of his unemployment to search for Walter. He did not know where to begin looking but knew he needed to do it. He assumed it made sense for him to retrace his steps back to each location he and Walter had crossed. This included Beauty & Essex, Carbone, and possibly even the apartment in Jersey City.

Just as he was looking to begin his search, other urgent priorities arose at their home which occupied his attention.

*****

Two months had gone by, and Oliver still had not received a call back from Singular Staffing. His search for Walter had also proven unsuccessful which began to frustrate him. He began to feel as if he was wasting away, and the feeling amplified when Amerie returned from Louisiana. The heat that August also did not help.

What am I doing with my life? Now Amerie's home and I'm still in the same place.

She had come home at the beginning of the month and began supporting the two of them. She knew Oliver was a proud man and reassured him that the money she earned was for both of them. As long as he gave her enough love and attention, she didn't care if he was employed or not. Oliver was happy to hear this, but deep down inside, he was still embarrassed.

As a man, how can I allow this? I need to find work immediately, he thought to himself regularly as he filled his afternoons with job searching and visits to the hospital to take her lunch.

"Since we got together, I've realized you have been more than just my partner," remarked Amerie one afternoon as they discussed Oliver's frustration with his continued search for work. "You've been a fresh breath of air, an inspiration, my reason. Everything I see you doing and what you plan to do for that young man means more to me than dollars. You don't need to ever make another dime and I will still be happy with your love. I think I can live in your love," she joked placing both palms on his warm cheeks. Despite her caring words, Oliver knew that it would not be enough for him to just support her emotionally. He had to do more.

In late August, he once again contacted Singular Staffing and told them that he wanted to expand his job placement availability to roles outside of just Manhattan. He agreed to jobs as far west as Newark, New Jersey, as far east as Queens, and as far north as Eastchester, New York. The placement manager felt bad for not being able to place him when he originally called and could hear the desperation in his voice. She announced that his expanded options had proven helpful because she saw a job opportunity in upstate

New York. Oliver knew it would be a long commute to get to work and back home every day, but he also knew it was work and he was desperate.

When Oliver asked what type of work he would be doing, he was told he would be a gravedigger. He was skeptical at first, especially having to be a gravedigger during one of the hottest summers New York had seen in a while, but when the administrator informed Oliver that she would continue searching, he accepted the assignment. He needed the money, and his plan was to take the job until he could find something closer to his home. Fortunately for him, full-time status as a gravedigger meant he had to only work three twelve-hour shifts a week and he would be paid by the hour. When she told him this, he accepted and made one last iteration of his interest in securing more local work when it became available.

*****

Labor Day weekend had arrived, and Oliver was hopeful that he would be able to find Walter Benine before his first day of work which was scheduled for right after the long holiday weekend. He wanted to start at the beginning and made his first stop Beauty and Essex.

When he arrived at the restaurant early that evening, he spoke with the manager, Demitri, who was very cordial, but also uncooperative.

"Unfortunately, I'm unable to provide personal information on our clients."

"I know, but I'm not some sort of stalker. I'm trying to help him," replied Oliver, who was frustrated at not being provided the information he sought out. "I can't go into details, but I really need to find him."

"I'm sorry I can't be more helpful, sir. As an establishment, we have a responsibility to safeguard our clients' information. Any breach in that could hurt our reputation and damage our relationship with our patrons. I hope you understand?"

"I do understand, Demitri. Thank you."

"My pleasure, sir. Maybe there's a friend of his who may be able to provide you with the information you seek?"

Just at that moment, Oliver believed Demitri had given him a helpful clue. He realized asking for personal information was not the best approach because of the security. He knew the next best way to find Walter Benine was through the people or things closest to him.

When Oliver arrived back home, he typed Walter Benine's name into Google. Right before he left Chicago, he had just started using the search engine to locate information and was hopeful this would spur useful results. He was right.

There were three results with information about Walter. These included an article from the New York Times which spoke about Walter and a fundraiser he had been a part of organizing in Bryant Park. Another one of the results had produced an article similar to the news clip he watched about Santina's death. Both links helped Oliver understand the type of person Walter was, but neither provided details that were new to him. Both simply confirmed what Oliver had already known, that Walter was a good man.

The third and final Google result that had Walter's name on it was one Oliver was not familiar with. It brought him to a page called LinkedIn with a picture of Walter's face beside his job title and company.

Associate Director of Client Relationship Management at Karot Advertising Agency, he read as he perused the page for any useful information. Karot was a very well-known agency and Oliver believed he had finally taken a step forward. He also read up on other details surrounding Walter which included his volunteerism, hobbies, and education.

His next search was for Karot Agency's New York office address. He realized that their office was very close to his apartment in Manhattan. Like Beauty & Essex, he knew he probably would not make it past the main security desk but still planned to try.

This has to work.

Fortunately for him, when he looked in Singular Staffing's directory, he noticed they did staff security in the same building that Karot was based in. His plan was set. He was going to visit the office right after Labor Day weekend and see if he could finally meet Walter Benine.

CHAPTER 25:

WEIGHT OF THE WORLD

Oliver Burke

Labor Day that year fell on Monday, September 4th and Oliver was excited to also have that Tuesday off. He was looking forward to relaxing before he found himself back in the work force. He knew he may not have had a better opportunity and decided to visit the Karot office that Tuesday.

As he approached the building security desk that morning, Oliver exchanged glances with the security guard who he noticed was not smiling and seemed uninterested in anything and anyone. He was slouched at the desk with what seemed like a nonchalant demeanor toward approaching visitors. Oliver noticed the guard was watching a video on his cellphone while he leaned back in his chair.

This is going to be harder than I thought.

"Hi, good morning. How are you?" remarked Oliver in a very excited tone.

"Hi, morning. How can I help you?" replied the guard in his carefree manner.

"I'm hoping you can help me find someone."

"Ummm… who are you looking for?"

Before continuing, Oliver looked at the guard's name tag and saw it read, "Rodney." He remembered a previous conversation he had with Eugene in which the fallen father of two mentioned there was a Rodney who used to work security at their building downtown before Oliver began. He knew it was a longshot but decided to ask anyway.

"By any chance, did you used to work security at the Triage Tower building downtown?

"Ummm yeah, I did. Why? Do I know you?"

"No, I don't believe we've met. I actually got your name from Eugene Garry."

Suddenly the expression on Rodney's face softened and his demeanor changed. A smile appeared as he found himself at the intersection between the excitement of being noticed and the anonymity surrounding this unknown stranger. "Oh yeah! Eugene Garry! He's a great guy. How's he doing?"

"Oh, you haven't heard? Eugene passed away. Long story short, he died from an accident in the office. I also worked security for Singular Staffing and was one of the last people to see him alive that day."

"I can't believe it. He was so nice. How could something like that happen to him?" remarked Rodney in a somber and surprised tone. His body language had also adjusted, and he now sat up while speaking with Oliver.

"It was a very sad day. Listen, I need your help with something. Do you know someone by the name of Walter Benine?"

"Yeah, I know Walter. Why, did something happen to him too?"

"No, he's okay. I was just hoping I could speak with him about something. Is he here?"

"I think he may have taken the day off to go somewhere. He was in the office very early this morning and left with a bunch of his coworkers. I think he may be traveling for work. He does a lot."

While Rodney was explaining, another elderly man who was also at the lobby desk approached the pair.

"Hi, gentlemen. I'm sorry to interrupt you. I believe I may have overheard you mention you are looking for Walter Benine? I'm also looking for him. I learned he worked in this building and was hoping to speak with him as well. Sorry to hear he isn't in today. I was hoping to thank him."

"What did you want to thank him for?" questioned Oliver.

"Let's step to the side so we aren't in the way," the elderly man replied with a smile on his face.

"Ahh, you're right. The story must be good then," mentioned Oliver as he shifted his attention back to Rodney. He extended his hand in appreciation, wished him luck, and thanked him for his assistance.

"So, what did you want to thank Walter Benine for?"

"Well…my family and I are street performers who regularly play music in Times Square. My wife, son, daughter, and I love to come into the city together to make beautiful music that others can enjoy. One evening a few months back, Walter Benine and his girlfriend came by and listened to us perform. I watched from my drum set as he wrapped his arms around her holding her tight. After we wrapped up our set, they approached us and thanked us for the music. His girlfriend had a huge smile on her face as she held onto his arm which made me happy to see. There was pure joy at this moment. That's how my wife and I started. There's nothing like young love!

"Later that evening, while we were wrapping up and getting ready to go home, a young lady approached us. She handed me an envelope and disappeared. When

I looked in the envelope, I saw that it contained a letter and a check for $10,000. Shocked and confused were probably the first two emotions that showed on my face. It wasn't until I read the letter that the shock and confusion turned into appreciation and gratitude.

"The letter spoke about how the music we played that night meant so much to him and his girlfriend. It also spoke to how it brought her so much joy that he felt compelled to act. The check's memo said, 'college tuition for the children' and had the note signed by 'an appreciative admirer.' I would not have known who it was from if the check didn't have the name 'Justice Benine' on it with a Jersey City address inscribed. When I searched the address, I saw it was registered to a Walter Benine and after doing some further research, it brought me here. That gesture meant so much to us that I wanted to personally thank him on behalf of my family. I've been looking for him for a while now and finally made my way here."

Oliver was amazed at what he heard. He gazed as the man spoke about Walter with such reverence and resolve. He was happy to see there were others who saw Walter for what he truly was. A man with a purpose.

The entire time the man spoke, Oliver thought to himself how much of a coincidence each of his crossings with Walter had been. Although they had not met, he knew all the previous almost-encounters were just the prerequisites he needed. What impressed him the most was the fact that Walter's selflessness was not found on the front page of any newspapers by his own accord, nor did he go around bragging and boasting about his efforts. Each act was done through the kindness of one man's heart without any apparent return or expectation.

Oliver and the elderly man shook hands and then parted ways. Despite not being able to meet with Walter, Oliver was satisfied with the results of his visit. He had finally met the infamous Rodney, gotten one step closer to Walter, and reconfirmed what he already knew. While departing, he confirmed to himself that he still had plans to return in hopes of finally meeting Walter Benine. Just not that day.

He smiled as he thought about the details of the elderly man's story. It reran in his mind and as it replayed, he heard the narration transition from the elderly man's raspy voice to Ma's gingerly tone which ended every sentence with young man, honey, or my sweet Obie. He smiled.

When he arrived home, Oliver shared the details of his day with Amerie. He could tell she was almost as excited to hear about this step forward as he was to tell it. The next day was his first day of work and he knew he had some long days of work ahead. Before bed that night, he gave Amerie a kiss on her forehead and thanked her for always being patient with him as he chased the goals, he set for himself.

*****

It was now October and after only a few weeks of work, Oliver began to think about his fatigue. He had only worked for a short time but felt like he had already been working for many years because of how rigorous the tasks were. He was able to work independently which was good, but the long workdays mixed with the temperature made it challenging on his aging body.

He was originally informed that he would work three long days a week but shortly after he began, a colleague who worked the other shift had resigned from Singular Staffing and Oliver was left to pick up the available overtime shifts until a replacement was found. Unfortunately, not many qualified people had an interest in working that far away from Manhattan which delayed the new hire process a bit.

He enjoyed making money but knew he wasn't doing work he was passionate about. His goal was to go back to the Karot office after he began this assignment, but since he began work, he couldn't find any time during the days he was scheduled to work. On days he was off from work, he didn't want to do anything but rest or spend time with Amerie.

When he woke up that morning, he felt more fatigued than normal. His head ached, his muscles were weak, and he could barely keep his heavy eyelids open. Although he was committed to his work, this day, he just couldn't do it.

He reached out to his supervisor and told him he didn't want to work any extra shifts because he needed to rest.

"I'm sorry, but I've been really tired lately. I think the extra shifts have taken their toll," he exhaled.

There was then a silence over the phone and Oliver was hopeful that his supervisor could hear his fleeted energy levels through his voice. He was right.

"I'm sorry to hear that, Oliver. You've been doing an amazing job and I think you've earned the time off. Get some rest. I will chat with you again soon."

Although his plan was to rest, he knew he had some unfinished business at the Karot Building. After hanging up his phone call, he went back to bed and when he woke up a few hours later, he felt more refreshed and was ready to restart his search.

*****

When he arrived at the Karot building that same early afternoon, he once again approached Rodney, who now had the look of an old friend after a long absence. He exchanged pleasantries with the guard and followed up by reminding him that he was there looking for Walter Benine.

Rodney told Oliver that he believed Walter was upstairs and when he directed his call to Walter's office number upstairs, he was surprised to hear a woman's voice.

"Hi, may I speak with Walter Benine please?"

"Ummm… I don't see him anywhere. Think he may have already left. Can I ask who's calling for him?"

"Sure, it's a friend he met at Beauty and Essex. I wanted to follow up with him on some stuff and kinda just popped by unexpectedly while I was in the neighborhood."

"Oh okay. Well, I'm sorry it doesn't look like he's here. I think he may have had a family emergency and may have already left for the hospital."

Family emergency?? He thought to himself. *What else can go wrong for this guy?*

"Okay, thanks. I can try him again at a better time. Who am I speaking to by the way?"

"My name is Malia Lowell! I work with Walter. Who am I speaking with?"

Just before he could answer, the line abruptly cut. Oliver, who now had a look of surprise, peered into the phone receiver and then back at Rodney. When he connected his eyes with the indolent guard, he looked beside him and saw that Rodney had accidentally disconnected the phone cable line while casually leaning back in his chair.

He asked Oliver if he was able to get in contact with Walter.

"No, but I did speak with Malia Lowell. Think she works with him. She said he left already."

"That's weird. Walter usually says goodbye before leaving for the day. I hope I get to see Malia though. She's gorgeous."

The two men shook hands and Oliver departed the building.

While standing outside, he considered the closest hospitals to their location and realized that New York-Presbyterian in lower Manhattan was nearby. He knew this was also the same hospital that Amerie worked at, which gave him another incentive to visit. He knew it was a long shot, but he had to try.

He decided to give her a call and playfully asked her if she was free for lunch. She loved when he was spontaneous like this and informed him that she wasn't hungry.

"Is there anyone with the last name Benine who was recently checked in?"

"I knew there was a catch," she replied with a giggle. "There is a Justice Benine who was checked in recently. Oh my! Is he related to Walter?"

"I think so. I think that may be his brother we saw outside of Carbone."

Oliver remembered hearing the name from the elderly man and knew this was his intended destination.

When he arrived at the hospital, he contacted Amerie who came outside to greet him, as she normally did. He briefly recapped what had happened earlier that day, sparing no detail, and told her he needed to meet with Justice. She knew it was against hospital policy for him to access a patient in this manner but made an exception for him. She knew what he was there for and was ready to support her man any way she could.

He walked past the reception and waved at the young, cute receptionist who, like Amerie's other colleagues, knew him as her well-mannered, unicorn boyfriend who treated her like the queen he believed her to be. He visited Amerie often and always made sure to say hi to her colleagues. They found no need for him to sign in.

Amerie walked him to the room which listed "Justice Benine" on the clipboard and also detailed information related to the patient and his injury. With a stern look on her face, she gave him a kiss and advised that he behave himself.

Oliver knocked lightly and without waiting for a response, he slowly cracked the door open, entering the room. As he walked in, he noticed Justice was laying on his back watching the television which sat on a dresser in the corner of the room. On his head were wrapped bandages and a glass of water beside his bed. Oliver noticed Justice didn't peer over at his arrival, so he announced himself. He watched as Justice diverted his attention away from the television in his direction.

"Hi, Justice. Sorry to spring on you like this. I'm Oliver."

"Hi, Oliver. Do you work with the hospital?"

"No, I don't. I'm a friend of your brother, Walter, and was in the neighborhood so I figured I'd drop in to check on you even though we've never met. What happened to you?"

"Okay…thank you. Nice to meet you. I'm still trying to piece things together. The last thing I remember was running toward a lady and her son to move them out of the way from being run over. I was in an incident downtown, and I guess I may have been hit?"

"It doesn't look like you were run over," replied Oliver while examining his body. "But it does look like you did hurt your head."

"Ahh, that's right." Justice reached the back of his head touching the moist bandage. "There was some blood coming down from the back of my head when I was with David and Moriah. How are they? Are they here?"

"Who are they? There was no one else here when I arrived."

"They're the mother and son I saved from being run over. That's right, they stepped out some time ago, I think to get some food or something. There goes my memory. I'm sorry, remind me how you know my brother again."

"I must admit, I haven't actually met your brother yet, but I was hoping he would be here with you. This may sound weird, but our paths have been indirectly crossing for a while, starting with Beauty & Essex.

Most recently, I saw your brother had recently lost someone close to him. Santina?"

"Yeah, it was horrible. Everything that happened with that was horrible. She was killed by her ex-boyfriend. Walter was so hurt. What do you mean your paths have crossed indirectly?"

"Well, the first time I was introduced to Walter was at Beauty & Essex. He was hosting a party and I was a patron at the restaurant. I sat and watched how you all enjoyed the evening. The next time I saw him was actually with you again. It was right outside of a restaurant around Houston Street in downtown Manhattan. You were leaving Carbone. The next time was when I heard what happened to Santina Sanchez."

"So that made you want to meet him?"

"Yes, but there's more. I lost a lot of people who were very close to me over my lifetime, but there was one loss that was almost too much for me to deal with alone. The pain in your brother's eyes closely resembled the look I had in my eyes, and I figured I may be able to help him like a few others have helped me. Although we don't know each other, I want to be there for your brother. I want to save his life."

"Wow. That's so dope. He was crushed after her death, and I didn't know exactly how to help. I stayed close to him and I think that helped. I'm happy you want to be there for him also. He needs good people in his life."

Oliver nodded in agreement as Justice continued.

"He should be coming by in a few hours. I called him not too long ago and he said he was going to finish up his day at work and then head over. I too wanted to be there for him because he helped me when we were much younger and reminded me how important family was. He's always helping people. That's just who he is."

"Yeah, the more people I speak with about him, the more I see how true that is. Right before I came here, I spoke with someone who mentioned he wrote him a check for $10,000 to help with college tuition for his children."

"$10,000?! I didn't realize how much he donated that day. I knew he gave money, but 10k?! That's crazy," he exclaimed.

"What impressed me the most wasn't the amount," replied Oliver. "It was the fact that he signed as an anonymous admirer for the children's future and didn't even deliver the check and letter himself. I love the fact that he didn't need to be the savior in that situation."

"My brother typically signs these types of donations as an anonymous donor or in someone else's name because of his belief in Maimonides' Eight Levels of Charity. He prefers to live his life as the person delivering the gift versus the person giving the gift because it allows him to give without any expectations. I admire this about him. You're more than welcome to stay and hang out until Walter arrives."

Oliver saw Justice yawn a few times during their conversation and knew he grew tired in his weak state. He thanked Justice for his time and took his contact number down, which he planned to use after he was healed. He asked Justice not to disclose the details of their meeting.

"Please don't say anything. When I meet your brother, I really want it to be organic. Please."

"Sure, I won't say a thing."

"Thank you, thank you! I'll see you soon."

On his way toward the hospital exit, Oliver peered into the waiting room, through the open door, and froze. As he stood there, he was flooded by a sea of emotions but was unable to identify which one made sense at that moment.

Was it confusion or was it fear? Was it joy or was it hope?

He couldn't exactly place his finger on how he felt and turned back around to look into the room.

When he peered in, a ball of doubt, with a small bit of hope, formed in his throat as his heart pace began to increase. He felt his stomach turning and his hands become clammy. There, in the corner of the room, sat an elderly woman facing away from Oliver, toward the television. From the back, she looked exactly like Ma which frightened him. From the white hair that flowed down the back of her head to her curled shoulders which were covered by her light pink cardigan. *Can't be.*

As the woman slowly turned around toward the commotion at the door, Oliver's eyes met hers. He finally exhaled when he realized it was not Ma. She closely resembled his deceased mother, but she wore a few more wrinkles on her face than Ma had the last time he saw her. The woman's back was also slightly hunched which was Oliver's indication that she too bore the weight of the world on her shoulders. Like Ma, she also wore the troubles of others, so they didn't have to.

He wiped the slow perspiration that began to form on his forehead and smiled back at her. He knew his head was filled with the ghosts that remained in the shadows left by his broken heart. Although the many years of faith, love, and hope had addressed his sorrow, there was still a hole in his heart that he knew could never be repaired. He accepted this fact and convinced himself that it was best. He told himself that he never wanted to forget Ma's memory. He could never forget his angel.

CHAPTER 26:

FALLEN

Oliver Burke

More than a week after meeting with Justice Benine, Oliver found himself on a long stretch at work. It was the morning of his eighth day in a row and he was once again exhausted from the long twelve-hour shifts he was pulling. The graveyard was about an hour and a half commute each way, which meant he was out of the house for more than half of the day. The overtime was good and his weekly paychecks were substantial, but it was not enough to completely satisfy him.

When he woke up at 5 o'clock that morning, he looked over at Amerie and saw her peacefully sleeping. She had just come off a sixteen-hour shift and he knew she would most likely sleep until about noon. He kissed her on the cheek and realized he was too exhausted to go to work today.

She's so beautiful. I'm so lucky.

He picked up his cellphone and decided he was going to call out of work. He wanted to just stay with her. When he dialed his supervisor's phone number, his supervisor did not pick up. He dialed him again and was once again directed to voicemail after a few rings.

He preferred to speak with someone directly instead of leaving a voicemail because it would confirm that the message was received. He decided to avoid any issues with not showing up and committed to going to work.

He again kissed Amerie on the forehead and whispered in her ear that he was heading into work. In a groggy manner, she replied with an "OK" that satisfied Oliver.

During his commute to the graveyard, Oliver thought back to his life and considered the decisions that had led up to him going into a job he did not care about. He had met so many great people who were truly passionate about the work they did yet he was not happy. From Eugene's modesty to Ms. Mary's compassion, they always made work seem like less of a job and more of something enjoyable.

The graveyard was different though. He worked alone and was left to just his thoughts. This level of isolation reminded him of his days in the isolation chamber at PACC. As he grew closer to the graveyard, he found it harder and harder to convince himself why he was leaving the love of his life to go be alone.

Why am I doing this? The work I do doesn't even matter.

*****

This particular afternoon, Oliver was having a late lunch on a bench while the sun beamed on his head full of salt and pepper-colored hair. On most days, he could hear birds chirping or the sound of visitors moving between tombstones, but this day was different. This day wore an unusual silence that was both eerie and peaceful. All he could hear was the noiseless sound of the sun's rays shooting down on the open space around him.

The sun was at its highest point for that day, which made Oliver glad that he had packed a few extra bottles of water in his bag.

As he sat in silence, enjoying his sandwich, he could faintly hear a man's voice. The voice was a good distance away and Oliver was unable to make out the words, but from what it sounded like, there was some level of distress in the tone. He ignored it and returned to his sandwich.

A few moments later the same voice was back, but this time it was louder and sounded as if the person behind the voice had yelled, "How have I wronged you?"

Oliver's curiosity peaked and he assumed there was a conversation being held between two or more people. He became giddy at the fact that others were there, and his afternoon was not going to be spent alone. He decided to locate the source of the unusual plea to quench his thirst for information.

He wrapped his half-eaten sandwich, placed it back in his knapsack, and grabbed his shovel. He proceeded in the direction of the voice and continued to peer around as he motioned. As he grew closer to the source of the sound, he saw what looked like an African American man sitting under a tree. The man had both hands covering his face as if he was crying, so Oliver assumed he was upset about something. He didn't know what was going on and knew he had no business there.

He turned around and just as he was about to walk away, he heard the sniffles of the man. He could sense the man's sorrow and knew that deep down inside this man needed help. He also remembered something Ma told him, that "most people are fallen angels looking for a way home. Sometimes you need to be the one to teach them how to fly."

He nodded as he understood his responsibility and turned back towards the man, walking forward until he was directly behind the mysterious gentleman and could reach out and touch him. He placed one hand on the troubled man's shoulder and when he did so, the man jumped back in surprise, dropping his hands from his face. At the same time that the man's hands dropped, so did Oliver's jaw in surprise.

There, in front of him, was the benevolent Walter Benine, sitting in what seemed like a distraught and defeated position on the ground sobbing his sorrows. The man he had come back to New York to find was within arm's length, but Oliver could not have felt more lost.

The two men stared at each other and as they did Oliver thought back to the many scenarios that had previously run through his mind detailing their first encounter.

What is he doing here? This cemetery in upstate New York is the last place I would've expected to find Walter.

Despite that, he was pleased to see their stories had *finally* found an intersection.

Oliver peered around but did not notice any others around them. He realized Walter was alone, and speaking with himself, which was slightly concerning, but did not come as a surprise. Oliver saw the distress in Walter and his cries for help. There were dark bags under his eyes. He wasn't taking care of his appearance—his clothes were rumpled and dirty. He had been drinking, too. Oliver could smell it. The half-empty bottle of bourbon was sitting on the ground nearby. Oliver noticed how Walter's face now wore a new level of pain, which was different from what he could remember seeing on the news broadcast.

Oliver, still at a loss for words, forcefully blurted out the first thing that came to mind.

"You're not asking the right questions and the answers you seek won't come unless you ask the right questions." He wasn't entirely sure where this came from but stood behind his claim as if he did.

Walter looked at Oliver, dumbfounded by his interruption. The two men continued to analyze each other. Oliver held compassion in his gaze, but in return, only received a blank stare which he knew was hiding a cocktail of Walter's emotions. Eventually, Walter found his voice and finally said something.

"Whatever, leave me alone."

Oliver replied, "What purpose will that serve?"

"The purpose of being alone," snarled Walter, "is so I don't have to answer dumb questions from old men who don't make any sense, so leave me alone. I just want to visit my parents' gravesite in peace. I don't want to talk about it."

This isn't how our first conversation was supposed to go, Oliver thought to himself. *Our first interaction was supposed to be meaningful, but here we both stand on what seems like opposite sides of pain, both with our own struggles.*

"Well, maybe so," said Oliver, gathering. He could tell Walter was there for more than just a visit to his parents' gravesite. "But I see a lot of people come to the graveyard. People don't come here to leave the way they came in. I think you're here searching for something."

Assuming he was at the graveyard because of what had happened with Santina, Oliver continued with his dialogue. He figured it couldn't have been Justice because he seemed fine during his recent visit.

"This isn't you, Walter, and if peace is what you seek, you won't find it here. You won't find it where you're looking."

Walter stubbornly ignored him, looking down at the grave in front of him. Oliver looked intently at him and noticed Walter was clutching a length of coiled rope that was sitting near him. He knew he needed to help Walter and pulled out as much empathy as he could muster.

"You've been hurt, and your heart has been broken, but that rope won't repair your pieces," explained Oliver. "You will not find the peace you seek in the bottom of a bottle, the bottom of that grave, or at the end of that rope. You believe your truth is in this perfect image of yourself, but I want to help you see that it's the times we realize our imperfections that give us all the absolution we seek."

"Listen, old man, you don't even know me. You talk about imperfections, but you're just a gravedigger."

Oliver still had a face full of sorrow as he looked at a grieving Walter. He thought he knew the pain the young man was feeling inside, but also knew it was much deeper than just pain. Like himself, he could tell Walter knew he didn't want to be alone. He could tell Walter was afraid.

In Walter, Oliver saw himself on the night he arrived to Chicago. The night that a lost teen on the verge of a breakdown told himself he wanted to be alone. Fortunately, Father Nana had had other plans. He knew he could not leave Walter alone.

"I may be 'just a gravedigger,' but I know more about you than you think, young man," he echoed Mabel-Ara's words. "I know that you have a pure heart and that you have a lot more to contribute to the world. Your potential is just being realized, and the fact that you've been hurt recently should not dissuade you from the good you're doing in the world."

"What do you know about anything?"

"Well, I know what pain looks like. You're asking God, 'How have I wronged you,' but you don't understand what that means. That statement implies that your current situation is a result of some sort of punishment bestowed upon you. I'm here to tell you that you're wrong. You're not being punished for anything."

"You don't even know me, old man. What makes you think any of that is true?"

"Why are we here?"

Walter stood there with a confused look at the question received. He looked like he was preparing a well-thought-out speech, but after moments of silence, he did not respond.

"Listen…. I don't know why we're here, and also, I do NOT need a lecture. I want to be alone, and I want you to leave, old man," demanded Walter. "I really don't want to talk about it."

Oliver folded his hands in front of him. "I'm not going to make any assumptions, but if you came to this cemetery to do what I think you came to do, you'd be ripping the world off. You'd be robbing the world of your ideas, creativity, empathy, compassion, innovation, drive, and best of all, your love."

"I don't care about my purpose, net worth, or what the world thinks of me. The only person I'm worried about is lying in a hospital bed teetering on the edge of life and death. He's supposed to be Superman."

Oliver could now tell where Walter's pain was coming from. He could see this was far beyond just what happened with Santina.

Something else must have happened to his brother since the last time I saw him.

With a look of disagreement, Oliver shook his head slowly.

"The reason your brother made the decision to save that woman instead of running away with the others was because of the example you set. Outside of firefighters and police officers, there aren't many other people who would risk their life for another person, especially a complete stranger. In the many years I've walked this earth, I think I can comfortably say I've met no more than ten people who I believe would risk their life for someone else without being told to or having some sort of incentive. I don't know him well, but I believe Justice may be the eleventh person on my list."

Oliver remembered the night the officers and fire department arrived to his burning home to save him and his family. Their courage and bravery was permanently tattooed in his mind and he knew Justice had these traits.

Oliver also realized he hadn't yet revealed to Walter that he had met Justice back at the hospital. He had spent so much time focusing on making their initial interaction meaningful that he had forgotten to explain and understand. He realized he was attempting to force help down Walter's throat, which he now began to realize was the incorrect approach. If Walter was going to accept his help, he had to first understand why he needed it. He needed to play the same role Father Nana played for him on his first night in Chicago. He knew he needed to do better.

"How do you know about my brother? How did you know what happened?"

"I know about what happened with Justice because I'm supposed to know. The reason we're both at this graveyard talking is because we need each other. In our overlapping story, both of us were meant to be at the same place at the same time because one of us seeks deliverance and the other seeks redemption."

Walter blinked rapidly and Oliver could tell he was trying to make sense of his claim, so he continued. "I was in your same position some time ago. I lost someone very close to me also. I think I can help you."

"What does that have to do with me though?"

The combination of the sun's beaming rays mixed with Walter's dehydration from drinking nothing but bourbon displayed his fatigue. In every word he spoke, Oliver could see his dry, cracking lips begging for hydration. His eyes were slightly bloodshot from the tears which made it difficult for Oliver to bear. He had seen Walter as a strong, confident man based on their few passing's. The Walter in front of him seemed more shattered than the Walter he watched during the news report.

"I will tell you. First, let's drink some water. You seem like you need it." Oliver turned around and began to walk toward the bench where he left his knapsack. Assuming he was leaving, Walter ran after him and attempted to stop him. Oliver smiled and proceeded forward to grab his knapsack, then returned with cool bottles of water. Walter opened one and drank thirstily—a good sign.

While they drank, Oliver thought. *I need to find some way to convince Walter that I can help him. Maybe it's his pride, maybe it's fear. I need to find a way. For this to work, Walter needs to want to receive help. For this healing process to truly be as effective as it was for me, Walter must first understand himself.*

Oliver continued. "I knew three other great individuals that remind me of you and Justice. They weren't great because of how they looked, how much money they had or where they came from. The thing that made them great was what was in their hearts and how they were using it to change the world."

Walter, who was getting impatient at the fact that his questions were not being answered, raised his voice in frustration. "Who are they and what do their stories have to do with my brother and me?"

"I'll share their stories because I believe you need to hear them. At the conclusion, if they have no effect on you, I'll walk away, leave you be and you will never have to see me again. You've already drank half of that bottle of bourbon so maybe you had better let me hold on to it. It's good to share, you know?"

A less depressed and more interested Walter agreed and handed over the bottle because he knew he wasn't going anywhere and was still interested in learning about how the gravedigger knew Justice. Oliver pulled out two cups from his knapsack and began to pour.

*****

He knew Tremaine, Eugene, and Peter at different periods of his life and briefly thought back to how much he had matured since first meeting Tremaine on a bus in Chicago.

Each of their endings was tragic, but Oliver knew the role they played in his life all led up to this very moment. Their deaths had to mean something. He smiled at the thought of him revisiting their memories through his storytelling.

He took another sip of water, cleared his throat, and started from the beginning.

CHAPTER 27:

MAYBE I COULD HAVE SAVED HIM

Oliver Burke

It was a little after midnight and Oliver was wrapping up his recount of the final moments Tremaine Morgan, Eugene Garry & Peter Castile were alive. When he was done, he noticed Walter wore a look of skepticism, which surprised and disappointed him. Although he cherished each of these relationships, he knew his young counterpart was not as emotionally invested, which he believed to be the root behind his reservations. He knew there was a certain convenience that the stories had to their present predicament, which made them difficult for Walter to believe.

"How did you know these people?" questioned Walter with a bit of doubt in his tone.

"Seems I didn't do a convincing enough job sharing my story," he chuckled. "Over the years, I've taken on many different nicknames and worn many different hats, but the name I was given from my father was Oliver Burke."

He saw Walter's face shift slightly and knew he was sobering up. He realized they would be opening many truths during their discussion and wanted to be as transparent as possible with Walter. Oliver followed the revelation of his name by revealing the truth about his past.

"I'm sorry, I meant my mother. I say my father because it is convenient and avoids questions about my past, but it was actually my mother who gave me this name. I don't want to lie to you, Walter. I feel I can be honest with you."

"Thank you. I appreciate that, but I'm still curious, how do you know these individuals?"

"I knew these individuals and can tell you their stories because I was there and I was unable to save them. It has been something that has kept me up most nights, and I want to change the way the story ends for you. The two of us being here is not simply a coincidence. We were meant to meet today."

When Oliver looked at Walter, he saw a mirror image of himself. The young twenty-something had the same look that he, himself, had displayed many times before. He knew the look to be a cocktail of emotions which included: confusion, sorrow, doubt, and shame, amongst several others he could feel but couldn't explain. It saddened him to see this downfall, but what pained him, even more, was the fact that he could tell there was also something going on that he could not see, which was preventing him from truly delivering the help Walter required.

In Walter, he could tell that something was different. Something seemed darker. His eyebrows were raised, and his eyes displayed a certain heaviness, which painfully imprisoned each tear filled with burden.

Walter asked Oliver for the third time how exactly he knew each character and Oliver could hear the impatience in his tone. He apologized and joked that the bourbon must have been getting to him.

"I told you I knew these individuals, but the stories go much deeper than just us being acquaintances."

He spoke about how to Tremaine he was a bus driver who went by "O" because of the nickname he was given by loved ones in Chicago. He shared how sad it was for him to see another promising young black teen taken before his time. "What hurt most was how hard his mother had worked to keep him safe. It was as if her sacrifice was worth nothing with his passing."

With Peter, he described how he was very fond of Peter and when he learned of his death, he was at a complete loss for words because he had the nightmare days before. "What shocked me most was the nightmare. I was absolutely horrified to hear of my friend's death because it was like I had a premonition of it. My dream did not have Peter in it, but I should have known. When I spoke with Ms. Mary, I thought the dream had something to do with her grandson and left it alone. I don't know how, but I was probably the one person who could have saved him, but I didn't and now I live with that for the rest of my life. He was so excited about the meeting with the bank, I couldn't bring myself to disrupt his energy."

Lastly, with Eugene, Oliver described how he went by the nickname Obie, which was the nickname his mother had given him. He joked about how Eugene pronounced the name using the two letters "OB" instead, which made him laugh every time he thought back to it. Oliver described how Eugene made him feel like he was more than just a security guard who came out of the shadows to protect people so far above him that most couldn't tell the difference between him and

Rodney. Oliver expressed how he was forever grateful to the fallen father of two. "As a security guard, I used to think about how I was wasting time protecting people who didn't care to know who I was. Eugene changed that for me. He helped give me a name and face in a place where it was very easy to find yourself in the shadow of others. I just wished I'd gotten to him even two minutes sooner. Maybe I could have saved him too."

As Oliver wrapped up his stories, Walter realized he had finally lowered his shield. He could hear the regret in Oliver's voice and appreciated his vulnerability. Oliver was honest about the role he failed to play in each story, which Walter knew had begun to affect him. He realized that Oliver simply wanted to make amends for the lost friends he could not save. Because of his descriptive storytelling and vibrant emphasis on each of their respective impacts on his life, Walter found it very easy to see a piece of himself in each of the characters.

The two men were kindred spirits who were brought together through their individual relationships with pain and loss. Walter, on one end, a broken socialite trying to come to terms with the feeling of belonging and learning to accept the fact that he was not always in control. On the other end was Oliver, a well-mannered old-timer trying to change the way the story ended for those he cared about because he could. The two of them were brought together at the crossroad of their deliverance and redemption which made their graveyard meeting that much more significant.

"Truth be told, when I saw you on the news describing Santina's murder, I knew I *wanted* to find you. Then, when I heard about your brother, I knew I *needed* to find you, and our meeting needed to be a priority. The pain you felt when Santina died and when you learned about your brother was not derived from your heart or your brain. The pain you felt came from the fact that you believe you failed them. You believe you failed to protect them and failed to save them just like I felt with Eugene, Tremaine, and Peter. I'm here to tell you that you did not fail them.

"You may not believe me, but I feel Santina's life was most fulfilled when she was with you," remarked Oliver, as he attempted to convince Walter. He wasn't entirely sure if this was true but figured it was the best thing to tell Walter.

"You showed her that she deserved more than she was given up to that point. I could tell this by when I saw you together. Earlier you said your brother was dead. Is this something that the doctors told you?"

"Pretty much," Walter replied. "They said they've never seen anyone recover from his type of injury and they were suggesting I allow them to take him off life support. He had a serious brain bleed and was placed in a coma."

This was news to Oliver, since the last time he saw Justice, he was full of life, relaxing in bed in his hospital room. He was surprised to hear of these unfortunate changes in his condition but knew he needed to play it off to continue to come off as confident and supportive because that's what Walter needed at that moment.

"Is that what you want, though? Do you think your brother would give up if presented with the same option?"

"No, I don't," Walter responded, lowering his head shamefully. "In fact, I think my brother would have taken me to another hospital if the current doctors were giving up."

"So, what are you doing here? I hope not giving up. Your brother's still fighting, and if you leave him, you'd be putting him at a handicap to fight this battle alone. Listen, Walter, I know you're a smart guy. You may have come here to do something you cannot take back, but I want to tell you that a lot of people are depending on you to change your mind."

Walter, who was now crying uncontrollably, told the elderly man how bad he felt. Deep down inside, he knew Oliver was right.

"How do you know my brother again?"

Just then, Oliver began by describing the series of events, starting with him seeing Walter at the restaurant on New Year's Eve up to the moment he watched Walter on the news describing Santina's death. As he began, Oliver now also recalled why he remembered Walter from somewhere. Before their New Year's Eve dinner, he remembered seeing Walter helping an elderly man at a bus stop. It was a scene that unfolded so fast that pieces of that occurrence were slowly beginning to come back to him.

"When I saw you on the news describing Santina's murder, I came back to New York to find you. I saw a pain that was very familiar to me and thought I could help you. When I returned to New York from Louisiana, I went searching for you and my search led me to the hospital where your brother is. We had an opportunity to meet and I told him everything I'm telling you. He told me the story about what caused him to be in the hospital and how he had spoken with you that same day. When we spoke about you, there was so much enthusiasm and pride in how he described you. He mentioned the woman and child who he saved had also come with him to the hospital but stepped away so I did not get a chance to meet with them.

"The way Justice and I spoke, you would've thought we were long-lost friends who just reconnected. It was great cause in reality, we were two strangers who were connected through you."

Oliver stared with sad eyes.

"I asked him not to tell you I visited or that I was looking to meet you because I needed our meeting to be organic and meaningful. It needed to be real. When we finally met, I wanted us to connect in the right way."

"What do you mean real?"

"Just that I didn't want to force anything. It should've flowed. That's how life is."

"I guess…"

"This was ironic because I searched for weeks looking for you and came to find you in the one place I would not have searched. You may not believe me but after the death of my mother, I also considered suicide. Why did I deserve to live and she didn't? With the help of loved ones, I was reminded that I had a greater role to play in this world and I believe you do as well.

"Earlier tonight, you were ready to end it all. I hope that our conversation has shown you how significant of an impact you've made on this world. Because of this impact, the role you will play in the future is more important now than it's ever been."

"Thank you, Oliver. Words cannot express how grateful I am for you and everything you've done for me this evening. I suppose my problem is that I'm not used to having no control and I can't come to grips with the fact that so much of the life I've spent years perfecting is unraveling. Justice always knew how to handle these situations better and you're right, he's depending on me. I know what I must do. I can't fail him."

It was now very early in the morning and the sun was beginning to rise. Neither of them had realized they'd spent so much time in the cemetery speaking but knew their meeting had been purposeful. The two men embraced with a big hug and finally released all the tears they'd held back that night. When they let each other go, Oliver looked at Walter and smiled. Both men knew they had finally concluded their meeting.

"I plan to go back to the hospital and be there for my brother. No matter what the outcome, I know that I want to be there to support him. Will you join us at the hospital? When Justice wakes up, I'm sure he'll be happy to see we finally met and are both there for him."

Oliver smiled and replied, "I have something to do now, but no matter what, I plan to be there with you."

Walter smiled back, picked up his things then departed. As he watched Walter walk away, Oliver thought back to how everything in his life had been intertwined and had led up to that one fruitful moment that made every experience in his life worth it. He was overjoyed that their long-awaited meeting had finally happened.

Oliver's shift the day before had ended at 7 p.m. and it was now close to 7 a.m. the next day. He knew Amerie must have been worried sick when she had not heard from him. He looked at his phone and realized he had three missed calls and two voicemail messages. Two of the calls and one of the messages were from Amerie and the other call and message were from a random number that had a 917 area code. He grabbed his items and made his way back to the bus station to return Amerie's call. When he called back, she did not pick up, so he decided to leave her a voicemail.

"Hi, my love. I'm so sorry I missed your calls and message last night. You'll never guess who I ran into tonight! I love and adore you. I want to give you the life you deserve can't wait to see you when I get home. Love you."

As the bus pulled up, Oliver decided to play the voicemails. The first voicemail was from Amerie and was her inquiring if everything was okay. In the message, she asked him to call her back as soon as he received it, which he had already done.

In the second message from the unknown number, Oliver listened as the message began in an unusual silence which almost made him stop it and hit the delete button. Just as he was about to do that, there was a very low, and somewhat familiar voice. As the message played, the shock in Oliver's face flared as his jaw dropped and his phone almost slipped through his grip.

"Hi Oliver, it's me. It's Lenny…."

The End

Topics and Questions for Discussions:

1. What does '*The Angels Are Flying So Low*' mean to you?"

2. The book highlights the key principles of morality through the characters who influence Oliver. How did Oliver's morals change throughout the novel?

3. What role did Rahzmel serve in the novel? What role did Mabel-Ara serve? Were there any similarities in these roles? What were the differences?

4. There were four main females in Oliver's life, who found him at different phases. Salena, Monica "Minnie", Mabel-Ara, and Amerie. What type of character was Oliver during each of these encounters and how did they factor into the person we met in the end of novel?

5. In Chapter 17 (**Everyone We Lost in The Fire Pt. 1**), fire was referenced in a different manner from how it was referenced in Chapter 18 (**Everyone We Lost in The Fire Pt. 2**). What were the main differences?

6. After the house fire, the doctor describes how Oliver's burn will become a permanent scar. What do you believe is the significance in this?

7. Throughout Oliver's story, we see a change in his attitude towards the people he idolized. In what ways did Oliver seek to fix or escape the realities of his upbringing?

8. Consider Oliver's time in prison. Why was it so hard for him to fully break free from the previous life he no longer wanted to be a part of?

9. The first day he was released, Oliver was taken to Mabel-Ara's home. He was given a meal, a bath and a bed to sleep on. What made him almost leave that night? How

10. This novel was broken up into five parts. What were the general themes of each of these segments of the novel?

11. After reading the novel, do you believe was the significance of the book cover?

12. What did you find the most troubling about Oliver's life?

13. In Chapter 25 (**Weight of the World**), the narration mentioned Oliver had come to grips with the fact that the hole in his heart may never be repaired. Why did he accept that fact and how did it factor into his overall healing?